Potatoes, Come Forth!

Inconvenient Magic I

H. Jonas Rhynedahll

Published by Rhynedahll Software in the United States of America.

Other Works:

The Key to Magic: An epic fantasy series
  Orphan
  Magician
  King
  Emperor
  Warrior
  Wizard
  Thief

Chronicle of the Rider
  Dead Rider's Debt
  Rider's Journey (Revised Edition)
  Rider's Doom (Forthcoming)

Inconvenient Magic:
  Potatoes, Come Forth!
  Magic, Unfettered?
  Technology, Begin:
  Something or Other…
  Not This Side of Never, (Forthcoming)

To End a War (science fiction novella)

Not Your Typical, Scantily-Clad Virgin Sacrifice (short story collection)

Time Travelers' Currency Exchange and Pawn

A Triptych
  The Rabbit Hole
  Tunnels (TBA)
  The Long Way Around

Forthcoming:

No Babes in the Apocalypse
Zombies Don't Shoot Back

ONE

As the early morning breeze blew the last of the fading mist from the open expanse of the field, Everett strode forth, slid back the frayed sleeves of his work shirt, and raised his rough hands to the cloud-laced sky. After a perfectly timed dramatic beat, he intoned the magic words in a clear, well-rehearsed commanding tone.

"Potatoes, come forth!"

The sounds carried, cutting through the warming air, and echoed faintly from the distant tree line.

And then...

Nothing happened.

Unimpressed, the gruff farmer hawked and spat, then rubbed his mouth with a grimed sleeve. Olin Ghemenson was a solid, practical man who worked the earth. He had confidence in it and the efficacy of a strong back, but in little else. "That's all there is to it, is it? So when does it start workin'?"

"Most spells aren't very complex," Everett contended, somewhat defensively. "That does not diminish their power."

"Sure. So where're the potatoes?"

"Give it a minute, will you?"

Ghemenson shrugged, but his significant glance at the mule teams conveyed his meaning well enough. The middle buster plows would turn out the crop efficiently, but the ten acre field would take the four mule drivers most of a day. Everett had claimed to be able to magic them out of the ground in less than twenty minutes.

Everett had felt the magic coalesce and knew that the spell had actuated, but nevertheless, as always, the wait wracked his worn nerves. He could not escape the illogical fear that his spell would fail. None of his ever had, and there were only whispered rumors of suspicious provenance to suggest that such an occurrence was possible, but the anxiety still made his heart race and his hands tremble in persistent doubt. Grinding his teeth in annoyance, he crossed his arms to clamp the traitorous appendages in place, rocked back on one heel to proclaim his nonchalance, and started to count under his breath. The longest the spell had ever taken to evince was forty-seven seconds.

At thirty-nine seconds, the ground beneath his feet stirred, producing a feeble, almost imperceptible roll.

Ghemenson looked sideways at Everett. "Is that it?"

"No, that's just the beginning. Perhaps you should brace yourself. Depending on the density of your soil, there may be some displacement."

Ghemenson drew his lips into a thin line. "What does that mean?"

"Some shaking, normally. A minor earthquake on occasion."

"*Earthquake*? If there's damage to the barns, I'll be deductin' it from your fee."

Everett's heart raced faster. For all practical purposes penniless, he desperately needed this fee. Without it, he would once more go to bed hungry. "Oh, no, not that sort of quake, I assure you. Nothing to be concerned about at all."

The ground heaved and Everett staggered to regain his balance. Ghemenson, weighing at least seventeen stone, did not budge, but his expression became disapproving.

The next shock was milder and immediately followed by a steady, low-key vibration of the earth. Across the hedge-bordered field, the dried potato vines, the hilled rows, and the cultivated soil between the rows began to stir.

"Any second now," Everett promised the frowning Ghemenson.

The first red spheroid oozed from the shifting soil less than a chain from the dirt work lane on which Everett, the farmer, and his workers waited. The potato shook itself, somewhat dog-like, to shed the clinging sandy loam and rolled down the slope of its row into the furrow between. As the vibration increased slightly in intensity, another potato popped out two rows to the east of the first, then dozens began to appear, some wiggling forth like gophers from burrows, others leaping out of the ground like breaching fish. The potatoes trailed fragments of roots and those with rot or other wounds burst as they fought free, but even the smallest seemed fixedly determined to escape its subterranean existence to find a new destiny in the clear sunshine. As the activity increased, tiny geysers of potatoes, dried vines, and soil erupted in many places across the slightly rolling ground. Small clumps and then larger piles of potatoes formed as every spot of the field became involved in the desperate migration and a low noise of sliding earth, colliding potatoes, and rustling vines filled the air. Slowly, the collecting tubers began to roll and nudge themselves toward Everett, eventually coalescing into knee-high waves that washed over the rows, crushing the rare weed, as they swept with apparent inexorable force toward the waiting men.

Ghemenson took a step back. "My yield is better than two thousand pounds an acre. That's a good ten *tons* of potatoes, there, Magicker. You sure you've got 'em under control?"

"It's not actually a question of *control*, so to speak, Monsieur Ghemenson. I don't direct the potatoes. The spell simply requires them to gather at a focal point, or locus."

"I see. And where might this 'focal point' be?"

"Well, generally, it's about where I'm standing when I cast the spell."

"Hmm, then unless you have a spell that will let you breathe potato, I'd think you'd better move." Taking his own advice, the farmer headed back at a quick trot along the track toward his farm buildings, waving the mule teams ahead of him.

Everett, indecisive, stood his ground for a moment as the crests of the potato waves climbed higher. The highest wave was already over four feet, with a churning froth of smaller spuds at the top. Prior to this, he had only cast the spell on small garden plots and the harvest had been no more than a few wheelbarrows of potatoes that had piled themselves in front of him in a more or less orderly fashion. He had not considered the problems that scale might bring.

The leading potatoes thudded against his boots and subsided as their magical impetus faded, then were shoved aside as more potatoes rolled in. Yet more crowded close within seconds, jostling their fellows, overtopping his boots, and thudding insistently against his ankles. When the first of the waves was only a few yards distant, Everett decided to abandon his post. He did not run to join the waiting men, but his pace was faster than the casual stroll he would have liked. It had been difficult to convince Ghemenson, given the generally impoverished state of his appearance, that he was indeed a Journeyman Magicker. As he hoped to entice Ghemenson to recommend his services to the farmer's neighbors, failing to display confidence in his own magic now would certainly be counterproductive. He was careful not to glance back as the roar of the gathering harvest intensified.

Everett nodded casually to the four stocky, weather-beaten men and turned, taking care to appear unhurried, to view what his magic had wrought. A mound had formed across the work lane, landslides of potatoes tumbling to fill the low ditches to either side. The mound grew rapidly to a small, irregular hill as much as ten feet high, and then, abruptly, the noise, the earth, and the potatoes became still. A hovering dust lingered over the field and an aromatic starchy hint wafted on the wind, but otherwise the spell seemed complete.

Ghemenson gave the field a once over, then turned and gave Everett a curt nod. "I'll say this, for you, Magicker," the farmer conceded. "You did get the crop out of the ground in under twenty minutes."

Everett inclined his head serenely. "It is *magic*, after all."

"I don't suppose you'd have a 'Spirit the potatoes all into their bins spell', would you?"

Everett hesitated, instinctively if irrationally reluctant to acknowledge his magical shortcomings, then begrudged, "I'm afraid not."

"Thought so. That's the way it is with magic. Never quite finishes the job, if you know what I mean. Well, next time, maybe we can get them closer to the cellars."

Ghemenson turned to his men. "Jack, Charlie, Tim, go fetch the wagons and we'll get started." He looked back at Everett, gave half a smile, and made a rumbling noise that was probably a chuckle.

"Did you bring a cart, Magicker?"

Everett felt suddenly uncomfortable. "Sorry, *cart?*"

"Your fee of two hundred pounds of potatoes weighs *two hundred pounds*. You're a good-sized fellow, but I doubt that you can carry that much very far at all."

"Oh! No, I, uhm, hadn't thought of that." Mentally, Everett kicked himself.

"Well, I've got an old homemade wheel barrow that I can let you have, but you might want to think about getting your own, if you intend to deal in potatoes much."

TWO

Everett's insistent hunger prompted him to stop just two miles along the dusty, gravel-topped farm road from Ghemenson's farm.

Most of the moderately sized Barony of Heimgelberg was open flood plain country. Situated close to the dead center of the two thousand mile long Edze River, the demesne occupied one of the most fertile sections of the river's broad valley, the Edzedahl, and extended nearly a hundred miles west of the river and an equal distance north and south. Vegetable farms, livestock pastures, and cornfields divided by ten foot high, decades old hedges abounded and opportunities for shade from the relentless summer sun were few. When a woodlot of mixed hardwoods came into view around a wide bend in the road, offering a respite from his trudging march and deadfall for a cook fire, he surrendered to the gnawing demands of his empty belly and turned the barrow off the road.

Pushing with considerable extra effort through tall, already browning grass and brambles, he reached an almost cave-like area of shade beneath a large, spreading red oak. He took care to settle the barrow so that it could not tip, shrugged out of his pack, and set it atop the burlap sacks of potatoes. He then took time to securely tuck the legs of his trousers into his boots; the thick carpet of brown leaves probably harbored ticks and while the hard leather of his boots would discourage them, he had no desire to tempt the tiny black stowaways with easily climbed cloth. Plenty of dry branches lay about and it took only a few minutes work to gather sufficient fuel for a small fire. After raking a good-sized area clear of dead matter with the edge of his boot, he scuffed out a small depression in the loose loam with his heel and then used some of the half-rotted leaves as tinder to set the branches ablaze.

Keeping one cautious eye on the fire, he took his copper pot from its strap on the back of his pack. The hook-eyed steel rod to hang it above the fire also served as a hip stiffener for his pack, and he had to flip the pack and release two cinches to remove it, but his familiarity with the maneuver reduced the task to a matter of seconds. Likewise jamming the rod into the ground, hanging the bail of the pot, and filling it with water from his canteen. By the time he had peeled and cut two large potatoes into chunks, the water was at a simmer. Dragging a denuded log by the stub of a limb up to the barrow, he settled down on it to wait, licking his lips unconsciously.

He would have liked to have had coin from Ghemenson, but a promise of a millage of the harvest was all that the farmer had been willing to venture on unproved magic. Taking produce in trade, as he often must, left him feeling somewhat *unprofessional*, but at least he would be able to eat today.

He had cooked the last of his grits for supper the day before and had had no breakfast when he arrived at the Ghemenson farm. Absent the potatoes, he would now be scavenging for black berries and dandelion greens. The sometimes bitter fruit and the rather tasteless greens did not make much of a meal, as he had realized often over the last several weeks, but would at least allow him the illusion of having eaten.

He tested one of the potatoes against the side of the copper pot. The simple fare would be softened to his liking in perhaps a minute more. He flipped open the flap of a side pocket in his pack and dug around for his salt. He found the small glass vial under the cloth bag that held his razor. Holding the container up to a sunray pin-holing through the canopy, he shook it and frowned. There might just be a pinch left, hardly enough to suggest a hint of savor. Still, he set it out alongside the log on which he sat.

The nearest good-sized town, Pylton, was a two to three day's walk. Having to push the creaking barrow might make the journey take twice as long, but he had little practical option in the matter. With the local harvest in full swing, he could not sell the potatoes for anything resembling a decent price in any of the nearby villages. Nevertheless, he was fairly pleased with himself. The magicking that he had performed for Ghemenson had been the first paid work that he had done in a month. His Major spell was only useful for a few weeks every year and he had yet to establish a regular clientele for it here in the lowlands. The fee that he had been compelled to accept was almost a humiliation, but if worse came to worse and no one in the town was willing to purchase the four bags of potatoes, he at least would not starve till they were gone.

As he finished the last bite of supposedly salted boiled potato, he heard the sounds, probably a mile or two distant, of a steam mechanism approaching along the road. Jumping up quickly, he dumped the water from his cooled pot onto the smoldering ashes, quickly stowed it, the hanging rod, his empty salt vial, and his fork, shouldered his pack, and then pushed the barrow back to the edge of the road. With nothing but scattered farmsteads along it for better than twenty miles, there was precious little traffic on the road, technological or horse drawn, and he dare not miss any chance of a ride.

It took more than a good fifteen minutes for the large steel mechanism, clanking and smoking, to reach Everett. It was a grader, working to knock down the ruts and ridges in the loose macadam. On occasion over the past few months, he had seen it or its twin at work in the distance as he made the rounds of the farms soliciting work. He took a prominent but non-obstructive place halfway into the lane and raised his arm in a congenial wave, a neighborly grin clearly displayed. In his experience, most people did not mind hitchers, but a cheerful attitude and a ready smile always seemed to help.

The operator allowed a well-used smile to broaden his flat cheeked, sun-browned face in response, waved back, and then reached past his portly belly to shift levers to let the long, angled blade bring the grader to a grinding halt.

Waiting until a screeching blast of white steam from a side relief valve trailed off, the man called down pleasantly, "Good morning! How are you today?"

"Just fine, Monsieur!" Everett replied in the same tone. "My name is Everett de Schael. Might there be any chance of a ride? I'm headed toward Pylton."

"Well, Pylton is to the south and I'm scheduled to go

west along the Trebblety road today, but I could let you ride to the crossroads of the highway. That might save you about ten miles."

"Thank you, Monsieur! That would be great!"

The operator slid from his seat, walked a lateral brace to the starboard catwalk, and then hopped down to the roadbed with more agility than his size might imply. He stuck out his hand.

"I'm Chauncey Wiggins. But folks just call me Bob, after my dad."

Everett shook hands, contributing a polite laugh. "Glad to meet you, Bob. Thanks again for the ride."

"No problem. What have you got there? Potatoes?"

Everett forced a smile through an instant of chagrin. "Yes, I'm off to sell them in town. They're my fee for a spell. I'm a Journeyman Magicker."

"You don't say! Why, I'm a Common Magicker myself! Got one Minor and two Insignificants. It's one reason I got this job. My Minor spell is a Non-Visible Flammables Ignition. I can light the entire firebox for this beast's boiler in one go!"

In the general population, only one in three had any spells at all, and those with the three required to earn the rank of Common Magicker were equally as rare among spell casters. Everett knew that an appropriate amount of praise was expected.

"Excellent! That's a very handy spell!"

Bob chuckled. "It's not the best, but it's always had its uses. Like I said, it got me this job and the Barony pays civil workers pretty well. Now, let's see, I'd imagine that we can stow the spuds in the portside locker. I think it's empty. Let's have a look."

Hanging alongside the wood bin just aft of the rear man-tall iron-clawed wheel, the locker was indeed empty. Bob popped the latches and opened the doors to reveal a space that proved just large enough to hold the four sacks of potatoes.

"We'll lay the barrow on the catwalk," Bob suggested. "The grader doesn't bounce much and I think that it'll ride."

The operator climbed the ladder-like claws of the wheel

and Everett hoisted the barrow up to him. Bob turned it upside down and then lodged it against the handrail.

"I might as well stoke the firebox while I'm stopped," Bob told Everett. "Care to give me a hand?"

"Sure. What do you need me to do?"

"Take an armload of wood from the bin there and bring it around to the rear platform. One armload should build up the fire, but it might take two."

"I'll be right there," Everett assured the driver.

Bob followed the catwalk back behind the boiler and skipped down an angled ladder to the rear platform as Everett pulled two-foot sticks of split oak from the bin. The driver had the corner-hinged double doors of the firebox open when Everett arrived with his first armload and a jet of hot air shot outward well beyond the end of the platform. Standing to one side, Bob took the fuel a piece at a time and slung it adroitly into the maw of the furnace, soliciting a burst of fire from the coal bed with each toss. He sent Everett back for five sticks, added them, and, announcing his satisfaction, jerked on the coil-handled linked rod that let the heavy doors slam closed.

Just making conversation, Everett inquired, "This is fairly new, isn't it?"

"That's right! One of only two north of New Zindersberg. The Baron imported it all the way from the Republic just two years ago to use for his *Our New Highways* program."

"The complexity of the mechanisms that they have nowadays is amazing."

"You're dead right about that, Everett," Bob agreed as he headed forward. "Never saw anything like this when I was a kid. I just about believe that there's nothing that technology can't do."

Everett gave an unseen half-nod to the driver's back. He had long ago come to the same conclusion.

There was only the single seat in the cab of the mechanism, but Everett assured Bob that he would be just fine sitting atop his pack and leaning against a stanchion on the narrow starboard catwalk.

Just as soon as he had spun valves and shifted levers to set the grader in motion once more, Bob turned to Everett and said, raising his voice to a near shout to be heard above the noise, "I've always wondered, is there much money in doing magic for a living?"

Everett wanted to say, "Magic is inefficient, inconvenient, undependable, and frequently quite useless. Only an idiot would try to make a living at it."

But, rather than confess his own spite-filled dissatisfaction, he simply shrugged and said, "For some there is. I know most of the Wizards do well and I've seen where some Journeymen have set up shops in the bigger towns, but it all depends on the utility of their spells."

"I know what you mean. My two Insignificants are Unclassifieds – Roasted Peanut Creation, and Boiled Egg Summoning. They get me a few laughs on occasion, and boiled eggs and roasted peanuts of course, but aren't really what you'd call marketable. You know, I've only met one Journeyman Magicker before. He came through my hometown about ten years ago. He could mend pots and all sorts of metal items, brew a decent beer from hog slops, and, if I remember right, repair teeth. I don't recall what his other four spells were, but it seems like they were just party tricks like mine. What kind of spells do you do?"

Everett sighed. He generally avoided talking about his trade, because the conversation inevitably arrived at this final embarrassing question.

"Nothing quite so useful, I'm afraid. My Major spell is an Item Translocation Variant. I have two related Liquid Transubstantiation Minors, and four Insignificants that produce nothing of any utility whatsoever."

Bob looked interested and grinned. "You said Liquid Transubstantiation? Can you make beer? I've got a barrel of drinking water hanging off the port aft. Wouldn't mind a mug or two with my lunch."

Everett hesitated, dreading the admission, but then sighed again and told the operator frankly, "No, I can do wine, but it's undrinkable."

"Wine? Not that fond of it, but I suppose it would do. You know, 'undrinkable' is sort of a relative term. To tell the truth, I've downed a lot of swill in my time. Why don't we magic up a batch and try it?"

"I'm sorry, Bob, but I know it's undrinkable. My wine smells like pig urine and tastes about the same."

The man burst out laughing. "Yes, I'd guess you'd be right, then. Pity. What does your other Minor do? Any chance of a tea or fruit juice?"

Everett felt his mouth press into a tight line. "No, sorry. The other is wine into olive oil."

"Olives don't grow this far north, do they? Only ones that I've seen have been brought up from the coast, pickled, and are fairly pricey. It's the same with the oil. Seems like that spell would generate a good bit of income for you."

"It would, if my oil didn't taste and look like axel grease."

"Haw! That's a tough break, Everett. There must be something wrong in the world when a man gets two Minor spells and both turn out crap."

Everett said nothing. There was nothing to say. He had earned the rank of Journeyman Magicker by manifesting the minimum seven spells, a feat achieved by only one in ten magicians, but all of his spells, including the required Major, were, to be brutally honest, utter and total crap.

"I guess that's one way where technology clearly comes out on top," Bob mentioned offhandedly as he shifted gears to climb a slight grade. "The W-W-W."

"*Www?*"

"Oh, sorry, just a short hand we use in the road service. Job assignments come down to three things, the What, the When, and the Where, and it seems to me that those three apply to just about anything. In magic, though, the three W's are generally locked up out of reach like fine spirits in a chintzy joint. First, a magician never gets to choose *what* a spell does. The effect is what it is and that's that. Since we actually have to say a spell out loud the *when* is always restricted to the minute we cast. Sure, you could say we get to pick the *where* because every spell needs a locus and a focus, but I'd imagine that more than half the time those are already set too. Why, my Aunt Matilda had only one spell and it only worked on a Tuesday by a red barn!"

Bob gave the whistle chain a quick jerk to scare a rabbit from the path of the grader. "On the other hand, a technician can do just about whatever he wants. He can pick and choose elements from schematics to make his mechanisms and can pretty much decide exactly what he wants his mechanism to do, when he wants it to operate, and where he wants it to operate."

Everett made a noncommittal noise. Though he had never considered the three W's, in his estimation everything that Bob had said was accurate.

Having exhausted his interest in discussing magic, Bob launched into a detailed commentary on the best taverns along his route.

The remainder of the ride to the crossroads took better than two hours, as Bob occasionally had to back up the grader laboriously to go over particularly rough stretches more than once. The operator of the big mechanism was a gregarious fellow but seemed content with Everett's natural reticence. Everett laughed politely in the appropriate places and made simple encouraging comments as required while Bob regaled him with his admittedly tired repertoire of jokes, aphorisms, and grader anecdotes.

Still, all in all, Everett rather enjoyed the ride. Bob's stories and jests, as formulaic as they were, were a welcome relief from the usual solitude of his itinerant trade. In addition, as self-mobile steam mechanisms were a relatively recent innovation, he was moderately fascinated by the grader's workings. He had only seen his first steam tractor a year previously, when its technician creator had demonstrated its ability to pull a ten-foot disc harrow at twice the speed of a mule team. Of the three mystical trades, technology was by far the most utilitarian.

When they arrived at the stone paved Baronial Highway, the loss of both the ride and the company left Everett a bit morose. Bob helped unload the barrow, refill it with the potatoes, and then stuck out his hand.

"Good luck with your magic, Journeyman. I'm sure that one day you'll find some place where you can get full time work."

Everett shook hands firmly, knowing that the man meant only kindness, but still the words stung.

As Bob guided the grader across the highway and to

the farm track beyond, Everett settled his pack firmly on his shoulders, picked up the handles of the barrow, and pointed it determinedly south. He had balanced the weight of the potatoes as far forward as he could over the single wooden wheel and he was comfortable with the moderate strain. Having labored strenuously most of his life, both in his father's orchards during his youth and in the monastery boarding schools where the proctors had believed that a Magicker should train his body as well as his mind, he was well accustomed to physical work. He also had inherited his father's height, thick shoulders, and endurance. As long as he could maintain a decent pace, he was confident that he could get his burden to Pylton in a reasonable length of time.

The highway was one of the recent civil works of the current Baron, who Everett had heard had populist leanings. Although a hereditary aristocrat and granted his rule by his title, he apparently wanted to be liked by his subjects and had begun investing heavily in projects designed to win the favor of the average commoner. Running almost forty miles from the river ferry at Ingleside to the agricultural hub of Pylton, it was a single granite paved lane with sloping gravel shoulders and shallow drainage ditches. The joints in the interlocked pavers made a constant clattering sound against the wooden wheel of the barrow, but the hard surface was considerably easier going than the dirt and gravel farm road had been. It was no doubt much appreciated by any that might have need of traveling regularly between Pylton and Ingleside, but from the lack of visible traffic, it appeared that there was not an abundance of such persons.

After about four miles, he was trudging along at a determined, steady pace, easing the boredom of the march by mentally calculating whether he could walk straight through the night and reach the town by dawn, when, without warning, the wooden axe of the barrow snapped clean in two. With a rending crash, the barrow snagged and dumped the load of potatoes over sideways.

Shocked and unbelieving, he stood for a long moment shivering in inarticulate fury.

Eventually, after taking a deep breath and blowing it out, he declared in disgusted exasperation to the world at large. "That's the trouble with Technology. It's all crap too!"

Then, having no other option, he gathered his frayed nerves, took another deep breath and forced his anger to cool further. To tell the truth, he did not actually believe that technology was crap. Technology was unarguably the more robust and utilitarian trade. As Bob had more or less said, where magickers and wizards were forever constrained to a single set of static and unchangeable spells, mechanics and technologists could combine and adapt their schematics and even share them among themselves. Useful purpose could be found for many Insignificant technology schematics through inclusion or modification, but nearly all Insignificant spells were doomed to be, in Bob's words, no more than party tricks.

No, his anger was directed solely and completely at magic. He was just plain *mad* at magic. Mad because it promised fantastic success but delivered humiliating failure. Mad because it had condemned him to a life of want and embarrassment. Mad because of every scathing moment of disappointment that he had endured because of his worthless spells.

If, by some chance swing of fortune, he had manifested as a mechanic rather than a magicker, then he might have been able to earn money instead of potatoes! At the very least, he probably would not be here wondering how he was going to lug more than his own weight in farm produce twenty miles.

"Why," he complained again to the open fields and distant farmsteads, an attentive if unresponsive audience, "couldn't I have had a *real* spell? Why couldn't I have Gold, come forth! Or even, Cornbread, come forth! I thoroughly *like* cornbread and I'm beyond *tired* of potatoes!"

Grumbling, he began to sling the bags into a pile to one side to see if he might repair the barrow. As he grabbed hold of it, the stitches of the third bag burst, scattering its contents across the pavement. Outraged once more, he stood there in renewed rigid indignation and glared witheringly at the utter calamity that his life had become.

"Besides that," he griped to the uncaring soybeans, "I'm lonely. Why couldn't I have *Beautiful Woman, come forth!*"

The abrupt vibrating nerve sensation of the actuation of

a spell frightened away his anger. Before he could complete a curious thought, a wisp of air fluttered his clothes and hair.

Then, not three yards in front of him, a young woman, wearing not a stitch, appeared.

THREE

She was indeed beautiful, with the perfect face and lithe figure of a goddess. Her eyes were the color of a warm summer sky after a rain, her lips the color of clover honey, and her long hair the color of sun-splashed white oak bark. Not a single feature was out of place or body segment out of proportion. She was not a fantasy; she was an *ideal*.

She was also, oddly, dripping wet.

And quite surprised.

But not more so than Everett. He was literally stunned. This was impossible.

"Who are you?" he demanded.

"Who are *you*?" she snapped back at him, planting her fists firmly on her hips. Her expression declaring that she would brook no nonsense whatsoever, she swung her head about to survey the scene. "And where am I?"

"Uhm, this is the Barony of Heimgelberg and I'm, uhm, well, Everett de Schael."

"That's one of the small eastern demesnes, isn't it? That's more than twelve hundred miles from …from … from my bathroom." She eyed him suspiciously, taking in the mean cut and rough stitching (he had made it himself) of his once blue shirt and the threadbare state of his brown trousers. "You're a wizard?"

"What? No, of course not."

She tilted her head to the side and with casual grace began squeezing the water out of her hair. Her every movement fascinated Everett.

"Only magic could transport me out of my bath to this filthy road," she accused. "Are you saying you didn't do it?"

"Well, uhm, I'm not sure."

"Stop saying 'uhm.' It makes you sound like a dolt."

"U..*right*."

"Well? Answer my question."

Remembering the magical actuation, he felt a moment of heart constricting panic. The last words that he had uttered before her appearance *had* had the semblance of a spell. Had it been a First Enunciation? But why had there been no Epiphany? "I...suppose I could have."

"So you *are* a wizard!"

"No, I'm a Journeyman Magicker."

"Nothing but a Potent spell could transport a living mass my size across this distance. Only the Wizardly ranks have Potent spells."

Everett grasped at this solid, commonly known fact to steady himself. "That's correct."

Eyes widening slightly, she whipped her head about, aborting in mid-flinch a reflexive reaction to cross her arms across her breasts. *"Is there someone else here?"*

Not quite following, he looked around at the vacant road and fields, then ventured, "No?"

She relaxed slightly. "Then you must have brought me here."

"No, that's absolutely impossible. I don't have a *Transport an extremely beautiful and unclothed woman into my presence* spell." Though it definitely would be welcome, he added silently to himself.

The woman examined him with a jaundiced eye. "Your gaze is beginning to wander. Give me something to wear."

Everett spread his arms apologetically. "I don't have anything but the clothes I'm wearing."

"Then give me your shirt. Quick! Before anyone comes along!"

Trying to find a reason to refuse that would not make him appear unchivalrous, he did not comply immediately. When nothing remotely plausible occurred to him, he sighed, shrugged off the straps of his pack, and set it to the side. Then, fingers fumbling slightly, he loosened the upper buttons of the baggy shirt, pulled it over his head with care so as to not poke any extra holes in it, and handed it to her. He started to cross his arms, felt awkward and self-conscious, and dropped them to his sides. It was an odd thing for him to be standing in front of a woman with his shirt off.

Acting for all the world as if she were dressing in her own boudoir, the woman poked her head through the shirt and then slid her arms into the sleeves. She did not bother with the upper buttons as she tugged it down to suit her, leaving an entrancing triangle of collarbones and skin exposed. Finally, she combed her still damp hair back over her shoulders out of the way. As she was about a foot shorter than he, the tails of the shirt extended only to her mid-thigh. Her legs were athletic and, of course, also dazzlingly beautiful. And utterly fascinating.

Rolling up the sleeves at the wrists, she wrinkled her nose and gave a loud sniff.

"Sorry," he explained with a wince. "I've been on the road for a few days."

She rolled her eyes in exaggerated comment, then seemed to recollect the problem of her current situation and her mood quickly darkened. "Why did you bring me here?"

"I'm still not sure that I did, but *if* I did, it was entirely by accident, I assure you."

"What do you mean 'by accident'? Either you did or you didn't. There's no such thing as 'accidental' magic."

"I know that! The First Fundamental Precept of Magic states clearly: *Magic cannot be adapted, improvised, or modified.*"

"So you *did* bring me here?"

Everett stopped short. He could not deny that magic had been done. "It is *potentially* possible that I may have facetiously and inadvertently cast a spell," he admitted.

"Fine," the woman responded, her tone indicating that it was anything but fine. "Joke's over now. Send me back."

Everett slowly shook his head. "I can't do that."

"Look – what was your name?"

"Everett. And yours, Mademoiselle?"

"Look, Everett, sorry to let you down, but you have *absolutely* no chance of developing a romantic relationship with me. I know you magic types have difficulties in social situations, but this is just not going anywhere. End of story. So, send me back and we can both forget this whole mistake happened."

Everett's ire rose up. "You don't understand,

Mademoiselle *Whateveryournameis*, it's not that I don't want to send you back, it's that I *can't*. I don't have a spell to send you back."

"Of course you do. The spell you used to bring me here must be a Gross Vital Transportation derivation, right? There's nothing else that I've ever heard of that could move a person from one point to another without passing through intervening space."

"I suppose that you're right, but if I transported you here – and I'm still not admitting that I did – then the spell just manifested to me only a moment ago."

"Aren't you a little old for that?"

Everett stiffened. "There are well documented cases of spell Manifestation all the way up to the age of forty-five."

"Yes, but those have to be extremely rare. Most manifestations, magical or technological, occur between the ages of twelve and twenty-six."

The authoritative nature of her statement irritated him yet more; nowadays it seemed that every passing vagabond considered himself an expert on magic. He had not participated in a theoretical discussion of magic since he had left *Friar Albert's Advanced Academy of Magical Study* and having one now with a young woman that he had summoned out of thin air seemed decidedly ludicrous. Nevertheless, he felt behooved to assert his own official expertise on the subject.

"Yes," he noted in his best pedantic tone, "but manifestations outside those ranges do take place. For instance, I manifested my first spell at the age of *three*."

"And now you've manifested a Potent spell at the age of, what, forty?"

"I'm only thirty-one. Men in my family gray prematurely."

The woman waggled a hand at him. "We're straying. Cast the obverse of your first spell and send me back where I came from."

Everett straightened from his habitual slump to his full height and looked down at her with he hoped came across as an imperious air.

"You might have a vague acquaintance with some

aspects of magic, *Mademoiselle,* but it's clear that your information is simplistic, misguided, and incomplete. Magic simply doesn't work that way. Had you studied magic as a profession, *as I have,* then you would know that the Second Fundamental Precept of Magic clearly states that *Manifestation is unpredictable, arbitrary, and random.* Yes, it's true that Potent spells sometimes appear to manifest in pairs, or compliments, with one positive spell, or reverse, and one negative, or obverse, spell, but that's purely a statistically anomaly."

"All right. But how do you know you don't have the obverse spell? Couldn't you have also *inadvertently* manifested a second spell that will send me back?"

His thoughts churning, Everett clamped his mouth shut on an automatic denial. There was nothing in settled magic theory that covered this situation and the circumstances of the casting of the spell that had brought her here seemed to violate generally accepted magical norms. If he accepted as a given that he had manifested a Potent spell with a weak Epiphany that had simply gone unnoticed in his distracted state, then it was entirely possible he might also have similarly manifested its complement.

"I suppose it's could happen," he allowed.

She smiled for the first time. "So let's try it!"

"Okay, but I'm not making any promises. Where do you want to go?"

"Back where I came from."

"Right, but where's that?"

"I'd rather not say. You obviously didn't know where you snatched me from, so logically you shouldn't have to know where you're sending me. For your privacy and mine, let's keep this as anonymous as possible. I think it'll be better for both of us that way."

Everett shrugged, then, with no confidence whatsoever, concentrated to select the woman as a focus, extrapolated the potential terms of the obverse, and said, "Beautiful Woman, go forth!"

She tapped her foot. "Nothing happened."

"My spells are very seldom instantaneous."

"Well, how long will it take?"

"I have no idea, but most of my spells actuate quickly

and then generally evince in under a minute."

The woman waited another half minute, clearly counting silently, then inquired, "So it didn't work?"

"Obviously. As I expected, I felt no actuation."

"Are you sure you did it properly? Shouldn't you make a commanding gesture or strike a dramatic pose?"

Almost certain that she was making fun of him, Everett declared, "That part is just what my Commercial Aspects of Magic instructor called 'salesmanship.' Most employers expect something more than an enunciated incantation, but, truthfully, as the Third Fundamental Precept--"

The young woman rolled her eyes again. "Could we dispense with the lectures?"

Everett gritted his teeth. "Right. The key part is that *only* the words matter. The effects of the spell are initiated by the complete enunciation of the syllables."

"Well, did you say the words correctly?"

"Again, I have no idea. In my previous manifestations – and this is normally the case with magicians -- the terms of the spells came as an unpresaged inspiration, what we in the profession call an Epiphany. That didn't happen this time. Frankly, based on this lack of Epiphany and considering the additional evidence of the failure of the experiment with the obverse, I'm now convinced that I have not manifested a new spell, and, therefore, am not at all responsible for your involuntary transportation."

"Okay, we need to get beyond this. Try the first spell on me again. If it works, then we'll know."

He shrugged. Her suggestion was a simple and obvious way to prove his innocence.

The nature of the terms of the purported spell hinted that it, like his seventh spell, would summon its target to a locus rather than dispatch it to one as the failed obverse would have done, but this distinction was, now that he considered it, probably irrelevant for practical purposes with a single target. He turned and concentrated on a discolored paving block at the center of the highway.

"Beautiful Woman, come forth!."

Expecting nothing, he felt shock again as the actuation of a spell sent a subtle shiver through his body. There was no denying it, the particular nuances of the sensation identified it clearly — *the spell was indeed his!*

With no delay whatsoever, the as-yet unnamed woman appeared above the stained block, swaying slightly as her footing changed.

"So you *can* transport me!" she accused.

"Hold on! Let me check something."

Nerves vibrating, Everett turned and selected a spot a hundred yards out in the soybean field to the east of the highway. *"Beautiful Woman, come forth!"*

The young woman appeared at the locus in the midst of the knee-high soybeans and began jumping and shouting.

Everett felt like jumping and shouting himself. He *had* manifested his eighth spell! And it was indeed a Potent! Magickers with Transportation Variants could demand exorbitant fees. He would be rich!

Even better – the manifestation of a Potent spell meant that there was an excellent chance that he would manifest at least one more and earn the exalted magical rank that he had dreamed of since his first manifestation -- *Wizard!*

But – and with his magic there was always a *but* – he could not shake the worry that something was not quite right. Why should this spell be any different? Why would it not, like all his others, have some value-draining limitation?

Though classified into Variant families, spells could and did manifest in myriad variations through the expression of primary characteristics and the modifying effects of Component sets. In short order, he ran some conjectures through his head concerning the terms of the spell and devised an experiment to determine the nature of a key primary characteristic. Choosing a pebble atop the highway curb some three feet in front of him to establish a locus, he concentrated on the image of a comely young woman he had seen a few weeks previously on the street in Pylton, and pronounced carefully, "Beautiful woman, come forth!"

The comely woman did not appear. There had been no magical actuation whatsoever. His heart sank.

Then, to further define the bounds of the spell, he thought of the place where Bob had given him a ride, some miles away, and locked on the location using a meditation technique that the monks of *Friar Albert's* had taught him before their high estimations of his potential had evaporated. "Beautiful Woman, come forth!"

Out in the field, his original victim continued to wave at him unaffected and unmoved.

Dejected, he selected a locus immediately before him and cast the spell again.

She appeared, slightly breathless, and caught his arm to steady herself.

"I'm starting to get dizzy." She grinned. "It's sort of fun though." She awarded him a warm, interested smile, then sobered, let go of his arm, and straightened. "Okay, no doubt about it now. Congratulations on the new spell. Send me back, please."

Everett shook his head hard. "Sorry, it won't work."

"What? Why?"

"The first problem with the spell is that it's a Specific."

"How's that?"

"All spells can be classified as General or Specific. General Spells, like my Major, will operate on any item that fits their descriptive identifier. Specific Spells only operate on one particularly defined item."

"I know that!" she snapped. "What has that to do with sending me home?"

Everett blew out a slow breath. "My Major Spell is--" He paused a moment and blanked his mind to prevent the establishment of either a focus or a locus. " -- Potatoes, come forth! It works not on one specific set of potatoes, these here for instance, but on any potatoes within its range, which is about a thousand feet. If it were a Specific, it would only work on one particular group of potatoes and never on anything else."

"Fine, but--"

"Think about it. A General spell would bring a random beautiful woman each time if I had no focus. Instead, it only worked when I focused on you. Tell me your name."

"I thought we decided that, under the circumstances, I should remain anonymous."

"It's important."

She stared hard at him for almost three minutes. "All

right, if it's absolutely necessary, you can call me Sally."

"No, your full formal name please."

The woman hesitated again. "Why do you need to know my full name? It seems to me that --"

"I have a suspicion concerning the enunciated terms of the spell. Trust me, I'm a magicker."

She did not answer immediately, but after a further moment of quiet thought, she relented. "Sarah Louise Mathilde de Bisghfaem Monte-Jaune."

"That's a mouthful. Bisghfaem?"

"It's an ancestral surname on my mother's side. In ancient West Phagaellean, it means ..."

Everett held up a hand. "I know. *Beautiful Woman.*"

"So, you're saying...but that's absurd!"

"I know, but it's true – my new spell will transport you, and only *you*, because your name is *Beautiful Woman*. But the part that really matters is that this spell, like all my others, expressed with a Visual Restriction Component and I can only establish a locus in my own vicinity. In other words, I can only transport you to a spot that I can physically see."

"But that's utter and total--"

"Crap," Everett finished sourly. "Of course. It's just like my other spells. Utter and total crap."

FOUR

Everett refused to leave his potatoes.

"I don't think you understand," Sarah argued, "I must return home. It's vitally *important.*"

He crossed his arms to indicate that he had no intention of rising from his seat on the overturned barrow. "I've already apologized for bringing you here, Mademoiselle Monte-Jaune, but it really isn't my fault. I have no choice in which spells manifest to me. Settled research has determined that manifestation is a natural process whose results are for all intents and purposes random. In other words and at the risk of anthropomorphizing a force of nature, Magic determines which magician gets what, not the magician."

Sarah stared at him hard. "I understand that, but it also seems to me that you should feel obligated to help me to return home."

"And I undoubtedly will, when I've gotten my potatoes to market."

"But I need to get back as soon as possible!"

"And I need to sell my potatoes as soon as possible."

"That's ridiculous. Surely you can't believe that the pittance you'll receive is anywhere near as important as my…"

"Yes?"

"Fine, I suppose I must tell you, but you must swear to keep the information confidential."

Everett shrugged. "Sure."

"Swear and be bound."

Feeling a slight unease, he hesitated at the odd wording, but finally said, "All right, I swear to keep what you tell me a secret."

Sarah nodded and seemed to relax. "Tomorrow, I'm to be married."

"Congratulations. I'm happy for you. Happy nuptials

and all that. But I'm sad to say that there is no way, aside from a magical or technological miracle, that you're going to be able to cover twelve hundred miles in one afternoon. You're going to be late."

"Well, it's *certain* that I'm not going to find a wizard capable of sending me home here!"

Everett shrugged off the insinuated insult. He had no pride to injure where his magic was concerned, having long since accepted his status as possibly the worst magicker in the entire world.

A maxim that his father had customarily bestowed upon his sister popped into his head. "If it's love, he'll wait. If it isn't, then good riddance."

"Don't be ridiculous. Love has nothing to do with it. My betrothed, Burgrave George-William D'Orth, is twice my age, an unrepentant bore, and a confirmed lecherous drunkard."

Everett's mouth dropped open.

Sarah gave him a sour look. "It's a marriage of state."

"I see," he replied slowly. "What a pity." That such dazzling beauty was to be wasted on something as mundane as diplomacy must surely be a crime.

"What's that?"

"Nothing. Hey, wait a minute! I've heard this story. So you're actually a princess who's in love with the common but brave son of the gardener but is forced to marry the evil heir to the throne of a rival empire?"

"Stop trying to be funny. You do it badly. And, besides, that's just silly. No one could force me to do anything. For your information, I volunteered. I'm the only eligible female in our family that has the moral rectitude to put up with a total idiot."

"But you are a princess?"

"Wrong again. I'm the grand-niece of the Elector of Kleinsvench."

"I've heard of that place. It's one of those tiny city states wedged between the Kingdom of Alarsaria and the Republic of Zheria, right?"

"Our nearest neighbors are actually the Grand Duchy of Filingham, a close ally of the Kingdom, the Principality of

Gainsfield-Schloss, and the Potentate of Yarb, but, yes, you're essentially correct, and that explains why I must wed an idiot tomorrow."

"I don't follow."

"Everyone knows that the Kingdom and the Republic are on the verge of war. You've likely even heard this here in the hinterlands. All the buffer states are making alliances with stronger neighbors in order to weather the storm. We've cut a deal with the Principality, which is aligned with the Grand Duchy and thus the Alarsarians. Lands of the Principality lie geographically between us and the Zherians and we hope that they will be able to shield us from the fighting."

The small, sovereign demesnes where Everett had lived his entire life, both in the coastal highlands where he had been born and here in the plains along the River Edze, were, apart from an occasional fuss over trade duties, serenely peaceful. For almost ten years, there had been talk of open war among the major powers but the prospect had never caused great concern; it was generally accepted that no war in the metropolitan west could greatly disturb life in the agricultural east.

However, there was one thing Everett was sure of: if there ever were a war, he would not be involved. He might be just a mediocre magicker, but he had sense enough to keep himself out of the insanity of war.

"Now," Sarah continued. "Is it clear to you why we need to get to a town where we can find a wizard that can send me back?"

"No," Everett answered honestly. Really, did she think that her problems were more important to him than his own?

"Fine!" She seethed, once again using the word to mean something entirely at odds with its general definition. "Suit yourself." She spun on a heel and started marching in the direction of Pylton.

"You won't find any wizards in Pylton," he called after her. "There isn't enough business for one. You would have to go to a city."

She stopped and spun about. "All right, where is the nearest city?"

"I suppose that would be the capital of the barony,

Eriis, which is on the Edze River about seventy miles from here."

"All right. How do I get there?"

"Go north along this road about fifteen miles. At the ferry landing, which is on a tributary of the Edze called the Green River, you can probably buy a ride on a riverboat all the way down to Eriis. It's probably twice as far as an overland route, but easier. I've been told that the trip takes close to a week."

Sarah stalked back to him and thrust out a hand. "Give me money for the fare."

"Sorry, I'm broke."

She sighed heavily. "Of course you are." Without another word, she began walking north.

Everett remained sitting. It might technically be his fault that she was here, but he had his own troubles. After a further few minutes of self-commiseration, he got up resignedly, began gathering the scattered potatoes, and tried to figure out what he was going to do.

There were houses and barns visible in the distance in just about every direction. He would have to hike to one of the farmsteads to seek assistance: another wheelbarrow or, even better, a cart. His Material Consolidation Variant, *Manure, gather ye into a pile!*, was always worth a few pence. Maybe he could trade several castings for a ride to Pylton.

It was simply a terrible shame – no, it was worse than that, it was an *outrage* – that his new spell, a Potent with such potential, was not generic. What good would being able to transport one particular woman do him? He had to admit that it had been a sight to remember, her standing there before him suddenly, her smooth skin wet from her bath and glistening in the warm sunshine. He indulged in the exquisite mental image for a moment and then stopped in mid-reach for an errant potato.

"Beautiful Woman, come forth!"

Striding determinedly, Sarah staggered when she appeared. She did not look at all happy to see him again. "This isn't funny."

"Sorry, I brought you back because I have an idea."

"To help me get home?"

"Yes, or, at least, a way to get you to Eriis quicker."

"All right, I'm listening."

"First, an experiment. Here, hold this potato."

As soon as Sarah reflexively took it, he cast his new spell. She disappeared and instantaneously reappeared as a tiny figure on a knoll a quarter of a mile to the west. He cast his spell again and she returned to her original spot. She still had the potato.

"What was that all about?" she inquired in a prickly tone.

"Transportation Variants come in over a thousand documented forms. Almost all are unique in some aspect and it is difficult to immediately comprehend exactly which Component modifications a spell may entail."

"Are you quoting a textbook?"

"Well, as a matter of fact, yes."

"So what's your point?"

"Well, when you first arrived, you were ... you know."

"What?"

"Well, naked."

"Hmmph."

"Anyway, after we started talking, I suppose I was distracted and certain key facts didn't register."

'For instance?"

"A small amount of water came with you the first time and my shirt stays with you –"

"Obviously. Most of them work that way."

"Right. Clothing Retention Component. But the potato was also transported. It's clear that my new spell also has an Associative Component."

She nodded seriously in agreement. "So anything I'm carrying will be transported. That makes sense, but how does it help me get to Eriis?"

"If you can carry me somehow, we can leapfrog to the city in jumps as far as I can see. We might be able to reach it by this evening."

"Hmm, what do you weigh? Fifteen stone?"

"Thirteen and a half."

"There's no way I could carry you. I'm strong but not that strong. Here, let's try this. Raise your arms."

Everett did as he was bid. Sarah stepped in close, wrapped her arms around his chest, and clasped him tightly. He felt her warmth through the thin shirt.

"All right," she told him, her lips near his ear. "Cast the spell."

The close contact was disconcerting, but with a major effort he pushed awareness of her soft form from his attention, focused, and enunciated the terms of the spell. At almost the same exact moment, he felt the spell actuation, experienced a brief instant of vertigo, and saw their surroundings whirl in a swift shift. When his vision settled, he saw an entirely different scene. They now stood on the knoll surrounded by knee-high grass and waist-high milkweed waving gently in an unenthusiastic breeze. A key fact, immediately apparent, convinced him that his scheme would work. Not only had she brought him along, but also his pants, boots, and the potatoes in his pockets.

Excited, Sarah released him and stepped away to look back toward the highway. "Great! It worked!" She turned and awarded him an approving smile. "Let's get going!"

"We have to go back for the potatoes," he told her.

Her smile vanished. "I was afraid that you were going to say that."

It proved impossible to move all the potatoes in one trip; Everett could only shoulder two of the sacks at a time and Sarah literally had her hands full. Even though the transport itself was practically instantaneous, the process of moving the potatoes in two trips and then orienting to locate a new locus in the right direction, and, eventually, resting from the strenuous task of picking the sacks up each time, made the trips last on average ten minutes. Everett compensated by pushing his locus as far out as he could identify a point, but even so, after three hours, with the sun well passed noon, he estimated that they had covered only about fifty miles.

As they arrived the second time on a tree covered hill, Everett sagged to the ground, slipping from Sarah's grasp, and let the sacks slide from his shoulders. He was exhausted. She stood looking down at him, not quite frowning.

"We'll have to rest for a while," he announced.

"We could move much faster without the potatoes,"

she reminded him for perhaps the eighth time. This time, however, her words were not burdened with reproach.

On all the previous instances, he had refrained from responding, but this time he felt moved to offer an explanation. "These potatoes represent the only money that I have earned in a month. If I abandon them, I won't eat today or tomorrow or for the foreseeable future."

"You've no friends or family that could help till you find other work?"

"Not within three hundred miles, no. I came to the lowlands because I thought that I might find enough work as a Magicker to pay my way. So far, I've been wrong."

"There's a lot of work for magickers near Kleinsvench. In Filingham, Grand Duke Elder isn't much fond of technology, they say, and bans it from his palace. I know that in Yarb it's quite easy to get a magic license. Maybe you should come along with me and try your luck in the west."

Everett briefly considered the proposal. It could not be worse there than it was for him here. But there remained the threat of war. "I might."

"Well, whatever suits you. How far do you think we have left to travel to Eriis?"

"Probably twenty miles."

"What kind of plan do you have to enter the city?"

"What do you mean?"

She looked meaningfully at his bare chest and then glanced down at herself. "I'm wearing your shirt."

"So?"

"Are you really that thick or are you pulling my leg? I'm wearing your shirt and nothing else and you're bare-chested. It looks like we've just been – *you know*."

Everett grinned lopsidedly. "I suppose it might, but what difference would that make? You don't know anyone there."

"I'd still rather not enter the place looking like a harlot."

Everett stood up, his annoyance giving him the force of will to push through the pain in his arms and shoulders. "We'll find a place to get you some clothes when we get close to the city. There are a lot of little hamlets thereabouts. Let's go."

Two hours later, just on the outskirts of Eriis, Everett found clothes for Sarah by the simple expedient of sneaking through a cornfield and stealing them from a clothesline behind a relatively modest fieldstone dwelling. The pants, shirt, and jacket were a man's work clothes, patched, stained, and much too large for her, but were the only clothes hanging on the line. Hidden several hundred yards from the farmhouse amidst the seven-foot verdant stalks, she made him turn around while she changed, which he thought rather silly, as he had already seen, as it were, *everything*. Nevertheless, presently he had his shirt back and she, though shoeless and with shirt and pants cuffs rolled up, had outfitted herself in a more modest if plebian fashion.

He did not have a watch, but the angle of the sun suggested that it was fast approaching four o'clock. Sarah had not said anything about lunch, so neither had he, but now his stomach, somewhat indignantly reminding him of the recent mistreatment it had suffered, had begun to rumble.

"Want to eat a bite before we go on?" he asked her as they wove through the clinging corn toward the low hill where they had left his potatoes. The pine-topped prominence gave a clear view of the sun-washed, red brick outer walls of Eriis, about two miles away.

"I thought you didn't have any money."

"I don't, but I do have--"

"Potatoes. Yes, *I know*. I think I'm beginning to hate that word. No, let's just press on."

Everett shrugged. He had missed many a meal and could do so again. "Right."

FIVE

As the lengthening shadows covered the cut-stone front of the shop, several younger men, apparently the sons advertised on the *Hirogo & Sons* sign, moved trays of ripe and green tomatoes, yellow squash, cantaloupe, egg plant, and sweet corn from the outside stands through the propped-open double doors and into the glass fronted interior. A heavy man with a full head of not quite gray hair, the grocer examined the potatoes that Everett had spread on an emptied tray. He picked up one, raised it to his generous nose, smelled it critically, and then rubbed its skin with his thumb.

"These are really fresh," Hirogo offered. "We don't often get the red potatoes here. I'm told they don't like the soil."

Everett did not comment. With Sarah determined to return to Kleinsvench, the usefulness of his newest spell remained problematic. He had decided that his best option was to refrain from acknowledging the existence of his Transportation Variant, and to simply allow it to remain disused and all but forgotten. Over the years, unkind souls had ridiculed his less than impressive repertoire of magic, and although he had learned to turn a deaf ear to the derision, the laughter still grated. The entire incident with Sarah and his new spell had all the trappings of a bawdy tavern joke and he had no desire to gain widespread fame in that manner.

The grocer seemed satisfied. "I'll give you one silver six pence to the pound, but you'll have to take most of it in banknotes. Coin is scarce since the Baron started sending hard money to Ferbam to buy steel for his new gunboats."

Making one intermediary hop to an unwatched spot atop the New City Wall, he and Sarah had spotted a neighborhood market in the eastern section of the city and then transported the potatoes to a blind alley near it. They had arrived about two hours before dusk just as many of the shopkeepers were closing up. The grocer, who lived in an apartment above his establishment, had been willing to take a look.

Surprised and pleased, Everett tried not to grin. This was very much more that he had expected. "That's a good price."

"Quadruple what I normally pay, but what with the Kingdom buying up all the grain, beans, and oil, and the Baron deciding that he's going to build a river navy, prices for everything are getting pushed up. It's getting ridiculous. The boatyard is paying big wages, so there's plenty of money around, but the price increases are hurting some of my regular customers. Everything that comes into Eriis nowadays costs twice or three times as much. Not much to be done about it, though. Let me get your money."

As Hirogo counted the last few coppers into Everett's hand, he glanced down at Sarah's unshod feet and grinned.

"Ah, I see! I'd wondered about the red potatoes this far west, but you must have come down the Green from beyond Pylton?" He clasped Everett on the shoulder. "Congratulations! I took a farm girl to wife myself, some thirty-two years ago, but her dowry was asparagus!"

The man chuckled in remembrance, smiling kindly at Sarah. "The day I met her walking down a furrow, Elie was barefoot too."

As Everett opened his mouth to stutter a denial, Sarah hugged his arm and glowed proudly at the grocer. "My dad isn't too fond of Everett, so we decided to move to the city."

"Well, don't worry girl. He can find work right way in the boatyard. Baron Fredrick has determined to take it upon himself to police the Edze from here to the gulf and he's building fifty steam gunboats to do the job. If you ask me, it was the Alarsarians who supplied the money, such as it is." He glanced significantly at the fold of ten crisp, twenty silver banknotes in Everett's hand.

"You'll need shoes in the city, girl," the grocer went on. "The cobbles will tear your feet to shreds. Tomorrow, go see a cobbler by the name of Bindston over on Elber Street. Tell him I sent you or he'll try to charge you twice as much as he should."

Sarah thanked Hirogo with a blissful smile and then started to steer Everett away up the street.

Having a sudden craving, he stopped before they had gone more than a few steps and turned back. "Monsieur Hirogo, have you any apples for sale?"

"I wish I did as they would go for a nice premium, but no, they're out of season."

"No storage apples left?"

"Not a one, sorry."

"Thanks all the same." Everett smiled through his disappointment and let Sarah tug him away.

When they had gone some distance along the flagstone sidewalk and were safely out of earshot of the grocer, he asked her "What's with the pretense?"

She released his arm but continued to walk on into the city. "I don't want it nosed about who I am. If Hirogo happens to mention us to others about town, which I don't doubt that he will, he'll speak about a young couple from the countryside, not a foreign girl. If there are Alarsarian agents here in Eriis, then there are sure to also be Zherian spies. If they learn that I'm here, they might try to prevent me from returning to Kleinsvench."

Everett made a face. "Isn't that just a little paranoid?"

Sarah laughed. "It did sound a little bit that way, didn't it? And a little pompous?"

"More than a little."

"Well, maybe I'm exaggerating the danger, but I'd still like to keep a low profile. Perhaps neither Kleinsvench nor I are of any significant importance to the Great Powers, but I'd still prefer this episode not to become public knowledge. My future in-laws are the sort of elitist nobility that would pretend to faint dead away at the slightest hint of scandal or irregularity. Kleinsvench is in a tough position. Without the alliance, one of the larger demesnes might decide to annex or occupy us when the fighting breaks out."

"What will happen if you don't make it back for the wedding?"

"I'm not sure. Since I just disappeared from my bath, I don't doubt that my family will suspect skullduggery. My

Aunt Louise is the hand-wringing type but my father is pretty sharp and I think that it'll be obvious to him that magic snatched me away. Hopefully, he'll be trying to find a wizard with a spell that can locate me or explain what happened. If I don't manage to return, I would imagine that the Elector, who is quite a shrewd old biddy, will try to convince the Burgrave to accept one of my cousins as a last minute substitute."

"So this mess is probably not a total disaster, then?"

"Maybe. But I still need to try to get back. Even if the wedding gets sorted out, I have other … responsibilities … that I cannot be away from."

"I'll help all that I can," he told her with utter sincerity.

She smiled in evident gratitude and then paused to look about.

Eriis was a pleasant little city, neat and prim. The current Baron's great-grandfather had spent half his treasury to demolish and rebuild much of it according to an ambitious master plan drawn up by one of the most famous architects of his time. Most of the buildings, some up to four storeys, were of brick and often sported balconies and sharply arched bay windows in the distinctive style known as "Heimgelbergian." Rooftop gardens and street spanning arcades were common, as well as decorative cornices, faux columns, and colorful mosaics. The long dead architect had laid out the remodeled section of the city in regular, precisely oriented blocks, and the streets and walks were all paved and guttered, with good drainage and sewers. Generous spaces had been allotted for parks and tree covered commons and overall the place had an open, breezy, and clean feel.

Everett had only visited the city twice in the twenty-eight months that he had been in the Barony, but had immediately taken to Eriis, and had resolved to rent permanent lodgings here, once his commercial fortunes turned.

"All of the wizards have shops on Boulevard de Berast," Everett informed her. "The avenue is in the wealthy neighborhood near the Baron's palace, but they don't keep long hours and are probably all closed."

"Do you think that any of them would open up for us?"

"Unlikely. All of the commercial enterprises in that

district cater to the affluent and are fairly prosperous. Living above one's shop is an economy the proprietors there don't need to practice and, as far as I know, none do. I would imagine that all have already scattered to their taverns, rooming houses, or apartments. But I don't think we need speak with the magicians directly. I seem to recall seeing a sign in one of the wizard's windows with a list of spells and prices. If the others do the same, then we could just window shop to find out if any of them can cast a Vital Transportation."

"Sounds good! Let's go."

As they moved deeper into the heart of Eriis, they encountered no significant vehicular traffic. On occasion, they merged into bustling pedestrian crowds as the populace began to head home for the evening. Though their appearance was somewhat meaner than the majority of the citizens, they drew little attention. Most seemed single-mindedly intent on reaching the shelter and succor of their houses. After a charging matron with several packages unconcernedly trampled her toes, Sarah clung to Everett's arm and let him run interference.

He made a couple of false turns but managed to navigate to Boulevard de Berast without mishap. Both the palace of Baron Winstead Heimgelberg, situated on the rugged, prominent rise at the center of the city, and the neighborhood of posh homes that surrounded it were inside the Old City Wall, but the propped-open gates were untended and no guards were present to offer challenge as they entered. A left at the first intersection beyond the gate brought them to Berast, a broad lane that wound around the foot of the hill. With wide promenades and a grassy median sprouting mature live oaks, the avenue was an opulent reflection of the character of the district.

It still lacked better than an hour before nightfall when they arrived, but two wardens in the butternut and gold livery of Heimgelberg had already begun to light the pole mounted oil lamps that lined the thoroughfare.

Seeing no need to rush, Everett, with Sarah still on his arm, began to stroll down the promenade on the left side of the boulevard, casually taking in the shop window displays.

Among the various milliners, chapelleries, confiseries, fine goods shops, and banks, there proved to be five wizard and four magicker shops. All of them, as expected, where shut tight, but all had printed cards or elaborate signs posted to advertise their wares. They checked each one in turn, finding everything from a Human Behavior Modification (*Loose that extra weight now!*) to a Plant Lifecycle Advancement (*Apples One Month Early Guaranteed!*) The last shop that they came to was that of a Master Wizard by the name of Gerald D'Ange. His list of eleven spells was on an ornately carved board mounted to the right of his garishly-red door.

Everett ran his finger down the silver inlaid letters. "Well, looks like it's your lucky day! Here's one – *Large Mass Vital/Non-vital Transportation (Group, Potent, One Way and Round Trip).*"

"Great! What does it cost?"

"Just a second." Everett read the next line. "Specific Location Only. Vacation on the fantastic equatorial Isle of Baelgru! White sand and warm sun even in the dead of winter!"

"Oh."

"Sorry."

"Not your fault. Well, I mean, it *is* your fault that I'm here, but you know what I mean."

"Right." He did not know what to say next, so he remained quiet while she stood in thought.

"Your spell is simply too limited. It would take forever to get to Kleinsvench," she pondered out loud.

Everett did some swift mental calculations. Transportation over a journey of twelve hundred miles probably would take no more than fifteen or so days, but being unable to carry more than a minimum of supplies and having no way to determine a proper course would no doubt cause the trip to take double or triple that.

Not that he actually wanted to attempt it. "Right."

"There's no other option, I suppose, but to head down the river and then catch a coastal steamer?"

"That would probably be the quickest way," he ventured, pleased that she did not press him to use his eighth spell.

"Do we have enough money to buy passage all that way?"

He gave a slight wince at the inclusive and presumptuous "we" and the claim that it implied to the banknotes in his pocket. Still, it could not do any harm to travel with her. Despite his best efforts, it was time to admit that he did not have the proper spells to earn his keep here in the Baronies. It was just possible that he might have better luck in the more populous and metropolitan western part of the continent. If the brewing conflict did explode into war, he could always return to Eriis or perhaps one of the coastal ports like New Zindersberg, the large trading port at the mouth of the Edze.

"I doubt it," he opined. "If prices are rising as sharply as the grocer said, then two hundred might not even buy us both a ticket on a boat from here to the gulf."

"Could we work our passage? Sign on as deck hands?"

"I don't know." It actually sounded like a really juvenile, half-baked idea to him, but he thought it would be better if she found that out for herself. "We could ask at the docks tomorrow, I suppose."

Sarah nodded. "Do you know of a place where we could lodge for the night?"

"Inns are fairly expensive here. I usually sleep in a hayloft outside the city." He did not think it necessary to mention that he did so without permission and always had to sneak out before daybreak to avoid begin caught.

"I'm tired enough to sleep anywhere. Let's go."

Away from the prosperous district, the streets were unlit, but the soft evening twilight of middle summer prevailed and they had no trouble retracing their steps. Once outside the Old Wall, Everett detoured south along Garker Street, the main north-south artery, explaining to Sarah that his preferred hayloft lay in that direction. Garker passed through several residential neighborhoods and then edged by an area predominated by small workshops and warehouses. By this time, the twilight had all but succumbed to full darkness and the streets were mostly deserted. The windows of the city began to show lights, mostly the yellow, inconsistent illumination of oil lamps, but occasionally the white glare of the new battery fed electric bulbs.

Just beyond a cotton warehouse, with the Main Southern Gate of the New City Wall in sight and the street otherwise vacant, a man sidled from a side road and stopped when he saw them. He was rather common: average height, work clothes, a fancy moustache. Smiling pleasantly, he said, "Good evening!"

Everett also stopped and laid a restraining hand on Sarah's arm, so that they were still several paces from the man. His father, afflicted by a terminal predisposition to adages, had had another frequent saying: "Just because a man looks friendly, doesn't mean he is."

"Evening," Everett replied neutrally.

"Out for a walk with the wife? Good night for it." The man had an even baritone and hands that danced as he talked.

"Right."

"I hate to ask, but could I bother you for a few coppers? I've lost my job and haven't eaten since yesterday."

Everett relaxed slightly. He had an intense, personal understanding of the man's plight and had once or twice had to do a little begging himself. He began to fish in his pocket and, without thinking, pulled out the fold of banknotes to get at the coins.

The man's eyes widened at the sight of the money, and, then he grinned, showing the patent enamel of a full set of false teeth. Then, with studied casualness, he slid a long dirk from a sheath at the back of his belt. His easy motions indicated that he was more than comfortable with the weapon. His tone still pleasant, he twitched the end of the knife at the paper bills. "That'll do. Just let me have it all."

Sarah sucked in her breath sharply.

Cursing himself for an idiot, Everett jammed the banknotes back in his pocket and raised his fists. He was not going to give up the money. He had *earned* it, for Magic's sake! No two pence thief was going to take it away from him! As he readied himself to attack the cutpurse, he heard a swift sound behind him and something struck him on the back of the head. Stunned, he staggered and dropped to his knees. Immediately, rough hands pinned his arms.

Sarah said loudly, "Flammables, ignite anon!"

White light flared and someone, maybe the first man, began screaming. The rough hands released Everett and, head spinning, he tried to stand. Sarah cast again. Again, light flared, brighter, and another man screamed in pain.

Sarah took hold of his arm and hauled him upright, then slung her arms about him. "Get us out of here!"

He shook his head, trying to clear it. "What?"

"Transport us!"

Looking about through blurred vision and ignoring the horrifying images of two men leaping about and swatting at flaming clothing, he caught sight of the pool of light from a lamp at the gate far down the street. He focused and cast.

When they appeared in front of them, the two Baronial Gendarmes lounging in the gatehouse jumped up, shouting, and went for their pistols. Beyond the gate, Everett saw the wavering glint of starlight on something far out in the gathering night and cast again.

Water exploded outward from them in a huge burst of spray and then rushed back, cold and solid, to swamp them. Sputtering, he kicked to bring his head above the surface, saw Sarah's head bob up near by, and swam toward her. Treading water, she sculled about and then launched herself in a practiced breaststroke. Following, he saw her emerge from the water after only a few yards and he also soon encountered the sloping bottom of the pond. He followed her up the cow-mucked bank and into the cropped grass of a large pasture.

As water dripped from the end of his nose, he glared accusingly. "Why didn't you tell me you were a Magicker?"

She pinched her lips together. "You didn't ask."

He choked back a curse, blew out air to ease his aggravation, and rubbed the painful swelling on the back of his head. A monstrous headache had already begun. "Well?"

"Well what?"

"What rank are you? How many spells do you have?"

"Six, currently."

"It might have helped if you had told me that in the beginning."

"I don't agree. None of my spells is any kind of Transportation Variant."

Seething once again, he stared at her gritting his teeth

for a moment and then with cold determination reached in his pocket to extract the soaking banknotes. He carefully separated five and tossed them down at her feet.

"That's half of what I have. Goodbye." He turned about and started marching across the pasture. He did not pick a direction; he just left her. She did not call after him.

After a hundred yards, Everett came to a rail fence. Beyond were another pasture and a large herd of dairy cattle settling for the night. Not wanting to disturb the animals into a racket, he turned and followed the fence and started looking for a place to bed down. He was cold, tired, and hungry and the only condition of the three that he could remedy at the moment was the second.

The fast Inner Moon had risen, and though not quite full, it provided enough light for him to see his general surroundings. There were the dark silhouettes of trees far ahead of him, but most of the land was given over to rolling pasture. Something more than two miles off of his left shoulder, the lights of Eriis were visible. Eventually, the fence guided him by a meandering path to a dark, sagging old cottage that had been converted to a hay shed. The windows were empty holes, no paint remained on the weathered siding, one entire end wall had been wrecked out, and the stars and moonlight shone through the slate roof, but the night had already begun to cool and it was better than sleeping among the cow patties. Most of the bales had already been taken out, but there remained sufficient loose straw scattered inside to ruck into a meager bed. He burrowed into it, damp clothes and all, and tried to relax in spite of his throbbing skull.

He was almost asleep when he heard steps stirring the grass outside.

"Who's there?" he called, sitting up. Sometimes these farmers could be rather unreasonable about uninvited guests. Their unreasonableness generally involved pitchforks and cudgels.

"It's me," Sarah, plainly visible in the moonlight, answered from the just outside the house. "I've come to return your money. I don't have any right to it."

Everett got up, stalked toward her, and stuck out his hand. "Suit yourself."

She laid the damp bills in his palm and then walked with calm assurance by him into the dim interior.

"*What are you doing?*" he demanded indignantly.

"I'm going to sleep. This is the only place close and I'm tired."

Flabbergasted, he followed her, rolling the bills carefully and shoving them into a shirt pocket. "You can't sleep here."

"Of course I can." She found his pile of hay, looked it over, then sat down and started rearranging it to suit her.

"That's mine."

"We can share it."

"Not hardly. Now, what did you tell me? *Oh, yes.* There's *absolutely* no chance of us developing a romantic relationship."

"Don't be absurd. All I'm interested in is sleep."

Grumbling, but not willing to throw her out bodily, he flopped down to secure claim to his own portion of the musty hay.

She slipped out of her jacket, spread it aside to dry and then began to tug the sleeves of the shirt in order to remove it.

"*Now what are you doing?*"

"I'm not going to sleep in these wet clothes and neither should you."

"*What?*"

She looked at him, smiled amusedly, and said, "*Good night and sweet dreams!*"

SIX

Everett woke just after dawn. Feeling rested and warm, he did not stir for several moments. When he finally deigned to open his eyes, he immediately saw Sarah sitting in her now dry clothes nearby, trying to comb out her fluffed hair with her fingers.

"You cast a spell on me," he said without ire.

"Of course."

"What is it, a Short Term Soporific?"

"Yes, but without a set duration. It makes the target sleep for a period of normal rest. It works great on babies. When I was young, I was in great demand as a baby sitter."

"Huh," he grunted. He started to sit up, realized that he was nude and covered only by his own nearly dry clothing, and clutched at them in sudden panic. "I'm naked!"

"I wasn't about to let you sleep in your wet clothes."

"But – you undressed me?"

"You've seen me without my clothes on," she pointed out.

This brought him up short. She had a point.

Managing to keep all the pertinent bits covered with his shirt, he drew on his small clothes and pants, then stood up to finish dressing, all the while marveling at the strange detour his life had taken. This thought raised logically obvious suspicions.

"Have you cast any other spells on me?" he interrogated while buttoning his shirt.

She awarded him an obviously insincere pout. "No, of course not."

Not bothering to mention that he did not believe her, he hopped on one foot to slip on one sock, then the other, and then slid on his boots. They squelched unpleasantly. If he walked far in them, he would wear blisters. He noticed that

Sarah was also now wearing a pair of sturdy, lace-up shoes and white socks.

"Where'd you get the shoes?"

She did not smile. "I encountered them nearby."

"Ah." *Encountering* needed items was a practice he had often had to employ himself.

The night's rest had considerably lightened his mood. His headache was gone and he felt more refreshed than he had in some time, likely a side effect of her Soporific. He debated with himself for just a moment, then offered, "Help me transport myself back to the city and I'll buy breakfast." At least his spell could save him some foot sores.

"Deal."

Two clandestine hops and a short stroll brought them to Eriis's North Main Gate. On a previous visit to the Baron Heimgelberg's capital, he had eaten a very good meal at a place in the northern borough of the city. He could not recall the name of the street-side café, but he did remember that they had served excellent cornbread. After a ten-minute walk along the gradually awakening streets, he easily found it again and the two of them grabbed a small table as the morning clientele began to crowd in. Then, moved to benign largesse by the comforting and exhilarating feel of money in his pocket and cognizant of his many missed meals, he ordered pancakes and link sausage, biscuits with jam and bacon, grits, scrambled eggs, and a tall glass of milk for them both. He did defer, however, the offer of hash browns; he felt sure that his companion would not be enthused by more potatoes. He then surprised himself by eating his entire portion, finishing by swabbing the last dregs of the grits from his plate with his final bite of biscuit. Sarah also surprised him by devouring her own meal with a voracious appetite, except for the two biscuits and bacon, which she folded in a paper napkin and stuffed in her jacket pocket against, she informed him, future need.

The waiter, a shorter man with a crippled left arm and a cheerful disposition, nodded in admiration as he totaled up the bill. "My sister is the cook. It does her proud to see people finish their plates like that. That'll be seven and twenty."

"Ouch," Everett complained, handing the man a twenty.

The waiter shook his head in sympathy and made change from his apron. "At the rate things are going, it'll be twice that in a couple of months."

Everett accepted his change, all in crumpled banknotes except for the coppers, then handed the man back a five. "For you and your sister, for excellent service and an excellent meal."

When they left the café, Everett made his way back to Garker Street, in order to guide Sarah to the docks. His full stomach made him disinclined to be disagreeable and he deferred the question of whether he would part ways with her until they arrived.

As they made their way along the street, mixing in with the increasing but still light traffic of workmen headed to their labors, distracted accountants and other professional types, casual shoppers, school children, and the like, Sarah suggested quite seriously, "You shouldn't have given that man such a large tip. You can't afford it."

"It's my money. I'll blow it any way that I please."

"At the rate of twelve and twenty a meal, you'll be broke in four days."

"Not if I only buy *one* portion."

"Fine. You'll be broke in *eight* days."

"I'll find other work."

Sarah stopped abruptly alongside a patisserie's display window, grabbed his arm and pulled him out of the flow of pedestrians. Giving the semblance of examining the enticing arrangement of cookies and candies just beyond the glass, she told him, "You don't have to. Get me back to Kleinsvench and I'll pay you five thousand silver in coin."

"Do you *actually* have five thousand silver?" In his experience, the wealthy tended to have a generally elitist demeanor that she clearly lacked.

"Not in cash, no," she admitted easily. "But the Elector does and she'll honor my pledge."

Everett found the offer sorely tempting. Five thousand silver, even if the west were suffering the same rising prices as here in Eriis, would buy him an excellent fresh start. Such a financial cushion would give him plenty of time to research the demand for his spells and establish a regular clientele. Indeed, he might even be able to take some time simply to enjoy life for a while.

Still, Sarah was a major headache. She was unpredictable, deceitful, and entirely untrustworthy. Also, her magic remained a dangerous unknown. On the other hand, she was the most beautiful woman that he had ever met.

"If I take the job, I expect total honesty."

"Fine."

"Why did you set those thieves on fire instead of putting them to sleep?" he asked flatly, immediately enunciating one nagging concern.

Her response was matter-of-fact. "They attacked us and might have killed us. I reacted as necessary to prevent that."

"They might be dead."

"They probably received only moderate to severe burns. I didn't ignite their bodies, just their clothes."

"That sounds rather cold," he suggested carefully. The thought that she might decide to set him on fire at any second was somewhat intimidating.

"It was practical. Why didn't you immediately transport us? That would have been the simplest solution."

He started to say, "There wasn't time," but rejected the rationalization as soon as it occurred to him. If he expected total honesty from her, he would have to adhere to the same standard.

"I had some very painfully embarrassing experiences with my spells when I was young. As I told you, my magic is crap and spells are never my first reaction."

Just as Sarah opened her mouth to reply, an oddly dressed man with a strange cap on his head appeared beside her, shouted, "There you are! *Let's go!*"

Then the bizarre fellow and the Kleinsvench woman promptly disappeared, startling passersby and causing a general disturbance. Someone began shouting for a constable.

"*For Magic's sake!*" Everett cursed. There went his five thousand silver! "*Beautiful Woman, come forth!*"

Sarah popped back into his arms, disoriented, and he immediately cast again, transporting them both to the top of a multi-storey bakery a few blocks away. If Sarah's abductor showed up again or a constable or gendarme arrived, he definitely wanted to be elsewhere.

"Who was that?" he asked her as soon they landed on the flat gravel roof.

She held on to him unsteadily. "I don't know. A wizard I think."

"I think I deserve a small remuneration for my trouble before you go home."

"He didn't take me home! I didn't recognize the place and none of my family was there, just strange men with guns!"

Gravel rustled and dried bird droppings swirled as the wizard reappeared. *"Let's –"*

Reacting in a flash before the man could complete his spell, Everett set Sarah aside, stepped in, and punched the wizard so hard in the face that the man bowled over backwards. As the wizard started to get to his feet, Everett closed and drew back his arm again.

The wizard cringed, plopping on his backside, and threw up his hands with fingers spread.

"Don't hit me again!" he pleaded nasally through a bloody nose.

"If you try to cast a spell, I'll break your jaw this time so that you can't speak," Everett warned.

Sarah moved up beside Everett and demanded, "Who are you?"

"And what in the world are you wearing?" Everett added. The thing looked like some comically exaggerated costume from a theatrical farce.

Wincing, the wizard applied one of the long, voluminous sleeves of his chartreuse, symbol embroidered garment to his leaking and rapidly swelling proboscis.

"I'm Grand Master Wizard Wendal Pourfrey, Recognized Specialist in Retrieval, and this is my wizard's robe." The wizard produced the statement with a certain amount of resurgent pomposity, and then shook the hem of the robe, encouraging the gold tassels to dance. "They are all the rage in the capital."

The wizard spit out some blood, searching about until he found his hat, which looked something like a cross between a dunce cap and an old woman's bloomers. Perching the hat on his head seemed to lend him a measure of strength and the man almost visibly gathered his dignity. "May I rise?"

"All right, but remember what I said," Everett warned.

"Certainly." Wizard Pourfrey hiked his robe to plant one sandaled foot, then levered himself up. Suddenly, he shot Everett a truly venomous look, and spat out rapidly, *"Be ye wood, now and for all time!"*

Everett froze, sucking in a frightened breath. However, nothing happened.

Pourfrey's eyes grew large. "Wha--?"

Everett snapped his arm back again and the wizard ducked his head, crossing his arms protectively over it. Everett dropped his feint and kicked the man lightly in the groin. The slack of the overlarge robe dampened the blow somewhat, but still Pourfrey collapsed, retching and moaning as he clutched pitifully at his injured testicles.

"Set fire to him," Everett told Sarah loudly, implicitly trusting that she understood that his words were meant only as a threat. Though the wizard's failed attempt to turn him into a wooden statue made him feel less than charitable, he was not angry enough to want to watch a human being burn alive.

"Wait!" Pourfrey cried, trying to scramble away. "No more spells! I swear!"

"Only the truth, cretin," Sarah told the man.

Everett felt the light jangle of a spell actuation. Quite often, he could do that – feel the magic actuations of others. The uncertain ability had never been more than random and the sensation barely detectable so he habitually disregarded it. This time he made careful note; a second of Sarah's spells was an Imposition of Veracity.

"Who hired you?" Sarah questioned.

The wizard goggled as his mouth opened to respond, apparently in violation of his own wishes. "The Chief Minister of the Republican Directorate of Security and Technology, Donald de Grosivna."

Sarah frowned. "The Zherians?"

Unsteadily, Pourfrey got to his feet a second time, but seemed unable to straighten completely. "Yes." He sucked a long, shuddering breath. "More accurately, however, I must note that I believe the Chief Inspector to be operating more or less independently of the office of the President or of the Parliament."

When he finished, he made a little humming noise to verify that he was again in charge of his own mouth and swung his head to look curiously at Everett. "Why didn't my spell work on you? That's never happened to me before."

"We'll ask the questions," Everett growled, trying to appear as menacing as possible. He had been wondering the same thing himself, but decided that bluster would suit the situation better.

Pourfrey winced and shrunk into himself slightly. "Certainly."

"Why did de Grosivna hire you to find me?" Sarah continued.

"He did not say and I did not ask. My Location Revelation spell needs only your name to produce a locus. I simply provide a service and do not concern myself with my customer's motivations."

Mindful of the exacting nature of truth spells, Everett crafted as general a question as he could. "Is there anything else that you can tell us about the motives, plans, objectives, or intentions of your employer?"

Again, Pourfrey's lips worked under the influence of Sarah's spell. "No." Then, from all indications, voluntarily, he explained, "Curiosity tends to be negatively received by the sorts of people who engage me."

"Is it necessary that I burn you alive to prevent you from trying to find me again?" Sarah asked in a deceptively casual manner.

The wizard stiffened, trembling slightly. "No, of course not. Absolutely not. Positively not under any circumstance, no."

"Will you attempt to harm, locate, retrieve, disturb, discommode, or otherwise injure us in future?" Everett verified.

"No. Certainly not."

"Then swear and be bound," Sarah told Pourfrey.

Again, Everett sensed the slight vibration of a spell actuation and seemed to detect a flavor similar to the first. So! She had cast upon him when they had first met! He wondered what other spell she might have used upon him.

Pourfrey nodded eagerly, with evident relief. "I swear."

"Get out of here," Everett commanded.

Pourfrey reached into a side pocket in his robe and pulled out a small cage. Inside was a contentedly corpulent and thoroughly bored black mouse.

"What's that for?" Everett demanded.

Still under the compulsion of Sarah's spell, the wizard replied, "My Vital Transportation Variant has a Paired Duo Component. The spell always transports live creatures in pairs." Before he could be further questioned, Pourfrey quickly looked at the mouse and cast, *"Let's go!"*

Once the man and his mouse had vanished, Everett relaxed.

Sarah smirked. "I guess I'm not so paranoid after all."

SEVEN

Whether the result of paranoia or not, extreme caution seemed justified. Throughout the remainder of the morning, Everett bounced them around the rooftops of Eriis until they settled finally at a sheltered nook on the bell tower of the Steam Fitters Guild Hall. The position offered both a solid brick wall at their backs and a clear view of the surrounding roofs and streets.

For good or ill, he had firmly decided to throw in his lot with Sarah and see her back to Kleinsvench. If she had not lied about the payment, then he would come out of the affair flush with cash. If she had made the offer simply as a pretense to encourage him to help her, then he honestly would be no worse off than he was now. Also, the fact that the utility of his most powerful spell would forever be dependent on her cooperation remained a strong incentive. Were he to go with her to her home, perhaps from time to time she could be persuaded to assist him with commissioned courier work. Aside from these reasons, there remained a certain element of self-preservation in his decision. The parties that had sent Pourfrey would likely not take a positive view of his role in thwarting Sarah's abduction and might try to take punitive action against him. Having seen the ease with which she cowed and completely dominated a Grand Master Wizard, the most powerful magical rank, he had little doubt that he would be safer with her than without her. He did not bother to tell the young woman of his decision; by all appearances, she had already taken it for granted.

Given the possibility that they might be required to flee at an instant's notice, they stood close together, arms wrapped loosely around each other. Everett, though he dare not mention it, found the contact remarkably pleasant.

"I think we're safe enough now," Sarah suggested. "I

don't think any other wizard is coming for me, at least in the short term. Let's find lunch."

As Everett was beginning to learn, the young woman tended toward practicality. "Perhaps we should leave Eriis altogether. Return to the country side, that is."

"Another wizard with the correct spells could find us no matter where we are. I think our best bet is to find a way to reach Kleinsvench as soon as possible and we won't find that in a cotton field or a cow pasture."

He had to accede to her logic. "Right. The same café?"

"Sure, as long as you promise not to leave a five silver tip. We're going to need every copper."

After a filling meal of fried catfish, grilled squash, snap beans, fried okra, and, of course, excellent cornbread, Everett spelled them with only three hops to the top of an apartment building near the river docks. They had taken care to cast only when unobserved and had remained as much as possible out of sight of the inhabitants of Eriis. Paranoia, of course, was not simply an occasional pastime, but a vocation.

"There's Baron Heimgelberg's new boatyard," Everett identified, pointing south over the New City Wall and along the bank of the river to a dusty area of raw earth about half a mile out.

The yard covered forty or fifty acres of former cotton fields and the hulls of several shallow draft riverboats were already under construction. Stacks of timbers and lumber abounded and by Everett's raw estimate more than two hundred men worked on the scaffolds about the gunboats. Other crews were in the process of laying brick ramps from the water to the dry docks and still more labored in the construction of foundry buildings.

"All that activity takes a great deal of money," Sarah mused.

"The grocer said that the Kingdom was putting it up."

"I'm sure they are. This isn't good."

"Why do you say that?"

"We're convinced in Kleinsvench that this war is going to be a big one, not just an extended border skirmish like the last two. The Kingdom gets a lot of cotton, grain, meat, and farm produce from the demesnes along the Edze and they wouldn't be spending all this money to secure their supply lines if they thought it would be another single season conflict."

This left Everett wondering anew what type of mess he might be putting himself into by going west.

"We should head for the docks," Sarah prodded, stirring.

"Right."

Eriis was the major transshipment point for nearly all goods that moved along the Edze. Bellow the city, the low, mounded hills of the morainal ridge known as the Continental Spine confined the river and it ran much deeper, permitting the easy passage of the larger riverboats whose draft forbade the shallow and winding course to the north of Baron Heimgelberg's capital. Hemmed in by warehouses and freight yards, the city's docks lay in a shallow, artificial inlet just outside the New City Wall. Among the many small launches, barges, and punts were more than a dozen of the often gaily-painted large steamboats, most continuing to waft dark smoke from their stacks.

This morning, a great mass of cargo was on the move along the quayside, shifting on and off boats of all sizes, into and out of warehouses, and to and from other parts of the city. Many of the largest riverboats were piled high with cotton bales, wine casks, sacks of grain, and assorted crates and boxes. Indeed, the main business of the river traffic was the transfer the production of the agricultural demesnes down to the coast so that it could be shipped west to the more populous regions of the continent.

As they walked from the secluded cubbyhole of an alley onto the quayside, Everett noted with interest that among these major vessels were two of the newer side-wheeled type. He had heard that these had a top speed twice as fast as their older stern wheeled cousins. He had always had a more than casual interest in technology, and considered the possibility of observing the improved mechanisms at close range a treat.

The *Edze Princess*, a broad single stacked stern wheeler, wallowed heavily in the first slip, its decks piled twenty high with hundredweight sacks of corn. Crewmen, bare-chested in the burgeoning heat, worked to secure nets over the grain. She had the look of a well-aged craft and her upper decks had not seen a fresh coat of paint in some years, but as far as Everett could tell, the boat was river-worthy. A bald man with rough blue trousers and a high-collared, brass-buttoned white shirt sat at a fold-out metal table alongside her gangplank, entering bills of lading in a ledger. Perched beside the ledger was a faded blue, broad-billed captain's hat with the leaping silver dolphin insignia of the Free Port of New Zindersberg.

As they approached, the captain looked up and awarded them a jolly smile. "What can I do for you folks?"

Sarah smiled brightly back at the man. "We wanted to inquire concerning the cost of passage to the coast."

"I'm sorry, Madame, I've no berths available. Not even deck space. The New Zindersberg Consul has hired everything for a load of new recruits for the NZFC. I couldn't squeeze in another soul."

"What's the *NZFC?*" Everett asked. He had never heard of it.

"New Zindersberg Free Corps. The Assembly voted three months ago to fund infantry regiments and I'd say that was a wise decision, the way things are looking. Enlistment is open and recruits come from all along the Edze. You know, you're a strapping fellow. If you're interested, there's a five hundred silver signing bonus. They'll sign you up at the offices of the Consul over on Beal Street, just other side of the gin. If you go and if you don't mind, mention my name – Captain Gerard Corveille. There's a twenty-five silver referral bounty."

"Thanks, but I've no desire to soldier. I'm a Journeyman Magicker."

"Even better! I heard last trip that the Assembly is also going to raise a company of magickers and wizards."

"Sorry, still not interested."

Corveille nodded. "Don't blame you. I'm not anxious to see the Great Powers' troubles come east myself, but I don't think we'll be given any say in it."

Bidding the convivial man good day, they moved on.

The next boat in line had a generally ramshackle

appearance and the name on the blazon board atop the wheelhouse had peeled so badly that Everett could not read it. Except for a deckhand shoveling cattle droppings and hay from a pole coral that covered the entire aft cargo stowage, there was no activity aboard. When hailed, the man informed them that the boat's schedule called for a cruise upriver with a pilot to the cattle landing at Pennsbrook Town.

The third slip held a flat-decked punt with a modest open steam engine and stern wheel. No one was about, but chains and locks secured the boat to a bollard. Obviously, this craft worked upstream and would be of no use to them.

Everett and Sarah made their way down the quay, finding only boats fully booked or fares priced beyond their means. It seemed that every restless farm hand and dissatisfied laborer in the Barony had decided to try their luck in the expanding armies of the south and west. The cheapest quote was one hundred silver each for a spot atop a cargo of cotton with the proviso that they must bring their own food and water for the two-week trip.

"I'm beginning to think that I should have asked more for the potatoes," Everett told Sarah.

"We could always enlist," she told him with a crooked grin. "That would get us to New Zindersberg and then we could desert."

"And probably be shot," he responded sourly.

As they turned onto the jetty to which was moored the last of the large riverboats, they came upon a commotion at the gangplank. A tall, well-built young man in fine clothes and a rounded, mustachioed boatman were engaged in a strenuous discussion. Nearby on the quay, a large flatbed wagon and mule team waited. Several quiet men in matching light gray trousers and buttoned-collar jackets leaned against it as they watched the exchange. Though unarmed, Everett thought they had the look of esnes, an aristocrat's household soldiery recruited from his personal lands.

"Purser Stewell, I will *of course* not accept delivery of ten barrels of *apple vinegar* when I ordered *olive oil*," the young man, quite composed, insisted in a strong and determined voice.

"Now, see here, Baronet Rorche, if you have a problem

with the shipment, then you need to contact the shipper."

"I have not the time. But in any case, as it seems that there is some difficulty in communication occurring, I will state again that I will not pay for this cargo nor acknowledge delivery."

"This load is Cash on Delivery, Freight Included," Stewell blustered, turning his clipboard to show a form to the Baronet. "If you don't pay, we're out the freight and have to haul it all the way back to New Zin to try to get our money!"

"I am sorry that you will be discomfited, Purser Stewell, but the error is not mine. Good day to you sir!"

With that, Rorche spun on a heel smartly and marched back toward the wagon, agitated but not angry. Stewell threw up his hands but did not try to detain the nobleman, instead scuttling up the gangplank of the riverboat as he called for his captain. When the Baronet passed Everett and Sarah, he nodded politely and somewhat distractedly wished them a Good Morning.

Everett, to his mild disgust, noticed Sarah's appraising glance flick over Rorche. He had seen identical looks from horse breeders at livestock auctions when a champion stud came up for bid. The man was classically handsome, obviously moneyed and well educated, and exuded confidence like someone who had never suffered anything less than complete success at any task that he had attempted. It was natural that a beautiful woman would find him attractive.

"Just my luck," Everett mumbled.

"What's that?" Sarah asked.

Not willing to explain what he actually had been thinking, he improvised, "That man needs olive oil and I have spells to transubstantiate from water to olive oil. If the quality weren't so poor, I could probably snare a fat commission from him."

Sarah came to a stop. "Why don't we ask? We do need the money. Maybe he doesn't need the best oil." Before he could protest, she took his arm and steered him around.

"Baronet Rorche!" she called. "Excuse me, do you have a moment?

Without the slightest sign of pique, the young aristocrat halted and turned about. "My pleasure, Mademoiselle, but I must confess that I am pressed for time."

Sarah smiled and when she spoke, her speech was not the common plebian jargon with which she conversed with Everett, but the same stilted aristocratic mannerisms that Rorche employed. "Please forgive the intrusion, but I happened to overhear your discussion and may be able to provide some assistance. Am I correct in understanding that you have need of a large quantity of olive oil?"

As he focused on her, the young Baronet looked at Sarah in a manner that immediately caused Everett to take a disliking to him. In demeanor, Rorche was the very epitome of a gentleman and clearly would never have done anything so crude as to ogle the young woman, but the signs of his appreciation – the slight dilation of the eyes, the straightening of the spine to emphasize height, the quick inhalation to swell the chest – gave proof enough of his passive interest.

Rorche nodded once, a precise, almost mechanism-like bob of his head. "Indeed. Five hundred gallons of it, to be exact. Have you some idea where I might acquire such a large quantity? I was under the impression that I had already bought up all the not significant free stock available here in Eriis."

"We can perhaps assist you. Needing so much, dare I say that you have no intention of using it for cooking?"

"That is correct. I require it for technological purposes."

"Then the culinary quality of the oil is a secondary concern?"

"This is also correct."

"Excellent!" Sarah beamed. "Then I believe we can help you."

"How so?"

She indicated Everett. "Everett is a Journeyman Magicker and has spells capable of producing olive oil from water."

At this, Rorche focused on Everett with the single-minded intensity of a house cat tracking a bird beyond a closed window. Everett was pleased to note that the Baronet seemed to dismiss Sarah from his awareness entirely. Around the man's eyes, a slight tension gave the faint suggestion of the fanatical as he examined the Magicker. Then the young Baronet did something that Everett had only seen theatre actors do previously -- he clicked his heels in salute. However, Rorche did so with such sincerity and flair that, rather than farcical, the gesture impressed Everett as serenely dignified.

"As you already have mine, might I inquire as to your surname, Monsieur?"

Reluctantly, Everett gave it.

"I am very happy to make your acquaintance, Monsieur de Schael. Might I trouble you further for a demonstration of your magic?"

"I'll need a small quantity of water."

"Should it be pure?"

"It makes no difference."

"Then let us adjourn then to my wagon, where I believe there is a bucket for the mules."

There was perhaps a half a gallon left in the stiff leather bucket. Rorche set it atop the wagon and then he and Sarah, with his men in a circle behind, watched expectantly. Everett, purely for appearances sake, waved his hand slowly over the tepid liquid and cast his first spell. *I bid cool water become sweet wine!"*

After a long twenty seconds, the water clouded from within and darkened to a leprous purple. Before Everett could stop him, Rorche leaned over the bucket and took a tentative whiff. Straightening swiftly, the man made a muffled retching sound and turned his head away politely for a moment to clear his throat.

"Somewhat disagreeable odor, I must say," he judged, though not with rancor, when he had recovered.

Without comment, Everett cast his second spell. *"Wine, make ye oil anon!"*

It took more than a minute, but finally the texture and color of the liquid transformed again. This time, obviously having learned his lesson, Rorche dipped only the tip of his finger in the viscous, slightly greenish, translucent fluid and carefully brought the dampened digit to his nose.

"It does indeed appear to be olive oil, Magicker, though I think I shall exercise due caution and defer a taste test. What are your limits on quantity per cast?"

"The range of the spell is short, only about three feet, but I could, I think, handle a couple of barrels at a time."'

"Excellent. Now, are you committed to a commission basis or would you consider a long-term position? My requirements for the olive oil go beyond a set quantity."

"I'm afraid I'll need a flat fee. We're about to make a journey west."

Rorche smiled the broad, exceeding pleased smile of a man who has discovered steak on his plate when he expected turnips. "Coincidentally, I and my compatriots are also about to set out in that direction. Perhaps we could come to some sort of mutually beneficial arrangement."

"Have you a riverboat?" Sarah asked.

"Oh, no, not at all. We intend to fly."

EIGHT

"I've seen a hot air balloon," Everett admitted. "There was one at a fair when I was twelve."

"Then you understand the principle of lighter than air flight? This is similar, but instead of heated air to propel our craft upward we will use – well, for the moment, I should just say that we intend to use certain derived vapors. Our mechanisms and procedures are proprietary, you understand."

"Is that why you need the olive oil? To make the vapors?"

"Not specifically, no."

Baronet Rorche's rented warehouse was a tall building with brick columns and steel trusses, but the walls were splintered, weather-beaten wood. At both ends, by appearances recently, the entrances had been remodeled with sets of twenty-foot tall sliding doors to permit the passage of large loads. Guarded by two of the gray uniformed esnes, who, Everett took careful note, also had no visible weapons, the doors at the street entrance were cracked just wide enough to admit them single file and then immediately closed. Unfamiliar gargantuan mechanisms with numerous intricate protruding parts, large reinforced steel tanks, and a web of interconnected copper piping covered about half the building's scarred and uneven black brick floor. Nearest the door, several long tables crowded with odd glass tubing, small and large vats, and steaming pots were camped in a rough octagon, tended by a number of men and women. All were quietly and intently engaged in complicated activities, decanting, mixing, measuring, and stirring, but Everett had no clue as to what, exactly, they were concocting.

"Then you are a technologist?" Sarah inquired in a casual tone.

This was the second tier of technician ranks, the equivalent of a wizard, and it was clear, at least to Everett, that she intended the presumption as flattery.

Rorche smiled without pride. "Yes, though I see myself as more of a *synthesist*. Our group includes some magicians as well as technicians, but we also have a few representatives of non-mystical trades and have hired the services of many others: smiths, carpenters, ironmongers, and so forth. When I began this project to manufacture the world's first flying mechanism, I realized that I would need the talents of many different fields to realize the full potential of my schematic. The great success that we have had in this melding has challenged me to a new goal -- to systematically blend the efforts of all of the professions in order to produce greater advancements for mankind."

From a lesser man, this statement would have seemed no more than pretentious bombast, but from the striking Baronet, who cut as heroic a figure as any man that Everett had ever met, it struck the magicker's ears as the unabashedly optimistic declaration of an altruistic idealist.

But that did not mean that Everett believed it.

An older man stepped out from the camp of tables and apparatus and scurried toward Baronet Rorche. Perhaps twenty stone, he had thick jowls and the waddle of a man who had been heavy since childhood. He had thick white hair, but only in an arc that circled at the latitude of his ears, and he walked as if both knees pained him.

"Ah, excellent!" Rorche enthused. "Here is Monsieur Edwin Van Kelder, our *chemist!*"

Everett found himself intrigued. Of the three mystical trades, Chemistry was the most rare. This would be the first time that he had met a chemist, though chemical concoctions were quite commonly manufactured from printed formula books and available in nearly every hamlet and town.

Edwin Van Kelder was an emotionally demonstrative man. He embraced Rorche like a son, grasped Everett's hand and shook it energetically while clapping him on the back as if they were old chums, and then, quite the gallant, bowed low to kiss Sarah's hand. This last was also something that Everett had never seen outside the theatrical stage and he began to wonder what other eccentricities might be revealed by these new acquaintances.

"Edwin," Rorche introduced, "this is Magicker Everett de Schael and his, ah..."

"I am Everett's sister, Susan," Sarah supplied.

Everett covered his startled reaction to the lie with a cough into his hand, understanding her need to keep her identity secret, but wondering distrustfully why she chose to portray him as her blood relation.

Edwin craned his neck to look beyond Rorche, a quizzical expression on his face. "Franz, where is the oil?"

"The factor in New Zindersberg shipped apple cider instead of the oil, but I think that I have found a remedy in the person of Magicker de Schael. He can transubstantiate water with only one intermediate step into olive oil."

"Incredible!" Edwin cried, ecstatic, and, seemingly overcome with his joy, wrapped Everett in a lung-crushing bear hug. Everett suffered the contact stoically as Sarah watched with some amusement. Then the chemist released him and declared, "We must get started immediately!"

Everett was not so enthused. Fly to Kleinsvench? Simple curiosity had convinced him to accompany Baronet Rorche to his warehouse, but the idea seemed fancifully unlikely at the very least. As he recalled, the balloon at the fair had risen only when safely tethered to the earth with a cable. On one particularly blustery day, rising gusts had forced the daredevil pilot to descend to avoid being dashed against nearby trees. How would one navigate such an undependable craft cross country when subject to the fickle wind? Instead of an intended destination, one might more likely end up in the middle of the ocean or on some frigid mountaintop.

"We haven't yet settled upon my fee," he demurred.

Edwin's face fell. "Franz, we must have him in our group! He would be the key to the fuel processing chain!"

"I heartily concur, Edwin, and was in the act of explaining our project when we arrived."

"You must show them the air carriage! That will convince them!"

"Indeed," Rorche agreed, smiling. "I trust that would

be the very thing."

The air carriage proved to be in a spacious storage yard outside the rear doors. A high board fence and the blank-sided walls of adjacent warehouses fully enclosed the scuffed earth yard, effectively guarding it from outside view.

"We just rolled it out this morning," Edwin boasted proudly, as a father would of a child. "We are to begin inflating the vapor cells this very afternoon."

The term "carriage" led Everett to expect some type of wheeled conveyance, but only in the sense that it rested upon a linked line of wagon frames, did the air carriage indeed have wheels. The craft itself had only stubby, skeletal metal posts extending downward from its slightly rounded bottom to support it. All of seventy-five feet long from tapered nose to blunt tail and thirty wide, it resembled most closely the hull of a ship. A line of portholes and doors at middle and rear indicated that there was but a single enclosed deck, though a waist-height rail encircled the roof of the construction, indicating a second open deck above.

Rorche pointed out key features, not without a certain amount of subdued enthusiasm. "My schematic specifies a design that emphasizes strength while keeping weight to a minimum. The panels of the outer skin are the thinnest laminated wood available and we have shaped them with the application of steam to be slightly convex for added rigidity. We have chosen the term 'scales' to identify these new panels. These scales form an interlocked shell with an inherent structural advantage similar to an arch and thus the need for additional ribbing or bracing is greatly reduced. The skin has also been treated with a bonding shellac created from one of Edwin's formulas that makes it completely waterproof. As you will notice, the shell also has an oblong curvature that will greatly reduce air resistance. The view windows fore and aft and the portholes are manufactured from a layered resin material made by one of our Mechanics, Roger Binsyen, and have a third the weight of glass. Each and every component of the structure contributes to its strength. There is not one ounce of wasted weight. With no danger of boasting, I may safely say that this is the strongest manner of construction, measured by unit of weight, thus far achieved."

"Still," Everett pointed out. "It must weigh, what, several tons?"

"Dead empty, the net weight is five thousand, three hundred pounds, including the nets and rigging to restrain the vapor cells, which we have yet to attach, and the not inconsiderable empty weight of the rubberized fabric vapor cells. With a crew and passengers of thirty and baggage and supplies, and full tanks of fuel and ballast, we estimate that the gross weight will be some less than eighteen thousand pounds."

Everett raised his eyebrows. "Why, it seems to me that you'd have to have a hot air bag the size of Eriis to raise that much."

"But," Edwin injected gleefully, "we are not using hot air but a much stronger vapor derived from an aqueous solution! Millicent, our mathematician, has calculated that we will need only two hundred and forty-seven thousand cubic feet of lifting vapor to raise her!"

Everett did rough calculations in his head. "What's that, a bag one hundred by fifty by fifty?"

"Exactly," Rorche confirmed. "That is, the actual dimensions of our lifting area are slightly greater than that, taking into account the use of small, slightly pressurized cells rather than a single large volume, the physical bulk of the rigging, and additional vapor cells to permit a ten percent safety factor."

The numbers sounded astronomical to Everett. Despite the fact that it was something as ephemeral sounding as a "vapor," he found it hard to believe that Rorche and the people with him could produce such a huge quantity. All of the magical and technological processes of which he had knowledge generated outputs of nowhere near that scale.

His doubts must have been evident in his expression.

"The mechanisms in the warehouse are capable of a production rate of ten thousand cubic feet of the lifting vapor per *hour*," Rorche informed. This time, he did not make any effort to hide his pride. "Their design, as is that of all of the processes and mechanisms that we use here, is the result of our collaborative method of *synthesis*, the melding of Magic, Technology and Chemistry. We have discovered great efficiencies and refinements that each of the trades is incapable of alone. I do not believe that such a combination of disciplines has previously been accomplished to such a degree in all of history."

In spite of this selfless and grand but not grandiose manifesto, Everett remained unconvinced. For reasons he could not quite enunciate, he mistrusted Baronet Franz Rorche, about whom he actually knew practically nothing. Another favorite adage of his apple growing father had been, "If it sounds too good to be true, start looking for worms."

Still, if he accepted at face value the assertions that this new mechanism could indeed fly, and the implication that it would be able to make a controlled voyage, it sounded like a perfect opportunity to return Sarah to her home. His investment in the project would only be his time and spells, whose value under any circumstances was miniscule.

"How far west will you go and when will you leave?"

Rorche smiled triumphantly. "Tomorrow, as soon as all the vapor cells are filled and secured, we shall take a shake down cruise above the city to learn her handling characteristics. Should there be no difficulties, and we foresee none, then we will depart at full light the following day, bound for the capital of the Kingdom of Alarsaria, Eyrchelle. The voyage should provide adequate proof of the mechanism, and once we have risen additional funding, we plan to establish a regular passenger and mail route between the east and west. Eventually, we expect to expand to all of the major cities."

Everett glanced at Sarah and received an almost imperceptible but firm nod.

"Then, I suppose," Everett told Rorche and Edwin, "that we should start making the olive oil as quickly as we can."

An ecstatic Edwin spontaneously distributed bear hugs all around.

NINE

"But we don't know anything about Rorche," Everett argued.

"I don't care if he's the Mad Prince of Hweuland," Sarah rejoined. "The air carriage represents my best chance to get back to Kleinsvench before things go totally widdershins."

In a surprisingly short time, Rorche's men had presented Everett with ten barrels filled with river water. Spelling two at a time, within thirty minutes he had completed the task. He had continued to wonder to what use they would put the product, but had refrained from pressing the issue; he thought it certain that at some point, the synthesists would share the information. After a brief spate of testing, the Baronet had thanked them profusely and then had asked one of his esnes to see them out.

"Who's the Mad Prince of Hweuland?" Everett asked, dodging around the signpost of a darner's shop as they made their way back to the sheltered alley near the quay.

"Oh, I thought they told that children's tale everywhere. The Mad Prince of Hweuland was a silly old man who fell in love with the Outer Moon and swore to have it for his very own. He does a great many strange things to attempt to capture it, but always fails. In the end, he flies away into the sky on a giant swan and is never heard from again."

"Oh, yes, I've heard that one. Only the fellow's name was Crazy Count Cravon."

Sarah rolled her eyes melodramatically, "Regardless, the point is that whoever he is and whatever he's up to, I want to be aboard when Rorche's air carriage sails."

Everett shrugged and fell silent. He did not, however, cease mentally examining the afternoon's events and Baronet Franz Rorche himself for worms.

With members of the petty nobility -- barons, counts, viscounts, minor lords, and the like -- there was the general presumption of wealth, or at least that they had a decent income from their demesne, though Everett had heard of quite a large number of cases where aristocrats were in fact nearly as penniless as he was. Rorche had mentioned something about needing additional funding. Perhaps --

"Everett," Sarah prompted.

"Yes?"

"We're here." She waved her arms at the scattered trash, hardy weeds, and abandoned junk that decorated the dead end of the alley.

"Right. So, what's our destination? The café for supper?"

"No, I think we should go shopping."

"You can't be serious?"

"*Think*, Everett. We each have only the one set of clothing that we are wearing and nothing else. We're going to need more than that to travel half way across the continent."

"Well, I have the stuff in my pa—*for Magic's Sake!* I left my pack on the side of the Baron's Highway!"

After visiting a clothier along the northern end of Garker Street, Everett had barely twenty silver left. Two sets of clothing for each of them, including small clothes and socks, and a shoulder satchel to put them in had nearly cleaned him out. Though thoroughly discouraged and still angry with himself for losing his pack, he did not permit the low state of his finances to ruin his enjoyment of what he expected to be his last hot meal for some time.

"You mark my words," he assured Sarah, emphatically waving a bite of sweet potato speared on his fork. "There'll be nothing but cold rations on the air carriage."

Sarah had ordered the fried catfish again and she threw a pained look across the table at him over the sparse remains of her meal: three well-gnawed corncobs. The fish, fried okra, spiced new potatoes, and cornbread with honey had all vanished. Her process of consuming food could almost be termed a frontal assault.

"Are you always this negative?"

"I'm not being negative. I think it only makes sense to

understand the potential drawbacks and hazards. For instance, if the air carriage does manage to fly, what's to say that it won't come crashing back to earth when we're a hundred feet up? Mechanisms, unlike magical products, *are* subject to wear and breakage."

Sarah took a pose. "How could a man as handsome as Baronet Franz possibly build something not perfect?"

"Now you're just making fun of me again."

Leaning forward intently, Sarah looked him squarely in the eyes. "Your obvious adolescent jealousy, though it might be marginally flattering under other circumstances, is simply a waste of time and effort, both yours and mine. I'm not some immature, vapor-headed girl. I don't swoon or pine or mope over men and you can rest assured that I am *not* irrational enough to become involved emotionally or otherwise with *any* man under *any* circumstances. As I've told you time and again, my overriding objective is the protection of my family and to do that I must return as soon as possible to Kleinsvench. It doesn't matter to me whether Baronet Rorche is some evil genius with nefarious schemes or is simply just another doomed crackpot. If his air carriage doesn't get me home, then I'll find some other way."

Everett blinked. "Me? Jealous? That's just absurd."

Sarah shook her head wearily. "Fine. Suppose we did sit here and enumerate all the things that could possibly go wrong. What would that gain us? We don't have the resources to provide for any potential problems and trying to plan for them without having a clear understanding of what could go wrong is an exercise in futility. If something happens to the air carriage or some other difficulty crops up, we're just going to have to adapt and improvise, as we already have. We're both magickers and somehow or other we have to win through or die trying."

Rebuffed, Everett focused on his plate, filling his mouth with sweet potatoes. He had not actually equated his reservations about the air carriage with the conception of personal danger. A fall of ten feet could kill a man, if he were unlucky enough to land on his head. A fall of a hundred feet would very likely not leave much that the undertakers could use for a respectable funeral. Somehow, the sweet potatoes, despite being drowned in his favorite brown sugar and cinnamon sauce, no longer seemed quite as palatable.

He caught their waiter's eye and the plump young woman swept around to their table.

"Ready for desert?" she asked with a not entirely professional smile.

"Do you have any apple pie?" he asked with little hope.

"We have a great one in season, but now all we have is blackberry."

As one of his rations of last resort, the thought of blackberry pie did not appeal. "I'll pass."

Sarah likewise deferred desert and they concluded their meal in studied silence and departed. Everett started walking automatically toward the North Main Gate.

"You've lodgings for the night in mind?" Sarah asked evenly. "Another hayshed?"

"There's a barn on a hill about two miles to the north-west. The homestead is vacant and falling down, but the roof of the barn is still in decent shape."

Once they had reached a secluded spot on the highway north of the city, Everett pointed out the prominent hill and its orphaned barn and transported them there straightaway. While Sarah investigated the interior, he trotted towards the half-collapsed old farmhouse. When he returned to find her eyeing a musty pile of forgotten hay in the sagging loft, he offered her a pick of his harvest, a handful of tiny crab apples.

She shook her head determinedly. "No, thank you. Aren't those terribly tart?"

With evident relish, he consumed one in three surgical bites. "Incredibly sour and not quite ripe too."

She wrinkled her nose and made a face. "You're quite fond of apples, aren't you?"

He devoured another apple and cavalierly tossed the core off the loft platform. "For me, apples are a special treat. Most of the time they're hard to come by here. I grew up on an apple farm along the eastern coast and back then I had them just about whenever I wanted them."

Her eyes trailed across his face. "How long have you been away?"

"Three years this last spring. There's not much

opportunity for a Magicker out east so I came to the Edzedahl to get established in the trade."

She glanced around at the windblown wrack, dust, and cobwebs that had collected in the desolate barn to emphasize her point. "Not having much luck?"

He lifted one shoulder in an unconcerned shrug. "I get by."

"On potatoes."

"It takes a while to gather a clientele."

"Have you thought about going home?"

"No."

"You weren't happy there?"

He remained silent for a drawn-out moment, then admitted, "Just the exact opposite. I suppose that you could say that I have never experienced a more prosperous, contented, and secure time in my entire life."

Sarah looked wistful for a moment. "With the always looming threat of conflict between the Great Powers, my youth was one of continual tension and upset. I hardly remember more than a few moments of what I would consider to be peace in the first two decades of my life."

This comment amended a ponderous mood onto the gathering dark, and without any further conversation, they settled to sleep, reposing on opposite sides of the hay pile. At first light, they transported back to the city. A street vendor, a stocky man who did not bother to disguise his appreciation of Sarah's trim form, allowed himself to be bargained down to a price of Everett's last two silver fifty-seven for a loaf of fresh bread and a half-gallon of milk for their breakfast. They ate sitting on a bench in a tree-shrouded park at the center of a plaza, idly discussing Kleinsvench and the vagaries of passersby, then returned to Baronet Rorche's warehouse a bit before eight o'clock.

The first thing that Everett noticed was the unanticipated lack of activity. Except for some of Rorche's esnes, there was no one about in the warehouse and the thicket of apparatus that had been present the day before was gone, with the tables themselves shoved carelessly into an abandoned clump along the side wall. The large mechanisms that he had expected to see belching smoke, spitting oil, and clanking as such always did, were quiet and still. When one of the taciturn young men in gray ushered them into the presence of the Baronet, they found him standing at a well-used wooden desk tucked into a corner. Drawings on drafting paper, ledgers, and stacks of handwritten notes covered the desk's battered top in a tangled heap. With Rorche was a trim and charmingly elegant woman of indeterminate age who Everett took to be the mathematician, Millicent. Talking quietly, the pair appeared in deep contemplation of a set of figures on a clipboard. After but a bare moment, apparently receiving the clarification she required, Millicent rushed away after tossing them a quick I'd-love-to-talk-but-have-business-that-can't-wait smile in greeting.

"Excellent!" Rorche approved eagerly as he turned and caught sight of them. "I had hoped you would be on soon. We are far ahead of schedule and plan to launch in little over two hours. Once we had optimized the material flow, the production of our vapor mechanisms proved to be fifty percent higher than our previous calculations. Edwin was so enthused that he convinced the rest of us to work straight through the night with our other preparations and the manufacture of the fuel! Almost everyone has gone home to sleep, but you must come see the air carriage!"

The Baronet himself appeared as fresh and energized as he had the day before. He wore the same suit of clothes, but the pressed creases in his jacket and trousers were still sharp.

Everett had imagined how the completed mechanism would appear, but he was still taken aback when they walked outside. Casting a huge shadow over the yard, the great mass of the vapor cells, black globes two yards in diameter, hovered above the air carriage, extending high above the adjacent buildings. Rather than the loose random clump he had envisioned, the cells were confined and arranged within a compactly ordered tubular matrix by innumerable nets and lines. The cell matrix itself had been secured to the open upper deck of the air carriage at eight points along each side, with the lowest row of cells only perhaps fifteen feet from the railing. The wagons had been pulled away to the side and two low, wooden platforms erected adjacent to the side and rear doors. Resting only on its six spindly legs, the air carriage appeared barely restrained by dozens of heavy ropes. These ties led from steel rings along the underside to stakes twisted corkscrew-like into the ground. Shifting ponderously in a mild breeze, the now much more imposing craft did indeed give the impression that it could leap for the sky at any moment.

Rorche seemed pleased by their reaction. "Come, I should show you the engines that your oil will fuel."

A number of Rorche's were loading boxes and crates through the cargo doors at the stern, but only one small group of those the Baronet named "compatriots" were present and it was toward these that Rorche steered. The group, an older man, two middle-aged women, and a younger woman who was pretty in an industrious way, were in the process of securing a large, blocky mechanism to a tapered strut that protruded ten feet from the port side stern. About the size of a hogshead of beer, the mechanism rested on a metal stand with an unconnected halo of wires, cables, and fitted copper tubing draped across it. An identical mechanism, completed and covered in a slick metal shroud, had already been mounted to an identical strut on the opposite side of the air carriage.

The older man, one of the middle-aged women, and the younger woman all shared similar sandy hair, sharp cheekbones and strong noses. All paused, wrenches in grimed hands as they attached mounting bolts, as the Baronet approached.

Rorche introduced Everett and Sarah, using the alias she had supplied the day before, then indicated the others in turn.

"This is Algis Coldridge, a Journeyman Mechanic who has created the engine from his own schematic, his wife Ellen and sister Josline, who are both also mechanics and whose schematics have greatly enhanced the efficiency and output of the engine, and his daughter Eylis, who is a Common Magicker with spells that affect metal fabrication."

As handshakes were exchanged all around, Everett, wondering where the firebox and boiler were, commented interestedly, "I've never seen a steam engine this small."

Algis grinned catlike. "But that's the important part! It

isn't a steam engine!"

Ellen, who was as tall as her husband but had dark hair and darker eyes, elbowed him playfully. "None of your guessing games, Algis. Everett, the engine produces torque by the sequential driving of four internalized pistons through controlled explosions of a mixture of liquid fuel and air instead of a blast of steam. This method produces a greatly increased power to size ratio. For want of better, we call it an oil fueled engine."

"You made the fuel from the olive oil?"

"Yes," Rorche confirmed. "Edwin has a formula that uses the oil, alcohol, and lye to produce a stable combustible liquid."

"It *is* quite amazing, when you think of it," Josline Coldridge suggested. "Algis manifested the schematic when he was only twenty-three and we have been working to build and refine it for two decades with only the vaguest conception of what it would burn. When Baronet Franz brought us together with Edwin, it almost seemed like our moment of destiny had finally arrived."

"It was the moment of *synthesis*," Rorche corrected politely. "We all know that the great limitation of the mystical trades is that manifestations occur in isolation, without any correlation, logic, or interconnection. There must exist literally thousands of spells, schematics, and formulas whose potential cannot be realized because they depend on mechanisms, concoctions, or magical creations that are unknown at large or do not yet exist. A prime example is my air carriage. I manifested the design of the air carriage without any knowledge of its engines or the nature of the lifting vapor. Only with the contributions of other technologies, chemistries, and magics has it been possible to produce this working prototype."

The Coldridges, one and all, followed this discourse with the bright-eyed reverence of committed believers.

"I gather that these will propel the air carriage?" Sarah asked, moving about to studiously examine the new engine.

"Yes," Josline answered. "On this shaft we'll bolt an air moving vane that I manifested. It will push air backwards to create force in a similar fashion to the way a paddle-wheel on a steam boat pushes water."

Sarah looked impressed. "How fast will it go?"

"Because of the scarcity of the oil fuel, we have only operated the engines with the vanes attached for a very short period on a test stand," Algis replied, taking a turn, "but Millicent's calculations suggest a top speed for the air carriage under ideal conditions of twenty-five miles per hour."

"Remarkable!" The comment escaped from Everett of its own accord. Twenty-five miles per hour was just slower than a horse at full gallop but no horse ever bred could keep that pace for more than perhaps two miles. No land-bound steam mechanism that he had encountered had been able to best fifteen.

Sarah raised an eyebrow. "Will you be able to operate the engines continuously?"

"Once we confirm that all of our metal fabrications are sufficient to the heat and stress, yes," Ellen answered. "Initially, however, our plan is to run them only for regulated intervals during daylight hours. We will descend and moor at night."

As Sarah continued her questioning, Everett began to worry that her single-minded intensity might offend the family of mystical tradesmen.

"So we will cover approximately three hundred miles a day?"

"Perhaps more nearer two hundred and fifty," Rorche supplied. "But we fully intend to eventually run the engines from beginning of voyage till end. We conservatively expect to be able to travel between Eriis and Eyrchelle in less than three days!"

"But this first trip will take five days?"

"Yes, that is correct." Rorche looked as if he were about to expound, but the approach of one of his esnes, a grizzled, solid looking fellow with a long, prominent scar on the side of his neck, caused him to turn about. Coming from the warehouse at a fast trot, the man gave the impression of restrained agitation.

"What is it, Sergeant Tekle?"

The sergeant clicked his heels. "Sir, a squad of Baronial Gendarmes is at the street entrance. They're demanding admittance."

Rorche scowled briefly. "I expect that the vapor cells have finally been noticed. I must ask all of you to please excuse me. I will need to attend this matter. Eylis, would you do me the favor of showing Everett and Susan to their cabin? Algis, I think it would be wise if you tried to complete the installation in as short a period as possible. Once the Baron's men leave, I am going to send word to Edwin and the others. We may need to launch on short notice."

The elder technician clenched his brow. "Franz, we probably need at least another hour on this engine."

"Do what you can. I suspect if we do not launch quickly that the city officials will enforce ridiculous delays." The Baronet nodded tersely to them all and moved off rapidly with the sergeant.

While Algis, Ellen, and Josline attacked the engine with controlled urgency, Eylis set off briskly, striding to the temporary platform and mounting the stairs in two energetic bounds.

As he and Sarah rushed to catch up, Everett quickly asked the younger magicker, "Will there be trouble with the Baron?"

Although she did not slow her pace, Eylis did not appear concerned. "I wouldn't think so, but we neglected to seek licenses or permits for our work here. We thought it best to keep the air carriage project out of the public eye. It's going to be a new business venture, after all, and we didn't want word getting out till we were ready. I've heard that the Baron is having cash flow problems and they may try to make a fuss about fees and taxes. That might make it difficult for us. Our budget doesn't have allowances for any extra expenses."

"I thought the Alarsarians were footing the bill for the gunboats?" Sarah asked.

"That's the rumor," Eylis confirmed. "But Baron Heimgelberg has been pretty close-mouthed about the subject. All of the new bank notes have been printed by his own banking house, so who's to say?"

As they reached the rounded metal door, the sharp report of pistols rang inside the warehouse behind them.

TEN

Shocked, Everett whipped his head about.

Within moments, Rorche and Tekle ran at full speed into the yard, dragging a staggering man with a nasty scalp wound that leaked bright crimson blood down the front of his gray jacket. Half a dozen of Rorche's esnes charged out following them and hurried to slide the tall doors closed.

"Come on!" Eylis yelled, snatching open the door and leaping inside.

Sarah clasped Everett's arm. "Let's go!" She lunged through the door after Eylis.

Everett followed into a corridor hardly wider than his shoulders that ran forward the length of the port side. Light from the doorway and the portholes lit the passage dimly. Two men rushed from the bow, their pounding steps making booming sounds on the sheet metal deck and sending bouncing vibrations through the soles of Everett's boots.

"Eylis! What's going on?" the one in front cried. He was a shorter, stocky man with black hair and a full, trimmed beard.

"I don't know, Bennett! There are Gendarmes at the front entrance!"

Bennett turned about. "Aldo, get back to the bow and close all the circuits on the batteries! We'll have to launch!"

The second man whirled and ran back without a word. Bennett slid by Eylis and sprang for the still open exit. Without glancing back, Eylis immediately bolted after Aldo. Sarah, having backed up to get out of Bennett's way, jammed against Everett, forcing him aft against the lightweight door that closed the end of the corridor. He reached to catch both her arms as she made to follow the Common Magicker.

"We'd better get out of here!" he hissed at her.

Sarah twisted loose from his grasp. "You can leave if

you want. I'm going with the air carriage." She sprinted to catch up with Eylis.

Cursing, Everett vacillated for a moment and then went after her.

At an open compartment in the windowed bow, Aldo and Eylis were frantically closing large knife-bladed switches on a floor-to-ceiling panel mounted on heavy insulators to the rear bulkhead. Arcs flashed and the space began to fill with an acrid smell.

"What can I do to help?" Sarah gasped.

"We're going to have to dump all the ballast at once to gain altitude quickly," Aldo told her. "Open those eight valves all the way. I'll have the water pumps going in just a second." He pointed at a manifold of two-inch diameter pipes that rose out of the deck at the starboard bulkhead.

As the last electrical switch closed, Sarah dashed to the manifold and began to spin valve wheels. The manifold rattled as water began to surge through it.

Eylis turned to Everett. "Come with me!" Without looking to see if he followed, the young woman disappeared down the starboard side corridor. Drawn by her intensity, he raced to follow.

Eylis skidded to a stop in front of a one-foot square metal panel inset into the hull at about waist height. Everett had vaguely noticed similar panels all along the port corridor.

A finger-ring handle protruded from the upper right corner. She snatched on the ring to swing the panel open, pulled a now revealed hammer from a clip, and with one sharp blow drove a tapered brass bin out of a shaft that extended through a round support. The shaft, under tension, disappeared suddenly down into the support, leaving a round circle of daylight shining through. The deck beneath Everett's feet jolted slightly.

"We must release all the mooring rings! Do just like I did on all the panels along this side but leave one in the middle! I'll get the port side!" With that, Eylis sprinted toward a cross-corridor and vanished.

"To the Outer Moon with that!" Everett mumbled. He decided, five thousand silver or not, that he did not want to be involved with Baronet Franz Rorche, his insane flying

mechanism, or the niece of the Elector of Kleinsvench any longer. He trotted down the corridor seeking an exit, found a door, flung open the latch, and found himself face to face with a man in the black trousers, jackboots, and red trimmed butternut tunic of one of Baron Heimgelberg's gendarmes. The startled man raised his pistol and pointed it at Everett's head.

Everett threw up his hand reflexively, knocking the gun aside as it went off with a deafening roar. Luckily, it wasn't a double-barreled model and so the man only had but the one shot. Everett grabbed for the weapon, but the gendarme kicked him viciously in the belly and he doubled over, gagging.

Backing up on the wooden platform, the gendarme broke open his pistol with a practiced slap, snatched a cartridge from a belt loop, shoved it home in the chamber, and snapped it shut. Panicked, Everett rammed headfirst into the soldier with all his weight before he could bring the pistol to bear. The two of them crashed onto the rough planks. More afraid than he had ever been in his life, Everett fought the man for the pistol as they grappled and rolled. With savage desperation, he managed to grab the mechanism just as the hammer slammed down again, pinching his index finger excruciatingly but not driving the pin into the cartridge. Within seconds, his opponent, larger and stronger, abandoned the pistol, wrenched around, and wrapped the magicker in a strangling hold. The edge of Everett's vision dimmed and began to go dark.

"Give me strength!"

The terms of the spell whispered unbidden from Everett's lips. A shock surged through him as he sensed the most powerful actuation that he had experienced in his entire life. Sudden energy infused his arms with phenomenal power. With unbelievable ease, he ripped the gendarme's rock hard bicep from about his neck, snapping both forearm bones in the process. As the man screamed hideously, Everett raised him above his head and threw him ten yards out into the yard, where he bounced, rolled, and flopped.

Then, just as suddenly, the magical energy that had made Everett inhumanly strong evaporated and he was left standing impotently as he wondered what had just happened.

"Impressive."

Everett whirled.

Sarah stood in the doorway, her expression guarded and unreadable. "Are you coming?" A shout echoing down the corridor inside the air carriage drew her away from the opening. The flying craft shifted, swaying. On this side, only one mooring ring and its ropes remained attached.

He drew a deep, ragged breath, but did not move.

A pistol cracked and a bullet splintered the handrail a few inches from his left hand. Reflexively, he leapt for cover, diving for the doorway and landing inside just as the air carriage heaved and rocketed upward. With the sounds of other shots and the chilling *zing* of bullets passing through the hull ringing in his ears, he rebounded off the corridor wall, scrambled to catch hold on the nearly featureless wood panels, and felt himself falling back toward the banging door.

Sarah's arms encircled him and she used her weight to pull them both away from the opening as the air carriage surged skyward. For several terrifying moments, the vessel rocked and danced erratically, tossing them about. When the violent movement finally subsided, Sarah released him but remained seated with her back against the outer corridor wall and her feet braced against the inner. It was clear she was taking no chances.

As the craft continued to shudder and creak ominously, but with gradually diminishing force, she regarded him as if seeing him for the first time. "Congratulations."

"Uhm, thanks."

"What's it like?"

"Being a wizard?"

"Yes."

"Just the same."

"Thought so."

Everett sat quietly for a few moments then said, "You released the mooring rings?"

"Yes. Bennett sent me to help you. He thought you'd fallen behind Eylis and said that there was a danger that the uneven strain might warp the frame of the air carriage."

After a few more minutes, when it seemed that the air

carriage had steadied, they rose and looked out.

The ground was far below and rapidly falling away. The buildings of Eriis, tiny and fading, were still visible in the far distance but were sliding toward the horizon at a rapid pace. Below, a checkerboard of fields and pastures unfolded somewhat leisurely. At least, that is what Everett thought until he took into account the effects of scale.

"We must be traveling thirty or forty miles an hour," he said.

"I wonder why there's so little sound from the wind?"

"No idea. Seems like there should be quite a bit of noise though."

The air coming through the door was cooler than the balmy temperature that had prevailed on the ground in Eriis and it continued to cool as the air carriage climbed. Within another couple of minutes the light dimmed as if they had passed into shadow and the air became progressively damper, then filled with mist, and finally a fog abruptly cut off their view.

"Clouds!" Sarah exclaimed in amazement.

Everett caught hold of a stanchion alongside the door, leaned out to catch the latch, and swung the door closed.

"This doesn't seem right," Everett told her. "The air carriage isn't under power. It's just drifting with the wind. We should go find the others."

A full complement crowded the forward compartment: Aldo, Bennett, the Coldridges, Millicent, Baronet Rorche, Sergeant Tekle, and the eight gray clad esnes, including the injured man, who reclined against one wall as one of his comrades tended the bullet crease in his scalp. Some were looking out at the clouds shrouding the forward view; others were simply standing or sitting quietly. Conspicuous for their absence were Edwin and the other magicians and technicians of Roche's group, abandoned in Eriis due to the abruptness of the crisis.

Baronet Rorche, who stood in the center of the compartment, looked around as Everett and Sarah emerged from the corridor. "Everett, Susan, I am pleased to see you. We did not know if you were still with us. It seems that indeed all present at the warehouse managed to board."

Everett wanted to say something to the effect that he was not at all pleased to be aboard, but kept his mouth shut.

"A gendarme tried to get in through the starboard exterior door," Sarah told the group with no animation or emotion. "Everett had to throw him out."

Everett kept his face blank. He knew intrinsically that the young woman continued to keep secrets from him, but was glad to see that she was also willing to keep his. At that moment, it seemed wise to keep the capabilities provided by his newest spell to himself.

"We were just discussing our predicament," Rorche went on.

"We're adrift?" Sarah asked.

"Yes, the *unexpected* nature of our departure prevented the completion of the installation of the port engine and thus far we have been unable to start its starboard companion."

"Why are we still rising?" Everett wondered aloud. "I'd think that you would want to bring the air carriage back to the ground."

Aldo, standing with Bennett at a curved panel of gauges, levers, and rotary dials in the forward section of the compartment, made a disgusted face. "That was my fault. I was only thinking of launching quickly and was blind to my obvious error. I shouldn't have dropped *all* the ballast."

"I don't understand," Everett admitted.

"We control the altitude of the air carriage by releasing ballast or vapor. The first causes it to ascend. The second causes it to descend," the Baronet explained.

"So what's the problem? You can still release vapor, yes?"

"Yes," Bennett groused. "But if we release enough vapor to descend to the ground, with no ballast to compensate, we'll be unable to ascend again. We'll be stranded wherever the air carriage comes to earth. Due to the inherent complexity of the conduit system, it's only possible to release the vapor at a moderate rate and therefore such a descent will take hours. At the speed that the wind is carrying us, once we land we might be two hundred miles or even more from the city."

"Which means," Rorche emphasized, "that the air

carriage might never fly again. The vapor production mechanisms in Eriis are too large and heavy to be transported whole and would need to be disassembled and brought overland. This almost certainly would take months, provided that Baron Heimgelberg permitted us access to them. Considering the less than peaceful nature of our departure, his cooperation seems highly unlikely."

"What happened, Franz?" Algis Coldridge asked with some concern. "Why were the Baron's men firing at us?"

The Baronet looked grave. "I accept full responsibility for this disaster. When I arrived at the entrance, the warden with the squad announced that they had come to arrest me and impound the air carriage. Without warning, the gendarmes seized me. When my esnes tried to intervene, the Heimgelberg's men drew their weapons and one of them shot Wrelton. In the ensuing melee, we managed to hurl them back long enough to seal the doors and retreat to the yard."

Ellen Coldridge looked confused. "But why would they want to arrest you?"

Rorche shrugged. "I had thought that our efforts had remained unnoticed by the authorities but it appears that I had deluded myself. As we all know, the commercial potential of the technology of human flight is significant and my suspicion is that Baron Heimgelberg intended to insure that he controlled and profited from it. As lord and master of this demesne, he clearly has the legal standing to confiscate the air carriage."

Bennett, monitoring the controls, waved to get the Baronet's attention. "Franz, the Koerp's Mechanism shows that we have just passed eight thousand feet, but our rate of climb has slowed to seventy feet per minute and is still dropping. Also, we are traveling south by south-east by the compass."

"The gulf is only two hundred seventy miles due south of Eriis," Aldo stated. "If we are moving at twenty-five miles an hour, and it seems to me that we are moving much faster than that, we have perhaps only ten or twelve hours until we are out over the ocean."

Millicent pulled a pad and pencil from a pocket, and scribbled on it for a moment. "I can only estimate the bulk of the air carriage and its load, but I believe that we will level out around nine thousand."

When he spoke in response to these new facts, Rorche looked around to include all assembled. "We must decide what we shall do, and quickly. It appears to me that our only option is to descend immediately before we travel much farther. Once again, this will likely mean the complete loss of the air carriage."

Sergeant Tekle clicked his heels. "My lord, the men and I defer to your judgment."

The Coldridges held a whispered colloquium, then Algis announced, "There is nothing else to be done."

Bennett, Aldo, and Millicent all nodded without comment.

Then the Baronet surprised Everett by turning to him and Sarah. "I know you have only recently joined us, but in my opinion you have as much right to be a part of the decision as the rest of us."

Everett shrugged. The sooner he was off this doomed mechanism, the happier he would be.

Sarah, however, had quite a different idea entirely. "Forgive me for contradicting you, Baronet Rorche, but there is another option. Everett and I can save the air carriage."

ELEVEN

When the hubbub died down, Sarah explained. "I am also a magicker and have an Insignificant Liquid Materialization spell. I can create almost a quart at a time."

"You can magic water?" asked Bennett with a hopeful look.

"No." She seemed reluctant to go further.

"What then?"

"Everyone must promise not to laugh." Sarah's expression was deadly serious.

There were some odd looks, but all nodded or otherwise indicated their agreement.

Sarah sighed. "Urine."

Into the awkward silence that followed, Josline Coldridge said, "That would work, wouldn't it? Urine would have about the same weight as water, yes?"

"Logically, it would be denser and therefore heavier," Millicent said, "but I don't think the difference would be much."

"It'll work," Bennett declared, convinced. "But you'd need to cast your spell one thousand times. We had two thousand pounds of ballast, or approximately two hundred and fifty gallons of water."

Sarah nodded. "Then we had better get started."

There followed a rapid discussion of how best to refill the ballast tanks, as the tanks themselves were beneath the deck and their fill tubes only accessible from the exterior. Finally, Aldo and Bennett used wrenches to break a union on the valve manifold to access a pipe leading down into the tanks. Then, after a bit more discussion, Eylis ran to find a large, chambered funnel that she had used when filling the fuel tank. Aldo slid the spout into the open end of the pipe and stood back.

Then, as everyone watched expectantly, Sarah walked up to the funnel and cast, *"Pee pee, I see."*

There was no perceptible delay between the enunciation and the expression of the magic. Everett felt the tingle of the actuation immediately and a quantity of yellow fluid filled the funnel and drained quickly away, washing down the pipe with an echoing sloshing sound and a faint aroma of outhouse.

Sarah looked around, ignored everyone else, and focused on the smirk on Everett's face. She awarded him a severe glare. "I manifested this spell when I was only *two*." Her justification for the simplistic terms of the spell was almost a challenge.

Picturing a retributive quart of urine materializing above his head, he quickly blanked his expression.

Thereafter, the mood of the passengers of the air carriage considerably lightened and smiles began to appear on previously gloomy faces. The Coldridges went aft to investigate the trouble with the starboard engine while Rorche dispatched his men to inspect the rest of the mechanism for damage from the gendarme's gunfire. Then he, Aldo, Bennett, and Millicent busied themselves with checking the functions of the instruments and controls.

Everett, somewhat at a loss as to what was expected of him, simply tarried with Sarah while she chanted her spell repeatedly. After ten minutes, Bennett announced, "We are starting to descend slowly."

With occasional pauses for rest or a sip of water, Sarah completed her task in only thirty minutes, by which time the air carriage had dropped below the cloud layer and continued to lose altitude at a more or less steady rate.

"Using an estimation for the current weight of the air carriage, my rough calculations indicate that we will stop descending somewhere between five and six hundred feet," Millicent told those in the compartment. "Because we lack our full compliment of passengers and some cargo, we won't achieve ground level equilibrium. We must have more ballast."

"The tanks won't hold much more pis... uh ... *liquid*," Bennett cautioned.

The mathematician and the three technicians, Rorche, Aldo, and Bennett, all looked expectantly at Sarah and Everett.

Everett did not have any ideas, so he kept his mouth shut.

"Once we are within sight of the ground," the woman from Kleinsvench said with serene confidence, "Everett and I will procure ballast of some sort. It will in all likelihood not be liquid, however."

"That will not be a problem," Rorche assured. "But it will be better if the ballast comes in smaller amounts, so that it can be distributed about the air carriage to maintain trim."

"How much will you need?"

Millicent thought a moment. "Twelve hundred pounds should be sufficient."

Everett made a noise by blowing air out of the side of his mouth. "That's quite a lot."

Millicent looked apologetic. "Aside from the missing load, we also originally added additional capacity to the vapor cells as a reserve, believing we could exhaust the extra gas as needed during the journey to Eyrchelle."

Sarah shot Everett a warning look. "We'll manage it. We'll need help shifting the ballast about the air carriage, though."

"My esnes are at your disposal," Rorche agreed instantly.

Two hours later, Everett, Sarah, Sergeant Tekle, and four of his men stood looking out the port door, which faced in the direction of their travel. The landscape that passed beneath was prototypically rural: croplands, pastures, hayfields, a few snaking cart paths, and an occasional bayou or pond. Five hundred feet struck Everett as still dizzyingly high.

"It looks to me as if the wind is still pushing us quite fast," he said.

Sarah grinned. "That means that we'll need to transport as far ahead of the air carriage as possible. How far out can you get us?"

Everett raised his gaze toward the horizon. "Several miles, I think."

She clasped him comfortably about the waist. "There's

nothing to be gained by waiting longer."

He nodded, put his arms around her for no other reason than that it felt good, chose a locus on a distant swatch of green, and cast his Potent spell.

A herd of small goats turned interested gazes their way as they appeared on a gently sloping hillside. Munching disinterestedly on clover, one black and white doe glanced in their direction and then trotted toward them, stirring other animals to follow, until the pair found themselves the focus of attention of the entire herd. The goats nipped at their clothes and nuzzled their hands.

Sarah, clearly not accustomed to such behavior from livestock, flinched slightly as one nibbled at a finger. "They're friendly, aren't they?"

"Not really. They just think we might have feed grain. In my experience, goats have two overriding ambitions in life. One is to eat."

'What's the other?'

"To make more goats."

"Oh."

"Well, we're here. What are we going to use for ballast?" He was still slightly annoyed that she had promised his aide to preserve the air carriage without consulting him.

Sarah rubbed her chin with an index finger as she surveyed the pasture. High hedges bordered it and not much else was in view.

"I had thought that we might find rocks," she mused. "But there's no sign of those or anything else heavy enough to use."

Everett absently scratched a blue-eyed weather behind the horns. "Dirt?"

"How would we dig it? And we'd need buckets or boxes to hold it, which I doubt we can find. Besides, I don't think there's enough time." She pointed back toward the approaching air carriage. "It looks like it will pass over us in only a few minutes."

As he shooed away a persistent buckling that was trying to munch his trousers, he had an idea derived from the obvious. He suggested it to her.

She started to frown and then rotated her hands palms

upward. "Why not?"

When they transported the first of the extra ballast back to the air carriage, Sergeant Tekle and his men just laughed.

"Just make sure you don't separate the dams from their kids," Everett cautioned as he handed off a bleating animal. "Otherwise they'll never shut up."

With twenty-five or so assorted goats corralled in the two outer corridors, the air carriage ponderously sank nearer the ground. Two hours later, Everett found himself standing with Sergeant Tekle beside the cargo doors at the stern, which the esnes had opened inward and lashed in place. Already, twelve lines hung out the opening, cinched tight to vertical struts in the back wall.

The esne tossed another line outward, shook it to make sure that it dangled properly, then took a steel snap ring attached to a rope about Everett's waist and hooked it to the new line.

"Remember, sir," Tekle warned. "Don't let go of the line when you hit the ground. The knot at the end of the line will keep the snap ring from sliding off, but your weight must remain on the line."

"Got it," Everett assured the man.

Millicent had emphasized that any significant loss of load would cause the air carriage to rise. He wrapped his leather gloves around the line, backed to the edge of the deck, took a deep breath, and pushed himself off. His hands constricted automatically, arresting his fall with a sudden jerk. He eased the pressure of his hands as he began to swing, feet hanging, and allowed the friction of the gloves to slow his fall. It was only fifteen feet to the ground, but he still landed heavily and plopped on his rear. One of Tekle's men stuck out a hand to help him up before the moving air carriage, which scudded before the wind at a good clip, could drag him along. Careful to keep a heavy tension in his line, he started running with the others.

Because it came down to a matter of strength and weight, it had been decided that all of the men aboard, except for the injured Wrelton, would attempt to moor the air carriage while the five women monitored the goats and stood by aboard to provide any assistance that might be required.

According to the plan, once all of the men were on the ground, they would gradually bring the air carriage to a halt and then secure it in place with corkscrew steel anchors that were stored aboard for that very purpose.

After observing the ground in the path of the air carriage for some time, Rorche and the other technicians had chosen an open, fairly level meadow of about a hundred acres in size. A large space would be required for the landing to prevent the air carriage from colliding with trees, hedges, barns, or anything else that might permanently damage it.

Everett had been the next to the last and as soon as Tekle saw that he had made it without doing something foolish like breaking his neck, the sergeant belayed down on his own line, slowed almost to a stop a couple of feet above the tall fescue seed heads, and then alighted gracefully.

Rorche, on the far side of the line of running men, checked to see that all were ready, then called out, "Begin!"

As he settled his weight back against the line, the speed of the air carriage began to drag Everett along, the waist-high hay battering his legs. Ignoring his determination, the seemingly inexorable pull of the air carriage skidded his feet when he tried to set them, made him stumble, then jerked him forward so that he nearly flipped on his face. Hurriedly, he started running again to gain his balance, then bore down on the rope once more. This time he did flip all the way over and landed with a jarring crash. The rope dragged him for thirty feet on his arms, stems and rough edged blades of grass lashing his face, before he could get his boots underneath him.

Sheepishly, he peered around quickly to discover if the others had noticed his clumsiness, but was surprised to find that none of them was doing any better. Several of the young esnes had also fallen and were being dragged through the grass, twisting, rolling, and complaining.

"Franz, this isn't working! We don't have enough men to slow her down!" Algis shouted.

Aldo fell, cursing, and somehow lost his line. The man bounded up to chase after it, took a step, and collapsed with a yelp of pain.

The grove of long leaf pine at the far end of the field had been a comfortable three-quarters of a mile away when they began. Now, it was less than a half of a mile distant.

"It's going to hit the trees!" Bennett, to Everett's right, warned.

Reluctant to reveal his new spell, Everett tried to think of any other way to stop the air carriage. When Baronet Rorche tumbled and nearly lost his line, Everett knew he had no other choice and whispered the words.

As the magic flowed through him, he dug in his heels, pushing up deep furrows in the thick sod. The one-inch rope in his hands went taunt and began to sing as it neared its breaking point. He took a step to relieve the strain, cast his ninth spell again as the initial flood of strength faded, and then, holding his own line in one hand, reached across to take Bennett's.

As he continued to cast, plowing ruts through the earth with both feet, his cheap boots disintegrated, but he felt the air carriage begin to loose headway. Abruptly, the line in his left hand snapped with a sharp crack of tortured hemp. Sergeant Tekle rushed to press his own line into Everett's hand. Other lines were tucked into his grasp as he focused his concentration entirely on the ropes, spitting out the words of his spell over and over again.

Finally, after what seemed moments but could only have been seconds, the lines were no longer dragging forward, and he stood buried to his knees in a jam of earth and grass, holding in check the great mass floating above.

"Set the anchors, now!" Tekle barked at his men.

As Bennett, Rorche, and Algis gathered around to congratulate him, Everett saw in their eyes something he had very seldom before encountered – honest admiration for his magic.

TWELVE

Even with the aid of Everett's magical strength, it took better than three hours to secure the air carriage to Rorche's satisfaction. Just as Sergeant Tekle tied the final line to the final corkscrew stake, a large, curious delegation of gawking locals appeared, including families with children and the manager of the cooperative that owned the hay meadow. This worthy, politely explaining her reasoning that the new flying mechanism should be subject to the same mooring fees as river boats, agreed to accept a payment of forty-two silver seventy copper (all that could be scrounged from the crew's pockets) for the night. Afterwards, Bennett and Algis, with varied assistance from others, took the time to cook a hot supper over a campfire built a safe hundred yards from the air carriage. Though just the simple staple of pinto beans cooked with onion, peppers, and salted pork and served over browned rice, the meal took on the trappings of a celebration as the entire company, including most of the esnes, packed into the air carriage's three pace square galley.

Everett, finding himself unanimously appointed the de facto guest of honor, sat at the head of the long, bolted-down table, surrounded by cheerful faces and eager words of approbation. As he dug hungrily into his own bowl of beans, he absorbed with gratified contentment the attention and appreciation that his magical feat had brought him. All too often, his nearly useless magic had left him derided and ignored; he intended to enjoy thoroughly his moment in the sun.

"Newly manifested, you say?" Aldo, finished with his own meal and standing wedged into a corner between two of the esnes, repeated. "That's quite a fortunate occurrence for us, then. We'd have never stopped the ship without you." A fleeting, indecipherable look passed across the mechanic's

93

face.

"Personal Enhancement spells are a modern rarity. I've only read about them in historical works," Josline Coldridge, seated on the bench to Everett's left, declared. "Yours is obviously a Potent and, I must say, quite surprisingly utilitarian."

"Magic may not have the versatility of technology," Eylis, alongside her aunt, argued, defending her own trade, "but it's fully capable of magnificent accomplishments!" The young woman beamed at Everett, clearly charmed by his revealed magical prowess.

"Wizards have a high social standing in the Kingdom," Algis mused. "Franz, perhaps we should prevail upon Everett to accompany our team when we meet with the Alarsarian financiers. The association of a powerful magicker could only lend added weight to our proposal."

"Excellent idea!" The Baronet agreed. "Millicent, what do you think?"

"It could help, as long as we are subtle in our approach. We will need investors with deep pockets and those sorts tend not to be moved by extravagant displays."

"Exactly!" Bennett, across the room, declared triumphantly as if picking up an old disagreement. Then the mechanic launched into an enthusiastic diatribe concerning the inherent duplicity of bankers.

The remainder of the evening passed in unhurried and occasionally facetious discussions. Everett took it all in, saying little; he found the lively and intelligent company invigorating, especially since none of the conversations involved agricultural produce. Sarah likewise smiled and nodded more than she spoke, apparently thoroughly enjoying herself. Everett found his gaze repeatedly shifting to the young Kleinsvenchan, and she always seemed to know when he watched her, responding each time with a playful half-wink.

As the group dissipated in search of their bunks and much needed rest, the festivities slowly faded away. Eventually, Everett found himself alone, still basking in the satisfying afterglow of his success, but made no move toward the closet-sized cabin off the starboard corridor that Bennett had assigned to him. A vagrant thought passed through his mind that it would have been pleasant to have had the continued company of Sarah -- or even Eylis – but both young women had departed for the bunkroom they were to share, chatting animatedly about magic.

Nevertheless content, he interlaced his hands behind his head and leaned back against his chair, working through the revenue potentials of his newest spell.

After some time, Sergeant Tekle stuck his head into the galley, noticed Everett, and brought the rest of his body in from the port corridor, assuming a stiff, respectful stance that was not quite attention. "Sorry, sir. Might I ask if you'll be long? Monsieur Eyrwaeld has asked me to make sure all the lights are out to preserve the batteries."

"Monsieur Eyrwaeld?"

"That would be Bennett, sir."

"Right. No need to call me sir, sergeant. I'm just a tradesman."

"Yes, sir."

Everett smiled slightly, standing. "I'm not yet ready for the sack. I think I'll go up top."

"Fine, sir. I'll be joining you there shortly. I've first watch."

Everett nodded and exited the galley, turning right and moving forward to the first cross-corridor. He had to turn slightly sideways to maneuver through this even narrower passage, lit by a single half-power lamp, to reach the equally dim starboard side. Turning aft, he walked lightly to refrain from disturbing those behind the closed cabin doors that he passed and came to the ladder at the dead end. Climbing swiftly, he emerged through the lashed open hatch above into full darkness. Here in the open air with the mass of the vapor cells indistinctly sensed above, only vague black shapes registered to his eyes. The cells shaded the deck from the wane light of the Inner and Outer moons and the empty meadow provided no other illumination. The floor of the upper deck, formed by separated, thin wooden slats mounted on lightweight rails running the length of the roof of the air carriage, had a slight spring to it as he shuffled, carefully feeling his way, toward the bow rail.

Summers in the coastal highlands where he had lived the majority of his life had been uniformly moderate and wet, with frequent storms blowing in off the great bay formed by the thousand-mile spike of the Kyalt Peninsula. The Edzedahl and the southern coast experienced a long, normally sweltering midyear season that lasted from May till October and though he had acclimated over the two years that he had lived here, he still relished the relative cool that sunset brought.

When his questing hand found the bow rail, he leaned against it and let the sounds of an inconsistent breeze in an unseen distant tree line sift around him till he heard the almost imperceptible footsteps of Sergeant Tekle.

"I'd have thought that you'd have brought a light," he said to the esne.

"No, sir," Tekle replied quietly as he took a place a few paces to Everett's left. "That'd wash out my night vision and also make me an easy target."

"Ah." Then, despite relishing the quiet, but not wanting to seem impolite, Everett asked, "Have you been in Baronet Rorche's service long?"

"Yes, sir. Fourteen years. I signed on just after the passing of the previous Baronet."

"The Baronet must have been just a boy then."

"A stripling, sir, but quite capable of taking the reins of his demesne."

"Right."

Several moments passed.

"I've a spell myself, sir," Tekle mentioned without inflection. "I can dry socks."

"An Insignificant?"

"Yes, sir. It's more useful than it might appear, especially for a foot soldier."

"I think I see what you mean."

"If you don't mind my asking, sir, you're a professional magicker? I mean, that's how you make your living?"

"Right. I'm a Journeyman Magicker – well, Wizard, now."

"You do quite well, then, I suppose, sir?"

Everett chuckled in dismissal. "Not as well as you'd

think. Magic isn't really the path to riches and glory."

"Oh, I well know that, sir. My Dad used to tell me the right same thing."

"Your father was a magicker?"

"Indeed he was, sir. A full Journeyman with eight spells all manifested before he turned twenty-five. Most of them were an odd and unprofitable lot, though. He could barely make a go of magic. His Major spell let him make a block of ice the size of a pickle barrel."

"Really? Seems like ice would be a profitable commodity."

"It can be in summer, but not so much the rest of the year, and most folks don't have much need of a great lot of ice. His customers usually only bought one block a week for a silver and sometimes tried to bargain him down from that price. Most of the time he worked for butchers for set wages. Out of season he was a lumberjack."

"Right. I know how that is."

"He could also summon turtledoves from thin air. Not much meat on a turtledove, though."

"Large family?"

"There were nine of us. Might get two good bites from one bird, but they made a decent soup. Sometimes we had them for days straight. I've a brother who won't touch fowl of any kind to this day."

"Magic is a hard way to make a living."

"Yes, sir. I'd say that was true."

THIRTEEN

Sergeant Tekle raised his head over the parapet to check the top of the warehouse. "As well as I can see, it's clear, Mademoiselle," he told Sarah in a quiet tone. Still kneeling, she gripped the esne's hand and slipped her other arm around Everett's waist.

Everett snuck a look to select a locus and then enunciated, *"Beautiful Woman, come forth!"*

The three of them appeared just off the peak of the roof of the warehouse, shifting their feet and hands awkwardly to adapt to the gradual slope. Hopefully, they were out of view of the streets below and any potential wardens. All of them were dressed in dark clothing, but both moons were high in the sky and showing three-quarters full. Everett knew that they would be easily sighted.

Tekle rose to a crouch and began to move toward the gable at the yard end. He raised and lowered his boots with exaggerated care on the tar-slathered wood, lest the sound of careless footsteps give them away to any guards that might be inside the warehouse below. When he neared the edge, he lay down and crawled forward until he could scan the space beyond.

"No one in sight, sir," he whispered back.

Everett, trying to copy the sergeant's stealth, moved up beside him. Sarah followed and settled near the two.

The day following Everett's halting of the air carriage, Algis Coldridge and his family had had little difficulty in repairing the starboard engine (a stray bullet had punctured the fuel line) and completing the installation of the port engine. After freeing the now unneeded goats, the crew had launched the air carriage once more. Under power, the craft moved sleekly against the wind and, by an exacting process of throttling the engines' speeds, Aldo and Bennett had immediately steered back toward Baron Heimgelberg's capital at a comfortable altitude of two thousand feet. Rorche had suggested, with general agreement, that their first duty was to attempt to determine what had become of the other members of their group.

As they had neared the city that evening, the Baronet and his sergeant had come up through the hatch to find Everett and Sarah where they had sat to themselves on the upper deck. The two had just finished a bit of cold ham, bread, and some cached leftovers from the café in Eriis. Josline and Ellen Coldridge, immediately and unequivocally acknowledged by the rest of the company as the best cooks, had declared suzerainty over the galley. When they discovered that no firewood had been loaded for the compact, heavily insulated stove, they had further declared that supper would be potluck.

As soon as their simple meal would have been done, Everett had planned to make use of the opportunity to rebuke Sarah in private, having felt, perhaps illogically, misused by her ready offer of his services to save the air carriage. However, once his stomach had been full, he had lost all interest in being disagreeable. So they had simply been sitting without speaking, taking a rest from the uproarious events of the flight from Eriis, and enjoying a magnificent sunset made all the more grand by their high vantage point.

Rorche had had a special request to make of them.

"My demesne is a single impoverished village and two hundred acres of mediocre vineyards on the ocean side of the Chaelle Mountains," the Baronet had confessed. "I earn but seven hundred silver per year from my taxes and rents and most of that goes to maintain the constabulary and roads. In order to construct the air carriage and fund our operations, I have had to take a personal note with a usurer in Eriis. While I feel no great pain in association with a temporary default on the note, more than half of the proceeds of the loan remain hidden in a lockbox secreted in the warehouse. If we are to have any possibility of reestablishing ourselves in Eyrchelle, we must have that money."

Rorche's plan had involved the transport of Tekle to a point as close to the warehouse as was possible so that the sergeant might attempt to retrieve the lockbox. Once Everett explained that his spell would require that both he and Sarah accompany the esne, Rorche had looked uncertain.

"Will it be possible for you to transport all three of you at once? The sergeant weighs better than seventeen stone."

"Seventeen and one half exactly, my lord," Tekle had amended respectfully.

"I have been thinking about just such a problem," Sarah had said. "Everett's spell clearly has no Vicinity Component, since no portion of the ground beneath me nor the air around me transports, clearly ruling out the transport of items that do not have a significant connection to me, but the Associative Component seems to have no limitation whatsoever. It seems to me that I do not actually have to bear the weight of an object, but have only a firm contact and perhaps some enclosing connection."

"Meaning?" Everett, who had not considered this, had questioned.

"I think that I should just need to hold his hand."

And, indeed, experiments had proven this to be correct. Everett had fleetingly wondered why she had not brought this up before and consequently why she continued to hold him close when the two of them transported, but he had decided that he had a good thing going and had better just keep his mouth shut.

At that time, he had not been -- and yet remained -- unconvinced that he should enlist in Rorche's eclectic company of *synthesists*, but he had accepted the necessity of aiding them in order to see Sarah back to Kleinsvench, and had quickly agreed to assist in the proposed foray before the young woman could do so for him.

Now, hiding atop the warehouse and remembering the spine-shivering *crack!* of the Baronial Guardsmen's pistols, he began to think that he had been a little too hasty.

"The yard is clear also, sir," Tekle said quietly. "Can you put us there next to the wall, in the corner away from the door? It would be best if we avoided the opening. The moonlight would make our silhouettes perfect targets."

Covering a wince, Everett eased forward until his eyes cleared the flashing along the edge. "No problem. Ready?"

"Ready."

Sarah nodded.

Everett cast.

Once in the yard, they all straightened soundlessly and Sarah released her hold on Everett and the sergeant. Without pause, the latter sidled with exacting, stalking steps that made almost no discernable noise to the large doors. There the esne cocked his head to listen at the quiescent and apparently empty building for several long moments. Finally, Tekle leaned out to observe the dark and shadowed interior.

Everett, listening likewise, heard nothing but the slight brush of an insincere zephyr and the muffled, distant sounds of the resting city. After several more moments that wracked Everett's nerves, Tekle, apparently detecting no danger, waved them toward him. As a precaution, Everett caught Sarah's hand as they snuck to join the sergeant. She glanced at him but gave no other reaction than a quick, firm pressure on his hand.

Tekle held an exaggerated finger to his lips, received nods from them both, made a two handed "Follow me" motion, and then slipped inside.

Maintaining a firm grip on Sarah's hand, Everett followed, swiveling his head about to listen. The windowless warehouse was all but pitch black inside and he could see nothing but formless gray shapes where the massive mechanisms stood. To all appearances, the synthesists' work remained undisturbed. His stomach clenching tension and the unevenness of the brick floor made his movements unsure, and he gritted his teeth at every scuff and scratching step that he made. For her part, Sarah walked beside him with the contemptuous silence of a cat.

Tekle crept along the wall to the left. Rorche had revealed that he had secreted the lockbox inside a recess in the first vapor mechanism on that side. When they reached the end of the row, the sergeant knelt without pause and crawled beneath a large, protruding apparatus formed of concentric copper coils until only his legs remained exposed. After a few seconds, he wiggled back out, clutching the small, steel clad box, which reeked of machine oil. It was just barely larger than a shoebox and reputedly contained close to thirteen thousand, mostly in Alarsarian banknotes. The esne handed it to Sarah, who had to release Everett's hand to hold the heavy container in both hands. To remove even the slightest possibility that it would not transport, they had agreed that she should carry it.

Then, with a cursory look around, the sergeant whispered, "Monsieur Schael, should we return immediately or attempt to retrieve the drawings and papers?"

Baronet Rorche had also expressed a desire to recover the documents on his desk, important schematics and records of calculations, if at all possible.

Everett hesitated. "There appears to be no one here."

"We should get all that we can," Sarah urged. "It's not likely that we'll have another chance."

By all indications, the warehouse remained deserted. Surely if guards had been posted, the three of them would have already raised an alarm.

"Right," Everett agreed. "Let's do it."

Immediately, Tekle rounded the bulk of the vapor mechanism and led the way across the dark space, angling for the corner where the Baronet's desk had sat.

With an abrupt eye-blinking glare, a bank of actinic battery lighting flashed on to reveal a line of soldiers in green trousers and maroon jackets not ten steps in front of them.

More importantly, it also revealed their leveled line of rifles.

Everett froze. Sarah likewise became motionless and Tekle as well, though he seemed to bunch his muscles in preparation for action.

"Be so good as to remain exactly where you are!" an officer called out. He also wore the same utility uniform, but had silver insignia on his collars. "There is no possibility that my men could miss at this range."

The officer stepped forward, but to one side out of the line of fire. "Greetings. My Name is Captain Erick Van Ghest of the Royal Alarsarian Army and I am acting in the name and under the legal authority of Baron Winstead Heimgelberg. I must now inform you that you are all under arrest."

Everett flashed a look to try to get Sarah's attention. The two of them, at least, had a chance for escape. If he could get her to drop the lockbox and extend her hand so that he could grasp it, he could them transport to the yard and then away. Sarah, however, seemed focused only on the solders confronting them. He tensed, fearing that she would attempt to set the men on fire.

"Please take extreme care not to open your mouths," Captain Van Ghest added in a straightforward tone. "I must warn you that we are aware that you may be magicians and that if any of you attempt to speak at all, my men have orders to open fire immediately."

A cold sensation crawled along Everett's spine. He decided to take the man at his word and clamped his mouth shut. The black, yawning openings of the gun barrels had an indisputable persuasiveness all of their own. He cut his eyes back at Sarah and saw to his relief that she had relaxed and likewise pressed her lips into a tight line.

Within moments, gagged and securely bound, the three of them were hustled to an enclosed freight wagon waiting in the dark street. Once the Alarsarians had swung open the doors, they tossed first Everett, then Tekle and finally Sarah inside with rough efficiency. When the soldiers slammed the doors shut, the space was oppressively black, with only a few cracks in the wooden sides showing any light.

Everett got his feet under him and shifted around, bumping the other two slightly, till he found a bench and sank down upon it. As the wagon started forward with a jolt, Sarah and the sergeant found places beside him.

The ride proved not lengthy, if bumpy and uncomfortable, and their captors dragged them unceremoniously out into another dark street. The tall brick building to which the wagon had brought them had a vaguely residential look, like some of the blocky row houses that were common in the eastern boroughs of Eriis. Only the feeble glow of lamp light leaking around latched shutters softened its dark, forbidding facade. Immediately, the Alarsarians hustled them into the bright interior.

The sudden change in light made Everett squint, and he caught few details as two tall, blocky Alarsarians separated him from the others. Hauling him by the arms, the soldiers shuttled him without comment into a room off the long entrance hall and slammed him down into an armless wooden chair. Then the men took stances alongside him that indicated that they intended to make sure that he did not try to leave it. His chair was the only furniture present, and cobwebs in the corners of the undecorated ceiling and some undisturbed dust on the floor along the walls suggested that the place had until recently been vacant. Paneled in lightly stained pine and about twelve feet square, the room had no windows and no other doors save the one by which they had entered.

He sat quietly and made no move to resist. His thoughts were equally pacific; he had absolutely no idea as to how he might extricate himself from this predicament.

After some time, two officers entered. One was Captain Van Ghest. The other had similar silver badges on his collar but also had a gold and turquoise mobius insignia embroidered on his left sleeve.

"Thank you for your patience," Van Ghest told Everett, as if the latter had any choice in the matter. The captain was a tall, broad shouldered man with the cultured manner of a professionally trained Royal officer. He was probably a decade older than Everett, but trim and possessed of a full head of black hair under his slouch cap.

"This will only take a moment." His captor then took a brass watch from a button-down breast pocket and checked the time.

The second officer took a stance, raised his left hand to Everett as if in benediction and cast, *A revelation of magic I crave.*

Everett felt the feather light breath of a spell actuation, but nothing else, good or ill, and he saw no sign of any visible effect, magical or otherwise.

Van Ghest monitored his watch, while glancing up at Everett from time to time. When more than a minute had passed, the officer returned his watch to his pocket. "Thank you, Lieutenant Smythe, that will be all."

The silent subordinate, clearly a magician of some sort, saluted with precision and left.

The captain made a signal to one of the guards and the soldier removed Everett's gag, a sewn strip of canvas with multiple folds of cloth fastened in the center to suppress the tongue. Obviously created for the particular purpose of disarming magicians, the Alarsarians had cinched it painfully tight about his head, and it left him with a dry mouth and sore jaws. Working his mouth to get the kinks out, he waited to see what would happen next.

The captain smiled at Everett, not unkindly. "The lieutenant's spell has determined that you are not one of the magicians. Are you a technician?"

Everett kept his face blank. How could it be that Smythe's magic had failed? It could not be a coincidence that *two* spells, the wizard Pourfrey's and now this Characteristic Revelation Variant of the lieutenant's, had been somehow prevented from affecting him. *What in the world was going on?*

For a split-second, he thought about trying to bluff the captain, but realized that his ignorance of technological specifics would give him away instantly should he be subject to detailed questioning. "No, I'm not."

"Then what was your association with Baronet Rorche?"

"I was hired to be a cook on the flying contraption." He had worked as a cook several times when his magic had failed to generate any income. The pay had been often poor, but at least he had been well fed. It was a role he felt confident that he could play.

But Van Ghest simply nodded, apparently having little interest in anyone who was neither technician nor magician and thus unconcerned with any attempt to verify Everett's statements.

"Sadly," the Alarsarian announced, though his expression gave evidence that the term was no more than a polite formality, "I must tell you that you are to be detained indefinitely, pending the recovery of the flying mechanism and the Baronet."

Everett wanted to ask what had become of Sarah, but kept quiet. He had had a few encounters with various constabularies in the past and knew submissive silence usually resulted in less unpleasantness directed at sensitive portions of his body.

"Horst and Gavin will now take you to the room where you will be confined. Food and amenities will be provided as required. Thank you for your cooperation."

The two soldiers yanked him abruptly from his chair, marched him out the door, left down the broad entrance hall, and then up a curving stairway to another hallway. This had faded floral print wallpaper and a pair of guards armed with rifles stationed at both ends. At the fourth of seven identical rose stained doors on the right, the guards stopped, unlocked the door with a small brass key, removed the ropes binding his hands with practiced competence, shoved him in, and then slammed the panel firmly behind him.

Only a single, dimmed oil lamp lit the room. Three men were present and these crowded around him solicitously. He recognized the faces of two from the first day at the warehouse, though he did not know their names, and the third was Edwin.

The chemist wrapped an arm around Everett's shoulders in a supportive display of camaraderie. "Are you well, Everett? Were you harmed?"

"No, I'm fine."

"What happened?" asked one of the others earnestly. He was a shorter, older fellow with chin whiskers and a wiry moustache.

The last man was very young, thin but fit with plain features and a nervous tremble in his voice. "Where is Baronet Franz?"

"Come now, Harold, Mitchell," Edwin chided. "Let's give Everett a moment before we bombard him with questions."

"I'm all right," Everett assured the chemist.

Harold, the older man, immediately pressed, "Well, have they captured the air carriage?"

"No," Everett replied and then looked around meaningfully. There were Distant Listening spells and for all he knew there might be some type of technological mechanism that would permit their captors to overhear anything said in the room. "But I'd better not say more about it."

"Oh!" Harold peered about as if expecting soldiers to appear from the very walls. "Right you are."

"Can you tell us anything without giving too much

away?" Mitchell pleaded.

"When last I saw them, both craft and crew were in good shape," Everett said carefully as he took stock of the large room.

There were six cots and a privacy screen of the type used to conceal chamber pots, but no other furniture. With no windows and considering the orientation of the hallway, he did not believe that the wall opposite the door coincided with the exterior of the building, but rather probably abutted an adjacent structure.

"You're both technicians?" he asked Mitchell and Harold.

Mitchell nodded timidly. "I'm a mechanic, yes."

"I'm just a copper fitter," Harold admitted.

Everett frowned slightly. There would be no magic from these to help then. "Have you been allowed outside at all?"

"No," Edwin replied. "The guards bring our meals and take the chamber pot away to be emptied. But we've only been here since we were arrested yesterday, so that might change. Are you thinking of trying to escape?"

"Of course not!" Everett lied for the benefit of any potential listeners while nodding his head emphatically. Then he sat down on one of the cots to try to figure out how to do exactly that.

FOURTEEN

Now that his gag had been removed, Everett could transport Sarah whenever he chose. Using different combinations of his own and Sarah's spells, he ran several scenarios through his mind. Most struck him as simply ridiculous and a few seemed predestined to disastrous failure. The most straightforward – breaking down the door with his strength Potent and having Sarah sleep or set alight the guards – appeared likely only to result in both of them being shot dead. With four soldiers, it seemed unlikely to him that she could cast fast enough to incapacitate all of them.

However, the only other plan that occurred to him -- using his transportation spell to escape the building – required that he be able to see a distant locus. Could he get access to the roof?

"I didn't really pay attention when I was brought in," he asked. "Do any of you know if this building is three stories or four?"

Edwin gave him an odd look. "I'm pretty sure that there are four floors."

The other two nodded.

Everett looked up to study the ceiling four feet above his head. It was white plaster over lathe with a simple design texture of curving lines. Above that would be wooden joists and resting on those the sub floor of the next storey. The joists would probably be no more than sixteen inches on centers and might be as few as twelve. His magically enhanced strength would permit him to make a hole large enough for a person to pass, but the noise involved in ripping out the plaster below and the floor above was certain to alert the guards.

He shook his head, discarding the idea, and then realized abruptly that he should simply take a chance that the Alarsarians were not listening to the room at that precise moment and transport Sarah. She was good at thinking on her feet and was sure to have some idea as to how they might effect their escape. The guards might notice her disappearance, but it struck him as highly unlikely that they would think to search this particular room for her first.

"I'm going to cast a spell," he warned the others in a whisper. "Please don't make any sound that might bring the Alarsarians."

Edwin and Harold nodded seriously, but Mitchell simply appeared to freeze in panic.

Everett chose a locus in a clear space and incanted in barely breathed words, *"Beautiful Woman, come forth!"*

Sarah appeared, not bound or gagged as he had expected, but simply in a seated position with her legs crossed as if she had been casually occupying a chair. Her eyes went wide as she flopped down on her rear, her mouth wide but making no sound.

Everett's fellow prisoners were startled, but, as he had asked, made no commotion.

He rushed to help the woman up, telling her, "We need to figure a way out of here right now!"

Sarah brushed off his hands, tense and flustered, but only made an exaggerated nod in reply.

Suddenly worried, Everett demanded in a low voice, "What's the matter?"

Sarah tilted her chin up and made an X with her index finger across her voice box.

"You can't speak?"

She awarded him another strong nod.

"For magic's sake! Is it a spell?"

She threw her hands up in a gesture that he took to mean, "Of course you dope!"

"If you can't speak you can't cast!"

"This is indeed a dastardly act," Edwin condemned.

"You have to admit," Harold mused, "it is an effective way to keep a magician from using magic."

Mitchell, enthralled or perhaps stupefied, said nothing.

Rolling her eyes, Sarah made her mouth into a thin line, then stuck out a hand and tapped the side of her head with a finger of the other hand.

"Err, give you a minute, you're thinking?" Everett guessed.

Nod.

Shortly, she snapped her fingers and then pointed emphatically at him.

"Me?"

Nod.

She raised her right arm to shoulder height, made a fist, flexed her bicep, and pointed at it.

"Strong?" Edwin guessed.

Nod.

She pointed to Everett again, then held up nine fingers.

"Got it. My ninth spell is strength."

Edwin looked pleased. "Oh, you're a wizard, Everett? I had thought you were just a magicker."

"Yes, but just recently. You see--"

Sarah waved both hands in a broad exasperated gesture.

Everett ducked his head contritely. "Sorry."

"My apologies, Mademoiselle," Edwin added.

She gestured forcefully with both hands at herself. *Pay attention!*

Then, in sequence, she pointed at herself, at the floor at her feet, and across the room at another spot. Then she held up eight fingers.

"My eighth spell transports you."

Nod.

Without another pantomime, she held up seven fingers.

"My potato spell."

Nod.

Finally, she raised an eyebrow while consecutively showing him six, five, four, three, two, and finally one.

"Oh, you want to know what my other spells are?"

Nod. Nod.

"Well, my fifth and sixth spells you also already know. They're the Liquid Transubstantiations."

Sarah made a *go on* gesture.

"My fourth spell is a Minor Item Translocation. It works on manure."

Harold burst out laughing, then caught himself and said, "Sorry about that."

"My third is an Unclassified Insignificant."

Sarah motioned. *Explain.*

Everett blew out a breath. "It makes beans sprout."

Harold doubled over, holding his sides, and then tried to stretch his guffaws into coughs, somewhat unconvincingly. Edwin went red in the face trying to maintain a polite stony expression. Mitchell simply looked confused.

"I told you my spells were crap," Everett complained to Sarah. Then, tired of presenting his magical shortcomings as the butt of amusement, he rushed on. "My second is an Insignificant Process Acceleration variant. It will cause a flower to bloom early. My first is--"

Sarah threw up her hands. *Wait.* Then, she grasped one of his and began writing letters on his palm.

Mitchell moved alongside Everett and tilted his head to see, calling out each letter as it formed. "W-H-A-T-W-O-R-D-S."

"You want to know the terms of the spell?" Everett asked her.

Nod.

"Which one?"

She held up two fingers.

In order to prevent an inadvertent actuation, he concentrated on *nothing* as he pronounced the words. "Fulfill thy destiny."

Sarah snapped her fingers again and pointed at him. *That's it!* She held up two fingers and then indicated her throat.

Everett shook his head. "That won't work at all."

She pointed at her throat again and then tapped her wrist where a watch would be.

"Okay, I see what you're saying. The spell that prevents you from speaking is a timed spell and you think that my Process Acceleration will, well, accelerate it?"

Nod.

"No. It only works on flowers."

She stamped her foot. *Try it!*

Everett threw up his hands. *"Fine."* He concentrated

on her lovely neck and said, *"Fulfill thy destiny."* To his profound astonishment, he felt his spell actuate.

Sarah coughed and made a throat clearing noise. "Good. Now, I think--"

"Why, that's amazing!" Edwin exclaimed. "It's unheard of for one spell to affect another!"

Everett could only manage, "Uhm."

"Not really," Sarah contradicted shortly. "Back to what I was saying--"

"But don't you see?" Edwin rushed on enthusiastically, "this is a fantastic breakthrough! It will turn everything we thought we knew about Magic and Technology upside down! Think of the possibilities!"

"I'd rather work out how we're going to get out of here," Sarah urged.

Unheeding and exuding a passionate glow, Edwin turned to Mitchell. "Remember this moment, young man, for it is truly an historic event! I had always suspected that the expression of natural forces was mutable rather than immutable as is the current consensus, but now I have seen positive proof with my own eyes!"

Once more, Mitchell looked confused. "I don't understand what you're saying."

"This proves, my dear Mitchell," Edwin barreled on, oblivious, "that Magic and Technology -- and surely Chemistry as well -- cannot be impersonal and random but must instead be guided by some unknown directed spirit! A Mystical Spirit, if you will! Does anyone have any paper? I need to write this down for a dissertation."

Harold, with a sour look, disagreed. "Balderdash! Are you trying to claim that Magic, Chemistry, and Technology are deities? I'm sorry, Edwin, but that simplistic notion was discarded centuries ago!"

Everett started to interrupt, but Edwin, in full oratory, cut him off.

"Of course not! Or, at least, not in the way the ancient civilizations did, as capricious, occasionally malevolent gods who awarded spells, schematics, and formulas according to selfish whims! I accept the fundamental precept of modern thinking: that the three primary aspects of nature cannot be personified in a human sense. The concept that I'm trying to explain is just an extension of that precept."

Harold made another face. "And what would be the difference between a malevolent god and a mystical spirit? It seems to me that you're still trying to assign human characteristics to a simple natural process."

"But that is exactly my point! If Magic, Chemistry, and Technology were simple natural processes like, say, gravity, then it would be impossible to see such evolutionary changes as we have today witnessed. Clearly, some guiding spirit that shepherds the advancement of humanity must be involved!"

"Poppycock!" Harold rebutted. "It has been thoroughly established by Wizard Randolf Eskin in his *Proof of the Metaphysical Nature of Magic* that--"

At that very moment, the door burst open and Captain Van Ghest entered, pistol drawn. Lieutenant Smythe and four soldiers rushed in behind him.

"Do not move!" the captain commanded.

Everett heard a barest whisper escape Sarah's lips and then Van Ghest and all of his men instantly collapsed.

FIFTEEN

Mitchell goggled at the sprawled men. "Did you *kill* them?"

"No, they're just asleep," Sarah assured him.

"I didn't know your spell worked that way," Everett protested. "I had the impression that it was a single target."

"That's normally the way I use it, but if I distribute my focus it almost always works on an entire group."

"Almost always?"

"Well, actually, the one time I tried it I put an entire pack of dogs to sleep once. Except for three puppies."

"I see. Well, don't you think we should get out of here? If we get to a window, I can transport us away."

"There must be other soldiers," Harold cautioned. "We probably shouldn't just rush out."

"He's right," Sarah confirmed. "We need to be careful."

"Could we possibly free the others?" Edwin asked. "It would be terrible to leave without them."

Everett began to shake his head. "No--"

"Of course we can!" Sarah promised the chemist. "How many are they?"

"There's Margaret, Roger, Stephan, Will, Suzette, and Beatrice," Harold said.

"We don't know where they are, though," Mitchell said. "We haven't seen the rest since we were arrested yesterday."

"I was in a room with two other women," Sarah supplied "Both were also mute."

Harold nodded. "That must be Suzette and Margaret. They are both magickers."

Edwin began, "Maybe we could--"

"Hold it!"

All three of them stared at Everett, jolted by his outburst.

"You can't seriously believe," he demanded, "that the five of us are going to be able to traipse through this building – *that is full of soldiers with guns* -- just as we please? Did I mention that this building is *full of soldiers with guns?*"

Sarah made a dismissive motion. "Don't worry, Everett. We have Magic on our side."

Shaking his head, he told her, "There has never been a spell manifested that can stop bullets. My spells are useless against soldiers and there's no way that you could sleep everyone in the entire building."

"Excellent idea. I'll try it."

"What? Wait ...what idea?"

Sarah's eyes went blank. "Good night, dear Alarsarians, and sweet dreams."

"That can't work," he argued stridently. "You can't change the terms of a spell." To his utter confusion, he felt her spell actuate.

Sarah refocused her eyes and nodded. "I think that did it."

"That's absolutely impossible! All competent authorities agree that the terms of a spell are a precise conception generated by the interaction between a magicker's conscious mind and the initial infusion of the magic. From the *Treatise on Enunciation* by Grand Master Wizard Thorgingra, 'A magical effect will only actuate and evince when triggered by the original unaltered enunciation.'"

"Don't be silly, Everett. Spells aren't mathematical equations! As my grandmother liked to say, 'The magic isn't in the words. It's in the magician.'"

"But –"

"Well, I'm going to go see." Without waiting for Everett to follow, she walked to the door, stepping daintily over the recumbent forms of the slumbering Alarsarians, and went into the hall.

"I don't see anyone," she encouraged. "Let's find the others."

Edwin, Harold, and Mitchell hurried after her.

Everett stood his ground, refusing to believe that such

an absurd notion could work. He had never heard of a non-specific spell that could be altered for a specific use. And the concept of adapting the terms of a spell was a clear violation of all the known precepts of spell casting. This was simply preposterous! Sarah and his erstwhile cellmates would unquestionably come scampering back at the first hint of alert soldiery!

When they did not reappear after two minutes, his nervousness got the best of him and he threw up his hands and followed. There was no one in the hallway, but he did hear incautious steps clattering in the stairway leading up. He caught up with Sarah and his erstwhile cellmates just as they reached the floor above. The guards here, one at each end of the hall, were also laid out fast asleep.

"I don't believe it!" The exclamation escaped his lips almost of its own volition.

"Believe it, Everett," Sarah rejoined. "I told you: we have Magic on our side."

"You know, this could be further empirical evidence to support my theory of the Grand Mystical Spirit!" Edwin exulted. "Just suppose that there were prime individuals whose contribution to human advancement was favored or supplemented by this eternal, all-encompassing Spirit. These individuals--"

"I've heard a lot of hooey in my day, Edwin," Harold scoffed. "But this is just a little too much, even for you. Next you'll be trying to claim that all of human history is some grand scheme, monitored and coddled by this silly spirit!"

"Why, I hadn't quite gotten that far, but you must be right! Excellent, Harold, I shall be sure to footnote you in my dissertation."

"Pah!"

The chemist and the fitter stopped in the center of the hall, blithely forgetting the matter at hand as they became consumed with their argument. Mitchell continued along behind Sarah, somewhat starry-eyed, as she counted doors on the right. She tried the knob on the fourth. It was locked.

"I think this is the door. Everett, open it please."

He blinked at her. "How?"

"Rip it off its hinges, of course."

"Oh. Well, all right. *Give me strength.*"

The brass knob crumpled in his hand and wrenched free of the solid oak panel, which rattled, but did not open.

Mitchell went wide-eyed at the display. "Wow! I've never before seen a Strength Enhancement Variant. Could you just punch a hole in it?"

Everett rejected that notion immediately. "That would probably break every bone in my hand."

"The brass didn't damage your hand," Sarah pointed out. "Your strength spell must have some sort of Invulnerability Component."

"Well, I'm not interested in taking the risk of being one-handed the rest of my life, if you don't mind."

"Then kick it open."

"And break my foot instead?"

"Fine. I'll just set fire to it then."

"That'll probably put the entire building to blaze!"

Sarah crossed her arms and glared.

"Oh, for Magic's sake!" Everett cast his ninth spell and pushed with his palms on the door until it splintered with a great racket and collapsed inward in a mangled pile, revealing two anxious but silent women. The younger one, blonde-haired and slim to the point of being gawky, caught sight of Mitchell and flung herself toward him, wrapped her arms around his neck, and proceeded to do her best to smother him with demonstrations of affection.

Margaret, a rosy-cheeked grandmotherly sort, simply shook her head and smiled.

"I see that you have met?" Sarah teased the two sweethearts. Then, dismissing the reunited couple with a single exaggerated lift of her eyebrows, she turned to Everett, "Give them back their voices so that we can find out what spells they have. And then we need to find Tekle."

None of the five spells that the two female magickers possessed between them, all Insignificants or Minors, proved obviously useful in the current situation, but Margaret did know that the other prisoners were confined on the same floor.

All of the rest of the doors were locked, but Everett simply and cheerfully smashed them in. He took some pleasure in doing so, reveling in the wanton but otherwise harmless destruction, and was slightly disappointed when the spree came to an end. Tekle and the other men, Roger, middle-aged with the shoulders of a lumberjack, Stephan, about the same age but less solid, and Will, a white haired man well up in age, were discovered in the last room on the left. Beatrice, a sturdy, older sheet metal worker with a very pragmatic attitude, called out from the room immediately across the hall when she heard the noise and was quickly released.

As the group gathered around Sarah and Everett, arguments and reunions, romantic, philosophical and otherwise, temporarily in abeyance, it was clear that all of them had accepted that Sarah was in charge and all of them were simply waiting for her to tell them what to do. She speedily obliged, asking the synthesists to stand by and dispatching Tekle to scout the lower floors. Tekle returned within moments to report that all the guards, including two exterior sentries, were indeed under the effects of Sarah's spell. For good measure, he had bolted the front doors and found and likewise secured a rear exit.

"Very good," she approved. "Now, Everett and I will transport you two at a time back to the air carriage. We'll need everyone to get up on the roof."

Sergeant Tekle clicked his heels. "Pardon me, mademoiselle, may I make a suggestion?"

"Of course."

"If possible, we should locate the lockbox. I would also suggest that we should gather some of the rifles and pistols and as much ammunition as we can carry plus anything else that might be useful."

Margaret looked startled. "Why would we need guns?"

Tekle grinned patiently. "One: we are now fugitives from Baron's Heimgelberg's justice. Two: It is clear that we are now also at odds with the Alarsarians. Three: As a consequence of Number One and Two, if we want to keep the air carriage, we must be ready to defend it."

Frowning, Margaret opened her mouth to reply, but Sarah cut her off.

"Sergeant Tekle is right. We'll face immediate arrest if we return to Eriis for any reason, and there can be no doubt that Baron Heimgelberg will publish warrants, so we won't be able to stop at any other towns in his demesne or any place where he has constabulary agreements. We need to take with us any item that might remotely be of use. Everyone scatter and gather up everything you can find. Particularly, take any money you come across."

"Are the soldiers dead asleep or can they be awakened?" Harold questioned.

"They can be roused with a good shaking or a sharp pain, but should remain asleep if you're careful."

In short order, the group divided into pairs and trios and began scavenging through the building, sifting through the pockets of the Alarsarians with the care of pickpockets, and searching every room. Happily, Tekle did discover the unopened lockbox in a room on the ground floor. While they began to haul their finds, mostly the weapons and some odd pocket change, up to the roof, Sarah pulled Everett aside.

"I think we should question that captain before we leave," she told him. "We need to learn exactly why the Kingdom has taken such a great interest in the air carriage."

Everett quickly agreed. The involvement of the Alarsarians had been a shock. First, the Zherians had tried to snatch Sarah, and now their enemies had been revealed to be actively working here in Heimgelberg. Evidently, the coming war to the west was not as distant as he had believed and now he and Sarah seemed inescapably embroiled in the clash of the two great demesnes.

To avoid any chance of waking the other soldiers, Everett carried the captain like a babe in his magically strengthened arms down to the very room to which he had first been taken. Once securely bound to the chair with ropes found in a hall closet, Sarah roused the officer by the simple expedient of slapping him repeatedly in the face.

Everett winced in sympathy. "Is that necessary?"

"Probably not, but it does make me feel better."

He shrugged. "Right."

Captain Van Ghest twisted his shoulders and threw back his head to avoid another slap, blinked, and focused on first Everett and finally Sarah. "Ah, I see the situation has changed somewhat."

Sarah was not interested in polite preliminaries. *"Only the truth, cretin."*

"A veracity spell? It appears that an attempt to claim my rights under the Treaty of Ghoot would be a futile gesture. However, before the interrogation begins, may I ask how your companion eluded detection by Lieutenant Smythe's spell?"

"No, you may not," Sarah denied. "What is the Kingdom of Alarsaria's interest in the air carriage?"

"We wish to control this new technology."

Van Ghest, while incapable of resisting the effects of the magic, clearly did not intend to provide any information that was not extracted by a specific question.

"Who informed you of its existence?" Everett asked. "The Baron?"

"No. Baronet Rorche and his group came to the attention of our operatives as a result of normal intelligence gathering activities."

Sarah evinced surprise. "Operatives? You have spies in Heimgelberg?"

"Yes."

"Where else?"

"In all the major capitals with roving teams in the larger rural regions."

"In Kleinsvench?"

"Yes."

Sarah's eyes narrowed, but she did not continue, biting her lip in thought.

Everett considered her reaction, grasped that she did not want her Kleinsvenchan connection mentioned, and detoured to another line of questioning. "So you had people watching the warehouse?"

"No."

"You used magic?"

"No."

Everett sighed and took time to devise a more precise and informative question. "How, in exact detail, did you keep track of Baron Rorche and the construction of the air carriage?"

"We insinuated an operative into the group and he has relayed regular reports of progress on the mechanism by means of notes that Lieutenant Smythe is capable of reading using his Distant Observation variant."

"You have a *spy* in Rorche's group?"

"Yes."

"Who is it?" Sarah wanted to know.

"His name is Jonnan Kreig, a technologist and Major in the RIC."

"There's no one by that name aboard the air carriage," Everett contradicted. "Is he using an alias?"

"Yes."

"What is it?"

"Aldo Serap."

SIXTEEN

At the time, Everett had thought that Sarah's assertion that they would transport two of the released prisoners at a time had been a simple misstatement, but the young woman actually had devised a scheme to accomplish this.

"Ready." she breathed into his ear.

"Beautiful Woman, come forth!"

By the simple expedient of riding piggyback on his back, with her legs wrapped around his waist, she could keep both hands free to hold onto her passengers, in this case the last two, Tekle and the mechanic Roger Binsyen.

They appeared alongside the previous transportees and their spoils on the roof of a large barn that stood a safe two miles from Eriis. Just as soon as the burgeoning day had permitted Everett to see his target from the roof of the prison building, he and Sarah had begun transporting the group on the first leg of the journey to the air carriage, which waited fifteen miles from the city.

"We'll take the sergeant and Binsyen on," Sarah announced to the group on arrival. "And return right away for the next two. Everyone get ready."

Everett cast.

The next locus was a clump of trees that projected above a ridge three miles across a swale. Without great delay, they transported the group there and then on to the next, the half-ruin tower of an old hilltop outpost, and then from there to half a dozen other prominent elevated landmarks, until finally they landed in a logged clearing below a set of low hills. With her engines idling against the wind, the air carriage was in sight, floating serenely above a small lake that was yet hidden beyond the rising ground. Rorche had chosen the sparsely wooded area to avoid the curious and thus perhaps keep word of the whereabouts of the air carriage from the Baronial authorities.

As the Baronet's rescued compatriots, sitting on stumps or standing casually in a rough circle, settled in to wait for the final transport, Sarah stretched ostentatiously and then gestured for Everett to follow her. "Everyone, take a few minutes to rest. Everett and I are going to fix our landing point from that hill."

Everett, who had been carrying her not inconsiderable weight for an hour and welcomed a walk to work the kinks out of his back, gratefully trailed after her through the cutover. Dodging stumps warded with the thorns of blackberry canes, honeysuckle encumbered piles of discarded limbs, and intervening sprouts of new oaks, sweet gum, and hickory, they walked for better than ten minutes. The top of the tree-shaded hill overlooked the lake and gave a direct view of the open rear cargo doors of the air carriage. Not coincidently, in addition to leaving Everett slightly winded, the upslope stroll also took the pair far beyond the earshot of the others.

Giving the appearance of fixedly studying the air carriage and without looking back toward the group, Sarah told him, "We can't tell them about Aldo."

Everett leaned sideways against the solid trunk of a sweet gum and did not try to conceal his surprise. "What? Why not? If we don't reveal the spy, the Alarsarians are certain to try to capture the air carriage again."

"Exactly."

"What do you mean?"

"Kleinsvench and the Kingdom are allies, or will be soon. I can't betray an Alarsarian spy and not expect negative repercussions. "

Indignant, Everett glared. "But you can betray Rorche and the others?"

"It's not a matter of betrayal. The two of us are simply bystanders caught up in someone else's problem. We bought passage on the air carriage with our magic, nothing more."

"Then why did you insist on rescuing everyone?"

"Because I knew that it wouldn't be difficult and it was necessary. If we returned without the others, Rorche would have resisted the idea of continuing the journey across the continent. Now, we return as heroes, and he and the rest will trust us implicitly. That will make it far easier to convince them to divert to Kleinsvench."

"That sounds cold-bloodedly mercenary and callous."

Sarah's eyes flared. "I've never claimed to be anything else. I've agreed to marry to cement an alliance and could very well likely spend the entire remainder of my natural life as a political bargaining chip. Why would I have any qualms whatsoever about using anyone and everyone to insure the safety and security of my family?"

"Right."

"No, Everett … I didn't mean--"

"Forget it."

If he had ever thought that her interest in him might be anything more than a dispassionate utilization of an available resource, then there was absolutely no question about the nature of their association now.

The corners of her mouth turned down as she watched his face. "Will you do as I ask and not tell them about Aldo?"

He looked at her without saying anything for a moment. Then, "My price is now ten thousand silver."

With no visible reaction, she said nothing for an equally long beat. "Eight."

"Ten."

"Nine."

"Ten."

She pressed her lips into a thin line. "Very well. Ten thousand silver to return me to Kleinsvench."

Consciously choosing to drive deeper the wedge of anger that now lay between them, he commanded her, "Fetch the others. I'd like this journey to be done."

A considerable outpouring of relief and excitement erupted when they began transporting to the cargo compartment of the air carriage. The esne keeping watch there immediately ran to the corridor to summon the Baronet. Rorche and the others crowded around in greeting, questions and explanations flying. The full transport took less than ten minutes; by now the rescued band had learned to wait in paired lines, weapons and other items held in off hands, ready to step up to take Sarah's grasp as soon as the magician duo reappeared.

Rorche called for an impromptu conference when the last two, Tekle and Binsyen, were transported.

"This is the only space aboard that is large enough for all of us to gather together and I believe that we must decide this very moment what we should do next," he said, once the noise of reunion had quieted.

"What do you mean, Franz?" Edwin asked with a mildly worried tone.

"Our original plan to travel to Eyrchelle is now clearly unwise. I do not doubt that we will again face arrest if we appear there."

"Are you proposing that we stay here?" Margaret asked.

"No, we still require the financial, technical, magical, and physical resources of the west in order to construct our fleet of air carriages and commence our commercial enterprise, which I am convinced is still the best opportunity that we will have to recoup our investments. We must determine which country, aside from the Kingdom of Alarsaria, is best equipped to enable us to do so."

"It will have to be someone on the Zherian side," Harold spoke up. "Any of the allies of the Kingdom would be almost certain to turn us over to the Alarsarians."

"Why not the Republic itself?" Algis, standing with his wife, suggested.

"They are said to be quite friendly to technology," Ellen added.

Several others spoke in agreement.

"Then a show of hands, please," the Baronet requested, once again demonstrating his democratic eccentricities, "to indicate that we shall voyage to Mrysberg, the capital of the Republic of Zheria.'

Everyone except Tekle and the esne, who would simply follow where Rorche led, and Everett, who did not care and made that feeling evident, raised his or her hands. Sarah, though Everett knew she had good reason to not wish to travel to the Republic, also raised her hand.

Preparations for the voyage were begun immediately, with Aldo, Bennett, and Millicent charting a course and the others finding assigned compartments, storing gear, or discussing watch rotations, technical matters, or, in the case of those with no clear duties, the trauma of their arrest in Eriis.

The remainder of the day passed without incident as the air carriage crossed the Edze at two thousand feet and continued flying on into the night and early morning. Rather than face possible attack and capture by mooring, the synthesists had made the decision to take the risk of running the engines continuously. Contending with crosswinds and headwinds, Bennett and Aldo, who rotated four hour shifts as steersman, could only manage an average of some twenty miles per hour, but by dawn they had passed above the smaller neighboring demesnes of (according to Rorche's maps) the Castilian of Shywd, the Countess Ethel Mac Toogln, and the Independent Oligarchy of Pshyun. Well into the High Shadowed Hills, Millicent proudly announced that the air ship had covered some four hundred and forty-six miles, plus or minus twenty-three miles.

Everett endeavored to stay out of the way, idling in the corridors chatting with Tekle, lounging on the upper deck (now labeled the Observation Deck by common consensus), or napping in the tiny room with two stacked bunks and little else that he now shared with Mitchell.

Around midday, when he chanced to catch Sarah in a private moment as they passed in the starboard corridor, he pressed without preamble, "Don't you think that you'll be arrested in Zheria?"

"Obviously. But we are going to leave the air carriage at the border and then make our way to Kleinsvench."

"I thought as much."

As she barged by him to continue on to the bow, she threw over her shoulder, "I pay you for magic, not for thinking."

He shrugged to her retreating back and walked to the dead end of the corridor to access the Observation Deck. Now that the air carriage flew under power, there was a steady cold wind across the deck, but he preferred the open air to the sometimes-claustrophobic interior and had resolved to spend most of the voyage there.

Several people were already present, most bundled in

heavy jackets and scarves against the wind. At a fold-out table fastened to the deck, Aldo, Harold, Josline and Suzette played some sort of bidding card game, interestingly holding down won tricks with pistols. Mitchell, Will, and Beatrice, hunkered on low stools behind a tarp draped as a windbreak over the rail at the bow, good-naturedly argued the validity of some effervescent and perhaps unfathomable point of an unfamiliar branch of existential philosophy.

Everett loosened the rope holding another stool to the rail and carried it to the card players, who greeted him with nods and smiles.

As he studied his cards, Aldo grinned. He showed the others the three of diamonds, tucked it face up under a pistol. "Three spades, four hearts."

Harold, to Aldo's left, grimaced. "You always seem to get the cards, Aldo." He showed a queen of spades and likewise burned it. "Four spades, seven diamonds."

Josline, Aldo's partner, folded her cards in a pass, leaving Suzette to declare, with some glee, "Thirteen no trumps!"

As the hand played out in an incomprehensible flurry of taking and refunding of tricks, Everett unobtrusively studied Aldo. As far as he had been able to discover by simple observation, the Alarsarian spy had as yet no inkling that he and Sarah knew his secret. It had occurred to Everett that it was almost certain that Aldo's flushing of the original ballast had been an intentional act of sabotage instead of the panicked error that he had claimed. This was also likewise the case when he had stumbled and fallen at the first landing of the craft. It had further occurred to Everett that there could be no doubt that the Royal Intelligence Corps officer would attempt other sabotage to prevent the air carriage from reaching Republican territory. Everett had considered that Aldo might seek to capture the air carriage, but had concluded that the Alarsarian could not expect to overpower the entire company, especially now that all of the esne and many of the passengers, at Tekle's urging, were constantly armed. Everett thought the man's only viable course of action would be to make an effort to disable permanently the flying mechanism.

He had originally thought to inform Sarah of his

conclusions, but had decided that it would be a waste of time to do so. Either she had already considered the spy's probable perfidy herself and planned accordingly, or she would be surprised with the rest. As she had just told him, she was not paying him to think for her.

As to when Aldo might carry out his treachery, Everett had no clue. Having no desire to experience the first ever crash of an air carriage, he had resolved to make every effort to forestall the spy's efforts. Thus, as now, he had begun to shadow the steersman, hoping that the undeniably compact space of the vessel would explain his frequent presence.

Suzette laid her last card, the jack of clubs, and raked in the final trick. "That's a double *and* a triple!"

With a melodramatic groan of defeat, Aldo pushed back from the table, glancing at his watch. "We'll have to finish the game later. I'm off to relieve Bennett." He picked up his pistol, slid it into the regulation Alarsarian holster, and snapped the flap, all with a practiced single-handed motion.

Everett thought the maneuver a bit too casual in its accomplishment, but none of the others seemed to notice.

He stood up and offered the imposter a friendly smile. "Hey, Aldo? Might I come along? I've wanted to learn how the air carriage is operated."

"Sure!" Aldo agreed with no discernable trace of guile. "I was just telling Bennett that we should train more steersmen. We'll need to eventually. The other air carriages will require dozens." He looked at his tablemates. "How about you all? Anyone interested?"

Josline shook her head. "Not me. I'll stick with the engines."

Harold rolled his shoulders. "I'll give it a go."

"Me too!" Suzette enthused.

"Great! Come along then."

SEVENTEEN

"These rotary switches control a series of electrically driven valves on the main vapor trunk," Aldo explained. "It is important to release vapor in moderate stages and to balance the release through all sections of the cells."

Though there was constant sighing of background sound in the air carriage while it was under power -- air crossing the hull, vagrant vibrations in the structure, the muffled burr of the engines – the interior had the acoustics of a monastery library and Aldo spoke in a conversational tone.

"How do you know how much vapor to release?" Suzette queried.

"We have yet to install mechanisms to measure the flow of the vapor exiting the cells, so calculations are necessary to determine this. Luckily, we have Millicent, who has prepared charts based on our current load, ambient temperature, and so forth." He pointed to a sheaf of papers on a clipboard next to the control board. "We simply cross reference to find a number of seconds of release per one hundred foot of altitude. Likewise, when discharging ballast in order to gain altitude, it is vitally important to do so according to the outlined tank balancing procedure in order to maintain the equilibrium or trim of the air carriage. Failing to do so might place stresses on the air carriage that exceed design parameters. Now, these switches…"

Everett listened to the remainder of the lecture with half an ear. Bennett had made it clear that none of the three potential trainees would be permitted to actually steer the air carriage until they understood the entirety of the control mechanisms with absolute and unshakable certainty. However, Everett already knew that, even if he had been truthfully inclined to become a steersman, his remaining time aboard would not be sufficient to reach that level of competence.

"I understand," Harold asked, "that the air carriage is steered by throttling the engines?"

"Yes," Aldo confirmed, and then walked to a position at the center of the forward console. He placed his hands on two large knobbed levers that extended from slots at the center of a flat wooden panel.

"These control one engine each by means of a braded steel wire that feeds back through a conduit to the engines. There are return springs on the throttles, so moving a lever back will reduce the speed and consequently the thrust of that engine. You will notice that the engines are slightly off balance now to compensate for a slight crosswind. Such adjustments are constantly necessary to maintain our heading on due west."

The technician continued for over an hour, naming all the controls and giving a brief overview of their use and function. Not once did he betray any hint that he was anything less than completely committed to the air carriage and his duties as a steersman.

By dawn of the next day, the vessel had crossed the gray and black stony prominences of the High Shadowed Hills and entered the easternmost territory of the Kingdom of Alarsaria, a densely forested province with scattered villages.

Everett rolled out of his bunk when the first weak light of day crept under the compartment door, flipped on the dim battery light, used the built-in basin to wash quickly while Mitchell grumbled and pulled his blanket over his head, and then scurried forward to the control compartment. He remained there for the greater part of the morning with Aldo, who was on shift monitoring the air carriage's progress, and Bennett, who had interpreted his continual attendance as zealous dedication and had cheerfully assumed the role of instructor.

He had not spoken to Sarah again. As she moved about the air carriage, she acknowledged his presence, but gave no indication that her ire had eased. His own anger had dissipated somewhat, but he did not feel any desire to make any attempt whatsoever to insinuate himself again into her good graces.

As noon approached and the air carriage began to pass over agricultural terrain, Aldo had as yet done nothing that might reveal his plan, but whatever the man had in mind must clearly be done soon. Bennett had already informed Everett he would apply a course change at one o'clock to turn slightly to the north. Millicent's plot would take them across the Alarsarian allied County of Llaele, avoiding the larger cities and towns, and then beyond the border to the state of East Lystra, a member of the Republic. There, Rorche planned to moor in an isolated spot and dispatch an expedition to explore the possibilities for negotiations with Zherian commercial interests.

Currently drilling him on the battery circuits, Bennett prompted, "And this?"

"The main starboard ballast pump," Everett droned.

"This?"

"The auxiliary starboard ballast pump."

Bennett pointed at a smaller knife switch.

"The starboard corridor lights."

Bennett raised an eyebrow.

"Sorry. *Port* corridor lights."

Suzette entered from the port side, energetic and smiling, carrying a silver tea service on a tray. "We finally managed a fire in the stove using some packing crate lumber and we have tea! Ellen said to tell you that lunch – sandwiches again -- will be ready in a bit."

"I'll take a cup," Bennett welcomed.

"Everett?"

"No, thank you." He liked tea fine, but preferred the iced variety, which only could be had in winter. Welcoming the break, though, he took a seat on a stool beside the vapor manifold.

"Aldo?"

"Sure. Any chance of a teacake?"

"I don't think so, but I'll be glad to go check." She set the tray on a small shelf next to the vapor controls, carefully filled two steaming cups, and then handed them to the two steersmen. "I'll be right back."

Aldo's eyes trailed her as she departed and Everett assumed, with a certain amount of condescension, that the steersman's interest was a simple admiration of the way her trousers fit her backside. Distractedly, the mechanic set his cup on the chart table that Tekle had had made just that morning from a modified packing crate.

Moving toward the table, Bennett sipped his tea, then took a long draught. "I wonder if they'll have as good a blend in the Republic?"

"Once we are settled, you might be able to import some from New Zindersberg. It seems to me that they will stay neutral."

Bennett took another sip. "You sound sure that the war will come."

"Not sure, no, but I cannot see any hope that the diplomatic conferences will resolve anything."

"You're probably right. I heard a story in a tavern just last week that they spent a full three weeks at the last one just trying to agree on whether the tables should be oriented on a north-south or east-west axis."

"Sounds about right."

Bennett set his cup down and caught the edge of the table. "Huh. Woozy there for a..."

Then, without further warning, he folded slowly as if his knees had given way and fainted over onto his back.

Before Everett could do more than be startled, Suzette appeared again from the head of the port corridor. Her expression more one of disappointment than of alarm, she glanced at Aldo's cup sitting on the chart table, and then shrugged.

"A pity," she said tonelessly. "I sort of liked you, Aldo."

Everett saw the steersman's hand flash toward his pistol, but Suzette was almost incredibly faster. Her gun roared, ear-smashingly loud in the confined space with an answering rattle from the clear material of the forward window. The blow of the bullet flung Aldo backwards into the pipes of the ballast manifold only inches from Everett, bright red spewing from a gaping wound in his chest. When the Alarsarian sagged to the floor in a spreading puddle of his own blood, it was clear that he was dead.

Then Everett heard the unmistakable metallic sound of

Suzette's pistol snapping shut. She had reloaded! Panicked, he dodged toward the starboard corridor. The pistol's hammer cracked, but there was no discharge. Suzette began cursing. Her weapon had misfired!

Everett fled. He reached the end of the corridor in seconds and swarmed up the Observation Deck ladder, expecting the hammer blow of a pistol shot to his back, but burst out of the hatch unharmed.

He ran toward the bow. Maybe he could climb up into the vapor cell webbing?

Steps heard pounding behind, he took a leap to one of the supporting lanyards and grabbed onto the cable. As he began to haul himself up, hand over hand, he again heard the crack of a pistol hammer but no corresponding bark of fire. Then he reached the bottom webbing and realized that he could only climb outward around the cell envelope. He reached out, upside down, to grab a hold on the netting, then hooked his feet and started to ease outward.

"Stop, Everett!" Edwin called.

In consternation, Everett jerked his head around to see the chemist climbing from the hatch to join Suzette. Mitchell, gun drawn, came immediately after.

"I shot at him twice but both cartridges misfired," the young woman told the two of them, her former persona of a harmless ingénue replaced by one comfortable with the business of killing. "I think he is using magic."

The young woman's lips curled in disgust as she pronounced the last word.

Edwin tapped his chin with a finger. "He *is* a wizard. While I have never read or been notified of the existence of such a spell, I also know of no magical postulate that could contravene the manifestation of one. Mitchell, you shoot him. That will establish another data point to allow us to build a hypothesis."

Everett lunged toward another hold, sure that he was about to die. He did not stop moving when Mitchell's pistol also clicked and failed to fire. He now dangled twenty feet out from the Observation Deck, nothing below him but empty air and the earth, two thousand feet below.

Above the wind, Edwin said, "Try the same cartridge

off in another direction. Then we will know whether the shell itself has been made faulty."

The gun banged, not as loud as the shots fired inside the air carriage, but Everett jumped all the same and then spidered further away from the deck, focusing on the webbing in front of him. The strain of holding nearly all of his weight had begun to make his arms shake and he had to stop to rest, fists clenched on a main cross weave. Belatedly, he remembered his ninth spell and cast it to gain relief.

"Try this, the both of you," Edwin suggested as if discussing a recipe for cake. "Aim at his boot, rather than him."

Two ineffectual and almost cotemporaneous clicks replied.

"What if we shoot away the ropes that he is holding?" Suzette pondered.

"You may try," Edwin conceded, "as long as you do not puncture a vapor cell. The vapor is highly flammable."

"I think it can be done if we climb up to get a good angle," Mitchell stated matter-of-factly. "His weight distends the webbing downward."

Everett, knowing that the three would not stop until he was dead, made a decision.

He let go.

EIGHTEEN

Everett had fallen for only a few seconds when the words of a spell sprang from his lips.

"Take ye flight!"

Instantly, the magic arrested his fall and he seemed to hover, looking down at the landscape below. Then, after perhaps a dozen seconds, he plummeted again.

"Take ye flight!"

Again, he floated, free of the draw of the earth far below. Marking seconds, he sculled with his hands, trying to adjust his orientation. By the count of thirteen, his fall resumed, but he had managed to assume an upright position, feet downward. After one more cast, he made it to the ground, falling less than five feet into a plowed field. The loose dirt cushioned the impact somewhat, but still his knees banged into his chest as he collapsed. He lolled onto his back, staring up into the sky and grinned.

He had survived!

Wait a minute.

He had survived?

He thrust himself into a sitting position. This could not be mere coincidence nor the random fluctuation of a natural physical force. He had manifested *exactly* the right spell at *exactly* the right moment to preserve his life. Nothing in conventional magic theory could explain that.

Come to think of it, his other recent manifestation, the strength spell, had been the same. That spell had allowed him to overcome the gendarme and had come to him just in the nick of time.

Three more extremely suspicious oddities immediately presented themselves as evidence of the unnatural state of the world: the failure of the Alarsarian magician's spell to detect his magic, the deviant adaptability of his and Sarah's spells in the Eriis prison, and the failure of the pistol cartridges of Edwin's cohorts. There seemed little doubt that these occurrences also must be the results of magic, though magic bereft of spell, manifestation, enunciation, or actuation. Such passive magical effects were entirely unheard of and until this moment he would have said that such a thing was impossible.

There could be only one explanation for these undeniably beneficial alterations in the natural order. Somehow, somewhere, something – *someone* – had manipulated the forces of nature in order to protect him.

No human wizard had ever been known to possess a spell that would permit a fundamental change to natural law, a change to magic itself. That devious villain Edwin had spoken of a Mystical Spirit. Could that preposterous idea have merit? Was there some disembodied being with intelligence, motive, and purpose that had determined to interfere directly and positively in his life?

If so, what reason could there be for such interference? Not until he had met Sarah had –

"For Magic's sake! Beautiful Woman, come forth!"

The young woman appeared in his arms, unresponsive and unmoving, her eyes closed.

His heart froze as he feared her dead, poisoned by the bizarrely transformed Edwin and his minions. Then he saw the slight rise and fall of her chest and realized that she must simply be locked in a deep sleep, overcome by some potion mixed in the tea. Likely, the same was true of Bennett and the others on the air carriage.

Save poor Aldo, of course.

Thinking of the craft, he looked up, scanned the sky, and found its tiny dark shape against high clouds some distance off to the north. It was still headed towards Zheria. To what fate it flew, he could only speculate. The revelation of Edwin, Suzette, and Mitchell – and perhaps others – as traitorous, heartless killers with some still unknown agenda had thoroughly annihilated all of his previous presumptions and assumptions.

He looked back down at Sarah. The soft lines of her face lay in peaceful repose and she seemed none the worse for the imposed slumber. Clearly, she was not in distress at the moment.

I need a spell to awaken her!, he shouted in his mind to the unnamed, unidentified, possibly non-existent disembodied being.

He held his breath in anticipation, but no magical inspiration burst into his consciousness.

After waiting a further futile ten minutes, he gathered Sarah in his arms and with some difficulty stood. Struggling with her limp form, he juggled her about until her head lolled against his shoulder. Knowing that they could not remain here in the open till she awoke, he took stock of his surroundings.

Huge and rolling, the field seemed to go on for a mile or more in every direction. He had often read the vast wheat lands of Alarsaria described thus and took it for granted that he had landed in the Kingdom. For whatever reason, it looked as if the early wheat had been already harvested and a second crop not yet sewn. Silos and buildings lay off to the west, so he started walking in that direction. He had to resort to his strength spell after about a hundred yards to ease the fatigue in his arms, but covered ground quickly and reached the buildings within half an hour.

The site might once have belonged to a farm. There were half a dozen grain silos, two larger buildings that had the shapes of barns, another that once had been a two-storey dwelling. Now, though, the place was obviously a fortress, with timber revetments occupying the porches and windows of the house, a palisade of logs and sandbags linking all the structures, and blockhouses of freshly lain brown brick covering every approach. A wide, deep ditch ran along the exterior, pierced only by a hard-packed road leading to the south. Soldiers were partially visible through firing slits and gun ports, and Everett soon identified the maroon field jackets of the Royal Infantry of Alarsaria.

He felt a moment's hesitation at that, but there was nothing to be done for it. He could not assume that the events in Eriis had not already been made known here, but hopefully he would be able to conceal his and Sarah's identities and avoid any unpleasantness

When he was only about three steps from the plank-shored edge of the defensive ditch and casting about for someone to hail, a four striper popped from a hatch in the top of a blockhouse that abutted a cut-stone silo on the opposite side. With the hardened look of a professional soldier, he was probably fifteen years older than Everett. The close cut stubble under his slouch cap was mostly gray.

The sergeant had the oddest expression on his face as he proclaimed, "You have to be the luckiest man alive!"

The Alarsarian was better than ten yards away but his strong baritone and innate friendliness carried easily.

Everett was somewhat taken aback. He had expected a more belligerent challenge. "What? Why do you say that?"

"Because you have just walked down the center o' a beebeefield."

"A what?"

"A beebeefield. That whole area is sown with beebees."

Everett shook his head in incomprehension. "What in the world are *beebees?*"

The man grinned. "Don't get to town much, I expect? I thought everybody knew about beebees. That's 'B-B.' Stands for 'Buried Bombs.' It's a mechanism filled with gun powder."

"And they explode when stepped upon?"

"Yeah, they surely do. A sow got loose when we were emplacing them. There wasn't enough left for a good stew."

"Oh." Whatever effect had preserved him from the pistols apparently also *–fortunately!* -- worked on any other similar mechanism.

"Like I said, you have to be the luckiest man alive. None o' my mates back at the barracks will ever believe this."

"Probably not."

"Well, I guess I had better tell you that you both are under arrest."

"Right."

"What's with the girl? Drunk?"

"Right, something like that."

"Well, stay right where you are and we'll lower the footbridge across. Then the Lieutenant will need to see you."

At a field desk in a small room in the former

farmhouse, the young officer, J. Jenkins according to a patch sewn onto the breast of her field jacket, accused the sergeant of pulling her leg.

"The fellows at the academy warned me about such pranks. The young woman is a nice touch. Excellent try."

"Honest, Lieutenant!" the underofficer swore. "He walked right out o' the eastern beebeefield."

"Balderdash! I should put you on report for bringing civilians up here, Sergeant Mallory. I'll overlook it this time, but let's not have it happen again, read me?"

The sergeant snapped to attention. "Yes, mam."

"Now, send them back to the rear where they belong." She waved a flimsy at Mallory. "This morning's dispatch warns that we should expect action by the Zherians at any moment. I want you to issue every infantryman quadruple ammunition and check on the sentries on top of the silos on every quarter hour. I don't want to catch anyone up there sleeping like I did yesterday."

"Yes, mam."

Outside the lieutenant's door, Mallory shrugged. "Best crazy story that I've ever had and everybody'll just think that I'm a bad liar. Well, come on. We'll get you headed back to Bayou Dorking, like she said."

Whispering his spell again to ease the strain of carrying Sarah, Everett followed the sergeant out of the farmhouse. Several curious guards watched without speaking as they exited through a timbered overhang covered in sandbags.

"Bayou Dorking?" he questioned. "That's the nearest town?"

"That's right. Not from around here, are you?"

"No, we're from …" Everett thought quickly, but his knowledge of western geography was severely limited and only one place name in the vicinity sprang to mind. "Bindleberg."

"Bindleberg? Isn't that the technological monastery way up in the High Shadowed Hills?"

"Exactly."

"So what are you doing way down here?"

"We're on a, uhm, holy pilgrimage."

"To where?"

"Kleinsvench."

"What, so the two o' you practice the doctrines o' the Old Style Dho Sect?"

"Yes," Everett agreed quickly.

Mallory laughed kindly. "Sorry, son, I just made that up. How about telling me the truth?"

Everett shrugged. What could it hurt? Even if they were imprisoned again, he had total confidence that sooner or later the two of them could use magic to escape. As Sarah had said -- whether she meant it in the same sense or not -- in some weird way Magic – or at least *someone* -- was on their side. As they walked toward the rear of the compound across a yard scuffed to bare dirt, Everett told the Alarsarian every detail from his initial transportation of Sarah to his blind leap from the air carriage, reserving only the self-incriminating encounter in Eriis with Captain Van Ghest.

"I was wrong," the sergeant admitted as Everett finished, stopping in front of the heavily fortified rear gate, a double switchback of sandbagged bunkers. "*This* is the craziest story that I've ever heard. Did I hear that right? *Potatoes*, come forth?"

Everett sighed wearily. "Right."

Mallory quirked his lips in amusement. "Amazing."

Everett grimaced. "What are you going to do with us now?"

"Send you on to town. If I went in and tried to tell the Lieutenant this whopper, she'd have my hide. Best to just get you and your problems out o' my hair. I'll have to send a couple of infantrymen with you, though, and turn you over to the Provost."

Mallory led him through the gate to a small area bounded on one side by a horse corral and on the other by a line of parked freight wagons. As two stablemen hitched a pair of gray draft horses to one of the heavy wagons, the sergeant called another man over to him.

"Percy, go get Privates Clay and Serheighmon. I'm sending these two to town under guard."

Percy scratched his bald pate. "She won't like that, Sergeant. You know she thinks you're just been trying to put her out of harm's way."

"In the King's Army, soldiers obey orders. You just go tell them to report on the double."

Percy shrugged, grinning, and went into the compound.

"Clay and Serheighmon will take you to the Provost in Bayou Dorking," the sergeant told Everett quietly. "I'll leave it up to you to explain what you were doing out here. My advice would be to come up with a better story before you get to town."

"At least we don't have to walk," Everett replied optimistically. While one of the stablemen held the horses, the other fetched blankets for a pallet in the bed of the wagon. Everett laid Sarah on the pallet with care, arranging her limbs in as comfortable a position as he could. He sank down beside her, stretching out his legs and leaning back against the driver's seat, happy for the opportunity to get off his feet. He was thoroughly tired and, having missed lunch, hungry.

"Sergeant, I don't suppose there is any chance of getting something to eat?"

"Cook's shut down the mess already. I might have a field ration on me, though." The Alarsarian patted his pockets in sequence and then grinned, shoving a hand down in a long outside thigh trouser pocket. He brought out a sealed wax paper covered rectangle about the size of a student's copybook and passed it over. "These are kind o' dry, but there are canteens under the seat."

Everett accepted the ration with an appreciative smile and tore the end off. The thin, grain, nut, and dried fruit cake inside was further protected by a wrapping of baker's parchment. Taking care not to drop any crumbs, he broke the cake along an incised line and then re-wrapped Sarah's half in the parchment and slid it back into the wax paper envelope. He only got four good bites out of his half and finished quickly, but the small snack took the edge off his hunger.

"Thanks again, sergeant. I appreciate it."

"No problem. I always keep a couple on me. I've missed a few meals in my time."

Private Clay, a tall woman who appeared to be not quite twenty, arrived at an agitated trot with her full kit and rifle and hauled herself up immediately onto the seat of the wagon, as if she already knew what the sergeant expected of her. She seemed none too happy with her assignment and, once seated, shot Mallory a hard look. This the underofficer blissfully ignored, pointing the other soldier towards the back end of the wagon.

Serheighmon was a fresh faced lad with a rumpled but clean uniform and he offered Everett a friendly smile as he settled onto the tailgate, his rifle cradled haphazardly across his lap and pointing in no particular direction. With one hand holding his weapon, he tucked off his cap and used it to wipe sweat from his forehead and black stubbled scalp. He seemed to have no objections whatsoever to a casual jaunt into town.

Mallory walked around to address the driver. "Clay, I want you to head over to Supply after you leave these two off and go through the requisitions. I think they shorted us ten cans of hash last month. Stay there until you find the discrepancy even if it takes a few days."

Clay's disapproval intensified, but all she said was a chilly, "Yes, sergeant." She snapped the reins angrily and the wagon took off.

South of the outpost, the croplands to either side of the arrow-straight road had been recently harvested, but had not yet been plowed. The complete absence of trees made the expanse of tan stubble and straw seem to go on forever. Rising and falling like lazy waves, the terrain caused a gradual up and down movement of the wagon that gave Everett the impression that they traveled across a lethargic earth colored sea.

"Is she sick?" Serheighmon, gesturing at Sarah, asked Everett after a few minutes along the rutted road. Clay had her eyes fixed on the path ahead of her and did not appear inclined to chat.

"No," Everett answered, then gave a very abbreviated and abridged version of the story he had told Mallory.

"*Air* carriage, huh? I saw something high up pass over the border earlier but didn't know what it was. I've always thought that technologists would figure a way to fly sooner or later. She's your wife?"

"No, just a stranded citizen of Kleinsvench. I'm helping her get home."

"You might want to reconsider going to Kleinsvench, given the war and all."

Suddenly alarmed, Everett asked quickly, "Has the fighting already started?"

"No, but everybody knows it'll be any day now. There's been a lot of activity all along the frontier, but the officers seem convinced that the main attack will come along the Eiae Plain smack through the Grand Duchy of Filingham. Kleinsvench, which is a close neighbor, is almost certain to be right in the thick of it."

Everett shrugged. "She's determined to return home and I don't think that anything will dissuade her."

"She'll be better off in Kleinsvench," Clay interjected without turning, apparently not able to ignore the conversation any longer. "The main thrust o' the Republican attack'll be either here in the east or through the Tghustan Forest in the far west."

The other private laughed. "Don't start that again, Clay. If the Zheries moved an army in this direction, we would already know about it. The road dust could be seen for miles."

"Not necessarily," Clay countered, turning her head to keep half an eye on the horses as she warmed to her argument. "If they broke it up into small units and moved them along separate routes far from the border, we'd not have any warning at all."

Serheighmon waved his free hand dismissively. "I suppose they could do that, but why in the world would they? Our main battle lines are too far from here to be flanked and if they moved too many troops this way, they would open up their center to a counterattack."

A distant sound, akin to thunder, came from the north.

Everett, wondering about rain, asked. "Is there canvas for the wagon?"

"No, but there're slickers under the seat," Clay replied, then looked back to the north curiously. "Not sure what that is, but this time o' year the rains usually move up from the south-west."

Awarding Serheighmon a feisty stare, she opened her mouth to return to her rebuttal, but before she could speak, a horrendous torrent of sound erupted from the direction of the outpost.

NINETEEN

The tremendous explosions bolted the horses and the wagon bed began to bounce and swerve, tossing Serheighmon, arms and legs flailing and his rifle arcing away, off the rear end. Clay cursed a streak as she fought to bring the team under control.

As the jouncing intensified, Sarah began to stir, moaning. Everett braced himself against the side of the wagon and took hold of her shoulders to keep the gyrations from throwing her about. Her eyes opened and blinked as she sought to focus on his face.

"Everett … what's happening?" She demanded, trying to sit up.

"I don't know. Just lie still."

She looked passed him to take in the open sky above. "Where are we?"

"In Alarsaria."

"Where's the air carriage?"

"I'll explain later. Right now we have other problems."

"I'm all right." She pushed his hands away. "Let me up."

The wagon slowed and came to an abrupt stop as Clay, feet braced and back arched, strained against the horse leads. The Alarsarian soldier hurriedly tied off the leather straps, set the brakes, and stood to turn about. Everett leaned away from Sarah and she sat up, not quite steadily, swiveling her head to examine her surroundings. When both women sucked in sharp breaths almost at the same instant, he whipped about to look back along the road.

The outpost was simply gone. Nothing could be seen of the quarter mile distant fortified compound save for billowing surges of towering smoke and the occasional shrouded flash of roiling fire. Small secondary detonations shook the ground as ammunition stores cooked off.

Fifty yards behind the wagon, Serheighmon, silhouetted against the black and gray clouds, rose slowly from the dust of the road, holding his left forearm with his right hand, and began walking unsteadily toward them.

Clay, perhaps unnecessarily, said in a dead calm tone, "It's the Zheries."

"We'd better get out of here," Everett recommended with some force.

As if to punctuate his suggestion, another salvo fell upon the former farm, sending up globes of fire and debris a hundred feet high. Blasts of sound and scorched wind again buffeted them. Spooked once more, the horses dragged the wagon a good dozen yards, throwing Clay back into her seat, before the friction of the locked wheels forced the animals to halt, wild-eyed, shivering, and dancing in fright.

As they righted themselves, Serheighmon trotted up, still holding his arm and now clearly grimacing in pain. "I think I broke my arm when I fell."

Everett hopped down to help the injured soldier into the wagon. "We need to get going," he urged. "The next barrage might land right on top of us."

The soldiers did not immediately react to his suggestion, and he began to consider transporting Sarah and himself far ahead out of danger.

Somewhat confusedly, Serheighmon wondered, "Maybe we should go back?"

Her face expressionless, Clay shook her head. "Shells that big only come from six-inch guns. Our deepest bunker was only three feet and that's not enough to survive six inchers dropped right on top o' them. The Zheries had the compound zeroed. Everyone there is dead."

The other private looked stricken. "Oh, crap. Your Dad was a good man, Clay."

Clay shrugged. "He was a good sergeant. Not so much anything else."

"Sergeant Mallory was your father?" Everett felt sick to his stomach. The man had been kind in his way and now he was abruptly, impersonally, and ingloriously dead.

"Yeah." Clay shrugged again, her face unreadable.

"And most o' the rest were my friends. It makes no difference."

"Everett," Sarah said, getting his attention. "We should transport out of here."

"Right." He climbed onto the bed of the wagon and stood, searching for a locus to the south. Then, thinking to get a better vantage and not considering any potential repercussions, he leapt upward and said, *"Take ye flight!"*

This time, rather than simply hovering, he soared upward a good ten feet, apparently spurred by his leap. At the top of his arc, he selected an unidentified rise on the horizon as a locus. As his spell expired, he rapidly spit out another cast to arrest his fall just before he struck the wagon bed and then clattered down just seconds later when it too expired. Serheighmon, Clay, and Sarah watched him with expressions of, respectively, amazement, curiosity, and calculation.

"You're a wizard?" Serheighmon asked, a bit in awe. "I've never been this close to one."

"He's a Master Wizard," Sarah confirmed. "Soon to be a Grand Master Wizard."

Everett eyed his companion, trying to divine her meaning. Had she also deduced that someone or something with the power to alter the normal operation of magic aided him?

"So, Master Wizard, you've a Transport spell?" Clay asked, her eyes lingering on the destroyed outpost.

"Yes. And with Sarah's assistance, it will work for the four of us."

"Then let's go. We've got five minutes or less."

Everett turned. Through the clearing smoke of the barrage, the shattered and heavily cratered farm had become visible. Perhaps a mile beyond the burning debris piles, a long line of advancing steam mechanisms could be seen, dense black smoke boiling from the stubs of smokestacks. With what appeared to be large gun barrels protruding from the front of their iron shells, the mechanisms were about the size of Bob's road grader and coming on rapidly.

Before he could restrain it, a needless question popped out of his mouth. "What are those?"

"Steam driven artillery o' some sort," Clay said distractedly. "It's a wonder that no one has thought o' it before. Those things are a major technological advance and will change the entire conduct o' the war."

As if struck by a sudden thought, she jumped to the ground, pulled a knife from a belt sheath and began slashing the horses free from the wagon. She swatted at the rumps of both and both bolted. As the two draft animals galloped off in different directions across, she climbed back aboard.

"Couldn't leave the poor beasts tied to the wagon. All right, get us out o' here, wizard."

The first hop took them less than three miles, but Everett spotted another locus without delay and cast again. Serheighmon and Clay, clasping Sarah's hands, navigated him toward the town of Bayou Dorking by the simple expedient of following the road. The rural center proved to be only thirteen miles from the devastated outpost and it was perhaps only half an hour later that they came within sight of it. Warned of the presence of beebeefields, he made sure that his last casting placed them atop a huge forward blockhouse on the outskirts of the town.

The second after they appeared on the slightly sloped tar-slathered crest, Sarah released the hands of the two soldiers and slid slowly from his back. As he turned about, she essayed a shaky step, stumbled, and would have fallen if he had not caught her.

She smiled weakly, holding his arm. "Sorry, I'm still a little woozy."

Everett smiled back and slid an arm around her waist for support. She seemed comfortable with this intimacy, draping her own arm about his shoulder. Events had clearly erased the strain that had existed between them on the air carriage. He dug in his pocket and offered her the remaining half of the field ration.

"Eat something. It'll make you feel better."

"Thanks, Everett." She did not attempt to move away as she began to chew the molasses bound cake.

Clay glanced about and then strode to an armored hatch cover and began banging on it with her knife hilt.

After a few moments, another hatch on the opposite

side of the blockhouse sprang open and several infantrymen armed with rifles boiled out and dropped prone to take aim at Everett and the rest.

A young officer stuck his head out of the hatch after a moment and pointed a pistol at Serheighmon, the nearest of the group to him. "How in the name of Technology did you get up here?"

The young private slowly raised one hand and looked around at the others.

"You should have said, 'in the name of Magic," Sarah, munching the field ration, corrected offhandedly by way of answer. "We are magickers, Everett and I."

There was evident pride in her declaration and she seemed to tighten the arm draped about his neck slightly.

Clay, hands likewise raised, spoke up quickly. "Privates Serheighmon and Clay, lieutenant, with two displaced noncombatants. We're Ninety-Second Scout Company, assigned to Forward Outpost Number Eight."

The lieutenant emerged fully onto the roof and waggled his pistol to bring Clay closer.

Without dropping her hands, (the other soldiers had not relaxed their rifles), Clay approached the man with hurried steps and saluted, somewhat awkwardly.

"Report," he barked at her.

"Lieutenant, Forward Outpost Number Eight has been attacked and destroyed. The Zherians are coming across the border in force."

The officer's countenance paled. "What? You must be joking?"

"It's a fact, sir," Serheighmon seconded.

In short order, the four of them were whisked from the roof of the blockhouse, down through labyrinthine narrow corridors, out an armored rear exit, and practically thrown onto a coach that was then driven at a gallop to the town.

Most of the sturdy timber and plaster buildings of Bayou Dorking, a borough about half the size of Eriis, appeared abandoned; apparently, the civilian population had long since been evacuated. At the outskirts, the coach passed lines of earthworks under construction, fences of hastily strung barbed wire on steel posts, large bivouac areas, and several hundred Alarsarian infantry engaged in diverse mundane tasks, from filling sandbags to hanging out laundry. Aside from a few bored sentries, most of the soldiers lacked weapons. No alarm had yet been given.

At the center of the town, the coach halted before an impressive stone building with four corner towers and a verdigris-greened sloping copper roof. The corporal and guards of the coach exchanged quick words with a sergeant commanding a detail of sentries. With but a single bit-off curse, this underofficer immediately rushed Everett, Sarah, and the survivors of Outpost Number Eight into the building, up a broad set of marble stairs, and into a red oak paneled conference room filled with a dozen or so Royal Alarsarian officers. The various accoutrements of a headquarters were in evidence: large marked and annotated maps pinned to walls, tables covered with stacks of multi-colored forms, writing instruments of all sorts, and trays designated with cryptic abbreviations, and numerous clerical rankers taking notes, rearranging stacks of forms, or simply being unobtrusive.

"Sergeant Burke!" snapped an older man wearing a dress jacket hemmed in gold. By the demeanor of the others in the room, Everett immediately took him to be the senior officer. "I hope you have a good explanation for barging in like this!"

Ramrod straight and tense as a banjo string, Burke saluted. "Major Schoenboerg! These infantrymen have brought word that the Zherians have crossed the border and attacked an outpost!"

A pencil snapped loudly and then gasps and general expressions of shock passed around the room.

Just under average height with a wide frame and dark hair, the major advanced to confront Clay and Serheighmon. "Details, now!"

Clay, with occasionally clarifying interjections by Serheighmon, relayed the events of the destruction of their post in a succinct fashion.

Schoenboerg, reacting instantly, rounded on a captain. "Sound a general alarm!"

Activity exploded, with officers rushing from the room, dispatch riders being summoned, and a general hubbub of rapid-fire discussions and decisions.

While this continued unabated, the major, who had not moved, returned to his questioning. "Steam driven six-inch guns, you say? How many?"

"I counted more than thirty, sir," Clay replied.

"What infantry and cavalry?"

"None that we saw in the short time before the wizard transported us here, sir."

"Wizard? What wizard?" Schoenboerg demanded, swinging his head to take in Everett and Sarah.

Clay turned slightly to single out Everett with her eyes.

Schoenboerg swung the confront him. "Who are you?"

"Uhm, Everett de Schael."

"You are a wizard?"

"Probably."

"They're both magickers, sir," Serheighmon supplied. "He's a Master Wizard but she's not mentioned her rank."

This earned the infantryman Everett's immediate ire for the unwelcome revelation of Sarah's magical status.

The major measured Everett with his eyes and was apparently unimpressed. "What type of spells do you have, offensive or defensive?"

"Sorry, I don't understand what you mean." His answer was honest, but he was afraid that it might sound obstinate so he smiled slightly in order to hopefully convey the fact that he was harmless to these armed men.

Schoenboerg cocked his head slightly. "Your accent is not Alarsarian nor Republican. Where are you from? New Zindersberg?"

"No, ...sir. From Eriis along the Edze River."

"What are you doing here along the border?" The officer's suspicions were plain.

"I have engaged him to assist me in traveling to Kleinsvench," Sarah explained while Everett was trying to think of an answer that would not under any stretch of the imagination implicate him as a Republican spy. "I am a citizen of the demesne and have urgent business that requires me to return home from a trip abroad. We have been traveling overland but have encountered some difficulty. If you would be so kind as to aide us to continue our journey, I am sure that the Elector will be significantly grateful."

Schoenboerg altered his stance slightly, becoming less overbearing, but remained stern. "Kleinsvench is now a member of the Grand Alliance and as an allied citizen you will certainly be provided with all support due you under treaty. However, considering present conditions, you must realize that that support may be severely limited."

Sarah smiled winningly. "I understand completely, major."

A corporal dashed in at that moment and passed the officer a note. Schoenboerg read it hastily and then, clearly having more important matters that demanded his attention, pointed in dismissal to a set of ornate, padded armchairs shoved into a corner. "You two have a seat over there. I will decide your disposition shortly."

Sarah, to Everett's surprise, meekly complied. After throwing a quick eye toward the armed sentries that were suddenly very much in evidence, Everett decided not to attempt to argue and followed her. While the Alarsarians made ready for war and hardly before he sank completely into his comfortable chair, Sarah required of him an accounting of the events that had led to their leaving the air carriage.

"What is the last thing you remember?" he asked her.

"I had sat down to eat lunch with some of the others. I noticed an odd aftertaste in the tea. And then nothing. A potion had been added to the tea?"

"Yes. Edwin, Suzette, and Mitchell -- that I know of – are the culprits. They killed Aldo."

Sarah grimaced. "You clearly used your spell to rescue me, but how did you escape?"

"They had guns and chased me up to the Observation Deck. I climbed into the rigging and then jumped."

"*You jumped?* Did you already have the flight spell?"

"No."

"You expected to manifest a spell that would save you?"

"No."

"Then that was really stupid."

"Yes."

In the ensuing uncomfortable silence, Clay appeared

out of the hectic crowd of soldiers and handed them both a small slip of paper.

"What's this?" Everett asked, without bothering to read his.

The young woman smiled apologetically. "It's your emergency conscription notice. You've both been drafted into the Magicker Company."

"We're not citizens of Alarsaria!" Everett protested.

Clay shrugged. "I mentioned that to Major Schoenboerg. He said that if you did not serve the Crown then you must be Zherie spies. In which case he would have no choice but to have you shot."

"Tell the major," Sarah announced with a chilly smile, "that we will be proud to serve with the Royal Alarsarian Army."

Clay braced to attention and saluted Everett. Her manner was stern and from all appearances authentic. "Sir, as you're our highest ranking magicker, the major's brevetted you to lieutenant and given you command o' the Company. Serheighmon and I, since we're currently without assignment, are to be your liaisons with the regular forces."

Everett's mouth dropped open. "Don't be absurd."

"These were the major's orders, sir."

Sarah stood up quickly, resolute and decisive. "Everett should take command of the Company immediately."

As far as Everett could tell, there was not a single trace of sarcasm in her voice.

TWENTY

"Of course we can defend the town with four magickers and a half grown boy!" Sarah declared.

As far as Everett could tell, there was not a single trace of sincerity in her voice.

The entirety of the other members of the Magicker Company – all three of them -- stood in a single, casual rank in a small ground floor room. Outfitted in intricately carven black oak molding and carnelian tapestries depicting some ancient saga of lost love, the salon had a "lived in" look, with half-open books scattered about, tidily stacked but used dishes on a serving cart, and articles of clothing draped neatly over various furniture. Clay and Serheighmon, who had had his arm splinted by a corpsman, had complied without question, comment or delay with Sarah's demand.

All of the Company appeared to be also conscripted civilians, rather than the professional soldiers that Everett had, remembering Lieutenant Smythe and perhaps naively, presumed.

Everett cleared his throat, addressing the two women and adolescent boy in an encouraging tone to ameliorate the severity of Sarah's pronouncement.

"Well, maybe we should begin by introducing ourselves, giving our magician rank, and indicating which spells we possess that might prove useful for … in the defense. My name is Everett de Schael and I am a Master Wizard with two Potent spells that have proved useful in situations of conflict."

With an approving nod of professional respect, the woman on the left smiled. "Glad to meet you all. I'm Abigail Gallow. I'm a Common Magicker with four spells and I generally work in the agricultural industry. Don't think any of mine will help with the war, but here they are. I can calm horses for shoeing, settle the stomachs of livestock and infants, invigorate grain crops up to ten acres, and cure the winter sniffles."

Abigail had long left middle age behind, was plump in a comfortable but sturdy way and had the appearance of someone who had spent most of her life in practical work. Dressed in heavy trousers, shirt and short jacket, her mud stained boots suggested that she had come straight from the fields.

"Are we going to get to see any shooting?" burst out the boy standing between the two women. He was probably no more than fourteen, red haired to a fault, and full of unrestrained energy.

"Shush, Artie!" the second woman scolded. She smiled apologetically at Everett, Sarah, and the two infantry soldiers. "Not knowing any better, he thinks this whole thing is a lark."

"He'll learn better soon enough," Clay commented flatly.

The magicker frowned then looked worried, draping an arm protectively about Artie's shoulder. She was about ten years younger than Abigail and had a trim figure and dark hair tied back in a single braid.

"Show them your spell, Artie," she ordered, squeezing the lad's shoulder for emphasis. Her gesture was entirely proprietary and it was clear that she had assumed responsibility for the youth.

"Sure!" He stuck out his hands, palms upward and cupped in the shape of a bowl. *"To the blazes!"*

Everett felt a strong but shallow actuation.

Throwing off curling wisps of scorched air from teasing flame crests, a white-hot globe of fire about a span across formed above Artie's hands, floating unmoving as it rotated and twisted irregularly. The globe threw off a wave of white light that brightened the room remarkably. The contrast dimmed the room's oil lamps to insignificance.

Sarah perked up interestedly. "Can you throw that?"

"Huh? No, it's not real fire." The boy, withdrawing one hand slowly, poked and arm through the globe with no visible effect on either the globe or his arm. "It's not even hot. It's just kinda a light."

"Most of the effect is pure illusion," the second woman explained. Then, slightly defensively, "The light, however, can be quite useful. It is, by the way, inexhaustible."

"I see." Sarah tucked the corners of her mouth back in mute comment and gave Everett a sidelong glance that expressed concisely that she thought the situation now hopeless.

"Right, that's fine, Artie," Everett complimented, keeping his expression carefully neutral. "Must you cast another spell to disable it?"

"Oh, no, I just take my hands away!" The boy dropped his hands and the globe promptly vanished.

Everett raised his eyebrows. "That's rather unusual."

"We think that the spell is corporeally centric," Abigail provided. "Such spells are rare, but not unheard of."

"Right." Everett turned to the second woman. "And your name and spells, Madame?"

"I am *Mademoiselle* Silvia Borus."

Everett bobbed his head. "Your pardon, Mademoiselle."

"*Think nothing of it.* For myself, I have two spells. The first is a Vital Entity Location Variant and the second is a Ferrous Metal Manipulation Variant and both are Specifics."

"Could you elaborate?" Sarah prodded.

Silva gave a brief chagrinned smile, displaying transitory dimples in her cheeks. "I can find lost pets and fix broken iron skillets."

Before anyone could say anything else, an orderly entered, handed Clay a note, and exited immediately.

The female Alarsarian infantryman scanned the scrap of paper and then announced, "The Republican forces are in sight. We are ordered to move immediately to our forward position, which this says is an observation bunker adjacent to the All Seasons Inn, and provide all possible aid to the defensive forces."

"Do you know where the Inn is?" Sarah asked the woman.

"I do," Abigail supplied. "It's at the crest of Rolf's Hill on the north-eastern side of town."

"Right," Everett acknowledged. He considered the

situation. Both RAI soldiers had retained their rifles and side arms and he had the firm conviction that the fundamental definition of "liaison" in this instance was to insure the continued fidelity of Sarah and himself to the Kingdom's cause. While it seemed nonsensical to advance closer to the battle, there was little doubt that if the two of them were to extricate themselves from Alarsarian custody, it might be easier if it were somewhere other than their heavily guarded headquarters building.

"Let's head up to the roof. To save time, Sarah and I will transport us to the bunker."

The only accessible part of the roof was above one of the towers and they had to climb a tall, spindly ladder through a scuttle hole to reach it. Some of the rungs were cracked and the rails thinner than they should have been, making the climb a less than sanguine experience. Nevertheless, everyone managed to ascend in a manner consistent with their general demeanor: Clay and Serheighmon attacked the task with military efficiency and alacrity; Artie swarmed up like a squirrel that had a dog chasing it; Silvia mounted the rungs in a methodical and careful manner; Abigail approached it as simply another unavoidable task.

Sarah, however, surprised Everett by casually wrapping both arms about his neck and saying, "Magicians, remember? Just transport us up there."

He could not see the roof deck because of the angle through the scuttle hole, but reasoned that a spot in the air would serve for a locus just as well. Thinking ahead, he leaned down, caught Sarah under the knees, and picked her up. She gave a startled laugh as he cast, *"Beautiful Woman, come forth!"*

Appearing six feet above a small, level platform ringed with a low wall, he immediately cast again. *"Take ye flight!"*

With a sudden, dizzying view of the surrounding precipitously sloped roof of the headquarters, the lower adjacent buildings, and the streets far below, he then cast the spell in rapid succession, so that he and Sarah appeared to float slowly down until his boots touched on the deck of the tower. The three Alarsarian magickers, crowded together on the small space with the soldiers, spontaneously rewarded his performance with a brief spate of appreciative applause as he set Sarah on her own feet once more.

"I've never seen anyone that could fly!" Artie enthused, rushing up to Everett, who could not keep a triumphant grin from his face.

"It's a sort of controlled fall, really. Not what you would actually call flying." Thoroughly pleased and flattered, he focused on the adults. "Right, we'll have to make a couple of trips. Where's the inn?"

Abigail pointed over the parapet to the north. "You can see it there on the hill. The building with the red tile roof and large gables."

"Right. Got it."

"Lieutenant, it might be better if we were to send a scout ahead," Clay suggested as he examined the distant target.

"Do you think the fighting has already reached the inn?" he demanded tensely. It might be time for he and Sarah to escape. There was no way that he was going to transport into the middle of a battle.

"Just standard operating procedure, sir."

"Oh, uhm, sure. You could go first then. Since I can establish a locus on the inn from here, it's not necessary that I accompany the two of you. I can send you and her and then bring her back immediately."'

"Might want to wait about fifteen minutes before transporting her back, sir, so that I can send word with her that it's clear."

"Right. Whatever you think is best. Sarah, are you ready?"

"Good to go." She gestured Clay to her and locked her left arm with the Alarsarian's right.

"I can make out a big veranda with dining tables. I'll put you there. *Beautiful Woman, come forth!*"

Posted along the parapet and looking keenly, Serheighmon declared, "I see them. Looks like no problems. Clay gave a wave and they've gone into the inn."

Artie dashed to the soldier's side. "I can't see them. Where are they?"

"Get away from that edge young man!" Silvia scolded. Nipping his ear, she encouraged him back toward the perceived safety of the scuttle hole.

Chuckling, Abigail walked over to Everett. "That was impressive magic, there, Master Wizard. I take it that your wife is a magician too? She never said."

"Sarah is a Common Magicker, yes, but we aren't married."

Abigail shrugged. "Reggie and I never had the Royal Sanction on our household either, but that didn't stop us from having five sons and thirteen grandchildren."

Everett reddened. "No, I mean, well, Sarah and I are just traveling companions. We're not romantically involved."

"Really? You had me fooled then. From the way the two of you stand together, I'd have said that you were well on the way to starting your own family."

Clearing his throat to cover his embarrassment, he immediately changed the subject, "We'd better keep an eye out, in case they try to signal us."

TWENTY-ONE

Dug into a formerly manicured lawn adjacent to the elegant and shuttered inn, the observation bunker seemed secure enough. The Royal Engineers had utilized creosote planks half a foot thick to construct its sides and overhead and had packed the spoil a yard deep on top. A single sandbagged entrance without a door led down into a room twenty feet square floored with river gravel. A reinforced observation port looked out over a brush covered slope and the roofs of the houses at the bottom of it toward the north.

As the group, Serheighmon leading and Clay lagging to the rear, trooped down a steep ramp into a deeply shadowed interior, Artie cast his spell, brilliantly lighting the bunker to reveal only empty space.

"I'd put that out," Clay cautioned. This late in the afternoon, that light'll shine out like a beacon through the port and I don't think we want the Zheries to notice us here."

Artie gasped and abruptly dropped his hands.

As his eyes readjusted to the dimness, Everett walked to the observation port, an opening two feet by six framed in riveted steel plate, and stepped up onto the firing step to look out. The vantage of the hill gave him a view of two or three miles and he could see much of the Alarsarian entrenchments and fortifications. Beyond, the smoke and dust of the advancing Republicans was unmistakable. He turned about to face the others. All were watching him expectantly. He realized quickly that he had better distract the two soldiers before they began making helpful suggestions.

"Serheighmon, come up here and keep watch on the battle. Relay information to us as needed."

"Yes, Sir." The man took his post, unslinging his rifle and leaning it against the wall within easy reach, then focused toward the coming battle.

Everett walked back to the tense group. "Clay, take position in the entrance ditch. I don't want anyone sneaking up on us here."

"Yes, sir." She hustled out and went prone at the top of the ramp, rifle cradled and ready.

"What do you want the rest of us to do, Lieutenant?" Abigail asked. The sincerity and intensity of her question gave him pause.

"I'm not really a lieutenant. Just call me Everett."

Abigail grinned. "And I'm not really a soldier, but we have to do what we can. Do you have a plan?"

A quip slipped out before Everett could restrain it. "Retreat?"

The rustic Common Magicker gave him a hard look. "I can't say that I'm enthused with this war, Everett, but I was ten when the Republic tried to seize the wheat fields in the province of West Nyllean and I saw the burning farms and the dead. I'd not like to see that again. My magic may not do much to stop the Zheries this time, but I intend to do what I can."

This was not an affected declaration of patriotic fervor but a simple explanation of practicality and as such it struck him as all the more unsettling.

"Right."

"You volunteered for the Magicker Company?" Sarah, her expression one of simple curiosity, asked the woman.

Abigail nodded proudly. "That's right."

"Both of us volunteered," Silvia inserted. "During the civilian evacuation, there were all kinds of requests for volunteers. When I saw the placard announcing the Provisional Magicker Company, I signed up right away."

"I volunteered too!" Artie contributed.

Putting an arm around the boy's shoulder, Silvia smiled sadly at Everett and Sarah. "Artie was found wandering about town by a patrol after everyone had gone and was turned over to us because he is a magicker. He is an orphan."

"I think the Zheries are about to loose a barrage," Serheighmon, warned. "The steam mechanisms have all lined up and stopped."

Artie twisted from Silvia's grasp, ran to the firing step,

and began hopping when he proved still too short for a clear view.

"Artie, get down from there!" Silvia admonished, taking his arm and pulling him, complaining, away from the opening.

"Everett, you probably should call Clay back inside," Sarah advised. "She's totally unprotected out there."

"Oh! Right." Everett immediately strode to the exit and ordered the Alarsarian infantryman back into the presumed safety of the bunker.

"Should I take guard here at the entrance, sir?" Clay asked.

"That's fine."

"Might I suggest, sir, that--"

"Everybody take cover!" Serheighmon yelled, diving for the floor. The distant rippling booms of the big guns followed his words.

Instantly, Everett crouched down with Clay, Abigail, and Sarah against the heavy timbers that lined the rear wall, while Silvia huddled with Artie along the right wall.

The explosions of the shells followed quickly but did not sound close. The ground vibrated mildly with each detonation.

When the blasts trailed off, Serheighmon crawled over to the forward wall and stood up for a quick look. "They targeted the beebeefields and wire. Now they've started moving again, heading for the breach they opened. They're coming on pretty fast. I bet those things are doing thirty miles an hour or better!"

Sarah swung around to question the other infantryman. "Why isn't our artillery responding?"

"The brigade has got only one battery o' six two-inch field guns. Nearly all of our big artillery is emplaced along the fortified lines out west of here. I was told that the major has positioned our two-inchers at key positions in the town. He's thinking that at point blank range that they might be able take out the road wheels on the Zheries' mechanisms. If that works, then the disabled mechanisms will block the advance of those following."

Sarah eyed Clay frankly. "Do you believe that we have

any chance of holding out against the Republican attack?"

The woman rolled her shoulders in a half shrug. "I'm guessing that they've got heavy armor on the mechanisms that will leave them unharmed by rifle and pistol shot. If that's true, then they might plan to roll right through the infantry positions and bypass the blockhouses. Our defenses're designed to repel an infantry and cavalry assault, not something like this. If they can punch through to the town, they can easily cut off the forward units, disrupt our communications, and break our chain of command. After that, it would simply be a matter o' mopping up."

Everett listened and did not comment.

More artillery shots echoed in the distance.

"They're firing point blank into the block houses and blowing them apart!" Serheighmon exclaimed.

This time, the explosions were louder, the shaking stronger. Dust filtered down from the overhead.

Abigail locked eyes with Everett. "If we're going to try magic, it might better be soon."

Sarah took hold of his arm. "We need to get out there and stop the Zherians."

For a moment, Everett mentally recoiled from the suggestion that they rush to the battle, but then realized that this must simply be a ploy to get them away from the two armed Alarsarians.

He nodded. "Right. Let's go, then."

"I'm ready." Abigail declared.

Sarah smiled, but shook her head. "Stay here. You'll need to take charge of the Company while we are away."

Abigail grinned sadly, as if she did not expect to see Sarah and Everett again. "I'll take care of them."

Clay stood and cinched the strap that held her rifle to her shoulder. "I'll come with you."

Sarah frowned. "Everett and I might be able to protect ourselves, but you would only be a target."

The soldier settled back, not completely concealing her relief. "All right."

Catching Everett's eye, Sarah hurried out and he immediately rose and followed. Once through the door, she bounded up the ramped slit trench and then trotted up the sloping mound of the bunker to its apex. The view of the outskirts of Bayou Dorking and the battle lines beyond opened up before them.

"What's your plan?" he whispered to her.

Sarah looked at him in askance. "What do you mean? I don't have one yet."

"So we just transport out?"

"What, into the midst of the battle? Of course not. We need to--"

"Hold on. Are you *actually* thinking of using our magic to attack the Zherians?"

"That's what I said, wasn't it?"

"The two of us against an army?"

"Magic is on our side, Everett."

"How do you know that?"

Sarah rolled her eyes. "Sorry, it's just an expression."

"Wait, so...but when...oh, never mind."

"We can't just run, Everett."

"Why not?"

"The Zherians are my enemy, whether I want them to be or not. All of my family are in danger because of their aggression and the best thing for Kleinsvench is for this invasion to be stopped here."

Everett shook his head tiredly at her patently selfish but impeccable logic and looked out toward the advancing Zherian mechanisms, which showed no sign of slowing as they raced through the Alarsarian defenses. He saw tiny flashes from the entrenched Royal Infantry and heard the distant rattle of their rifles, but apparently, as Clay had speculated, the large mobile artillery had armor plating that shrugged off small arms fire.

His and Sarah's situation, if anything, could only get worse. With her determined to stay, he could not and would not leave. That meant that the two of them would almost surely perish like the Alarsarians beneath the crushing wheels of the attacking mechanisms.

He considered himself a rational man. He had no fundamental opposition to action; in certain circumstances it was the only rational choice. But in this particular instance, it seemed to him that the steadfastly rational decision was to abandon the hopeless plight of Bayou Dorking and its doomed defenders. No matter how powerful his magic, the onslaught of the Republic of Zheria was without question unstoppable.

But what of the thus far unnamed patron who had altered nature itself to provide him with spells in time of need? Could it be possible that he would manifest a spell that would overthrow the entire Zherian invasion?

Was Magic really on his side?

He looked back at Sarah, searched her face, and gazed into her beautiful eyes. She looked back with a patient and unwavering confidence. Did she somehow know that this magical patron would intervene once again?

It was clear that he needed to know, one way or the other.

He made a decision, which, rational or not, seemed unavoidable.

"Stay here," he told her.

Before Sarah could respond, he ran toward the front of the bunker and cast, *"Give me strength!"*

His next step hurled him forward in a great bound, the force shaking the bunker roof. *"Take ye flight!"*

He experienced a moment of authentic flight this time, propelled by his magically enhanced leap, and soared at great speed over the battle. He could now see clearly the wedge that the Zherian mechanisms formed as they lanced toward the town. Behind them came irregular skirmish lines of troops bearing the green and orange diagonal striped flag of the Republic.

He cast his flight spell again as he began to descend, using it to time his return to earth so that he landed just behind one of the clanking mechanisms.

Up close, the Zherians' steam-mobile artillery was much more impressive. His estimation that they were the size of Bob's road grader was off by a factor of at least two, and the weight of such a mass of metal pressed deep ruts in the ground behind it. Mounted on eight twelve-foot cleated steel wheels, it towered over him, a fright-inducing monolith that chugged dark smoke from stubs of smokestacks at its center. The construction's armored sides sloped up to an arched roof and were crisscrossed by large rivet heads and occasional round-cornered hatches. Several rotating blisters extended out from the sides, each bearing a small gun barrel and slotted view port. One mounted on the blunt rear of the mechanism swiveled to track on Everett in obvious menace.

When the gun continued to point at him impotently, he relaxed slightly. The unspoken spell that had warded him from the guns of Mitchell and Suzette apparently continued to function.

"Give me strength!"

As he cast, he ran toward the mechanism and took a hold beneath a girder on its trailing end just under the gun port. When he made to raise it, the incredible weight pressed his feet down into the soil, making him stumble and lose his grip. He needed a firmer base to lift such weight! With an inarticulate growl, he ran to catch up, seized the edge again.

"Take ye flight! Give me strength!"

This time, as he hovered a fraction above the broken ground and the power of magic flowed in him, he was able to raise the multi-ton vehicle, the girder groaning and crumpling at the strain. Its wheels continuing to spin, he hurried to hurl it over, so that it flipped, end over end, smashing with a terrible rending of metal through the wreckage of bunkers and trenches and came to rest on its side. Steam hissed through rents in its armored skin and then blasted violently outward as a muffled explosion, the boilers giving way, split it wide open. Other explosions followed, as the large gun shells and other ammunition began to detonate, and the mechanism became involved in a massive expanding globe of fire and smoke.

A six-inch shell struck alongside Everett, showering him with clods of dirt as it plowed through the churned earth. His heart froze, but the shell simply buried itself without going off.

He whipped his head about. A hundred yards away, another mechanism had changed course to charge across the advance directly toward him, its forward gun depressed so that he looked straight up its barrel. Clearly, the unidentified magic that protected him from gunfire had also protected him from the explosive artillery shell, but equally clearly there must be a limited range to the spell! He dodged to the side, his magical strength carrying him more than two hundred feet, as the big gun fired again and the shriek of the hurtling shell sounded. It might not explode, but if the round struck him, he would be just as dead.

He landed in the midst of a group of helmeted Zherian infantry in red-brown and suddenly found himself the target of more than a dozen rifles. Triggers clicked uselessly all around and confusion seized the faces of the soldiers. Several immediately ejected cartridges, reloaded, threw rifle butts to shoulders and took aim again.

Everett recast his strength and jumped straight up, casting flight at the top of his leap so that he hovered hundreds of feet up in the air with the battlefield, now washed with the red hues of the setting sun, once more spread out beneath him. His destruction of one of the mechanisms had done little to stall the attack; the remainder continued, firing constantly as they bridged the Alarsarian earthworks. He was instantly convinced that he would be able to do little to disrupt the attack with the spells available to him. There were simply too many of the steam-mobile artillery; sooner or later one would get lucky and either run over him or hit him with a shell. He could not stop the Zherians and must return and compel Sarah to escape with him, even if he had to use his magic to carry her away bodily.

And then he experienced the most intense magical Epiphany of his entire life.

The spell was magnificent and strange, an incomprehensible and difficult collection of word sounds and tone syllables that suggested no familiar language. Frightened by this bizarre manifestation and not knowing what effect the spell might accomplish, he tried to repress the First Enunciation, but the words had a dark, almost malevolent energy of their own and would not be denied. They screamed from his lips with jolts of sparkling energy and their magic actuated in a vast shock that almost seemed to fracture the sky.

Light flared, casting sharp shadows across the darkening ground and then the whole of the battlefield disappeared in an enormous outpouring of light and ash that rushed upward to envelope him. Blinded, scalded and suffocated, he felt his consciousness fade as the entire world went black.

TWENTY-TWO

Everett woke with dirt covering his face.

Frantic, he thrashed about until he could suck an unobstructed breath and then pried his eyes open against a crust of caked ash. He saw a morning sky gray with dust and smoke, the rising sun totally obscured. Craning his head, he peered about to discover that he lay on his back, partially buried in loose soil and debris. He struggled free of the confining earth, slowed by aches and pains in every part of his body, and stood up. He was filthy with dirt and soot, scratched and bruised. His clothes were likewise tattered and scorched with one of his boots missing, but he appeared to have suffered no grievous wounds.

In front and below him stretched a great gaping hole in the ground, a crater at least five hundred feet across and greater than seventy-five deep. Beyond it lay the still smoldering wreckage of several Zherian mechanisms, many partially covered by ejecta, and a landscape burned and blasted by flame and wind. Though he immediately saw nothing that he could readily identify as a body, nothing living moved within his sight.

Whatever the newest spell had been, it had caused a great and devastating explosion larger than anything any human had previously created, either with magic or with technology.

Realizing that he had lain senseless through the night and into the next morning, he looked back along the line of the Republican advance to see what his magic had gained. The scope of the destruction extended, with diminishing effect, for a distance of perhaps a mile, but beyond that he could still see many of the steam-mobile artillery mechanisms and accompanying infantry. Fortunately, they were not moving toward him directly across the violated ground, but were cutting across the flanks of the area. Even if his spell had given them pause during the night, their advance had resumed with the new day and the Republicans looked to have lost none of their determination to capture Bayou Dorking.

Swinging around, he found that the town appeared mostly unfazed, though some of the leading buildings looked to have suffered wind damage. One or two had been set ablaze, and tall pillars of black smoke still rose from them, spreading a grimy haze across the area. Near the town edge, about half a mile from the crater, many of the bunkers and blockhouses still stood in what seemed good shape and the trench lines, though mangled, were visible. The majority of the defenders had been concentrated in this area, so hopefully most had escaped the brunt of the spell.

Having had more than enough of magic, he eschewed his spells and started slogging across the uneven, blackened terrain. Favoring his bare foot as he skirted heaps of earth and mangled metal and surmounted low ridges sculpted by the blast, he had gone only a hundred yards toward the town when his sluggish thoughts cleared enough for him to realize that he should summon Sarah.

"Beautiful Woman, come forth!"

He felt the actuation, knew the enunciation was correct, but Sarah did not appear.

"Beautiful Woman, come forth!"

Again the same.

He almost screamed the spell another desperate time. *"Beautiful Woman, come forth!"*

On his locus, a charred patch of dust only inches in front of him, nothing stirred.

Overcome by such dread as he had never before experienced, he fell to his knees, moaning.

Vital Transportation Variants only worked on living things. The spells would transport non-living items, but only with a breathing target. The only reason that the spell would not transport Sarah was if she were dead.

She had not appeared.

So she must be.

Dead.

When his father, the anchor of his life, had died, he had felt a great, staggering blow. This was infinitely worse.

He had loved Sarah.

Another might have argued that it was simple infatuation, but he knew it was not.

He would never have told her, would hardly have admitted it to himself before this, but he *had* loved her, perhaps from the very first moment. Hopelessly. Foolishly. Dementedly.

Certainly, his feeling was a gross violation of all common sense. He knew that she would never reflect his sentiment, that he was to her simply a means of returning to Kleinsvench, and that she would pass from his existence and forget him as soon as she found her way home,

Throughout his life, he had suffered the burden of the expectation that he would, one day, achieve greatness in magic. His family had hoped for it, his chums in primary school had teasingly suggested it, and his instructors in the study of magic, at least at first, had practically demanded it. *He was a prodigy, one of the rare ones that had manifested early, undoubtedly destined to enter the ranks of wizardry!* As each of his spells manifested and proved unsatisfactory, the repeated refrain had been, *"Don't worry. The next one will be a good one!"*

Driven by the crucifying knowledge that a magician could do nothing to improve his magic, he had thrown every ounce of his energy into improving his *study* of magic. He had memorized dissertations, sought rare monographs, and bored ever deeper into a single-minded pursuit of the collected wisdom of the great magicians who had come before. Rather than indulging in recreation and ease as had all the other students at *Friar Albert's Advanced Academy*, he had spent his free time buried in the sepulchral library surrounded by a shielding wall of books. On graduation, he had hardly known the first names of three of his fifty-seven classmates. He had told himself that he would have time for friends, family, and marriage after he found his key to success.

That discovery had never come. As he had grown older, the self-imposed isolation of the first half of his life had simply become a habit.

Sarah had been an aggravating, irritating, but

entrancing addition to his monkish existence. Only a man with no heart at all could have failed to have fallen in love with her.

And now she was forever taken from him.

With a dead voice, he tried one last time. *"Beautiful Woman, come forth!"*

After a moment or two, he stood and walked woodenly toward Bayou Dorking, leaving the dark spots of silent tears in the dust along his path.

The defenses of the Alarsarians were vacant and he went unchallenged as he negotiated wire, traversed trenches, and circled bunkers. There were no bodies either, just smoldering trash, shinny brass shell casings, and large chunks of metal and stone hurled from the site of the explosion. The Alarsarians, it seemed clear, had been able to retreat, taking their wounded and dead with them. He wandered across a road paved with tan brick and followed it.

Up close, he found the damage to the town to be more severe. Almost every house and shop on the leading edge of Bayou Dorking had sustained heavy blast damage. Roofs had been ripped away, windows disintegrated, and walls collapsed. Shattered bricks and splintered lumber were scattered everywhere and drifts of debris often blocked the road. After a block or so, however, the destruction lessened, so that he began to pass buildings that were in the main untouched, though empty and quiet. He considered returning to the bunker at the inn, decided he had no wish to discover Sarah's body, and listlessly continued walking.

"Everett!"

The sound of his name brought him up short in front of a butcher's shop with a fanciful façade of a hunting scene made out in multi-colored tile.

"Lieutenant!" Clay hissed at him from the open doorway. "Get over here!"

He stared at her dully. Presenting a generally grubby appearance, as if she had spent a lot of time crawling across the ground, she still had her slouch cap, though it looked like it had a bullet hole in it, and the cartridge belt around her waist was mainly empty.

Cursing, she ran out, rifle in one hand, and grabbed his

arm. "Come on! Get out o' sight! There're Republican skirmishers on some of the buildings! They've taken a shot or two at me!"

Without caring, he let Clay drag him into the shelter of the shop, whose bare dusty shelves and empty counter gave evidence of the length of time since its owner had been evacuated.

Clay made him crouch behind the counter, then grinned and slapped him on the back. "I thought you were dead."

"I might as well be. Sarah's dead."

The soldier took a long breath and let it out slowly. "She might be. I'm not sure."

"What do you mean?"

"The brigade started moving out just after midnight, but we hung on, mainly to see if you would show up. About dawn, the Zheries infiltrated something like a company o' skirmishers along the eastern flank of the town and they came across our bunker. I suppose they were just intended to create mischief in our rear. We got lucky and caught sight o' them as they came up the hill and pulled back to the inn right away. When it looked like they were going to surround us, we tried to make a break deeper into the town, but some of them cut us off in the middle o' the street. Serheighmon and I got off a few shots, but then Sarah cast a spell and a whole bunch of Zheries fell over."

"She just put them to sleep. That's one of her spells."

"Yeah, but the rest went to ground and started shooting. She just stood there in the open and started laughing like she was crazy. Then she started setting things on fire -- buildings, rifles, equipment, uniforms -- and they started running away. Serheighmon and I got the others into a house, but she hung back, saying she would cover us."

"Was she hit?"

"Not right away. I made Serheighmon take the magickers out through the back o' the house while I went upstairs to give her cover fire. She seemed to be about to run inside when a Zherie in a red tunic ran up on her blind side and threw something at her. I took a few shots at him, but he got under cover too fast."

"A bomb?"

"No, just a mechanism, I think, but somehow her magic stopped working. I saw her casting, but nothing happed. Then a rifle bullet got her and she went down. I'm sorry, sir."

"She was killed?"

"I don't know. They started unloading on my position and I had to bail out o' the house. After a while, I managed to get up on a roof a few blocks away and get my eyes back on her. The last I saw they were carrying her off on a stretcher, which makes me think she was only wounded. Then a wad o' regular Zherie infantry came up and I had to get out o' there. Right now, I think we're well behind their advance. I've been hanging around since, trying to gather intel. I was getting ready to pull out when I saw you."

"You haven't seen Sarah again?"

"No, sir."

Everett stood up. "I have to go find her."

Clay grabbed his arm again and tried to pull him back down into hiding. "Don't be stupid! That mechanism? It had to be something that neutralizes magic. No matter how great a wizard you are, you're powerless without your magic."

Knowing that what she said was true, he suppressed a lightning burst of irrational anger, and sank back to a crouch. "Tell me about that. Are you sure it was technological?"

"I don't think it was magic, if that's what you mean. It was metal, about the size o' a goose egg or maybe just a little bit larger. There were a few stiff copper wires hanging out, but as far as I could tell it didn't do anything."

"Did it make any noise of any kind? Mechanisms always make some type of sound."

"Not that I could hear from where I was."

He was unaware of the existence of any technology that could affect magic in any way, but now believed without a doubt that the natural order of things was out of kilter. If he could manifest spells in gross violation of the known rules of magic, then it was entirely likely that the Zherians could have manifested a schematic that allowed them to suppress magic. Granted that that was so, then that explained why he could not transport her and, he realized with a comforting wave of relief, she might still be alive.

Needing more information, he focused a hard expression on Clay. "But they had to get it close to her?"

"Yeah, I'd say within five feet or so."

"Then I just have to make sure that none of the Zherians get that close to me."

"You're not going to do another one o' those doomsday explosions, are you? I know most o' our guys have retreated out o' the town, but personally I don't want to be close to that and we've probably still got other stragglers like me around about. That *was* your spell, wasn't it, sir?"

"Yes, it was mine and no, I'm not going to do it again. At least, not unless I need it."

"Everett, I think the best thing would be for you to come back with me to our lines. If you try to find Sarah, you're bound to be captured or killed. If she's still alive, she'll be a prisoner and when the fighting slows down there'll be prisoner exchanges like we've always had."

Everett shook his head with unshakable certainty. "No, I don't think so. This war is different. No one has used mechanisms like the Zherian steam-mobile artillery before and even my 'doomsday' spell, as you call it, could only delay them. I think the Republic is going to crush Alarsaria totally. I'll have to find Sarah and free her somehow."

The expression on her face gave proof enough that Clay could not deny his prediction. "All right, sir. Do you want me to come with you?"

"No, it is best if I go alone."

Clay made no attempt to argue his point. "I can't stay here and I need to get what little I know back to our lines. There's a narrow alley out back. I'm going to try to make use of it to rejoin the brigade." She stuck out a hand. "Good luck, Lieutenant."

"Right. Good luck to you as well, Clay – wait, what's your first name?"

The soldier gave a half smile. "It's Pricilla, but no one's called me that since I was little."

"Good luck, Pricilla."

"So long Everett." She slung her rifle. "If we meet again, you'll have to tell me the whole story." It seemed clear that she did not expect this to occur.

"I will," he promised as she vanished into a hall at the rear of the shop.

He gave her half an hour lead, then walked back into the street, taking the chance that any Zherian sniper that might happen to detect him would not be beyond the range of his protective spell. He was still a wizard and Magic was on his side and he was determined that he would find Sarah if he had to break every Zherian in half to do it. Confidently, he began to march along the street back toward the northern part of town. If any hidden enemy indeed fired futilely at him, he saw no sign of it.

As he walked, he continually expected to be confronted by Zherians and so continually cast his magical strength. He did not know exactly what he would do, but he must be prepared. He was almost back to the damaged section of town when a squad exited a building and took firing positions blocking the way. All wore double-breasted bright red jackets instead of the more common red-brown uniform that he had seen on other Zherian infantry. One that Everett took to be an underofficer of some sort remained standing to one side. On one of the stiff collars of his jacket were black embroidered letters: E.S.A.T.

"Halt!" the man warned loudly in a melodious baritone. "Surrender immediately or be fired upon!"

Everett kept walking toward them.

The underofficer grinned savagely. "Fire!"

Triggers clicked without effect.

The underofficer gave a shocked squeak, then barked, "Reload! Fire at will!"

By this time, Everett had closed with the underofficer, and, as the red-coated soldiers hastened to open breeches and reload, he swung a roundhouse that clipped the Zherian's jaw while he drew his pistol. The underofficer dropped, stunned, and sprawled on the street.

Everett bent over the dazed Zherian and said viciously, "Lucky for you my strength spell had just expired or your head would have burst like a smashed melon."

The underofficer scrambled away from Everett, shouting to his men, "He's a *magicker!*"

One of them leapt to his feet, snatched something from

his belt, and hurled it at Everett. The thing flew toward him, metal shinny and spinning, with copper wires flashing in the sunlight at one end.

TWENTY-THREE

The Epiphany, the First Enunciation, actuation, and the evincing came in a single eye blink. *"Stay your passage, O Time!"*

The entire world froze in place: the underofficer in mid-scramble, his men in mid-reload, a blown scrap of paper in mid-scuttle across the cobblestones, the thrown object in mid-flight. There was also no background sound and an odd weakness and reddening to the sunlight.

Everett could still move and he did so, hurrying from the path of what could only be one of the magic canceling mechanisms that Clay had described. As his mind raced to comprehend the consequences of this new spell, he took a position beside the thrower and prepared to cold-cock the man.

Then someone tapped him on the shoulder, nearly making him jump out of his boot. He spun about to confront a short, rather dumpy, older woman wearing a frumpy housedress embossed with paisley daffodils.

"I *am* sorry, Everett," this new apparition apologized. "I just had to intervene. You were about to make a terrible blunder. Confronting the Esatis now will only needlessly delay you. Frankly, hero wise, you leave something to be desired."

"I've never claimed to be a hero and *who in Magic's name are you?"*

"Exactly."

Awareness dawned. *"You're Magic?"*

"Who else?"

"Well, I don't know –"

"Rhetorical question, Everett."

"Ah, uhm, right. You know, the way you talk is very familiar."

"No doubt. To save some time, here is the deal straight up: Sarah is my great-granddaughter. I have been helping you with spells so that you could help her. Now I need you to rescue her from Technology and not waste a lot of time bothering with this lot."

Not quite keeping up, he took a moment to review. "Right, I had already figured out some of that. Not the great-granddaughter part though. How exactly is that possible? Aren't you some kind of mystical spirit?"

The woman sighed. "Fine, I guess we have to do this the hard way. To answer your second question, it would be more accurate to describe me as a noncorporeal sentient entity."

Everett looked her up and down once more. To all appearances, she seemed entirely and mundanely human, from her worn, fur-lined house shoes to her thinning gray hair tied back in a practical bun.

"Aren't you 'corporeal' now?"

"No, this is just a convenient, non-contemporaneous light spectrum projection made possible by the disruption of physical time. A mirage might be the easiest term for you to understand. I do not actually exist presently in the corporeal realm."

"And the great-granddaughter part?" he prompted.

Magic sighed again in a put-upon way. "Eighty years ago I had the idea to embody myself as a corporeal biologic in order to obtain a greater understanding of the nature of residence in the physical realm. To facilitate that, I exceeded operational parameters and manifested a specific spell to a young, not un-handsome magicker. In the process of that, I engaged in the normal biologic prerogatives and produced a son, who, in the natural scheme of things, also later reproduced. And so on and so forth. I currently have some forty odd direct descendents here in the physical realm."

Everett shook his head. "You'll have to give me that first part again."

Magic gave him a highly displeased look. "You know, Everett, I would not have selected you if I had had any other choice."

"This does not surprise me."

"Well, in any event, I will try to simplify it for you. I gave a young man a spell to create a young woman out of thin air and placed a segment of my identity into that young woman. I take it that you can understand why a young man would be inclined to use magic to summon a young woman and that the natural consequence of that inclination is a baby?"

"Oh! Right. What did you mean, 'operational parameters'?"

"The residents – and I use this term loosely -- of the noncorporeal realm function according to an immeasurable magnitude of omnipresent operational parameters, or, I suppose you could say, boundaries of accepted behavior."

"So you broke the rules?"

"No, I cheated."

"And my new spells were also cheats?"

"Obviously."

"Right. So, did the other, ah, *residents* complain about your cheating?"

"No."

"So what's the problem?"

"At this rate, we will be here all day. Sure you don't want to just cut ahead to the part where I tell you what I want you to do?"

"No. I think I need to first understand this whole situation as well as I'm able."

This produced another drawn-out sigh from Magic. "Okay, from here on out just assume that I have simplified my explanations into human terms."

"Right."

"As I had created an exception," she continued, "Technology was now free to intervene directly in the physical realm."

"Technology could also cheat?"

"Yes."

"And that's the source of all these new mechanisms?"

"Yes. In this universe, Technology and I have a relationship that in many ways resembles a competition. In the vast majority of universes --"

"There's more than one universe?"

180

"Try to keep up, would you Everett? As I was saying, in most universes, only one of us holds sway, but here our influences co-exist. There is a lot more to it that you cannot possibly comprehend, but suffice it to say that in the normal scheme of things this competition would have concluded at some point in future. The result of that conclusion would be that one of us would be deemphasized and the other would become dominant. Still with me?"

"One of you would win?"

"Yes. Now, here is the key point. Technology is determined to accelerate the process. Since he can now also cheat, he has come in on the side of the Zherians, who have always favored schematics over spells."

"Come in? You mean he's become a human like you did?"

"Yes. Please stop interrupting. Technology intends to aide the Republic of Zheria to victory over the Alarsarians, who have always had a tendency to favor magical solutions, and then use that as a springboard to conquer the rest of the world. Once in total control, he will entirely eradicate magic users. This will leave Technology as the predominant aspect of nature and spells will no longer function."

"Sorry, I don't think I understand."

"Humph! Well, let me think a minute." She rubbed her chin for a second or two and then snapped her fingers. "I've got it!" Her eyes unfocused.

A spell manifested to Everett. He enunciated it. *"Behold the future!"*

Everett blinked once and opened his eyes in a different place.

Crouching below the stub of the parapet wall as the mortar shells continued to fall sporadically on the fortress, he struggled to bandage the gaping hole in Clay's chest. She had taken a shrapnel hit from the last bombing run. As her blood pooled obscenely beneath her, her face became pasty white.

"Leave me...," she gasped and then, with a choking rattle, she simply died.

Everett threw his eyes skyward as he again heard the drone of the air carriages. Another wave was coming in.

"Take cover!" he screamed at the few remaining defenders as

the bombs, with their bone chilling warning screech, began to fall.

Flame, hurtling earth, and rock mushroomed in sequential lines across the cratered courtyard and the already smashed central keep, ripping open the hastily dug trenches and medical shelters and hurling bodies and bits of bodies all about. A blast from one of the bombs brought down the old stone tower alongside the main gate, leaving a break in the curtain wall. Zherian infantry swarmed over the rubble and began firing at the wounded and dying Alarsarians. A red-coated Esati squad followed and quickly set up the tripod of one of their multi-firing guns. Immediately training the devastating mechanism on the wall platform, they began pumping bullets at over two hundred rounds per minute into the remaining Royal Infantry.

Everett felt bullets rip through his chest and then knew nothing.

He blinked again and found himself once more facing Magic, who watched him with a keen stare.

"That was the future?" he asked her.

"One short, relevant and significant segment of a potential future extrapolated from current circumstances. The extrapolation assumes that there will be no significant changes in existing behavioral trend lines. There are several more visions available to you at this time."

Everett felt an urge similar to the immediacy of a First Enunciation, save that this urge could be resisted, though not denied. Relenting, he cast again. *"Behold the future!"*

This time he was not himself, but an old man by the name of Hargrove, standing along the Grand Avenue of Eyrchelle with thousands of other cowed Alarsarians as long files of the hated, fanatical Esatis marched in triumph toward the Royal Palace.

A traitorous sky shown above blue and clear as the syncopated tramp of the invaders boots signaled the final humiliation of defeated Alarsaria.

Everett felt hot tears roll down Hargrove's cheeks. His home and neighborhood had been bombed into nonexistence from the air. Zherian mechanisms had crushed his fields and scattered his livestock. And his seven sons and daughters had died in defense of the hopeless cause of the Kingdom.

Hargrove pulled the old style single shot pistol from his tattered coat and fired at the marching Zherians. He laughed gleefully when one of them pitched over, blood erupting from a chest wound. The old man reloaded and fired again just before a dozen shots from the repeating rifles of the Esatis struck him down.

As he sprawled in the gutter, his life leaking away, he heard the Esatis begin shooting into the crowd. A young girl fell within Hargrove's view, her eyes lifeless.

Everett shuddered as the horrifying future faded, but did not resist as the urgency of another impending vision took hold and he cast once more.

Again he inhabited the body of another, a powerless witness, as the woman's hands raised a rifle at the shouted command of an Esati underofficer.

The next command came quickly. "Fire!"

Cyn O'Blen could not restrain a smile as her index finger stroked the trigger. The big rifle bucked against her shoulder and the bullet threw the filthy magicker in the center of her sights, a young man no older than twenty, backward into the wall. Her expert shot had pierced the scum directly through the heart. Some of the other members of the firing squad had not been so keen in their aim and Sergeant Perkins had to draw his sidearm to finish off three, an older man, a woman, and a girl, with shots to the head.

As Cyn gazed contemptuously at the bodies, Everett realized with a jolt that he recognized three of the executed magicians: Abigail, Artie, and Silvia.

"Come on, people!" Perkins sneered. "We've got to empty this ghetto today. Make your shots count. These magickers aren't worth two bullets! O'Blen, you and Shulm hit this next house."

Everett gasped as his stomach heaved. He managed to restrain the reflex, but still tasted the acid burn of bile in his mouth.

"Now do you understand?" Magic demanded.

"Not completely. Who are the Esatis?"

"Members of the Enlightened Society for the Advancement of Technology. The group has been around for a century and was founded as a social organization with the stated goal of fostering technological development. Along about the time that Technology embodied, they began to become radicalized and more political so that today ESAT is one of the strongest political factions in the Republic. As you have seen, they have created special military units that operate alongside the regular Republican Army." She gestured at the redcoats.

"And they hate and despise magickers?"

"Hate is a powerful tool, Everett. It is much easier to get humans to hate than to love."

Everett felt another urge to enunciate the spell. *"Behold the future!"*

This time Everett saw through the eyes of a young girl of eight named Caroline. She had run down to the fisherman's pier with all the other children and most of the adult occupants of the village to see the sleek warship that had anchored just beyond the breakwater. Eilbrek, her home, was the northernmost settlement on the Kyalt Peninsula and thus the most remote outpost on all the continent of Gheyr. A great stir of excitement passed among the crowd as a launch departed the low-slung cutter and sped without sail or oar toward the pier. A dozen red-coated marines bearing long rifles tipped with bayonets alighted on the pier, barged contemptuously through the crowd, and marched to the factorage where the standard of Lord Kelvan fluttered spryly in the inshore breeze.

Without ceremony, the marines snatched down the blue flag and raised a red one in its place. Caroline had begun to learn her letters, so she sounded out the black symbols on the new one.

"E-S-A-T"

Blinking back to the present, Everett interrupted Magic as she opened her mouth to speak. "Wait. There's one more." He cast.

Bargman Herk struggled through the knee deep drifts of ash and toxins, swinging his head in a slow oscillation to search for any recoverable, though he was certain that this area had long since been picked clean. The faceplate of his environment suit was scratched almost to the point that he could not see out into the dreary, nearly featureless rust-colored landscape. He had put in a requisition for a new one two hundred wake periods ago, but had not yet been granted a replacement. The rare spares went to scavengers with better production than him.

Bargman trudged on. He would have to go many miles to find unscavenged ground. There was a rumor of a newly found surface ruin beyond his normal twenty-five mile range. He was not sure that he had the strength for such a hike, but he had no choice. If he did not discover sufficient metals or plastics on this trip, he would not eat tomorrow.

He had come out during his normal off shift in an attempt to fill his quota. If he continued to fall behind, the Nutrition Section would be certain to withhold his work ration. He knew that that would be the beginning of the end. Scavengers who suffered denial of rations as punishment were doomed. Trudging the wasted surface of the world in the heavy environment suits burned extra calories that the normal food allotment could not provide. Such poor souls quickly succumb to starvation, many choosing to die on the surface rather submit to culling in the Underground. No one bothered to go look for them. Sooner or later, other scavengers would recover the corroded metals from their suits along with their nutrient rich bleached bones.

Everett blinked as the last vision faded, leaving him with the impression that it represented a far distant future, the final result of a technological triumph.

"Now do you understand?" Magic asked again.

"I think I do."

"Good. Now, just head on over to Zheria and find my great-granddaughter. Don't bother with trying to stop the invasion or anything else; you do not have the leverage to change events that are already in motion. You can only save Sarah and you must move quickly."

"Couldn't you just cheat and get someone closer?"

"No, the pogroms began almost six months ago. The Esatis have arrested most magickers in the Republic. The rest are in hiding or have fled to Alarsaria. Moreover, there are parameter constraints that prevent me from investing in a new hero. At this point, Everett, just believe me when I say that it is you or nothing. Now, get going."

"Hold on. One more thing. What does Sarah have to do with all this, aside from being your descendant?"

"She has been highlighted by Destiny, who is, before you ask, also a noncorporeal sentient entity, as a Primary Pivot, an individual whose actions can exert extraordinary leverage on events. This means, without getting into all the additional whozits and whatfors, that if Sarah dies, Technology is almost certain to succeed. If she lives, the odds remain even. I manifested your eighth spell in order to save her from assassins dispatched by Technology's minions. For me it was just a matter of the draw. Fortune, also a noncorporeal sentient entity, had already determined that you were due for a manifestation; I simply tweaked the process to present you with a spell that would get her out of harm's way."

"You're telling me that I became involved with all of this as a result of *bad luck?*"

"I suppose you could see it that way, but regardless we have to proceed with the task at hand using the resources available."

"Meaning me?"

"Yes."

"Back to Sarah--"

"Everett, you are beginning to be something of a bore."

"So I've been told. How is she going to stop Technology?"

"I know the answer but I cannot express it. The knowledge belongs to Destiny and they have neglected to become involved in the contest."

"Please stop talking in riddles."

Magic smiled sympathetically. "I am sorry, Everett. I *am* trying to be helpful, but I cannot tell you certain things that are outside my own scope. Why Sarah is important to the scheme of things is something I know, as we in the noncorporeal realm posses all knowledge in a communal fashion, but revealing that to you now without the permission of Destiny would be another violation of our operational parameters. If I cheat again then Technology will also be permitted to cheat in a similar way and this will remove all possibility that Technology will not prevail. Do you understand?"

Everett nodded begrudgingly. "Not really, but I guess that I'll have to accept the fact that to save Sarah I must defeat Technology."

"Fine. Now, let's get going, shall we? I will continue to provide you with spells according to my perception of your need and subject to sensible limitations. You just trot along and find Sarah and kill that sorry devil."

"Wait a minute. Did you say *kill?*"

"Physical elimination of his corporeal biologic is the

only way to get Technology out of this realm. If his inspired body remains alive, he will persist in his attempt to eradicate all magic. That means that he will continue to support and direct the development of new mechanisms of war like the steam-mobile artillery. The longer he remains in this realm, the higher his chances of success."

Everett did not comment. He would do whatever was necessary, but he was yet to be convinced that outright murder was necessary.

"Before you go, shouldn't you tell me who Technology is?"

"Did we not cover that?"

"No."

"Oh, sorry, Technology's corporeal biologic is Donald de Grosivna, Chief Minister of the Republican Directorate of Security and Technology."

"What? Are you telling me that Technology isn't Edwin or Baronet Rorche?"

"No, of course not. Why would you think that?"

"But I thought...oh, forget it."

"Fine. Goodbye, Everett. I will not appear to you again unless I feel the circumstances warrant another intervention. Now get to work!"

TWENTY-FOUR

As soon as Magic faded from his sight, Everett thought of dozens more questions that he should have asked her, but even so, his head felt dunce thick with information that he had yet to process fully.

He looked about. The Esati squad remained frozen in comical poses of interrupted motion.

"Perhaps I should have asked how I get time to resume its flow?" he mused aloud.

A spell manifested to him, somewhat apologetically. Along with it came the inspired knowledge that it was the paired Potent to the previous and no doubt would return time to its normal condition.

"You know, it would have been useful if you had given me this sort of helpful information with every spell." This comment, however, lured no further response from the noncorporeal realm.

He felt the insistent First Enunciation nudging at his lips, but repressed it. His current extra-temporal status obviously would give him numerous advantages, and it behooved him to explore its potential. For some time, he studied how he could utilize interrupted time to his benefit and when the First Enunciation nagged for his attention, he simply gritted his teeth to forbid it.

As he contemplated the Zherians, he could not help but think of the little girl who he had seen die through the old man Hargrove's eyes; the Esatis surely deserved some recompense for espousing a philosophy that had such results.

He began to experiment with the frozen world around him. He proved able to affect larger objects, at least to the extent of changing their location, though it took a great deal of effort to move anything more massive than a pebble. With his magical strength, he could pick up an Esati and reposition or reorient him, but was disappointed to learn that he could not in any way alter the soldier's stance or the position of the items on his person, even down to the tiniest wrinkle in his jacket.

The idea of simply rearranging the men in comical positions struck him as unsatisfyingly juvenile, but he discarded out of hand all notions that would see them come to grievous harm. He could not summon the ruthlessness to kill them in cold blood for unrealized potential future crimes. Thus, at best, he could only hope to inconvenience these fanatics.

He thought for a few moments. His strength spell functioned here in this nether world, so, logically, his other spells should as well, but which might he make use of?

Then he grinned, as the obvious answer occurred to him.

"Manure, gather ye into a pile!"

The size of the mound that formed, oozing and slithering from under doors, out of side streets, and from crevices and cracks in every direction, surprised him, until he realized that, in a town of this size, there must be literally hundreds of outhouses with associated cesspools. Moreover, the streets, subject to horses, must also produce a significant amount of droppings that would need to be stored in out-of-the-way piles.

Smiling as he took a great leap, he left the Esatis neck deep in the manure, much of it gleefully fresh.

As he soared upward, he reconsidered casting the spell that would free him from the frozen world. It seemed likely that his own personal time must continue to unfold, even though the lack of change in the world left him with no means of measuring it. He was thirsty, so logically he would grow hungry after a while, and become sleepy when his body determined that it should be night. If he stayed in interrupted time for relative days, he would surely age while all else and everyone else did not. Speculating, he envisioned himself somehow trapped in interrupted time, living his entire life in what would be to the rest of the world not even a single second.

This unnerving fantasy almost jolted a reflexive casting

of the counter spell from him, but he clamped his mouth shut and forbade it once more. No matter the magnitude of the risk, he would not abandon the power it leant him.

His flight-assisted leap brought him down near the great crater to the north. Depending upon his magically enhanced strength to absorb the energy of his impact, he struck the ground at speed and marveled as his landing disturbed the wounded earth only slightly, raising not a single speck of dust.

The battlefield had the almost artificial look of a posed museum display and he took a moment to take stock of the current situation. Some Zherian scouts had begun to move back into the area, but the bulk of the invading spearhead continued to flow around the scar like water around a bolder in a stream. For a brief moment, he played with the thought of attempting to disrupt the invasion by physically scattering the Republican forces. When he realized that such an effort would take a huge amount of relative time, weeks or even months of his life, he found himself unwilling to pay such a cost to achieve a victory that might prove, in the broader scope of the conflict between Magic and Technology, entirely irrelevant.

Sarah had to be his main priority. Above all else, he must find her and remove her to safety. After that, if necessary, he would try to come up with a means to deal with the Zherians and, eventually, Technology.

He doubted that Sarah's captors, without unusual magical or technological assistance, could have moved Sarah far in the time since her capture, which could only be hours at the most. Given the Esatis apparent abhorrence for all magic and all magicians, he felt that he could safely rule out the first. As for the second, it was an accepted fact that all technological means of travel were condemned to traverse physical space. Technological conveyances, as far as he was aware, could not, as magic routinely did, ignore real distance and were therefore subject to physical limits on speed.

Consequently, he was convinced that she must be reasonably close, within a radius of no more than a few dozen miles. He was equally convinced that she must remain in the claws of the Esatis, considering that she was known to them as a magicker. If he found the right batch of the fanatics, he would find Sarah.

Satisfied, he cast, *"Give me strength!"* and bounded into the sky.

Quartering the area in great flight-assisted leaps, he began to search over the invading force for the distinctive red jackets. As he sailed above columns of infantry, horse drawn supply trains, and steam-mobile artillery, he learned that the scope of the invasion was much larger than he had imagined, involving literally hundreds of thousands of troops and perhaps as many as a thousand steam-mobile artillery. To his surprise, however, there were relatively few Esatis and the small squads he did discover were scattered through the host and often not intermingled with conventional Zherian units.

Arrayed in a casual formation to guard a cottage, the first contingent that he found occupied a deserted hamlet only a mile to the northwest of Bayou Dorking. Thinking that he had lucked into finding Sarah at his first try, he swooped down, dodged around the statue-like guards, and pushed on the simple plank door of the stone building. When the door resisted his efforts, he cast his strength and slammed against it. The planks shattered into fragments but these did not fall or move farther than his initial impetuous and he had to shove the pieces to one side in order to open a hole big enough to admit him. In the small single interior room, he found a cowering young woman with ripped clothing and a tall Esati officer in the process of removing his pants. Incensed, Everett took the woman and moved her far to the south, leaving her near an unthreatened and still occupied village. On his return, he parked the officer in a nearby lake, barely resisting the impulse to plunge the criminal to the very bottom.

It took hours longer, relatively, and dozens of other equally fruitless searches, but he finally came across an Esati escorted wagon traveling north along a side road about ten miles from the front. With one of the magic canceling mechanisms mounted at each corner, the wagon carried a large cage constructed of riveted iron slats.

When he landed next to the cage, he saw but a single person lying within: Sarah.

In his haste to reach her, he ripped the cage apart,

leaving the splinters and mangled bars hanging in a cloud all about the frame of the wagon. Shaking from the effort, he scrambled onto the denuded bed and knelt beside her.

She appeared asleep, or, at least, her eyes were closed. Part of her shirt over her shoulder had been cut away and a large cotton bandage was visible. Gently, he took her statue-like form in his arms and bounded away, casting continuously to cover distance until he was perhaps fifty miles to the south of the invasion. Landing finally beside a tree-lined stream that ran deep and dark in sinuous curves along the border of a sheepfold, he placed her on a swatch of dried grass in the shade of a bank-clutching cypress.

"Time, resume thy flow!"

Sarah stirred and opened her eyes briefly, then sat up with a sudden start. Recovering quickly, she eased back into the grass, favoring her injured shoulder, and leisurely surveyed her new location.

"It's about time you showed up," she chided at last, grinning.

He wrapped her in his arms in a desperate hug.

She winced, her face tightening in pain. *"Easy, Everett!* I know that you're happy to see me, but let's save the festivities for later! When you squeeze me so tight it hurts."

He released her, reddening. "Sorry. Are you injured badly?"

"Nothing life threatening. The bullet went cleanly through without striking bone or artery, but it hurt when it hit and it still hurts now. Some Zherian medic patched me up and then those red coats tossed me in the cage. They didn't say where they were taking me, but I doubt that I would have enjoyed my reception very much."

"The Esatis are scum. They intend to kill all magicians."

She examined him thoughtfully. "You've gotten more spells, haven't you?"

"Yes."

"How many do you have now?"

He made a quick tally in his head. "There's four new ones, three that I can use whenever I want and one that might be too dangerous to use. I suppose I should also count the two persistent magical effects. So, sixteen."

"You have *sixteen* spells? *Nobody* gets more than thirteen spells, Everett."

"Well, I do. Magic is cheating in my favor."

"*Magic is cheating?* Tell me everything."

He did, though it took the better part of an hour. She questioned all and made him repeat much of his experience, particularly the things that Magic had told him.

"Amazing," she said finally.

"Did you know that Magic was your great-grandmother?"

"Not really. It has always been something of a family legend that we have been favored by Magic, but none of us ever suspected that great granny Miri was Magic itself. Are you going to do what she wants – kill Technology?"

He took a deep breath and let some of the tension ease from him. "Not if I can help it. You're safe and I'm not persuaded that I can do anything to stop this war. The Zherians are invading with hundreds of thousands of soldiers. No single man could hope to throw them back."

Sarah rubbed her shoulder, the muscles in her jaw tightening. "I used to think – well, it doesn't matter."

Everett rose and offered her a hand. As she took it and stood, taking care not to jostle her shoulder over much, he realized that some large measure of her former confidence was missing. Perhaps her ordeal had convinced her that there were indeed calamities that even her indomitable will could not overturn.

"What do *you* want to do?" he asked her.

"I ... I don't know."

Suddenly and deeply feeling the weariness of his long search, he chose to be blunt. "Do you want to go to Kleinsvench or fight the Zherians?"

She looked around for a moment at the bucolic sheepfold and the quiet stream and then turned back and nodded. "Let's go home, Everett. I've had enough of war for a while."

"Right. Stay your passage, O Time!"

It had not occurred to him to ask how she wanted to travel. The undeniable inherent logistical advantage involved in traveling in a timeless state made all other means of transport seem a waste of, as it were, time.

It also had not occurred to him at first that he did not actually know the exact location of Kleinsvench, but he did not concern himself overly with this problem as his spell gave him, so to speak, all the time in the world.

Luckily, the Alarsarians had a comprehensive highway system and a manifest dedication to signage. When he crossed the invested but unfortified border into the Grand Duchy of Filingham, he stopped at a crossroads outside a small town reputed to be Oakbrook, intending to resume time and get final directions from Sarah. Taking exaggerated care, he stood her posed figure back on her feet and took a moment to look around. The wider of the two routes led more or less north and showed the greenish discolorations of fresh horse manure and heavy wagon ruts in its packed gravel macadam. A great deal of traffic had passed upon it recently. No doubt, units of the Royal Alarsarian Army had moved up to emplace along the Republican frontier.

"Monsieur De Schael, might I have a moment of your time?"

Everett jumped at the unfamiliar male voice behind him and whirled about to confront this newest apparition.

The man appeared average in every aspect: height, weight, build and features. In fact, he seemed to possess no distinguishing mark of any kind. His bland, unblemished face was clean-shaven and his mouse brown hair moderately short. His eyes were no color in particular, simply dark, and his nose symmetrical, so much so that it struck Everett as odd; most noses favored one side, nostril-wise. The newcomer wore a plain gray jacket over equally plain brown trousers. It was as if he had been created to be the epitome of no-one-in-particular.

"I wish you people would pop into existence in front of me!"

"You have my apologies."

Everett made a not unfounded guess. "You're Technology?"

The fellow nodded without smiling. "Excellent deduction."

"You're also really not here?"

"Indeed. As referencing my current focus, the projected image is the product of the interaction of sympathetic vibrations in multiple light spectra that –"

"Right. I get the idea. What do you want?"

"Simply to correct some misconceptions that you may have been given."

"Right. Sure."

"I understand your reluctance to accept my statements at face value, considering that we appear to be on opposite sides of this contest, but I would at least like the opportunity to present my case."

Though he had not actually given it a great deal of thought, Everett had never entertained the expectation that Magic's adversary would appear polite and well-spoken; this fundamentally violated all classical conventions.

"What, no threats?"

Technology showed his empty palms. "I am not, as you may have been led to believe, the ultimate evil. My only goal is to see that corporeal sentients in this universe achieve the quality of life that they would have otherwise had without the handicap of a bastardized system of foundational underpinnings."

"Are you talking about the Magic-Technology thing?"

"Obviously."

In this persona, at least, Technology presented no apparent danger and, in fact, seemed only a reasonable man attempting to convey a reasoned argument. Everett decided to give him the benefit of the doubt.

"All right, have your say."

A thin box-like device with a black, glossy surface took shape beside Technology.

"What's that?" Everett questioned.

"In this instance, it is merely a simulacrum. I intend to employ it to facilitate in a natural and intuitive fashion the display of visual images that will lend support to my thesis. It and its variations and adaptive incarnations have many different identifiers throughout numerous universes, but this universe will not see it manifest, if it manifests at all, for at least another century. Consequently, it has no comprehensible descriptor currently. For the purposes of practical nomenclature, I will simply refer to it as a visual presentation device, or VPD. Primarily, the VPD will indicate certain calculated projections of forthcoming events derived from a given set of assumptions with approximations applied for variables whose randomness cannot be deemphasized."

"So, you're saying that you're going to show me more visions of the future?"

"I apologize. I had thought that my statements exemplified the communication that I desired to transmit."

"Why are you talking like a dictionary?"

Technology tilted his head and bumped the side of it above his ear with the heel of his hand. "Sorry about that. I am not directly experienced in the corporeal means of communication. My special area of interest lends itself to verbosity, that is, *wordiness*, and I seemed to have applied an incremental situational adjustment in the wrong direction."

Technology bumped his head again. "Okay, I think I've got it now. This better?"

"Uhm, I suppose."

"Good. Like you said, I'm going to show you scenes from the future."

Everett curled his lip in disgust. "I've already seen what the Esatis are going to do."

"I'm not going to show you visions of those fiends. Everett, I assure you, the Esatis, their twisted philosophy, and their reprehensible methods did not originate with me. Edwin is the prime culprit in the mutation of what was once only a social club into a genocidal political force. Men made the Esatis, not me."

"But they're doing what you need done, whether you're guiding them or not."

"To some extent, this is true, but you must understand that my corporal self, Donald de Grosivna, doesn't have the political clout needed to restrain Edwin and his fanatics. They're very popular with elements in the Intelligence Directorate and if he tried to suppress their excesses, he'd find himself isolated from key information and excluded from critical decisions."

To Everett, this sounded like a convenient, self-serving

rationalization, especially from a noncorporeal sentient being, but he simply waited for Technology to continue.

Technology nodded. "Let's begin with the most important scene." He waved his hand. Color and light blazed from the glossy surface of the mechanism. Everett watched closely, looking through a window into another time and place.

It took a moment for him to recognize the weeping man. "That's me."

"Indeed. The time of the image is less than one month from now."

The angle of the view changed so that Everett came to see the bier over which his doppelganger wept. Sarah lay upon it, her face lifeless and gray, her body thin and shrunken.

"How does she die?" Everett asked, unable to turn away.

"There's a type of life that is not yet understood here," Technology replied. "It's so small that it cannot be seen without mechanisms that have yet to manifest in this universe. This life, of innumerable sorts, grows practically everywhere about human beings and lives quite peacefully in its proper environment. However, if certain sorts are introduced into flesh where they should not be – by a bullet dragging scraps of contaminated cloth, for instance – then this life will infect and fester. These infections can and often do kill."

"Magic will give me a spell," Everett said in a dull monotone.

"I'd say you were right except for the fact that this projection is accurate based upon current circumstances. For whatever reason, as of this moment, Magic does not intervene and Sarah will die a difficult death in twenty-seven days' time."

Shaking his head, Everett rejected the idea. Magic had not gone to so much trouble to preserve her great-granddaughter's life to let her die to an illness that could be cured with a single spell. This false revelation must simply be a ruse to gain leverage by exploiting his feelings for Sarah.

He refused even to consider that it could be true.

Apparently reading the essence of his thoughts from his expression, Technology slowly nodded. "It's true, Everett. Unless something changes drastically, Sarah will die."

"Your sympathetic tone is wasted on me. I know you want her dead."

"Actually, this is no longer the case. There was only a small window where her demise would aid in the transition of this universe to a purely technological nature. That window has closed and her survival will not currently lower my chances of success. Whatever you may believe, I'm not inherently spiteful or callous. Just for your information, those conceptions don't exist in any form in the noncorporeal realm. I know how important she is to you and I assure you that there's nothing to be gained toward my cause by her death."

Everett, resolute, did not respond.

Technology, after a short pause in which he watched Everett with an open expression, continued. "The scenes that I'm going to show you now are not projections from current conditions. They're an alternative future created from a single change in the current time line."

"They're 'What if Technology wins?'"

"Very perceptive." Technology waved his hand again.

The vignettes that sprang from the imaginary mechanism described a future of plenty, of health, and of ease. Through the introductions of mechanisms that would tend to every need, the visions suggested, life for human kind would become comfortable, safe, long, and happy.

Everett grunted depreciatingly when the mechanism went dark once more. "I've seen the future beyond that. It's not so pretty."

"Men almost always fail to understand moderation, Everett. There are universes in which magical warfare has left planets barren of life. I can't tell you that humans will outgrow their own limitations, but I can tell you that millions upon millions in future generations have the potential to live longer and happier lives though the use of technology."

"They could do the same through magic."

"Do you really believe that? 'Magic is inefficient, inconvenient, undependable, and frequently quite useless.'"

Everett frowned. "I've never said that out loud."

"But you know it's true."

"Are you done? I need to get to Kleinsvench."

Technology sighed. "I've got one last bit of information to share and an offer to make, and then I'll leave you be."

"Get on with it."

"Very well, I'll keep it short. Magic didn't begin altering your spells with your eighth, but with your first."

"What does that mean?" Everett groused.

"According to Destiny, you've always been intended to be a great wizard. Magic couldn't alter that, it's outside her scope. She just changed your spells so that you would be receptive to her needs. Your first seven spells weren't supposed to be *crap*, Everett. They were supposed to be magnificent! You'd have been wealthy and powerful by the age you are now, a man secure in his place in the world. You'd have received your remaining six spells as a pair and the first ever quadruple within a year of your twenty-ninth birthday and become the most powerful Grand Master Wizard in history. Instead, you became an itinerant tradesman who could barely sustain himself, an unsettled individual dissatisfied with almost every aspect of his life, and a dreamer with unfulfilled aspirations who was primed and ready to become Magic's champion. She manipulated you into becoming a man who would literally jump at the chance to run away with a beautiful young woman."

Everett was speechless.

"I'm sorry, Everett, but it's true. What's more, at this stage the operational parameters relating to you are so far out of whack that you haven't been in the scope of Destiny and Fortune since your ninth spell. Magic has a relatively free hand with you; she can manifest any spell to you at any time. However, and this is the key part, the conditions that make these unlimited manifestations possible for her also make them possible for me."

Shaking his head as he dealt with the mental whirlwind thrown up by Technology's accusations, he argued, "I'm not a technician, so I don't see where that makes any difference."

"But that's exactly my point. I now have it in my power to make you the most powerful grand master technologist that this universe has ever seen."

TWENTY-FIVE

Everett shaded his eyes from the sun as he scanned the imposing pile of the castle. "I think I can see the balcony that you're talking about."

Sarah grinned, her arm linked with his, and seemed hardly able to contain her enthusiasm. The no-nonsense strength and determination that was the cornerstone of her character had given way to the bouncy excitement of a little girl. "That's the balcony to my family's apartments. The one with the red granite baluster. If you can get us up there, then we'll be home!"

Everett thought for a split-second of the place he thought of as home, his father's orchard. His sister Lessye and her family lived there now. He had not visited in more than three years.

The official residence of the Elector of Kleinsvench was the centuries old former stronghold of an extinct royal line. It occupied a dolerite crag that rose two hundred feet above the rest of the city, surrounded on the west, north, and east by high bluffs and on the south by a sloping fortified approach. A long narrow lake further defended the eastern side and it was from a bench on the lakeside main avenue of the city that they stared across at the square and generally featureless main building. It sat on the highest point of the crag, rising in plain view above the thick walls that surrounded it. Bulky, lichen-stained stone defensive towers of archaic designs sprouted all along the southern approach, but only one tower rose above the bluffs at the northern end, a distinctive, extremely tall tower built of red brick. This slender edifice narrowed in three steps and had large, cutout windows and a striking golden dome at its apex.

Over the course of two not hurried days, they had completed their journey to the city of Kleinsvench by means of

Everett's Vital Transportation Variant. This had permitted the two of them a quiet, comfortable time in each other's company and an opportunity to find proper clothing to replace Everett's rags and her ripped shirt. They had arrived early and strolled through the hardly stirring city, with Sarah shedding her restraint only when the Residence came into sight.

He had not informed Sarah of the appearance of Technology, the being's claims concerning the motives of Magic, or of his seductive offer.

"Let's go, Everett," Sarah prompted with an eager grin. "I'd like to sleep in my own bed for a change."

He concentrated on a locus in the right corner of the balcony. *"Beautiful Woman, come forth!"*

As soon as they landed, Sarah released him, rushed to a set of glass-paned doors, and cast them open.

The sitting room inside had a scattering of comfortable but worn armchairs, a card table whose varnish had been worn from the edges by decades of elbows, a chess board with exquisitely carven pieces, and wall-to-wall bookshelves filled to overflowing. Small signs -- books left laying about, a half-eaten sandwich forgotten on a saucer behind a lamp, a pair of beaten-up shoes under a footstool, a desk cluttered with paper held down by eyeglasses, a schizophrenic key ring, a magnifying glass, and a jar of sweets -- suggested that the room was the private province of a family rather than a place intended for company.

A high-pitched shriek erupted from a girl of perhaps thirteen. *"Sister!"*

Previously draped in a chair with a large book astride her lap, the girl exploded from her seat and threw her arms about Sarah's neck. A younger boy tumbled from a settee, scattering papers and a tablet, to join the fray. Their features matched Sarah's so well that there could be no doubt of their kinship. After much hugging, some weeping, shock and concern for her injury, and a general babble of questions and exclamations, the girl took notice of Everett and glared.

"Who are you?" she demanded in an accusatory tone.

"Everett's a friend, Emily," Sarah affirmed. "He's a wizard and helped me return home. Everett, these are my youngest sister Emily and my youngest brother Joseph."

"Oh!" Emily's eyes became large. "Wait, a *friend*, or, you know, just a friend?"

"None of your business. Where's Father?"

"He's down in the Lower Ward with the rest of the First Section of the Reserve Company. They're filling sand bags but we have to study for our end of term exams. You won't believe it, but Father said, war or no war, we had to get an education. How silly is that?"

Joseph, a year or two younger than Emily, marched to Everett and extended his hand, his demeanor frank and serious beyond his years. "Thank you for returning Sister to us, Monsieur."

As Everett shook solemnly, Sarah quipped, "Don't be too quick to thank him, Joseph, he's also the one that stole me away."

"Oh, I knew it!" Emily exclaimed. "He *is a friend!*"

Then there was nothing for it but that Emily and Joseph should catch Sarah's hands and run out through the richly paneled interior door into a spacious, portrait-lined hall.

Not feeling quite so energetic, Everett followed at a sedate pace, using the echoes of their laughter and juvenile exuberance as a guide. Their path led down through the building, out into an open court, and down a winding access road through weathered stone gates and arched passages to another larger courtyard, trumpeting all the while that *Sarah is home!*

Ravenous, he would have preferred to seek out the kitchens, but understood the priority of Sarah's reunion with her family. Curiously, he did not encounter anyone else in the splendid corridors, magnificent staircases, and grandiose entrance hall of the main building, nor were any sentries posted on the crenellated walls that marked the limits of the first courtyard. The smaller side buildings and gatehouses by which he passed appeared likewise deserted. Without any solid basis for the assumption, he had thought that the castle of the ruler of the city would be attended by a horde of servants, flunkies, and potentates.

In the Lower Ward, the boisterous charge of Sarah and her siblings had interrupted fifteen men and women at work. By the time Everett arrived, the group had abandoned sacks, shovels and a wagon of sand and had gathered around Sarah to exchange hugs and grins and demand a telling of all that had happened to her.

All heads turned to consider him as he approached. They were a varied lot of more or less ordinary-looking people dressed in worn work clothes, and while a few eyed him with suspicion, most appeared ready to give him the benefit of the doubt. Sarah broke free of her welcome and ran back to catch his hand.

"Come on, Everett! I'd like you to meet my father."

She led him through the still exultant gang to a tall, solid, older man with thick gray hair and a sun-browned face, interrupting him in the process of mock scolding the two youngsters for abandoning their studies.

"Father, this is Everett de Schael," Sarah introduced. "He brought me home. Everett, permit me to introduce my father, First Assemblyman Guillaume Monte-Jaune."

"He's a *friend*, Father!" Emily burst out and then giggled.

Joseph threw his eyes skyward as if to say, "Sisters! Heh.", then added aloud the clearly more important bit, "He's a wizard too!"

While Sarah shushed her siblings, her father reached out a work-hardened hand and took Everett's in a firm greeting that revealed considerable strength. "From the depths of my heart, Monsieur de Schael, I wish to thank you. Her disappearance was a major shock to us all and her return an incredible joy. Is there any way in which I could possibly repay you?"

Noting Sarah's quick look and tense expression and thinking wistfully of her original promise of a huge silver bounty, Everett wisely shook his head. "No need, Monsieur. It has been my pleasure to assist your daughter."

Sarah's grin resurfaced and the elder Monte-Jaune looked from her to Everett and back again. His eyebrows rose slightly. "I see. Well, may I at least invite you to supper this evening? We must have a celebration and though the meal may not be of the highest standard, it will be filling."

"I'd like nothing better."

Then Sarah led him around to make further

introductions. All proved to be family of one flavor or other, from a young man and young woman who were Sarah's brother Kyle and sister Meredith to cousins of all sorts, affiliations, and ages. Finally, she presented him to an older couple addressed as Aunt Louise and Uncle Alec, who confessed to simply being friends of Sarah's father. Louise was a tall, handsome featured woman who wiped explosive, happy tears while Alec, though marginally shorter than his spouse, had the lean bulk and steely demeanor of a former soldier. Their three daughters and son, all about Sarah's age or slightly older, were among those previously introduced.

"Sarah," Guillaume Monte-Jaune suggested when they had made the circuit back around to him, "why don't you find Everett a room in the residence where he can rest while the Reserve Company finishes up here?"

"Monsieur Monte-Jaune--" Everett interrupted.

"Please call me Guillaume. Everyone does."

"I'll be glad to help, Guillaume. How many sand bags do you need and where do you want them?"

"Well, we're trying to build firing positions here in front of the Yellow Gate. There have not been doors for the old Snake Gate there in more than a century and we thought –"

"Stay your passage, O Time!"

As soon as the spell took effect, Everett cast his tenth and twelfth spells and bounded away. His magical strength did not erase the physical weariness of his muscles, but seemed simply to overwrite it, and he fleetingly wondered without concern if he were doing irreversible damage to his body by insisting that it perform far beyond its normal limits.

Well satisfied of the inherent limitations on his ability to manipulate smaller objects in interrupted time, he had not bothered to attempt to divide the loose sand in the wagon in order to fill the waiting empty bags. That task would have simply been impossible. Moreover, he had already seen an abundance of ready-made sand bags along the miles of fortifications on the frontier between the opposing alliances. A few terrific leaps carried him north beyond the unmarked border of Kleinsvench, over the narrow neck of land appertaining to the Prince of Gainsfield-Schloss, and to the entrenchments of the Grand Alliance positions. Somewhat motivated by unadulterated spite, he considered but quickly discarded the idea of stealing the sandbags from the Alarsarians. Sailing over them and across a clear-cut no-man's-land of stumps and burn scar better than a mile wide, he entered into Republican territory. At a long closed and now fortified customs post astride the amputated stump of a major highway only a half mile back from the front, he found thousands of sturdy Zherian sandbags ready for the taking.

He landed alongside the twelve-foot sloped wall of a forward redoubt, refreshed his strength, and took hold of a bag on an upper course. However, instead of the single bag, a twelve-foot section a dozen courses deep pulled cleanly away in a single piece, with only a few bags ripped apart but unscattered in the process. He gave a half shrug and began liberating other sections of the wall, in the process leaving formerly guarded spyglass wielding sentries standing fully exposed. In several stages, he returned the sections to the Lower Ward and arranged them to protect the portcullis and curtain wall of the Yellow Gate. For good measure, he brought a few hundred extra sandbags in various configurations and set them out of the way on the eastern side of the courtyard.

Satisfied, he returned to his place in front of Sarah's father. *"Time, resume thy flow!"*

"—that we should—" Guillaume continued and then abruptly stopped at the shifting cloth sounds of the settling bags that now stood between the group and the lower gate with only a small gap at the center. He looked around for a moment, eyes widening, then focused on Everett once more.

"That is quite amazing, Everett. Master Wizard, did you say?"

"*Grand* Master Wizard, Father," Sarah corrected, smiling, apparently with proprietary pride.

"Excellent!" Guillaume beamed, and then with a suddenly serious mien, affirmed "Everett, we must talk."

"Could that wait till a little later in the evening? I know that you and your family would like to spend some time with your daughter and I've some shopping to do in town."

The elder Monte-Jaune regarded him calmly but

intently. "Of course. Perhaps after supper?"

"That'd be fine." Everett smiled at Sarah, bid all farewell, and started toward the flaking and cracked sandstone of the high-peaked arch of the Snake Gate. After murmuring something to her father, Sarah rushed to catch up.

"Everett?"

"Yes?"

"Are you coming back?"

"Of course."

"Do you want me to come with you?"

"No, I'll be fine. Grand Master Wizard, remember? I saw an apothecary's shop when we came into town and I want to see if they have a muscle lineament. I sprained one in my back sometime in the last couple of days."

"Are you going to be all right?"

He bestowed a confident smile upon her. "Sure, it's nothing serious."

"I'll see you in a little while?"

"No more than a couple of hours."

As Sarah, displaying noticeable reluctance, turned back, Everett strode with a steady gait out of the Lower Ward and down through the switchbacks and disused outworks toward the city. An impulse struck him to look back at her, but he did not.

As he moved along the uncluttered cobblestone streets of Kleinsvench among the mostly timber and stone buildings, he kept his eye out for a luncheon vendor's cart, but saw none. While he tried to persuade his empty belly that it would have to wait, it became clear that much of the city's populace was absent. He saw almost no wagon traffic and many of the houses and shops were shuttered or boarded up. The few pedestrians that he did encounter were often stopped in tense, compact groups, disputing quietly. He saw one matron on a second floor balcony hanging clothes to dry on a line that spanned between two buildings, but in general, the normal daily routine of the city was nowhere to be found. The longstanding expectation of the imminent appearance of the Republican juggernaut must have prompted the majority of the citizens of Kleinsvench to seek a less exposed abode.

Despite what he had said to Sarah, the apothecary lay

not along the main avenue by which they had entered the city but in its western quarter. Though he had never been there, he navigated to it without incident. It lay on the southern side of Rheen Street, in a four-storey brick building just across from a small park. Wedged between a locked librairie and an open but quiet boucherie, the shop, at the top of a set of half-circular stone steps, had a tiny display window and a broad parquet patterned door. The unadorned brass sign at the entrance read: Simon Mindelsen, Master Apothecary.

A bell attached to the door jangled as he pushed it open. A small space hardly bigger than a large closet, the interior of the shop was clean and orderly. On each side, floor-to-ceiling shelves packed with labeled boxes and tins made a slightly claustrophobic aisle that funneled customers directly to a marble-topped counter at the back. Behind that were additional packed shelves outlining a black-curtained doorway. Small, signed displays covered most of the counter: *Ervil's Patented Hair Restorer! Guaranteed Cure for Colicky Babies! Petifoy's Mange Balm (For Dogs Only).*

The proprietor was a wizened man of advanced age with hardly two orphaned strands of white hair on his age spotted bald cranium. No other customers were present and a professional but welcoming grin sprang to the proprietor's face as he looked up from a large book opened on the counter.

"Good morning, young man! What ails you today?"

"Uhm, actually, nothing, Monsieur Mindelsen. I wanted to ask--"

"Come, come, no need to be embarrassed. If it is a bedroom potency problem that afflicts you, then rest assured that I do not gossip. We have the latest formula bulletins from Eyrchelle and I am sure we can restore you to full vigor."

Despite himself, Everett reddened slightly. "No, thank you. What I need is some assistance with three formulas that I've found."

"Found, you say?" The apothecary eyed Everett guardedly. "You have not stolen them, have you?"

Everett offered the lie that he had prepared. "No, Monsieur. I came across them while studying the techniques of harmonizing. There's a book on ornithology in the library in the monastery at Gerabalde and I found them written in the margins."

"I see. I must warn you that proprietary formulas have been known to turn up missing. We apothecaries must work hand in hand with chemists and as a member in good standing of the Apothecaries Guild I am honor bound to report any formulas with undocumented provenance to the main Guild Hall in Eyrchelle."

Everett nodded with a blank expression. "I've no objection to that."

Mindelsen tucked one side of his mouth. "Let me see them then."

Everett handed the man the slip of paper on which he had copied the three formulas. Mindelsen studied it for a moment.

"Hmmm. This is standard chemist's script, but the characters are not the Modern Refined Set. An antiquated notation I would say, maybe from two centuries ago. The first formula has only three ingredients: sulfur, a nitrate, and sugar. The process directions seem odd though. One step introduces a bonding agent that I believe to be highly volatile. Were there any other notes with the formulas? Do you know if it is some type of throat lozenge?"

"My understanding is that it's a combustible substance."

"For what purpose?"

"To launch a projectile."

"Is that so? Hmm. Yes, I see. Though I must confess without shame that it is not my area of expertise, this second one is obviously an explosive. There are coded warning symbols throughout. However, this third one does not appear to me to be martial in nature. What is it for?"

"It's a potion to combat fever and infection."

"Ah! If you are not aware, a great many medical conditions do not respond to existing potions. Any new medicinal potion of sufficient efficacy will produce significant revenue. That formula may be the most profitable one, if you have a mind to set up production."

"I was actually hoping that you could concoct a set quantity of each of the formulas for me."

Mindelsen placed the paper carefully on the counter

and folded his arms. "I would be happy to, once I have verified that the formulas are not contraband. Regrettably, if I post a letter, assuming that the war does not disrupt the mail, it will take a month or more for a response to return from the Royal Capital."

Everett shook his head. "I don't have a month. I need the potion within a week and the other compounds within days."

"I am sorry, young man. I cannot see that happening unless you can find a wizard that can magic a response from Eyrchelle."

Everett smiled. "As a matter of fact..."

TWENTY-SIX

"At least the main invasion did not come through Kleinsvench," Sarah's brother Kyle told Everett. "We'd have been flattened here. Frankly, those mechanisms you described would have rolled through the Eiae Plain with hardly a pause until they reached the Cyheur Canal half way between here and Eyrchelle."

"Kleinsvench has no army?"

"We have the Residence Guard, who usually serve as gendarmes, border agents, and wardens. They number about two hundred and fifty, but three days ago the Elector took the Guard and enough volunteers to fill out a rump battalion and marched to the frontier to join the Grand Alliance forces. This stripped Kleinsvench of what few defenders we had – well, except for us in the Reserve and we don't count – we only have *two* rifles for Magic's sake -- but a military contribution was a condition of our inclusion in the Alliance."

"There was no way to avoid the Alliance?"

"No. When Sister's wedding fell through, the Alarsarian ambassador flat out said that the only way we could avoid full occupation by the Royal Army was to play an active role in the Alliance. It was basically an ultimatum and the Elector had no realistic option but to agree. The Alarsarians tend to be arrogant and overbearing but at least we can retain some semblance of sovereignty. If the Republicans overrun us, we'll become just another puppet state."

Everett sat across a large, otherwise vacant, circular table from Kyle in the ancient, cavernous banquet hall of the Residence. A complaining Emily and Joseph had already been escorted to bed by Meredith and Aunt Louise. Uncle Alec and some of the cousins had cleared the remains of the meal and then had left to relieve another team of Reservists keeping watch in the tower at the summit of the crag. This was, Kyle had been eager to explain, the abode of the largest set of great bronze bells in the known world, constructed at the decree of a centuries dead Queen Lydia d'Lho for the stated purpose of dispatching the Summer Doldrums, and referred to by one and all as Mad Lydia's Folly.

When Monsieur Monte-Jaune had mentioned supper, he had actually meant a full-blown potluck to which everyone remaining in the city had been invited. Ingeniously, the castle residents had apprised the populace of the event through a coded message of tones broadcast from the bells atop the monument to Queen Lydia's eccentricity. The thrice-repeated message had been simple: *Sarah's home! Let's have supper!* Within an hour, the several hundred attendees had begun to arrive for a cooperative gala equipped with their own food, drinks, tablecloths, silverware, and dishes. After shaking innumerable hands and enduring hugs from citizens of all ages, sorts, and sizes, Everett had been obliged to sample dozens of dishes proffered by preening amateur chefs. Despite this overabundance of appetizers, he had managed to clean his plate of the solid meal of boiled potatoes, pinto beans, and browned rice prepared as a communal effort by the Monte-Jaune extended family. Desert had been a magnificent fried apple turnover prepared by Sarah from a highly valued cache of sun dried fruit.

It was well after nine o'clock and it had been necessary to light the great chandeliers suspended high above, a task accomplished by Sarah in three casual spell casts as she strolled across the hall to the accompaniment of raucous applause. Beaming happily, she had been the prime focus of the evening and had been obliged to circulate continuously, chatting and smiling, while Everett had been allowed to retire contentedly to his seat. This had had the double consequence of allowing him to make an in-depth acquaintance of her family and for her family to submit him to a not so veiled scrutiny of his motives, history, skills, finances, goals, health, hygiene, and employment prospects.

At one point during the evening, Aunt Louise had patted him on the hand and said, "Don't worry, dear. I'm sure you'll prove fit for our Sarah."

Throughout, he had kept a watchful eye on his traveling companion, but she seemed determined not to let her wound, though still obviously painful, disrupt her homecoming. Now that most of the guests had finished eating, the more energetic revelers had migrated toward an open area at one end of the hall for an impromptu dance. A band composed of stringed instruments and a single xylophone had formed through carefully planned spontaneity and lively music now echoed along the vaulted ceiling and among the forlorn tables.

Enjoying the opportunity for a lately-rare moment of relaxation, Everett continued talking with Kyle concerning random casual matters for perhaps another hour as the hall began to slowly empty, the guests clearing their tables, setting the chairs atop, and carting away the fragments. Then he noticed Guillaume Monte-Jaune separate from the remaining die-hard attendees and make directly for him.

Kyle also took note of the approach of his father. "Father wanted to speak to you alone, Everett. So, I think I'll head off to bed. Besides, I have to get up before daybreak to take my shift in the tower."

Everett nodded. "Have a good night's rest."

"You do the same." Kyle strode off quickly to meet his father, exchanged a quick word that Everett could not overhear, and disappeared up the stairway that led to the family apartments.

Guillaume took a place next to Everett, sinking into the chair in a way that suggested he was tired enough to appreciate a quiet sit. His expression solemn, he wasted no time with preliminaries. "Everett, I wanted to ask you how long you might stay in Kleinsvench."

Having expected this question, he had a ready if imprecise answer. "I'm not sure, Monsieur Monte-Jaune. I had thought to set up a shop in Eyrchelle, but now with the invasion I think I might find better conditions for business in New Zindersberg."

"I don't doubt that you're correct, however I'd like to offer you a position here in Kleinsvench."

"Uhm, do you grow a lot of potatoes?"

Guillaume looked momentarily confused. "Sorry,

potatoes?"

Everett shook his head to clear it of an obsolete mind-set. "I mean, is there a great demand for magicking in Kleinsvench?"

"Not a great deal, as far as I know, but what I actually had in mind was an official position on the Elector's staff."

"What, like Royal Wizard?"

"Since Kleinsvench is a representative democracy with a hereditary head of state, the official title might rather be something on the order of Minister of Magic, although any title you prefer would be acceptable. Are you interested?"

"What would my duties be?"

"I won't sugar coat it, Everett. You'd be expected to defend Kleinsvench with every spell at your disposal. Sarah has told me of your capabilities and while much of her story seems impossible, I believe her implicitly and I trust her judgment. She declared that you were the most powerful wizard alive."

Everett opened his mouth to say, "That could well be true." But no words came out. As his entire body began to shake, blue and purple pinpoint sparks obscured his vision. Then he seemed to split from himself, his consciousness residing in a not quite solid doppelganger that floated away to one side of his physical form. He was able to observe his own body from a position several feet away as it began to spasm laterally, eyes open but vacant and oscillating violently. Still vital but uncontrolled, his body fell from the chair and a shocked Guillaume thrust his own chair away and knelt beside it, trying to press a fold of his belt between its clenching teeth.

As the elder Monte-Jaune began to shout for aide, Everett began to wonder if he were dying.

Magic appeared in front of him. "No, you are not dead. You are only suffering a seizure."

"Is this your doing?" he demanded heatedly.

"Not directly, no."

"What does that mean?"

Sarah, sprinting, passed disconcertingly through Magic's mirage and forestalled her response for a few seconds. When the young woman reached his body, she dropped and grabbed its flailing arms and tried to keep them from striking the rough flagstones.

"I need to ask you to remain calm, Everett," Magic told him with mild reproach. "There is no need to shout."

"I'm not shouting!" He thrust a finger at the anxious group that had collected around his body. *"If I was shouting, then they could hear me!"*

Magic squinted her eyes in a put-upon way and disappeared.

Everett fumed silently for a few seconds, then said, "Oh, for Magic's sake! Fine, I'll calm down."

Magic reappeared. "Good. Despite our trials, we should always strive to be civil."

Everett grumbled a barely audible reply.

"What's that?"

"I said, I seem to be the only one enduring trials."

"That sounds a bit petty, Everett."

"But true. Are you going to explain what's going on?"

"No shouting?"

Frowning, he promised, "I'll restrain myself."

"Very well. What you are experiencing is the first unmanifestation in human history."

"The first *what*?"

"Perhaps we should call it an *ex*piration? Does that sound better?"

"Wait a minute! Am I losing a spell?"

Magic pursed her lips. "Unfortunately, yes."

He sighed. "All right, why?"

"It is a combination of factors, really. As you must know, your last few manifestations have drastically exceeded the normally assigned compliment of spells. The thirteen spell limit is not just a random number that I pulled off the top of my head, but a factor of the ability of the human mind to channel the power of magic. Every spell requires a certain quantity of, well, *magical capacity*, for lack of a better term. As does every human, you have a finite magical capacity and any spell that requires more capacity than you have available would eventually be forced to un-manifest."

"So, after my sixteenth spell is gone, will I be back in equilibrium, or whatever?"

"Not exactly."

"What then?"

Everett's ethereal self began to drift back toward his body. He made frantic swimming motions, but these had no affect.

"Your seizure is about over, Everett," Magic informed him rapidly. "We'll finish our talk during the next one."

"Next one?"

Everett opened his eyes and moaned as his head suddenly exploded in pain. He felt the cold, hard stone against his back and knew that he was back in his body.

Sarah's voice drew his attention to her face. "Everett! Can you speak? Do you understand me?"

He croaked something inarticulate. He felt entirely drained, as if all strength had been sucked from his body.

Sarah's expression was grave, her worry clear. "If you understand me, nod your head."

He moved his head, not exactly a nod.

"Have you had a seizure before?"

He managed the barest whisper. "No."

"Could you have been poisoned?"

"No. Magic."

"You were attacked by a spell?"

"No. Lost one."

Then the second seizure struck. Again, his essence separated from his body and he had to watch helplessly as uncontrolled movements wrung his flesh. The only solace that he had was that he no longer felt the agony that his physical self endured.

An instant later, when Magic's mirage came into existence, he pounced immediately. "Why are you taking my spells away?"

"Because I have no choice. To put it in human terms, Technology has filed a grievance with an oversight committee and I have had to submit to binding arbitration. The ruling found that artificially overloading you with spells gave you an unfair advantage in the contest. The description that Technology used was 'invincible', though that's clearly not the case. In order to avoid ceding more important elements, I had to agree to reduce you to the normal compliment."

"So I keep thirteen?"

"For now, yes."

"So I *am* going to lose others?"

"I cannot say."

"Why not?"

"The ruling also found that sharing noncorporeal communal knowledge with you was also unfair. The good thing is that this also applies to Technology's corporal extension. He cannot share communal knowledge with his evil minions."

"The phrase 'evil minions' is somewhat trite, you know."

"I know, but I don't care. ' Evil Minions' has such a malevolent resonance all of its own."

"If you say so. So I've lost the second time spell and the future vision spell. Next, I'll also lose the first time spell?"

"Yes, and, happily, you'll be unconscious for that one."

Everett grunted. "Thanks a lot."

"Not my doing. The three closely spaced seizures caused by the un-manifestations will almost exhaust the energy in your brain and place you on the verge of death."

Once again, Everett began to drift back towards his body.

"One last thing," Magic added matter-of-factly. "I know all about the deal that Technology offered you. Do not betray me, Everett. If you do, I promise that you will regret it."

TWENTY-SEVEN

"Just one more bite," Sarah insisted. She pushed the spoon of broth into Everett's mouth.

"Mmmprh mwoh wmrr."

"What?" she asked as she pulled out the utensil.

"I said, 'I'm full.'"

"You've eaten hardly half of the broth. You need to eat more."

"I will later."

"If you don't eat, you won't regain your strength."

"Yes, mother," he teased.

Sarah tensed and instead of the witty riposte that he expected, she stood up. "You're tired. I'll let you rest."

"Wait, I'm sorry. Did I say something to offend you?"

Sarah hesitated and then slowly sat down again into the chair next to his bed. Drawing a large breath, she placed her hands on her knees and straightened her arms to raise her shoulders in a tension abating stretch. "No. It's fine."

He offered an encouraging smile but did not press. The morning sun, flooding through the open balcony doors, surrounded her with warm yellow light and he felt enraptured all over again.

She pressed her lips into a thin line. "My mother died of child bed fever after Joseph was born. As the oldest, I had to be more or less a substitute mother for my brothers and sisters. That's why they all call me Sister."

Then Everett finally understood her overriding imperative to return to Kleinsvench. The marriage had been simply a convenient, less personal excuse.

"Uhm--"

"I thought we decided that you weren't going to say 'uhm' any more?" she snapped. Then she relaxed and laughed when she saw his grin. "Well, if you're strong enough to joke, then you're strong enough to be by yourself for a while. I'm going to help Joseph study his lessons."

"That would be fine. I feel like a nap anyway."

As soon as she had left his room, pulling the large paneled door closed behind her, he threw back the quilt tucked up to his waist and swung his bare legs onto the floor. It had been two days since the seizures and he could not afford to waste any more time. A wave of transitory vertigo made him pause, but as soon as it had passed, he stood up.

"Give me strength!" The actuation came tardily, perhaps two seconds later, rather than instantly as it always had previously. He wondered at that but dismissed it as beyond his control.

After searching the room, he found his jacket, shirt and trousers hanging neatly in the armoire in the corner between the door and the balcony. He checked the pockets of his jacket to make sure everything was still there, dressed quickly, and went out onto the balcony. His room was just off the Monte-Jaune apartments and also faced out to the east, the height giving him a broad view of the city and its agricultural environs. Washed in the warm hues of the morning sun, the multi-colored roofs of the eastern half of Kleinsvench spread out before him. Though he could not see Mindelsen's shop, he felt sure that he could locate it once airborne.

Recognizing the possibility that he may have suffered some permanent brain injury and that therefore his spells may have been somehow debilitated, he decided against bounding away immediately. He should prove his magic by experiment first, lest he find himself a thousand feet in the air with no spell to stand on.

"Take ye flight!"

As before, the magic actuated immediately and with some relief, he felt the familiar sensation of floating as he rose slightly above the balcony. Reassured, he enunciated his strength again and leapt away.

He misjudged the timing of the final cast of his flight spell, landed with a heavy jolt, and had to shift his feet quickly to regain his balance. Trying to be as inconspicuous as possible, he had alighted in an alley just down from the shop, but as he walked out into the street, he realized that he should not have bothered. There was nary a soul in sight; apparently, a good many more of the citizens had left.

Monsieur Mindelsen's shop remained open for business, however, and the bell again jangled when he entered. Sipping a mug of something that smelled cidery, the apothecary smiled when he saw Everett.

"I am glad to see you up and about, Monsieur Wizard. You looked quite ill when I saw you at the castle."

"Just something I ate, I'm sure. I've come to settle my bill."

"Oh, no need. There will be no charge for the analgesics. Just consider it my contribution to the war effort."

"Thank you, but it's about the commission that I've come."

"Ah, I see. Well, I did tell you that it would be several days and I am unfortunately still in the process of gathering the ingredients, which will likely take a considerable time longer. Some of my regular suppliers have closed for the duration. Also, strong rumors have reached the city that the Zherians have crossed the border in the east and prices have begun to rise dramatically. I am afraid that I must tell you that my quote will, sadly, be terribly short."

"I understand completely." Everett stepped to the counter and put ten gold Alarsarian deca-crowns, one after another, in a line on the marble top. "I believe this should cover it."

The apothecary's eyes grew large; each of the fat yellow coins was equal to one thousand silver. He picked one up and held it up to a lamp suspended from the ceiling so that light sparkled from its pristine surface.

"Where in the world did you get these? I had thought that the Royal Treasury had taken them all out of circulation two years ago when they began issuing the new banknotes."

"Wizards have resources."

Mindelsen gave him a hard look as he placed the gold coin back on the counter exactly in the spot from which he had taken it. "This you have already proven to me. However, before I accept this money, I must also tell you that it is in all likelihood impossible that I will be able to concoct the medicinal potion under the time constraints that you have mentioned. As I warned you, most of the ingredients are rare compounds produced in distant locales. In particular, I have learned that one of the acids and an herbal distillate cannot be obtained locally for any price. I will need to write to a trade factor in New Zindersberg to negotiate the acquisition of those two. Even were you to magic the letters back and forth as you did before, it is likely to take months for the factor to find a source for the ingredients and as much as three months for normal freight methods to bring them here."

Everett reached into the pocket of his jacket and removed a small, wax-sealed tin and a green glass bottle with a stopper covered by copper foil. He set the two on the counter next to the coins.

"Luckily," Everett told the man without expression, "I anticipated this problem."

Mindelsen picked up each in turn, examined its label briefly, and returned it to the counter. "Monsieur Wizard, no offense intended, but prior to meeting you, my impression of magic was rather low, as it never seemed quite to measure up. Now, however, I am beginning to wonder if there is anything that it cannot accomplish."

"You mean you thought that magic was crap?"

Mindelsen chuckled. "Yes, that would be an accurate statement."

"It's true. Believe me, I should know."

"Yes, I suppose you should. In any event, I will get to work immediately. The potion will be ready day after tomorrow and the rest two days later. If any further delays arise, I will send word to the castle at once."

Everett thanked the apothecary and began to turn about to leave when he had a thought concerning one of the preparations that he had not been able to complete. "Monsieur Mindelsen, might you know if there's a gunsmith in Kleinsvench?"

The older man's face betrayed no comment. "There is one, a Monsieur Von Gylg over on Persimmon Street – three blocks north, four to the east, turn right at the intersection, third building on the right -- though he may have already gone to visit his relatives like a lot of folks."

"Visit his relatives?"

"Kleinsvench is no more than thirty miles from the front. It would not take much of an advance by the Zherians to place the city within range of their big guns."

"Right. If you don't mind my asking, why haven't you 'gone to visit relatives?'"

"If the fighting does reach the city, then my potions and salves will be required to treat the wounded. Besides, I cannot stand any of my relatives for longer than fifteen minutes."

Everett smiled humorlessly, nodded a goodbye, and left. Walking along quiet streets lined with darkened buildings, he found Persimmon easily enough and the shop of the middle-aged Monsieur Von Gylg without mishap. This last was mainly due to the fact that the gunsmith, along with three younger men who were obviously sons, was in the process of emptying his equipment from his sturdily timbered shop into a large wagon drawn up in the center of the otherwise vacant street.

Everett walked up to the older man, who watched him approach with little interest. The gunsmith was built like any man who had had to work steel for a living: strong, broad, and hard. He looked to weigh an easy eighteen stone, and not an ounce of that fat. Dressed in heavy cotton work clothes, he wore his fading blond hair long in a single ponytail. Distinctively, he had a tattoo of a serpent on his left forearm, with its tail wrapped around his thickly muscled forearm and its toothed jaws jutting along the first two fingers of his hand.

"Good morning, Monsieur Von Gylg," Everett began. "My name is Everett de Schael and I was told that you're a gunsmith."

The man started shaking his head before Everett had finished. "If you're looking for pistols or rifles, I've none to sell. The coming war has everyone running scared and I've sold nearly a hundred long guns and nearly as many side arms in the last month. I'm also out of cartridges. What little stock I've left will be kept for our own use."

The sons finished loading a long crate and then moved up behind their father, their stances clearly indicating that they were entirely ready to defend against any threat. Save for the tattoo, they were, one and all, simply younger and taller copies of the gunsmith.

Everett smiled his best harmless smile. "Actually, I've come to commission several metal devices. I can pay in advance and in gold."

Von Gylg shook his head again. "Sorry, son, I can't help you. We're packing up to move down into the Kingdom, other side of the Canal. The Alarsarians may not hold the border, but they're sure to hold the line of the Canal with the Green and Black rivers on their flanks. All of my tools are already loaded and you caught me just as I was about to lock up the shop."

"I could also offer quick transportation south," Everett proposed. "I could move the entire wagon, horses and all, to wherever you wanted to go."

"Eh, I thought I recognized you. You're that new wizard."

"That's right."

"I'd heard that you'd had some sort of fit?"

"Just a bad bit of meat, I'd imagine. What's your destination?"

Yet a third time, the gunsmith shook his head. "Thanks all the same, but I'd rather trust my horse team to get us where we need to be. I can't say as I've seen much in my life that honest work and sweat couldn't do better than magic."

"I'd mostly have to agree with you on that, but I do know that there are a few things that magic can accomplish that honest work can't."

The gunsmith barked a half-amused disbelieving grunt. "Oh, is that so? What might that be then?"

"Foresee the future, for one."

"Any man with good sense can figure out which way the wind is blowing," Von Gylg contradicted. "I don't need magic to tell me that right now the wind is blowing war, the extra nasty kind that chews up lives and spits out nothing but dust. I'm going to get my family and my business as far from it as I can."

Everett took a deep breath. "A spell has revealed to me a good bit more than that. By mid-afternoon today, the Republican forces will take the main Black River bridge at Braenbrakburn. By tomorrow night, they will overrun Morrison and drive on for the bridge at Szoerh and cross the

Green. Their plan is to encircle the main Alliance armies north of here by linking up with another thrust that is coming down from the west."

"Did you say *Morrison?*" one of the sons pressed with sudden intensity.

Everett nodded.

"Even if the Zheries have crossed the border in the east, there's no way they could reach Braenbrakburn," a second, standing to the left of his father, scoffed. "The city is nearly a hundred miles south of the border."

"Both of you, be quiet!" Von Gylg ordered, silencing the sons. He eyed Everett coolly. "All right, wizard, I'll need proof of what you say."

"I can take you to see the Republican forces. We can be there in an hour."

It took little more than forty-five minutes, and Von Gylg, cradled in Everett's magically strengthened arms like a babe, endured the trip without comment. The gruff tradesman showed neither fear nor excitement during the great leaps that carried them across miles-wide stretches of the occasionally forested countryside. When they landed on the crest of a tall, grassy hill about a mile from the new suspension bridge across the wide and muddy Black, he simply made a huffing sound at the sight of the dark clouds of smoke rising from Braenbrakburn. The city had clearly been heavily shelled; blast damage was visible throughout and much of the southern section burned. A thin, unfinished defensive line dug in across the main road along the Braenbrakburn side of the river also displayed the pockmarked craters of a heavy artillery barrage, but any defenders had long since withdrawn. A large force of Republican infantry rested within a few hundred yards of the eastern side of the city and some fighting, evidenced by occasional gun flashes, seemed to be taking place in the western fringe, but no major Alarsarian resistance remained.

As the first of the Zherian steam-mobile artillery began to roll across the bridge from the east, the gunsmith turned a grim face to Everett. "What are those?"

"Armored steam-mobile artillery. They're the spearhead of the Zherian invasion and also act as transports for the infantry. They can make twenty miles an hour across hard level ground. The device that I want you to make may be able to stop them."

Von Gylg pressed the heels of his hands against his forehead and raked his fingers back though his hair in a gesture meant to relieve pain. "All right, wizard, I've seen enough. Name your price."

Everett gave the gunsmith an odd look, confused. "Sorry, there seems to be some sort of misunderstanding. I meant that I wanted to commission you to create the metal components that I need."

The gunsmith tucked back one corner of his mouth in a sour grimace. "My wife, daughters-in-laws, and grandchildren are all in Morrison. We thought they'd be safer there and sent them off weeks ago. I want you to fetch them back to Kleinsvench. I'll do anything you ask in return."

TWENTY-EIGHT

Everett lowered the long freight wagon gently to the street. Immediately, Von Gylg dropped the tailgate and called for his sons to help the women and children from the bed. Some of the younger children began crying anew but the older ones had accepted the long, bouncing trip from Morrison as a wondrous adventure and began regaling their fathers with contradictory and boisterous reports of the journey. Their mothers and grandmother dismounted stoically, displaying the strained demeanor of those whose lives had been repeated upended by the calamity of war. Their reactions to the appearance of the gunsmith and wizard on the doorstep of the rented house in Morrison had ranged from weary acceptance to annoyance, but all had readily accepted the elder Von Gylg's curt instructions to pack and had quickly loaded both travel garbed progeny and household goods aboard the borrowed wagon with efficiency and alacrity.

As children carrying hand baggage and parcels were herded into the gunsmith's shop, Von Gylg presented his hand with solemn dignity to Everett, who shook it firmly and gratefully.

"Thank you, Monsieur Wizard. I'll start tonight on the launch tubes and trigger mechanisms. My sons will fabricate the shafts for the propellants and the shells for the heads and should have the first hundred in just a few days. When will the propellant and explosive charges be ready?"

"I'd think that Mindelsen should have some for testing by tomorrow or the next day."

"That will work. I'd like to be present when you begin your tests."

"Sure."

"I'd also like to accompany you when you put them to use."

Everett hesitated.

"I mean no insult, but it seems to me that one man can't do much without someone to watch his back, even if he is a great wizard."

"You should stay to watch over your family."

"My sons will do that. I'm fifty-one years old and I've reached a place in my life where I tend to do exactly what I want. In this case, what I want to do is to make sure that none of those Zherian mechanisms get within shelling range of Kleinsvench."

Everett nodded. "Right. Very well then. I'll come for you when it's time."

It was quite nearly dusk when Everett began the long walk up the approach road to the castle. Feeling the need to stretch his legs after the frenetic day, he had decided to neglect his spells. He had begun to suspect that the seductive convenience of his new magic was actually something of a wearing, difficult burden and he looked forward to the simple pleasure of an unhurried stroll. As he made his way along the still sun-warmed cobbles, he found a quiet comfort in the peacefulness of the nearly emptied city. Having grown up on his father's orchard-covered rural hillsides and spent much of his youth ensconced in the soft-spoken solitude of monastic schools, he had always found the raucous eruption that was urban life somewhat daunting.

He winced as a piercing pain stabbed his hip and limped another step before he could lengthen his stride to override the discomfort. Nagging aches and pains had developed in his knees and hips, and he thought the culprit to be the extensive period that he had spent in interrupted time before Magic had taken the spell away. Hopefully, the precautions he had taken to achieve an acceptable future would prove worth the cost.

He was within sight of the Snake Gate and the almost time eradicated giant serpent carving that gave it its name when the seizure struck. He collapsed immediately to the pavement, arms and legs jangling. As before, his connection to his physical body severed and his awareness separated from his convulsing form.

Magic appeared to him within seconds. "Good

evening, Everett!"

He eyed her sourly. "Which spell am I losing this time?"

"The *sound-like-a-strangling-cat-overlaid-with-the-screech-of-a-stomped-rat* spell. The one you call 'Doomsday.' It does not properly belong at this spatial-temporal juncture anyway and utilizes basic forces that ought not be accessed in this universe. Also, in strength, it ranks above Potent and therefore should be ranked a Suprapotent, a category of spells which humans of this era are not yet competent to wield. Because of the immediacy of the moment, I manifested it to you on the fly simply because it was available in an underutilized queue. But no need to worry; I am only taking that one to make room for a potential future manifestation. I want to hedge my bets when you face Technology's corporeal biologic."

"Well, *thank you,*" he cracked insincerely, "but I don't intend to do that. It's no longer necessary."

Magic displayed a suspicious frown, with the shades of thunderclouds in her eyes warning of a storm to come. "Oh?"

"Sarah is no longer in danger and I've come up with a way to prevent a Republican victory."

"Oh?" Magic repeated, not encouragingly. "What have you been up to Everett?"

Everett blinked virtually. This was an interesting development. "You haven't been keeping me under observation?"

Magic pursed her lips. "Your moment to moment life is not contained within my scope."

"Then how do you find me when you want to speak to me or manifest spells?"

"Targeting individuals for manifestation – or unmanifestation – is an essential element of my scope, so I intrinsically know where you are at those times."

"And otherwise? From what you've told me before, I had thought that you knew everything that there was to know about me. You know: omniscient, omnipotent, omnipresent."

"Noncorporeal sentient entities are not infallible deities, Everett. Under normal circumstances, the fate of all humans in this universe is the purview of Destiny and this predictive information is available to all noncorporeals through our link of communal knowledge."

Everett made an intuitive leap. "Destiny hasn't been watching me so you don't know what I've been doing."

"So what *have* you been doing?"

"Yes, do tell us, Everett," Technology chimed in. "What have you been doing?"

Magic made an exaggerated face and then utterly astounded Everett by sharing a friendly hug with her rival's simulacrum.

"Hold on!" Everett demanded. "What's going on?"

"Sorry, what do you mean?" Magic inquired sweetly.

"Well, aren't the two of you eon's long hated adversaries bent on the total and utter destruction of the other?"

"Why, who gave you that idea, Everett?" Magic demanded.

"As a matter of fact, you two did."

"Nonsense," Technology interjected. "All noncorporeals share an intimate and all-encompassing communal bond. Any conflict that you might perceive from your limited perspective is entirely a flawed transference of physical realm conventions."

"That's crap. Complete and utter crap."

"There is no need to get snippy, Everett." Magic rebuked.

"Oh, I disagree. In fact, both of you can get lost."

"Am I to take that as a rejection of my proposal?" Technology inquired.

"Without a doubt."

"Very well." Technology disappeared.

Magic smiled. "Excellently done, Everett. Technology can be such a bore. Now, back to what I was saying--"

"That's enough. I'm done with you too."

"Sorry, I am not sure that I understand your meaning."

"Go away. Leave me alone. Don't come back."

Magic's expression went blank. "Are you certain that this is what you want, Everett?"

"This is *exactly* what I want."

Magic's face remained unreadable. "Fine. So be it.

From this point forward, I will not involve myself directly in your travails. However, I am constrained to relay two key facts. One: there is an unavoidable inertia to human events and only great forces can disturb them from their appointed path. Two: with the proper lever and a place to stand, a single person can move the earth."

And then she was gone.

"*Wait!* What in the world does that mean?"

Gratefully, only silence answered.

Within scarce moments, he rejoined his own body, waking to thudding agony in his head and a painful pressure from swelling in his profusely bleeding nose. He had smashed it when he had fallen and the rest of his body felt as if he had also managed to bruise or scrape the majority of the protruding bits. He prodded a loose incisor with his tongue. The seizure must have banged his face against the pavement, dislodging the tooth. His left knee resisted movement, sending sharp jolts up his leg as he tried to flex it and his right elbow had grown to twice its normal size. Taking care to protect both, he rolled onto his back, tried to gather the strength to rise, had little success, and got up anyway. Swaying and swept by a surge of giddiness, he doubled over and retched green bile on the cobbles.

The light was rapidly fading and within moments he would not be able to see a thing. He held an internal debate for a moment and decided that he did not feel solid enough to finish the hike on into the castle. He cast about for a likely refuge and hobbled to the stoop of a house crowded between a boarded up chandlery and a featureless brick edifice. Covered with sea green paint that showed slight signs of peeling, the large, otherwise plain door appeared imposingly solid, but he doubted that it could resist his tenth spell. He tried the knob. To his surprise, it turned easily and he took a step into a darkened, vaulted entrance hall. Though the meager emerging starlight did little to relieve the deepening gloom, he left the door open. Practically blind, he took a few more tentative steps, shuffling his feet to search for trip hazards. The scuff of his leather boots on the tile floor echoed with the slight ring of sound bouncing off plaster walls.

He wished for a moment that he had Artie's light spell

and then morosely pondered what had become of the other members of the Provisional Magicker Company. It seemed unlikely that he would ever know.

Wanting something to drink and thinking to try to discover a kitchen or dinning room, he edged forward, unable to make out much other than indistinct black shapes. He bumped into something with his leg, ran his hands along polished wood filigree and identified it as a table, and sidled around it to the left with the fingers of his right hand trailing along its satiny top as a guide. His fingers encountered sold, cold metal and a moment's investigation proved the object to be a heavy candlestick and candle.

He grunted. Of course, he did not have a single match.

Even with all of the power that his recent manifestations had brought him, he still found himself in situations where his magic was useless to solve his problems.

Of course, if Sarah were with him, lighting the candle would be no problem.

Well, why not?

"Beautiful Woman, come forth!"

He felt the actuation and a breath of expanding air crossed his face. He sensed her presence, though he could not see her at all.

"You know, Everett, I think that we're going to have to establish some ground rules for your spell," her voice scolded from a pace just before him. "I was just about to sit down for supper." She did not, however, sound upset or bothered.

"Sorry. I needed a light. There's a candle on the table here by me."

He detected the movement of a darker shadow and her hand touched his shoulder. "Put it in my hand."

He did so.

"Flammables, ignite anon!"

Light flared from the wick and she returned the candlestick to the table, setting it down in the dust shadow that marked its original position, a clear decision to return it to its proper place. She glanced around.

"Where are we...what happened to you?"

"I lost another spell."

"For Magic's sake, you look terrible!"

"Thanks."

She took his face in her hands and critically examined his scrapes. "Why didn't you transport me right away? We could've transported back immediately."

"The option did not occur to me."

She released him. "Honestly, Everett, it seems to me that sometimes you blind yourself to what you can do with your magic."

"That's because my magic, unlike yours, is often of no use."

She gave him a hard look. "No, only magicians are limited, not magic."

Feeling a fresh onslaught of thirst, grinding fatigue, and the aches that seemed to vibrate from every portion of his body, he undeniably did not feel like arguing the point. "I wonder if there's anything around here to drink?"

"A glass of milk, please!" Within seconds of her cast, a filled crystal mug appeared on the table, its exterior frosting over instantly.

When he looked in askance at her, she replied simply, "It's my second spell. Wondrously practical in the middle of the night when you don't want to wake anyone."

The mug was just the size for a child. He laced three fingers through the handle and picked it up.

"It's cold!"

"That's the way I prefer milk. Almost freezing. In the winter, before breakfast, my mother would set the pitcher out on the window sill."

He drank it all in one swallow. The cold, flavorful milk washed the dryness from his throat but did not completely quench his thirst. Prescient, Sarah cast the spell five more times, lining up a row of small mugs and he drank them in succession, only savoring the last.

"Thanks," he told her as he put the final empty mug on the table.

"You know you can always depend on me, Everett. Do you want to try to transport back now?"

"Not up to it. I think that I'll just find a bed here."

"All right." She picked up the candlestick. "Let's look upstairs."

Upstairs proved to be a balcony around the entrance hall with four closed doors. Sarah opened the first and swung the candle to reveal a neatly appointed bedroom with a large bed, side tables, bureau, and settee. A colorful comforter with a fold at the head outlining pillows covered the bed. Other items in the room also had the semblance of normalcy.

"Looks like the owners expect to return," he commented with a voice that had the energy of a corpse, gravitating toward the bed. There was a slight patina of dust on the comforter, but when he threw it back, the sheets and pillows beneath looked freshly laundered. He sat down and began removing his boots.

She raised the globe of a lamp on a side table, tilted the candle to light it, and then moved toward the door. "I'll be right back."

Heedless, he lay back without bothering to pull off his socks and let his eyes close.

A noise startled him wake. Sarah had returned. The lamp revealed her to be carrying a tray with a quarter-round of yellow cheese, a jar of jam, a bowl of walnuts, a basin of water, and a washcloth. Incongruously, she was now wearing a floral print robe that clung to her curves.

"This is all that I could find."

"I don't feel like eating," he grumped.

She smiled slightly as she put the tray beside the lamp. "You might later."

She shooed him over and as soon as he had wiggled across to make room, she settled on the bed with care, then took up the washcloth, dampened it and began to tenderly wash his face.

"I wish that you would just let me go back to sleep."

She ignored him, finished cleaning the dried blood from his face, unbuttoned his shirt, and started to wash his neck and chest.

"All this isn't necessary," he complained again.

"Of course it is," she contradicted, and, apparently satisfied with the state of his toilet, dropped the soiled cloth onto the table as she stood up again.

"I promised you festivities, Everett, and, frankly, I'm in the mood for some myself."

She dropped the robe. She wore nothing underneath.

He stopped her as she moved to rejoin him on the bed. "Wait. One thing I need to know."

"What's that?"

"Did you use magic when we first met to make me … *interested* in you?"

Laughing quietly as she sank down beside him, she shook her head. "No, Everett, you're a man. A woman doesn't need magic to *interest* a man."

TWENTY-NINE

The basal thud of the first explosion shook Everett awake. He had only seconds to try to gather his wits when the bells of the Residence watchtower began a frantic pealing.

Now also awakened, Sarah shifted slightly and began, "Everett, what's --?"

The second explosion smashed through the house, crumpling walls, overturning the bed, and dumping the two of them to the floor in a tangle of limbs and bedclothes. The third made the floor heave and buckle and showered them with plaster and splinters.

"Give me strength!" Everett shouted, surging to his feet as a fourth explosion collapsed the room around them. He bowed his back and spread his arms to protect Sarah as snapped roof beams, sections of roof tile, masonry blocks, and other massive debris rained down. He felt jarring blows as the rubble struck but suffered no harm.

After a pause of no more than ten seconds, other explosions continued, but occurred beyond the wreckage of the house, the staccato booms moving off toward the south. Within seconds, the remains of the house had settled into a snarled mass around them and become still.

He shrugged his shoulders and straightened, throwing off broken wood and brick and forcing open a clear space around Sarah. Burgeoning fires lit the ruins with yellow, flickering light.

"Are you hurt?" he demanded as she stood shakily, pulling a sheet from under the remains of the bed and wrapping it around herself as an abbreviated dress that left arms and legs bare.

"No, I'm all right. I don't know how the Republicans were able to get close enough to the city to shell it, but we must return to the Residence immediately."

"It's not artillery," he countered. "Listen."

Sarah cocked an ear. High above in the distance, the fluttering sound of oil fueled engines was unmistakable. *"The air carriage!"*

Using the denuded lathe and decapitated studs of a section of canted wall for handholds, she scrambled up onto a sagging segment of roof for a better view. After taking the practical precaution of digging around to find his trousers, shirt, and boots and pulling them on, he followed her up to her perch into the open.

Fires and damaged buildings stretched out in a line for half a mile across the hill and down into the lower part of the city, cutting across streets and neighborhoods like a furrow. A few lights had begun to appear in various places, but most of the remainder of Kleinsvench remained dark and at rest. The sinister sounds of crackling wood drew his eyes around. Behind them, toward the front of the house, one of the blazes had begun to spread. The house would be engulfed in moments. He swung back toward the sound of the motors.

The dark mass of the air carriage could be made out easily against the star filled sky. No light shown from it, but occasional glints of the fires left in its wake reflected from its windows. It flew fairly low over the city, perhaps no more than two thousand feet, and as they watched, it started a ponderous turn.

"It's coming back," he warned. "We had better get out of here."

"No! Transport us up there, Everett! It's attacking the city and we need to stop it!"

He did not bother trying to argue; in any event, they could not stay here. He caught her around the waist as she hugged him tight, selected a locus on the barely perceived Observation Deck, and cast in rapid succession, *"Give me strength! Take ye flight! Beautiful Woman, come forth!"*

In pitch darkness, they appeared on the air carriage floating slightly above the deck. A chair, knocked aside by their arrival, clattered noisily across the flooring. In front of them toward the bow rail, a wedge of weak light flared at the sound and a vague figure began shouting as it rushed at them, its light jumping and jerking irregularly.

Everett released Sarah and braced to receive the attack.

"Good night and sweet dreams!" Sarah hissed.

Their would-be assailant dropped instantly and skidded a few feet from the force of his momentum. The light, clearly some sort of mechanism, bounced and rolled against the starboard rail kick plate, but did not go out. Everett swiftly knelt by the awkwardly sprawled, gently snoring man, rolled him over, and then pried a wicked looking boarding cutlass from his grip. Running his hands along a cartridge belt at the man's waist, he also found a pistol in a holster and quickly appropriated it while Sarah retrieved the light, a fat cylinder of glass and copper with shutters blocking three sides, and brought it close.

"*Esatis.*" She condemned disgustedly when the red of the man's jacket became clear. She looked at the pistol and sword in Everett's hands. "What do you intend to do with those?"

He shrugged. Aside from hunting with long guns as a youth, he had had little experience with firearms. Reloading a standard, single shot pistol such as this with any speed required a good deal of practice. Likewise, he doubted that his only possible technique with the sword -- swinging it haphazardly like a machete -- could possibly be effective.

"I'm not sure. Can you put the entire air carriage to sleep like you did to the Alarsarians in Eriis?"

"I don't know. I'll try." A look of concentration settled across her face. *Good night dear Zherians and sweet dreams!*"

Nothing from below could be heard above the drone of the engines and the wind. "Did it work?" he asked her.

She frowned. "I don't think so, or not entirely. There was a gap in the actuation, or at least that's what it felt like, toward the bow. They must have heard the sentry and activated one of the magic canceling mechanisms."

"What's their range?"

"Six feet or so."

"If we get close to that, we'll be helpless."

"*I know that much better than you.*"

He ignored her pique. "Is the effect persistent?"

"No, they seem to have some sort of charge -- not an electric battery though -- and expire. The Esatis replaced the ones on my cage exactly on the half hour. From what the guards said, I had the impression that they were in short supply."

"Still, they're bound to have others aboard, so simply waiting it out wouldn't work."

"No. But we have to capture the air carriage or destroy it. Everett, we can't allow the Esatis to drop any more explosives on Kleinsvench. A lot of the buildings are vacant, but a good many are not, and none of them could withstand this sort of attack, even the Residence."

Everett did not respond immediately. This event had not been revealed by his exhaustive casting of his now revoked fifteenth spell. Clearly, some major element had changed and the future visions that he had sifted through were no longer valid. There was also no doubt that his and Sarah's magic could be easily and devastatingly nullified by the Zherian mechanisms. He could draw only a single conclusion from these facts: all of his preparations may have been for naught. Sarah was undoubtedly once more threatened.

And, with equal clarity, he realized that her presence on the air carriage placed her in immediate mortal danger.

He could not have that. He must send her to a place where absolutely no harm could come to her.

He strode abruptly to the rail, identified a locus on the easily recognizable dark mass of the castle off to the north, and then pivoted right away to face Sarah.

"Stay with your family. I'll take care of the air carriage."

Her brow lowered. "Everett, what are you --"

"Beautiful Woman, come forth!"

She vanished before her anger could fully blossom. The lamp vanished with her, throwing the Observation Deck once more into obscure shadow. Grunting at the oversight, he felt his way to the incapacitated Esati, stripped the cartridge belt from him, buckled it about his own waist, and dropped the pistol in the holster. The cutlass he gripped in his right hand, inexpertly or not, as he peered at the closed hatchway leading down into the air carriage.

He shied from the idea of simply destroying the vessel

outright; it was still the crowning achievement of technology and probably remained unique. Moreover, in the hands of the Grand Alliance, it would provide an invaluable advantage, if only in its ability to provide intelligence of enemy movements. It could prove to be the key element in the defeat of the Republic.

The option of dropping through the hatch into the midst of a potential unpleasant reception from the air carriage's crew immediately declared itself a bad idea. He went back to the port rail and looked over the side. All of the small windows along that side remained dark. The hatch was only a few feet down. He tucked the cutlass through the cartridge belt and vaulted the side, keeping a hold on the rail. *"Take ye flight!"*

Slightly anxious, he cast the spell continually as he eased himself down within reach of the latch, at last hanging by one hand from the platted rattan kick plate. Hovering while buffeted by the wind and keenly conscious of the blurrily spinning engine vane only ten feet aft, he tried the handle. As expected, it was locked.

"Give me strength!"

Trying to make as little noise as possible, he pried open the lip of the hatch with his free hand. The lightweight bolt twisted from the jamb and as soon as the hatch popped open, he slipped inside, pulling it closed behind him. The corridor was dark, but apparently empty. The twisted frame of the hatch kept it from sealing and the sound of the air coming through the gap was surprisingly loud. Afraid that he had already given himself away, he stalked toward the bow, drawing the cutlass. Though some weak light came through the portholes, the pools of wane illumination provided only indistinct points of reference and he felt compelled to use his free hand as a guide along the outer wall.

At the first cross-corridor, he encountered another Esati, slumped against the base of the crosswise bulkhead; Sarah's spell had been at least partially effective. He stepped over the slumbering man and continued. He made it to the second cross-corridor without mishap, paused a moment, and continued. He paused again as he approached the control compartment and listened forward. Over the normal sounds of the vessel, he heard nothing.

Might Sarah have been wrong and her spell have taken effect on the entire crew?

He eased forward into the control compartment.

A knife switch closed with an arc flash and all of the lights came on, their intensity overloading his vision for a moment.

Mitchell, outfitted in full Esati uniform, charged at him from the right, his own cutlass slashing down.

Everett threw up his sword, managed to block the mechanic's first blow with a jarring *clang!*, but could not intercept the second, which bit deeply into his left bicep.

"Give me strength!" he cried.

No surge of power came as Mitchell continued to hack at him with unswerving intensity. Parrying desperately, Everett caught sight of one of the magic canceling mechanisms hanging from a snap on the breast of the young Esati's jacket.

"We expected you to attack the air carriage," Edwin announced, making his presence known. The chemist had leveraged his bulk into a swivel chair that had been added beside the control consol, a good dozen feet across the compartment. Rather than the bright red Esati uniform, Edwin wore a smartly cut tunic and trousers in midnight black that was surprisingly devoid of badge or insignia. He did, however, also have a canceling mechanism attached with a piece of cord to a large brass button on his left breast pocket.

"In fact," Edwin continued breezily while Everett gave way before Mitchell's attack and found himself pinned against the exterior bulkhead, "since we could not be certain of your exact location in the city and because it seemed likely that magic would prevent any of the bombs from exploding near enough to kill you, we depended upon the predictability of your reaction to the raid in order to make your verifiable elimination possible."

An instant late with a parry, Everett took a slight cut to his left cheek and drew back in pain. With a predatory grin, Mitchell disengaged, took two steps away, made a flourishing salute with his blade, and then shifted his feet *en garde* in preparation for a lunge.

"Now," the chemist insisted. "If you would be so good

as to expire without delay."

Left handed, Everett drew his pistol and fired from the hip, aiming for the mechanism hanging from Mitchell's chest.

The bullet pierced the mechanism dead center, but did not strike Mitchell squarely. Nevertheless, the blow spun the mechanic around and he dropped his cutlass and fell to his knees, clutching at blood welling from a hole in his jacket over his left ribs. As his face went white, he groaned and fell over.

"Now, Everett," Edwin disapproved. "That would have to qualify as cheating." Without pause, the chemist jumped to his feet and flung a jar at the magicker.

"Give me strength!"

The glass of the jar was paper-thin and it shattered into fragments when it struck Everett's chest. A thick, translucent fluid splattered all over him and onto the wall and floor next to him. Where the fluid landed on the wood and metal, smoke and a burning smell immediately rose.

Where the fluid struck him, however, there was no effect whatsoever. It simply slithered and dribbled down his shirt, over the leather and metal of the cartridge belt and pistol, and along the cotton of his trousers without leaving any mark or stain. The draining fluid leaked onto the floor and instantaneously eroded holes in the thin metal. Electrical flashes and water spurted out the holes.

"Ah, of course the acid would not affect you," Edwin realized. "By default, your strength spell must give you invulnerability. How else would your bones and flesh endure the stress of the tremendous physical forces?" The chemist brought up a pistol. "Just for fun, let us see if this functions, shall we?"

Click!

Everett froze at the sound, but when no bullet roared from the gun, he realized a key detail: the magic canceling mechanisms must only prevent the *actuation* of a spell and therefore would have no effect on his two persistent spells.

Edwin laughed. "Apparently, in the current circumstances, we have an impasse. You're protected by your magic and I'm protected by my technology." Edwin tapped the canceling mechanism for emphasis.

Not taking his eyes off the chemist and moving slowly

so as not to fumble, Everett broke the breech of his pistol, fished a cartridge from his belt, and reloaded.

Edwin frowned. "And then again, perhaps not."

With a speed that belied his size, the chemist whirled around and slapped at levers on the console. The engines changed pitch suddenly and the air carriage yawed in a violent surge, throwing Everett off balance and causing his finger to constrict on the trigger. The weapon discharged and a hole starred the forward window beyond the chemist's right shoulder.

Edwin leapt toward Mitchell's cutlass.

He never made it across the compartment. In the next instant, the bow nosed down and the entire structure shook and began to warp and scream under strain. Seams in the floor plating split and water sloshed through from below. Everett caught the edge of a vertical hull strut and kept his feet as the deck angled but Edwin lost his footing and fell back. The lights flickered and then went out completely as shorts arced across the battery board. Flames flared from the wooden scales of the bulkhead behind it and roiled across the ceiling plates and girders, flooding the compartment with smoke.

THIRTY

Everett was choking within seconds. He punched a hole through the hull, broke out scales to widen it, hauled his head and shoulders through to gasp at the rushing air, and then heaved himself outward free of the air carriage.

"Take ye flight!"

He fell perhaps a hundred feet before the magic evinced. Dragging in deep breaths to clear his lungs, he swam around to look back up at the air carriage. Slowing as the engines sputtered and died, the stricken vessel had gained only thirty yards from him. Already, a yellow-green inferno engulfed the entire forward end; evidently, the shellac coated wooden scales of the hull were highly flammable. As he watched, soot topped greasy spurts of fire began to lick the underside of the vapor bags above the Observation Deck.

Dreading what was to come next, he threw a quick glance downward to gauge his altitude. He was at least a comfortable fifteen hundred feet above the buildings below. When his flight expired, he did not immediately recast it, knowing that he wanted to be as far as possible from the air carriage.

Three seconds later, the vapor bags began to explode and the conflagration spread faster than an eye blink to involve the entire vessel. A blast wave of heated air tumbled him into a spin.

"Give me strength!"

As flaming debris rocketed passed him tailing expanding lines of stinking smoke, he righted himself and once more looked down. The city and one unlit tile-roofed structure in particular hurtled towards him at an amazing rate. Counting, he had only reached four when he plunged through the building, caving in the roof and bursting through floors, finally coming to rest driven up to his elbows through the ground floor and into the soil beneath. Wasting no time, he dug himself out, recast his Potent spells and bounded up through the gaping hole that his passage had made.

The air carriage had disintegrated, scattering burning wreckage over a large swath of the southern half of Kleinsvench. Some of the debris had impacted on streets or commons and looked to be quickly burning out, but a majority had fallen on flammable structures and ignited hundreds of fires. These were spreading at an alarming rate. If something were not done quickly to douse them, the entire city would go up.

He came to earth on a broad avenue within yards of a café whose terrace awning had been set alight. He cast about for someway to extinguish the blaze but found nothing to suggest itself in the blank stoops of the houses and shuttered shop front windows.

A light came on in a house across the way and a man about fifty and wearing only trousers ran out and rushed to Everett. He thought he remembered the man from the potluck.

"Monsieur Wizard! What is happening? Are the Republicans attacking?"

"Yes, but I've brought down their air carriage, their flying mechanism. Tell me, is there a fire brigade in the city?"

"Yes! Or, I mean, there was when everyone was still here. I don't know if there are enough left to operate the pump wagons."

"Do you know where the wagons are?"

The man pointed west along the avenue. "There's a depot fifteen blocks that way. It's a large stone building with an iron barred gate instead of a door."

Everett cast and bounded away.

He was back within ten minutes, dragging a heavy iron pump wagon with full tanks. A younger man and a gray haired woman, also looking as if the disaster had inopportunely wrenched them from their beds, had joined the first man. All were in a general state of agitation as they watched the fire begin to spread to the interior of the café. The windows of the upper storey had already burst outward from the heat, scattering the pavement with glass that twinkled in the flickering firelight.

"Here, one of you unlash the hose and direct it toward the fire!" Everett urged.

Acting with alacrity, the younger man did so, opening the two-inch valve and dragging out thirty feet of hose. The other man and woman ran up to one side and laid into the reciprocal pump handle there. Their efforts barely budged the handle.

"It usually takes ten men to build up a decent pressure!" The older man shouted to Everett.

"Give me strength!" Everett took the opposite handle and began driving the pump at a pace that rocked the wagon. The other two volunteers, their handle snatched from their hands and snapping up and down at a speed that they could not possibly match, ran to help the younger man direct the hose toward the café as a solid stream shot from its end. Within a few moments, the café, what remained of it, had settled into a steaming, sodden mess.

After a few abrupt surges, the pressure in the hose relaxed and the stream fell off to an inconsistent dribble. The tanks had pumped dry.

"Where are the tanks refilled?" Everett demanded urgently.

"The municipal cisterns," the young man supplied, then shook his head. "This one pumper won't help much, though. Look!" He pointed beyond the roofs of the buildings behind Everett, causing the magicker to turn about.

Surging smoke and the glow of the fires that vomited it up were visible in half a dozen locations, some distant, but some uncomfortably close.

"Monsieur Wizard, have you no magic that will put out the fires?" the woman pled earnestly.

Everett started to shake his head, but then realized that he actually might. Without another word, he cast his strength and leapt straight upward.

Floating at five hundred feet under the power of his twelfth spell, he once again could see the scope of the disaster. The growing fires threatened entire blocks and neighborhoods. He chose a particularly virulent conflagration that involved upwards of a dozen buildings on two sides of a narrow lane and tried a gambit that contravened all the basic assumptions of his magical education. He did not choose a single target for the spell, but rather fixated on multiple locus points and enunciated, *"Manure, gather ye into a pile!"*

After twenty-three seconds, the spell actuated.

The smell was atrocious, a gut wrenching miasma that settled over the lane like an evil fog, but when the various slithering, flopping, and mucking crap had returned once more to its non-magically enlivened state, the fires along the lane had unconditionally surrendered, smothered by an unyielding semi-liquid blanket at least a span thick at every locus.

Some few hours later when dawn finally broke, Everett, exhausted beyond words, surveyed Kleinsvench from an aerial perch over the south-eastern quarter of the city and saw a metropolis whose sewers and compost heaps were somewhat the worse for his efforts but which had been spared a fire storm. While squelching the fires throughout the early hours of the morning, he had occasionally come across groups of citizens working with pump wagons and on three occasions, the bells had sounded from Mad Lydia's Folly, indicating that the Reserve Company worked to organize the firefighting effort. Twice, people waved him down and begged him to assist in the rescue of loved ones trapped in buildings damaged by the bombing or the explosion of the air carriage.

In the first instance, he succeeded in clearing an entrance into the basement of a demolished three-storey apartment and freeing a dozen people that were bedraggled but without serious injury.

In the second, when he used his strength to raise the collapsed roof beams and fallen stone walls of a once modest dwelling, it was to reveal only the lifeless, broken bodies of two adults and four children.

The sight of the sheet and blanket draped forms laid in a line on the sidewalk surrounded by shocked neighbors and weeping kin was one that he thought would never dim in his memory.

After that, he had taken out the time to fly over the shops of the apothecary, Mindelsen, and that of the gunsmith,

Von Gylg. Located far from the main area of destruction, both were undamaged and their surrounding environs totally unscathed by the attack. Lights were on in both, but he judged that no harm had come to either and that there seemed little chance that they would be immediately threatened. Relieved, he returned to his task.

Now, with the red rays of the emerging sun camouflaging the blemishes of char and filth in an otherwise undisturbed cityscape, he was finally free to return to Sarah. Thinking of how indignant she would be when she saw him again, he allowed himself an anemic moment of mirth as he counted down to the expiration of his flight Potent. At this point, the timing of his casts had become almost automatic and he renewed his flight inches from the brick paved median of a boulevard, cast his strength, and then leapt in a great sailing arc toward the north, aiming for the lower courtyard of the Residence, perhaps a mile and a half away.

At the apex of his flight, he had an extended view of the territory around Kleinsvench. Like all cities, the area immediately beyond the unwalled limits was agricultural: grain fields, dairies, ranches, and sheepfolds that supplied food to the urbanites. There were some low hills and patches of forest, a large lake and a draining watercourse to the west, numerous small streams and creeks, but much of the area was relatively flat and open.

It was the perfect terrain for the steam-mobile artillery mechanisms of the Republic.

As the Zherians evidently also understood, since a large squadron of the smoke belching mechanisms was only a few dozen miles from Kleinsvench and coming on at full steam. Their path was unswervingly straight as they crashed through hedges, overthrew stone walls, and ground dark brown trails into corn and bean fields; they had a single target and knew exactly its precise location.

THIRTY-ONE

Everett landed on the esplanade that wound around
the bluffs at the height of the crag, only a dozen steps from the
arched pull-rope gallery at the base of Mad Lydia's Folly.
Kyle and another member of the Reserve Company, a young
female cousin, were standing at the parapet along the rim of
the esplanade and gazing out over the city. Rushing up at
once, they flooded him with excited questions.

"No time for that!" he snapped brusquely, cutting them
off. "Is there a code to warn the city to flee an immanent
attack?"

"*General Alarm* is three long peals of every bell," Kyle
responded immediately. "*Retreat to the Castle* is six alternating
beats of the three bass bells with the three soprano bells."

"A continuous cycling of the codes means *Without
Delay*," the cousin added. "But we can't sound any of those
without help. The bells are so large that it takes two people to
ring even a single one!"

Everett threw back his head to eye the belfry high
above. "*Ding Dong!*"

His first spell, manifested when he could hardly speak
more than the babbling language of babes, had made the
bronze chimes hanging on the porches of his father's house
sound randomly for an hour. He had not cast the Insignificant
in more than twenty years.

Now he needed the great bells above to sound an alarm
that all in the city could hear and understand.

The first tone of the *General Alarm* shook Everett with
its volume and echoed across the city like the condemnation
of an angry god, causing Kyle and his cousin to wince and
cover their ears with their hands. Then, half as loudly but still
sufficient to deafen anyone within a hundred yards, the bass
and soprano bells rang in sequence.

When the cycle began again with only a three-second delay, Everett shouted at the other two, *"WHERE IS YOUR FATHER?"*

Both shook their heads as they mouthed words lost in the blast of sound; nothing could be heard over the bells.

Exasperated, Everett cast and bounded toward the Lower Ward. As he cleared the bulk of the main building, he searched ahead and sighted First Assemblyman Guillaume Monte-Jaune standing between the lines of sand bags with about twenty men and women of various ages, many of whom looked to be members of the Reserve Company. Everett readily recognized the stalwart Uncle Alec and some of his grown children. The entire wearied group had soot covering their clothes, hands, and faces and shouldered shovels and other implements, apparently having worked in the beleaguered city much of the night. As he descended, Everett saw that all had been gazing curiously toward Mad Lydia's Folly.

Almost simultaneously, Everett and the senior Monte-Jaune demanded of each other, "Where is Sarah?"

Everett made a grimace that matched the one that sprang to Guillaume's face. "She's not here in the castle?" he asked quickly.

"No, she disappeared before supper last evening -- we had assumed that you had summoned her to you for some magical task – and have not seen her since."

Everett's frown deepened. "I transported her back here just after the bombing. Could you have missed her in the commotion?"

"No, she would have followed our emergency plan and assembled in the armory with the rest of those living in the Residence."

With a sinking feeling, Everett chose a nearby locus and enunciated, *"Beautiful Woman, come forth!"*

As he had dreaded, Sarah failed to appear.

"Some traitorous wizard must have taken her for the Zherians," he growled in sudden anger. "They've shielded her from me with a magic canceling mechanism, but I know who has her and I know right where he will be!"

Guillaume's expression hardened. "Can you get her

back, Everett?"

Everett did not hesitate. "Yes."

The older man nodded. "What assistance do you need?"

"None."

"Then I shall delay you no longer."

Everett contemplated Guillaume's earnest and unyielding expression and then the haggard faces of the others. Cognizant of an unavoidable truth, he shook his head. "There's another attack coming from the north. You can't withstand it without me."

"Is it another flying craft?" queried Alec.

"No, it's a group of steam-mobile artillery. They will be on the outskirts of Kleinsvench in less than two hours."

Then a small band of men, women, and children rushed into the courtyard through the Serpent Gate. They carried bundles, hampers, babies, and pets. Some led tethered goats or carried chickens in wicker baskets. All showed various levels of fatigue and anxiety. As soon as they saw the First Assemblyman, the adults began shouting questions and crowding around him.

While Guillaume and Alec tried to quiet the uproar, announcing the little that Everett had just told them, more townsfolk began to trickle in -- individuals with hardly anything but the clothes on their backs, prepared family groups with provisions, large well-organized contingents with packed wagons and horse carts who proved to be the remaining inhabitants of entire neighborhoods. Within half an hour, the courtyard was mobbed, with a logjam forming along the approach beyond the Snake Gate. The First Assemblyman and the members of the Reserve Company were completely engaged with the tasks of guiding the refugees to quarters in the Residence and its outbuildings, delegating volunteers to tend to the horses and livestock, procuring food and potable water, and implementing plans to secure the castle.

Everett found himself pushed to the fringes by the influx of civilians and claimed a becalmed wedge-shaped nook between the gatehouse and a heap of sandbags to try to figure out how he would confront the new threat. He had made little progress in his plans when the gunsmith, Von Gylg, found him. Accompanied by one of his sons, the tradesman brought a welcome surprise.

"Good day, Monsieur Wizard," he declared as if certain that it was, in fact, just the opposite. He proffered a metal apparatus about a yard long. It was one of the launch tubes that Everett had hired him to fabricate.

The magicker took it with a quick grin. "I didn't think you could possibly finish so quickly!"

"My sons and I worked throughout the night. When the attack began, it seemed vital to complete at least one."

"Have you any of the ammunition -- the lances?"

"Yes, but only eight. That was all of the propellants and charges that Mindelsen had completed." He gestured at his son, who shouldered a bulky canvas satchel on one side and a bundle of thirty-inch long one-inch diameter steel pipe on the other. "To make them easier to carry, we modified the drawings to add screw threads to the propellant shafts and a socket in the heads. The percussion charge must also be screwed into the head before you load the lance into the gun."

"All right. The Zherians are getting closer by the second and there's nothing to be gained by waiting. Are you still determined to come with me?"

"Without a doubt." The gunsmith turned and took his son's burdens to his own shoulders, then embraced the younger man. "Tell the family that I love them, son."

"Yes, Father." The younger Von Gylg nodded curtly at Everett and made his way back through the throng.

"Ready?" Everett asked, preparing to cast his spells, seize Von Gylg, and bound away.

"Yes, but if you don't mind a suggestion, I think we need an extra man."

"How so?"

"One to fire, one to load, and one to assemble. If it comes down to needing to fire the thing in rapid succession, that would give us a better chance."

Though anxious to proceed, Everett could see the truth in the gunsmith's argument. "I suppose we could ask for a volunteer from among the Reserve Company?"

"That would seem the thing to do."

Someone had organized volunteer guides to urge the stream of civilians to continue into the castle in an orderly manner, and the logjam in the courtyard had begun to clear. They found Alec, Kyle, who now carried a bayoneted rifle, and a handful of Reservists, who were variously armed with shotguns and pistols, setting up a position behind sand bags at the Yellow Gate.

"Where is Monsieur Monte-Jaune?" Everett asked without preamble.

"He's in the citadel sorting out quarters," Alec replied. "I can send word if you need him?"

"Not necessary. I just need one volunteer." He briefly explained the operation of the explosive lances.

"If Monsieur Von Gylg will assemble the lances, I'll load for you," Alec proposed without hesitation.

Thinking that the retired soldier would perform well under the pressure of combat, Everett readily agreed.

Alec's brow wrinkled in thought. "There'll be infantry with the smas?"

"The *what*?"

"*Self Mobile Artillery* is too much of a mouthful."

"Oh, I see. Yes, they support the *smas* with ground troops."

"Then it seems to me that you need at least a squad for fire support. How close do you need to get?"

Everett did not really know so he made a wild guess. "Fifty yards."

"The infantry will pick you off before you get inside of a hundred."

"I have magic that will defend me from rifle shots."

"Will it also protect the gunsmith and I?"

Everett pursed his lips and admitted that it would not.

"You intend to fly into the attack? How many can you carry?"

"We could commandeer a wagon as we did before, could we not, Monsieur Wizard?" Von Gylg suggested.

"We can, but we don't have time to assemble a large force. We need to get going right away."

"Six more could give us some cover in a prepared position," Alec asserted. "The eight of us would fit into that cart over there." He pointed through the slowly trudging line of civilians to a two-wheeled flat bed that had been abandoned by its owners and shifted to the far side of the courtyard.

"I'll go," Kyle declared.

"Me too!" insisted the very same young woman who had stood sentry with him at the bell tower. The other Reservists, three variously aged men and a woman of indeterminate age, volunteered practically in unison.

Recognizing that it would be quicker to acquiesce than to argue, Everett shrugged. "Load up."

Carrying the sturdy cart and its eight windswept, often tense, and occasionally anxious passengers above his head, Everett bounded from the city in a series of gargantuan leaps, arriving at the center of a bean field ten miles north of Kleinsvench. He chose a landing spot immediately in the path of the Republican advance, which was no more than three miles distant.

Alec, Von Gylg, and the Reservists hopped to the ground, crushing bean bushes without concern. Kyle and the others checked the loads of their weapons, tightened cartridge belts and satchels, and waited with grim but resolved expressions.

Everett scanned the area and selected a stand of good-sized pines that had grown up in an untrimmed corner of the field. A low fieldstone wall separated the rowed field from the pasture to its north and might provide some protection from Republican bullets.

"That might give you some cover there. I can fly forward to fire and then return for a reload."

"Yes, sir." Alec acknowledged. "Kyle, get them going, double time."

As the Reservists ran off, the gunsmith handed the launcher to Everett without comment.

He shouldered the weapon, cradling the forward end with his free hand, and found it less awkward than he had expected. His magic had only produced two visions that had shown the mechanism. One had revealed him finding the schematic and its accompanying formulas in an earthenware pot buried in forgotten ruins situated on a barren island off the western coast. The second had shown him test firing the weapon in a deserted field, a scenario invalidated by actual events. Neither had explained how the lances should be used against steam-mobile artillery. His intention was to figure out the proper procedure as he went along.

Weighing little more than a comfortable twenty pounds, it had no sights; aiming seemed to be simply a matter of pointing the business end at the target. A pistol grip backed the trigger but the weapon had no trigger guard or stock.

While setting his satchel and the lengths of pipe on the ground, Von Gylg advised, "Careful you don't jar the trigger once it is loaded. I made it with a light spring and it'll operate with very little pressure." He rapidly assembled a lance, proficiently screwing one of the heads onto a shaft, then inserting and locking a small red painted cone at the tip of the shell.

"Take care not to bump this. Any sharp blow will set it off. It should explode on contact with the target." Von Gylg handed the lance to Alec, who walked to Everett's front and, shifting to the side to be out of its path, slid the pipe stem into the launch tube. The mechanism cocked when a spring loaded pin locked the stem in place.

"It's ready?" Everett questioned.

"As ready as any untested piece of ordinance can be," Von Gylg confirmed with a crooked smile.

Everett gave a short nod to both men, cast his strength, and bounded toward the Republican smas.

Finessing his spells, he landed just sixty yards to the right of the lead vehicle, held the launcher steady, pointed the nose at its center wheel, and pulled the trigger. With the propellant exhaust thrusting from the open butt of the launcher, there was very little recoil as the lance flashed away.

Unfortunately, Everett had failed to lead his target, and he spat out an angry curse as the slightly wobbly lance and its long twisting tail of white smoke shot across the stern of the sma, missing it entirely.

Within a few seconds, the propellant burned out and the lance coasted on in a flat arc for an instant, finally diving into the grass and exploding five yards short of the next sma in line. The blast dug a large crater, showering the vehicle with dirt, but otherwise did not affect it. All of the score or so smas in the squadron began to turn into zigzagging courses, and some in the rear ranks stopped and began to disgorge infantry, who took stances and fired at Everett. Some were far enough away to be unaffected by his passive spell and at the first *zing* of a bullet, he bounded back toward the Kleinsvenchans.

Kyle and the other Reservists, crouching behind the wall or next to tree trunks, had taken watchful positions in a semi-circle around Alec and Von Gylg, who hunkered down next to the already assembled seven remaining lances in a small, pine straw covered depression. Each of the squad looked determined, but Everett had to believe that they would fare poorly against the trained Zherian soldiers.

"Did it work?" the gunsmith asked.

"I don't know," he informed the man unapologetically as Alec rammed the next lance home. "I missed."

Without another word, he flexed his knees and arrowed into the sky.

This time, he recast his flight spell on the downward slope of his arc, so that he hung hovering a hundred feet above the sma formation. As one of the mechanisms cut into a turn that would bring it directly beneath him, he took a bead on its twin smokestacks, followed it with the end of the lance, and fired.

The explosion ripped the roof of the sma open, and a huge outburst of steam and smoke expanded rapidly up toward him. He cringed slightly as the scalding cloud enveloped him, but the Invulnerability Component of his strength preserved him once more from harm. When the ejecta cleared, he saw that the mechanism had slewed sideways and was burning.

When his flight expired, he hit the ground and bounced back for another lance. In rapid succession, he destroyed or disabled six more smas in the same manner. He had attacked vehicles in the forward rank, hoping that the wrecks would block the advance of the surviving fifteen mechanisms, but without slowing these detoured slightly east on a line that would take them within yards of his loading team and the

Reservists.

Hovering at half a thousand feet, Everett realized he had only two choices: he could return at once and carry the Kleinsvenchans to safety, or he could figure out a way to disrupt the advance using his magic.

His experience had shown that the two most powerful spells of those he retained were ineffective against the steam-mobile artillery using obvious methods and he was blank of any other ideas that he thought might work.

The terms of his eighth and seventh spells defined their targets in incontrovertible terms; neither Sarah nor potatoes were available to him at the moment.

Likewise, neither bad wine nor putrid olive oil could possibly help in this situation.

Unlike the fires in Kleinsvench, a wall of manure would not halt the leviathan smas.

Nor would sprouting beans or blooming flowers.

Which left only his first spell.

Desperate for a solution, he considered the question of what the spell actually did. The terms did not define a target of any sort or describe an action. They were simply a child's interpretation of a sound produced by the clang of two wind chimes, two nonsense words that had specific magical meaning only in his mind.

He also now knew that the spell could be used to ring bells.

Could it be used to ring something else?

He chose the lead sma, concentrated a focus upon it, and cast, *"Ding Dong!*

He felt the spell actuate and then within a breath, the armored hull of the mechanism rang as if an invisible, colossal sledge had struck it. The hull continued to ring, generating ear-piercing, monstrous *CLANKS* on a two beat cycle. After another hundred yards, the sma skidded to a halt and its hatches popped open. The crew and infantry within staggered out, debilitated and holding their heads. Some had trickles of blood leaking from their ears and some were carried out unconscious.

For an hour, he rang smas, compelling their crews to abandon them and discouraging any that attempted to return to their vehicles. Finally, the dismounted Zherians collected their wounded, formed up, and retreated north on foot, leaving their magically cursed self-mobile artillery behind.

When the Republican soldiers were at least four miles distant, Everett respelled each sma so that it would ring for at least another hour and returned to the pine grove.

Von Gylg and Alec grinned when he landed.

"What is that great racket?" the gunsmith asked. "It sounds like you're smashing the mechanisms with boulders."

"Something like that. Alec, can you get the squad and Monsieur Von Gylg back to the castle on your own?"

The older man nodded. "You're off to find our Sarah?"

"Yes, and to kill the man who caused all of this."

THIRTY-TWO

As he flew north, reflection on his victory over the Zherian squadron convinced Everett to further examine his magic absent all of his preconceptions.

Sarah had told him that the magic was in the magician, not in the words. His own recent experience had made it clear that this had to be true, that a spell was only a *trigger* for a magical actuation. As alien as the concept was, the words must define the magic, rather than the magic defining the words.

In Eriis, Sarah had caused him to utilize his second spell to expire the Alarsarian magician's spell, interpreting the phrase, "Fulfill thy destiny!" for her own purposes. By extension, it seemed logical that he, at that moment, had had to share her interpretation in order for the magic to actuate as it had. Her confidence had planted doubt and that had allowed her suggestion of an alternate definition to wiggle its way into his mind, and thus the spell had produced an effect altered from its previous one but still consistent with its terms.

Why could he not, therefore, establish his own definition according to his own needs?

"Destiny" was, after all, such an expansive word.

When he reached the no-man's-land of the frontier, he found pirouetting cavalry groups exchanging long-range fire as the Republican forces made an insincere attempt to exploit the breach carved through the defense lines of the Grand Alliance by the sma column that had attacked toward Kleinsvench. With the bulk of their mechanized forces delegated to the two encircling thrusts, Everett suspected that they did not retain sufficient strength along the center to mount a determined offensive.

But he also did not doubt that the Zherians had kept a force of infantry and cavalry regiments in place that was strong enough to make it impossible for the Alarsarians and their allies to pull back. The army of the Grand Alliance would be unable to wheel to face the threat of the steam mobile artillery that had severed its supply lines without exposing its flanks. An attempt to break out of the encirclement to the south seemed unworkable and the static disposition of the Alliance forces gave sufficient evidence that the Alarsarian generals had already come to that conclusion. While Everett was no expert on military theory, he did know that any army that could not be fed and supplied with bullets was doomed. In effect, at least to his mind, the shrewd gambit of the Republic had already succeeded -- the Grand Alliance was beaten

He pondered the situation for a few moments longer and then bounded back to the Alliance rear and to an extensive compound, readily identifiable from the air as a headquarters. He descended into the center of the heavily defended redoubt alongside a pole flying the battle flag of the Kingdom of Alarsaria, a blue field depicting white stars in the shape of the Royal Constellation, Alar.

Squads of soldiers bearing bayoneted rifles surrounded him immediately and just to be on the safe side, he refreshed his strength.

An underofficer who could have been no more than twenty ran up, pointed a cocked pistol at his head, and screamed for him to drop to his knees.

Everett raised his hands passively. "Hold on just a --"

The underofficer's finger twitched, manifestly the movement inadvertent, and the hammer of his pistol snapped without effect. The underofficer's eyes went wide, but he did not attempt to reload, keeping the pistol aimed squarely at Everett's forehead.

Everett frowned. "My name is Everett de Schael and I'm a Master Wizard. I wish to speak to your commanding general."

Flummoxed either by his accidental but unsuccessful assassination of Everett or by Everett's request, the underofficer seemed at a loss for words.

A colonel insinuated himself between the scintillating bayonets of the surrounding infantrymen and gave Everett a once over. Like Lieutenant Smythe in Eriis, he had a gold and turquoise mobius insignia on his left sleeve. Tall and broad, with black hair peppered with gray and an open, expressive face, he had the air of someone well accustomed to authority.

"Stand easy, Sergeant Jones," the newcomer commanded. "I will deal with this."

"Yes, sir." Jones holstered his pistol and backed away. He seemed to some extent leery of the magician colonel.

The colonel turned to Everett. "Monsieur de Schael, you are in a war zone and hence are irrevocably subject to military law. As you have invaded this post without proper leave, I call upon you to surrender immediately or face lethal force."

"Listen, I don't have time for this. If you'll just fetch a ranking officer, I'll tell him what I need done and I can get back to my own pressing business."

"Monsieur de Schael, I overheard you describe yourself as a Master Wizard, though I personally have never heard of you and I have previously believed that I had met everyone of that rank alive today. Nevertheless, I will take you at your word, but I must also inform you that, first, I am *Grand* Master Wizard Thomas Haddrack, currently ranked as the most powerful magician in the entire Kingdom, and second, that I can immolate you were you stand."

This last came across not as a boast but as a simple statement of fact.

Everett had had enough idiocy. Every second he tarried here trying to help these thickheaded Alarsarians kept him from Sarah. He curled his lip in blatant contempt. "Go ahead, try it."

Haddrack's response was almost instantaneous. *"Jet of Fire, consume this foe!"*

From a focal point a foot from the colonel's eyes, a stream of blue fire two feet in diameter erupted toward Everett, forcing the soldiers to scramble away from the heat. When it reached Everett, however, the stream simply evaporated.

Haddrack's jaw dropped. "That's impossible!"

Everett laughed humorlessly. "Magic is on my side. *Ding Dong!*"

Every metal object within a hundred yards rang and the cacophony shook the ground like an earth tremor. While the crashes of falling objects descended from every direction, soldiers staggered and fell and the flagpole weaved like a drunkard.

"NOW," Everett shouted into Haddrack shocked countenance when the tonal assault quieted, "BRING ME SOMEONE IN CHARGE BEFORE I LEVEL THIS ENTIRE PLACE!"

Within five minutes, five generals and a Field Marshal named Reginald Kantenoy, the latter the titular supreme commander of all Allied forces, were staring at Everett in dumbfounded disbelief.

"You can't be serious," the Field Marshall argued. "Beans?"

Trying to rush things along, Everett offered, "Have some brought and I will demonstrate."

Five minutes later, the officers were convinced and made effusive promises to send out the orders by dispatch riders immediately. Not willing to expend another second with the Alarsarians, he immediately bounded away.

Knowing that the messages would not reach the majority of the Alliance forces for at least two hours, he spent the interval soaring above the Zherian lines and rather gleefully transforming their water supplies into nearly putrid olive oil. Finally, as a general mood of consternation and mild panic settled over the camps of the Alliance's foe, Everett jumped to a height of over three thousand feet. At that altitude, he could see at least fifty miles to both the east and west and cast, *"Sprout ye beans!"*

After a moment, he felt the actuation, a shimmer that rattled his bones.

If the Alarsarians had done as he had requested, then thousands of beans that had been scattered in front of the forwardmost Alarsarian positions had just sprouted.

"Fulfill thy destiny!"

This magic took almost a full two minutes to actuate and when it did, very little could be seen for another ten minutes, but eventually the lively green of the preternaturally growing vines became apparent, as if an emerald line had been drawn across the frontier by a titanic brush. The spiraling vines grew and intertwined, spreading, thickening, and hardening so that at their bases they became wider and more dense than the largest known trees. As clawing roots plunged deeply into the earth, the vines spread leaves larger than a house and glorious, verdant blossoms more than ten feet across. They climbed over and across themselves, sprouting new tendrils that eagerly sought to reach the sun above and within moments the spell was complete. Separating the Alliance and Republican Armies now stood a great, gapless, nigh impenetrable barrier one hundred yards thick and one hundred feet high.

The "destiny" that Everett had chosen to interpret for the bean vines had been magnificent: that they would grow unfettered and unlimited by the mundane boundaries of their common existence to become the most – of course -- magnificent examples of legumes in human history.

Content that he had done what he could to stave off the immediate defeat of the Alliance and thereby shielded Kleinsvench and its remaining citizens from further attacks, Everett resumed his flight north.

During the uncounted relative days that he had languished in self-imposed exile in interrupted time seeking solutions to the conundrums that he faced, Everett had discovered that the nature of the visions presented by the prescience spell could be adjusted simply by alterations in the locations of objects and people. Even the slightest change in the existing situation seemed to generate a change in the visions. By a tedious and time-consuming process of tweaking, he had been able to ferret out some extremely helpful pieces of information. One of those was a fleeting image of the probable current location of Technology's corporeal biologic, Donald de Grosivna. Recognizing the usefulness of such information, he had used the limitless convenience of interrupted time to quarter the Republic seeking to discover the spot detailed in the vision: an estate overlooking a valley covered in dense forest.

After what he had thought might be a week, or perhaps a month, of interrupted time, he had found the estate in a modest clump of granite hills fifty miles to the west of

Mrysberg. It was to this innocuous, at least to outward appearance, though grand residence that he flew now. He was determined to avenge the kidnap of Sarah and bring an end, even if only temporarily, to the nightmare that Magic and Technology had imposed upon his world.

Keeping a keen eye out for the enemy, he landed deep into the tree line, probably a mile from the estate. He settled quietly, without unleashing his spells to announce his presence. He had considered and discarded numerous combative scenarios, but had eventually concluded that his best chance for quick success was simply to spy out Sarah's confines, then sneak in and release her. Once she was safe, he could deal with Technology.

After skulking through the heavy shadow of the pine forest for close to an hour, he reached the concealment of a thick bramble of cane just across a narrow, tree-shrouded country lane from the estate. He was less than thirty yards from the six-foot iron fence that surrounded the manicured grounds.

It was immediately and abundantly clear that his original straightforward plan would not work. His original vision of the estate had shown only de Grosivna intently trimming white rose bushes in the spacious ornamental garden with naught but an abbreviated view of the valley and a section of the estate as a backdrop. When he had first identified the place and observed nothing blatantly untoward, he had tarried only long enough to confirm that it was indeed the one shown in his vision and had not engaged in any protracted scrutiny. At some point in the intervening two or three days of uninterrupted time, a company of Esatis had moved in, chopped down the white roses, daffodils, and irises, overthrown the stone benches, blockaded the black iron gates, and built sandbag revetments with clear fields of fire in every direction. The entrances, ground level windows, and second and third floor balconies were also fortified. As if expecting an imminent assault, the heavily armed fanatical technophiles patrolled or stood ready behind the revetments. Many served tripod mounted guns of a sort that Everett had only seen in visions: the revolutionary multi-firing mechanisms that vomited more than one hundred rounds per minute.

Technology had been expecting him.

As he considered possible routes for a brute force frontal assault, a curious party exited the front of the estate: a tall, regal man in a white shirt and trousers who walked in front, an Esati officer bearing a saber at salute, and six troopers in parallel files shouldering long, bayoneted rifles. This parade marched at an artificially stilted cadence down the steps from the columned porch, onto the gravel walk, and then crossed it toward a scarred, upright wooden post fixed incongruously in an oval section of lawn.

The Esatis stopped at ten yards and broke smoothly into a single rank facing the post. As the troopers brought their rifles to port, the leading man stalked toward the post, head high, and turned about when he reached it. At a command, the troopers raised their rifles to their shoulders and took aim. With an arm held stiffly straight, the officer raised his saber at a constant angle and held it high.

It took Everett two seconds to realize that he was about to witness an execution.

It took him barely one more to realize that the condemned man was none other than Baronet Franz Rorche.

THIRTY-THREE

"Give me strength!"

Everett leapt from his place of concealment, soared high enough to catch a brief glimpse of the roof of the mansion, and landed just in front of Rorche as the Esati officer brought the saber down with a flourish.

The six hammers on the leveled rifles snapped uselessly. Reacting instantly, the officer yanked a magic canceling mechanism from his belt and hurled it at Everett.

He strode forward, snatched the mechanism from the air one-handedly, experienced the bone chilling feeling of his magical strength ebbing away, and then pitched it aside, rapidly spitting out the terms to renew his strength spell just as the Esatis re-cocked their weapons and fired again.

When the brittle clacks of another misfired volley rattled down the line, the officer pointed his saber at Everett and shouted, "Charge!"

Everett grabbed the startled Rorche and leapt for the top of the mansion, leaving the rushing troopers to their own devices. He and the technologist alighted on a low-pitched swale between two sheltering, prominent gables, well out of sight of all on the ground.

As soon as the magicker set him down, the Baronet grasped his right hand in both of his and shook it enthusiastically. "Everett, I cannot tell you how happy I was to see you. I had become resigned to my fate, but no man wishes to leave this life with work undone. You have my eternal and limitless gratitude. If ever you are in need of any service that I might--"

"Your welcome. Now, where is Sarah imprisoned?"

"Who?"

"Uhm...Susan."

"Your sister?"

"She's not my sister and her name is actually Sarah."

"I see. I think I understand now. Unfortunately, I must confess that I have not seen her since Edwin took the air carriage. She was not with us when we woke from the potion."

"I know, but she was brought here last night."

"I am sorry. She was not placed with I and the others."

"She's here somewhere and I will find her. What others? I mean, who else from your group is here?"

"Excluding Edwin and his two cohorts, Mitchell and Suzette – you did know that it was the chemist who delivered us to the Zherians?"

Everett nodded. He saw no point in mentioning the chemist's recent presumed demise or his role in it.

"All of the technicians and tradesmen are here, save for Aldo, who we have not seen or heard from, but all of my esnes and both the magicians, Eylis and Margaret, were taken away and we have fears for their safety."

"Aldo is dead. Suzette beat him to the draw."

The Baronet grimaced. "So I had suspected, though I did not mention it to the others."

Shook by a sudden thought, Everett asked abruptly, "Are the others to be executed too?"

"No, the Minister had me tried before a show tribunal of Generals in this Enlightened Society of theirs for crimes against technology, the particular offense being my refusal to recreate my air carriage schematic. I was found guilty, of course. Minister de Grosvina told me out of earshot of the others that I was to be sacrificed as an example in order to convince them, specifically the Coldridges, to cooperate. It seems he found their engine of greater importance than the air carriage, which he said would soon be replaced by more advanced technology in any event."

Not at all surprised that the idealistic and egalitarian aristocrat would choose death over cooperation with the Esatis, Everett eschewed comment and concentrated on the task at hand. "Do you know where de Grosvina normally is?"

"I do not know his daily schedule, no, but he always met with me in a large hall in the cellars. It had the trappings of an office."

"I'll start there then."

"Will you be able to release the others?"

"I'll try. Where are they?"

"On the third floor, just below us."

"Right. You wait here. Stay out of the line of fire."

Rorche grinned wryly. "Rest assured that I shall."

Everett thought a moment, considering how it might be best to proceed. The Esatis were alerted to his presence and clearly making preparations to defend the mansion. He ran the terms of all his spells through his mind, trying to discern some unconventional use that might avail him of a way to disable the soldiers, their guns, or, preferably, both.

Slightly scratchy, highly amplified words interrupted his deliberations. Echoing lightly across the rooftop, the announcement, easily recognizable as the voice of Technology, originated from the ground at the front of the house.

"EVERETT DE SCHAEL, I WISH TO SPEAK WITH YOU!"

"That is the Minister," Rorche supplied. "Utilizing, I do not doubt, another of his unique technological marvels. If you were not aware, de Grosivna is a technologist of the highest caliber."

"I suppose I had better go see what he wants," Everett replied matter-of-factly. He cast his two Potent spells and bounded into the air.

Dressed in a smartly but conservatively tailored gray suit, Technology waited for him alone in the gravel drive, holding a mechanism with a large flared bell at one end.

When he saw Everett, he placed the mechanism to his mouth. "I WISH TO PROPOSE AN ARMISTICE BETWEEN YOU AND I."

Wary of approaching Magic's nemesis too closely, Everett arrested his downward arc by recasting his flight so that he remained hovering at about fifty feet.

"For what purpose?" he shouted down.

"TO DISCUSS THE TERMS OF AN AGREEMENT OF NON-INTERFERANCE."

"Between the Kingdom and the Republic?"

"NO. BETWEEN YOU AND I."

Everett was immediately suspicious. As far as he was

concerned, Technology's word was worthless. *"What surety do you offer?"*

"IMMEDIATE RELEASE OF ALL PRISONERS AND EVACUATION OF ALL ARMED PERSONNEL. WILL YOU AGREE TO NEGOTIATE IN GOOD FAITH ONCE THIS IS ACCOMPLISHED?"

Everett frowned. This would achieve his goal, but he believed that negotiating with Technology would be the equivalent of sticking his hand into a rattlesnake nest. Nevertheless, he seemed to have little alternative.

"In the open and beyond range of any of your mechanisms."

"DONE!" Technology's corporeal biologic strode into the house, leaving Everett with the distinct impression that he had just been suckered. When his flight expired, he enunciated his strength, hit the ground and bounced back to Rorche.

"De Grosivna has agreed to release everyone," he told the Baronet.

"So I heard. In my limited experience, he has always appeared the gentleman."

"He was going to have you *shot*."

"But not in a dishonorable fashion."

Everett snorted to display his contempt for this odd conception. "I'm going to take you to the edge of the woods. If nothing goes askew, I'll send the rest to meet you there."

"Very well." The technologist reached out and shook Everett's hand again. "Good luck, Monsieur Wizard."

As he flew back toward the mansion after depositing the Baronet, Everett, following some lengthy thought, made one preparation for his meeting with Technology.

Remarkably, at least to Everett's way of thinking, the prisoner release occurred with only one hitch: Sarah did not appear with the other former members of the crew of the air carriage. Algis, Ellen, and Josline Coldridge scurried from the house first, blinking as if they had not suffered direct sunlight in days. They were unescorted and Everett shouted directions to take them toward the rendezvous with Rorche. Then Will, Stephan, Harold, Bennett, Beatrice, and Roger all stumbled out in a self-supporting clump and Everett likewise encouraged them on their way. When the released prisoners had vanished into the forest, the company of Esatis, sans armament, debouched from the house, formed up quickly under the direction of two officers, and marched north at double time along the lane. Finally, after a further five minutes, Technology returned to the driveway, once again carrying his voice amplifying mechanism.

"NOW, ARE YOU READY TO NEGOTIATE?"

Everett was only interested in discussing one subject. *"Where is Sarah?"*

Technology's doppelganger appeared to do a double take. "I AM NOT SURE WHAT YOU MEAN. MADEMOISELLE MONTE-JAUNE IS NOT MY PRISONER."

Tired of shouting, Everett let his flight expire and dropped to the ground. No matter what nefarious scheme Technology had in store, there seemed little greater safety in being fifty feet away rather than five. The embodiment of patience, the man known to the rest of the world as Donald de Grosivna tossed his amplifying mechanism aside and smiled as the magicker drew near.

"Excellent! I would much prefer that our conversation be conducted privately. The members of the Enlightened Society can sometimes fail to appreciate the logic of practicality." The man smirked. "Evil minions can sometimes be such a bore."

Everett did not crack even a hint of a smile.

De Grosivna cleared his throat. "Well, be that as it may, let's begin, shall we? Now, my proposal is simple--"

Everett cut him off. "Where is Sarah?"

"My apologies. I believe that there has been some misunderstanding. I have not abducted the mademoiselle. As I once explained to you, the period of time in which control of her person could sway events in my favor has long passed. In point of fact, she ceased being a Primary Pivot once the two of you came west."

"You'll gain nothing by lying," Everett growled. "If you wish to escape this meeting alive, you'll hand her over right now!"

Technology wagged a finger. "Threats of that kind are rather meaningless. Even should some misfortune occur to this present biologic, my noncorporeal essence will continue to exist. We of the noncorporeal realm are not subject to death in the corporeal sense of the term."

Everett let a thin and cold smile slide onto his face. "Thanks for pointing that out."

"Certainly. We are both rational, intelligent beings and should always strive to utilize our intelligence and rationality to resolve our differences. Now, as I was saying, I propose that we declare an end to the hostility between us. I have no specific desire to cause you harm and the manipulation that you have suffered has only resulted in providing you with undue dislocation, unnecessary discomfort, and undeserved pain. I am sure that you will agree that the contest between Magic and myself is not properly now -- and should truthfully never have been -- your affair. I had hoped that the obvious correctness of my cause would persuade you to assist me in my efforts to better humanity through technology, but it does not necessarily follow that we should therefore be at odds. Thus the agreement of non-interference. You have been unfairly involved -- not of my doing I must reiterate -- and you should be allowed to pursue your own goals without further disruption."

"So, you're saying, we should just let bygones be bygones?"

"That would be the gist of it, yes. We shall enter into a binding agreement that neither of us will henceforward involve ourselves in the affairs of the other."

"What about the war?"

Technology displayed a sad face. "Human events of such a magnitude, once set in motion, cannot be easily halted. I will promise that I will do all that I can in this present guise to ameliorate the suffering of the citizens of both the Grand Alliance and the Republic by ensuring that the struggle comes to a swift and decisive conclusion."

"A conclusion in which the Republic – that is *you* -- win."

Technology shrugged. "As the case may be."

"No thanks."

"To be clear, I take it that you are rejecting the armistice?"

"*Right.*"

Sighing, Technology slipped a hand into the inside of his coat and withdrew a pistol. "Unfortunately, I expected this to be your response."

"You know that won't work with me," Everett pointed out, frowning.

With his left hand, the Minister withdrew a small blue box with a single red button and showed it to the magicker with thumb poised. "This device is an enhanced second generation magical dampener. I won't go into the specifics of the methodology – the particular technology that it utilizes is actually from another universe -- but suffice it to say that this is a significant improvement over its predecessor. The first generation mechanism suffered problems with inconsistency and duration, and the field it generated was entirely transitory. This, however, creates a permanent, magically dead zone that affects everything within a radius of a thousand yards. Once it is activated, magic will not function in this place for all eternity."

Everett did not move. "Why haven't you pushed the button? Why didn't you push it when I showed up?"

Technology smiled apologetically. "Due to some unavoidable and perverse side-effects of indwelling a corporeal biologic, my thought processes have become contaminated by human impulses. With some embarrassment, I must admit I am overcome with the need to gloat."

"You see," Technology continued, warming to his subject and driving his voice to a crescendo, "with this single mechanism, I have devised a way to achieve *complete* and *absolute* victory. Once these new dampeners are in mass production, I will be able to scatter them around the entire world and in so doing eradicate magic forever!"

Everett clapped his hands slowly in an overt display of sarcasm.

Technology's brow creased. "For some reason, your response to my monologue causes me to feel a hint of uncertainty."

"It should. You forgot the three W's."

"Come again?"

"The three W's. It's something that Bob told me just a

few days ago, though it seems like years."

Technology looked from side to side as if he had lost his place in some invisible script. "Bob?"

"Nice guy Bob. He doesn't mind giving a man a ride. He also holds the key to the entire universe."

"I fail to understand what you are trying to say."

"Don't worry, I only put it all together this morning myself and I'm not really sure whether it has always been this way or just changed recently. That doesn't make any difference though, because it's the way that magic works *now*. Funny thing: contrary to what I believed most of my life, magic is not actually crap. But back to the three W's. With most of my spells, the *what* is more or less determined – though I do now also know that there can be a lot of wiggle room in the *what* – and I have almost free rein in the *where*, but, and this is the most important part, the *when* is completely undefined."

"I do not see how any of these...questions ... are relevant."

"I see what you mean, but there's one question that I'm sure that you'll find relevant."

"And that is?"

"Can you breathe potato?"

For a moment or two, while a total look of incomprehension seized Technology's face, an awkward silence reigned, and Everett feared he had misjudged the passage of time.

Then, there came a mild rippling sound like soap bubbles popping, and a dozen or so potatoes appeared along the edges of the drive at different elevations and attitudes. These plopped to the gravel, milled about confusedly for a second or two, and then proceeded with accelerating energy to dash, bounce and skip towards Technology. Before the first had traveled more than a yard, hundreds more flashed into existence and the sound of their arrival graduated to the rattle of popping corn. Within seconds, the noise expanded to a continuous roar of ripping static.

Technology was visibly staggered as the first of the potatoes struck his chest with great force. A following shotgun-like blast struck the pistol from his hand, but he managed retain a hold on the canceling mechanism and savagely mashed his thumb on the red button. When the swarm of tubers failed to react, he crushed the button with the heel of his free hand, displaying signs of desperation, but again the transporting potatoes continued their assault undiminished

As waist-high drifts began to form around his body, Technology surged toward Everett and screamed, *"How did you do this?"*

Everett did not bother to reply, but simply turned and started running toward the lane as the swarm grew to a blizzard. A potato the size of a saucer careened off his forehead, almost knocking him to the ground. Barreling on, he threw up his forearms to protect his face from the pummeling torrent. With the noise now earsplitting, a constant hail smashed into his chest, arms, and legs with force enough to retard his forward advance, the slightly stunned potatoes tumbling and spinning around him to continue their unswerving obedience to the imperative of the spell. Almost swimming through the brown, tan, and red cloud as he strove to escape the fifty-yard radius of the spell, he was struck and bruised hundreds of times before he finally broke free. He gasped to regain his breath and then trotted onward a few dozen steps for safety's sake.

Only then did he turn to look back. Of Technology, nothing could be seen. Where the man had stood, a great conglomeration of spuds squirmed in an almost obscene parody of life. Already, many thousands of pounds crushed in upon Technology's corporeal biologic and soon there would be many more, compacting and smashing each other in a relentless effort to reach the central point of the locus, the man's breastbone.

Everett had had no choice with the *what*; there was no ambiguity in "potatoes." He could not by any stretch imagine that the word meant anything else – not watermelons, grapefruit, or even apples. What he had been able to interpret differently had been the quantity specified. In this case, he had taken the plural form to mean all the potatoes existing within a thousand miles, trusting in magic – or Magic, as it were – to provide the means for them to overcome the normal limitations of the spell's range.

The *where* had been a routine matter of selecting and concentrating on a locus at the moment of enunciation.

The supremely vital *when*, however, had been his free to select, and he had chosen a time an hour after actuation.

When facing Edwin on the air carriage, he had learned that the magic canceling mechanisms affected only the initiation of a spell and had guessed that any similar mechanism that Technology might bring to bear against him would function in the same way.

If he had been wrong, his life would have been forfeit.

Unluckily for Technology, he had not been.

THIRTY-FOUR

Everett dreamed.

At first, he chased a quarry that he could not see and could not catch through an endless ruin.

Then, he was sitting on his father's terrace, but there were no apples to eat and his father was long gone.

Finally, as he sat upon a bucket watching ripples in a pool, Magic and a thoroughly subdued Technology approached him from out of a green fog.

"Have you come to take my remaining spells?" he griped.

"By all rights, you shouldn't be able to keep them," Technology grumped.

Magic cut her eyes sharply to scold her fellow noncorporeal sentient being. "No, Everett, you get to keep everything you currently have. That is, for now. However, you must understand that these spells make you preternaturally powerful, and if in my judgment you begin to use them in an unseemly manner or in a manner that damages the cause of magic in this universe, I will be sure to revisit this decision."

"I could care less. Are you really here or am I just dreaming?"

"No, we're not," Technology replied blandly. "Most accurately, we should be considered a figment of your imagination rather than an intrusion of our noncorporeal essences into the physical realm. However, for all practical purposes, there's no difference."

Turning his back upon the two, Everett spit into the pool to express his opinion of that answer and then watched as the ripples collided and rebounded.

"Why are you here?" he asked without turning.

"As you have done me a great favor," Magic replied, "I

thought I would answer any questions you might have. All endeavors must have closure of a sort, after all. Technology is just along because I have been given charge of his parole. For a certain period, I will have veto power over his actions."

Everett only had one question. "Where in the world is Sarah? I've searched for her everywhere."

"I do not know, Everett. She is wherever you sent her."

"Is it even possible for you to give a straight answer?"

"That is a straight answer. I have no idea where Sarah is. Destiny cannot locate her and none of the other noncorporeals has a clue. I even questioned Weather, whose awareness of individuals is quite effervescent."

"Then I have no further use for your company."

Everett dove head first into the pool and woke up.

Throwing off his blanket, he sat up and gazed around dully at his cold camp. He had set up the night before among a stand of cottonwoods on a bluff above a river whose name he had not bothered to learn. Dry mouthed, he rubbed a hand across his still tired eyes and then reached for his canteen, draining most of the tepid water in one swallow.

After the death of Technology's corporeal biologic beneath the mountain of potatoes, he had spent most of a month combing the Republic for Sarah. Seeking out the work camps where the Enlightened Society had detained all Zherian magickers, he had found and released many, including the worn but otherwise whole Eylis Coldridge and Margaret who he had reunited with the other freed Synthesists in Kleinsvench, wreaked joyful havoc on uncounted Esatis, and sown great confusion in the Republican ranks.

But he had not found Sarah and no one he had taken the time to question had been able to provide any clue as to her whereabouts.

He stood up, walked out a short distance to make water, then came back to gather up his bedroll and tie it to his already stowed pack. He had encountered the pack along the way. It was a Republican infantryman standard issue and a serviceable if somewhat lacking replacement for the one that he had lost when he first met Sarah. He glanced around to make sure he had not left anything out.

Then, as he had every morning and every evening and

dozens of times every day for weeks, he cast his eighth spell.

"Beautiful Woman, come forth!"

And, as it had every morning and every evening and dozens of times every day, the magic failed to actuate.

After a moment, he shouldered his pack, cast his Potents, and bounded away, heading south.

He crossed over the frontier about mid-morning. The bean wall remained undiminished. Both armies had withdrawn; for now, the impenetrable barrier quite thoroughly dissuaded any attempt at attack by either side and little was to be gained by guarding an impassible section of border.

Passing over the bucolic Principality of Gainsfield-Schloss, he arrived in Kleinsvench hardly an hour later. The city had a demonstrably more energized air than it had when he had seen it last, three weeks earlier. A great number of its citizens had begun to return and with them the noise and life. He first visited Von Gylg's shop. The gunsmith, his sons, and around a dozen more people, none of whom Everett recognized, were busily mass-producing explosive lances.

"I've taken on contracts to export to the Alarsarians and others in the Grand Alliance," Von Gylg explained. "I took it for granted that you wouldn't mind."

"I don't."

"After costs, wages, and equipment fees, I've set aside the profits for you. We've received payment for the first two shipments of a hundred each and it comes to thirteen thousand three hundred and sixty-nine silver. It's all in coin in a strongbox. I wasn't really interested in paper, under the circumstances, and I didn't think that you would have any trouble with the weight."

Everett laughed hollowly. "Thanks, but by rights I should get no more than half. You can send that and all future payments up to the castle in care of Monsieur Monte-Jaune. I'll ask him to manage the money for me."

With a sad smile, the gunsmith examined Everett's face. "You'll be off to the Republic to search for Mademoiselle Monte-Jaune again?"

Finally putting to words the decision that he had already made brought a hard frown to Everett's lips. "No, I'm going back to the east. I may try to set up a magicking shop in New Zindersberg, but I haven't decided for certain."

Everett bid the man a quick farewell and started toward the apothecary's place of business. Along the way, he came across a café that had been shut tight the last time he passed. Today, it was open for business and well patronized. Not hungry but knowing that he needed to eat, he took a seat at a table for one beside the street and had a meal that proved disappointing. They boiled their okra, they had no fresh fruit of any kind, and they had never heard of cornbread.

Afterwards, he went to settle his account with Mindelsen. With a kind but resigned expression, the apothecary set a green glass bottle sealed with a screw lid onto the counter when he entered.

"I have your potion ready. The dosage is on the label," Mindelsen informed him in a business-like tone. "It will retain its potency for a year. If you need more after that, you have only to let me know."

Everett placed the bottle in his pocket without comment. "Will there be any additional charge?"

The apothecary chuckled. "Monsieur Von Gylg has been paying for the explosives and propellants in hard coin and I still have half of the gold you placed on account. With the drop in the value of paper currency, the deca-crowns have actually increased considerably in value. With interest and earnings from the formulas, the sum is something over fifteen thousand the last time I checked. As I have deposited the monies with a strongbox firm for safekeeping, it will be this afternoon before I can refund the balance."

"With my compliments, please consider the entire sum your just due for services well rendered."

"I thank you, Monsieur Wizard, but I expect to make a large sum from my commissions on the sale of the medicinal potion to foreign factors. Some of the physicians consider it a miracle cure. Here in Kleinsvench, it has already helped several dozen people with apparently terminal infections. However, if you do not object, I could put the balance to purchasing the ingredients to concoct the potion for those without the wherewithal to pay."

Everett nodded. "An excellent suggestion. What's

more, you can divert any future profits that might accrue to me for the same purpose."

The apothecary did not seem surprised. "It would be my pleasure. I should also tell you that I have applied by mail for registrations of the medicinal formula in your name in both the Kingdom and the Republic. Once they come through, however long that takes, I will license the formula for widespread production. The revenue will be more than significant."

"I'll have no need of it, though if there's much more than you need for distribution of the potion, I'd appreciate it if you could set aside a tenth portion and send it to Monsieur Monte-Jaune."

The apothecary inclined his head in understanding.

Finally, Everett wound his way slowly through the city and made the hike up the inclined approach to the castle. He found Sarah's father on the esplanade adjacent to Mad Lydia's Folly, studying the revived metropolis. The meeting was brief.

Nodding curtly as Everett, stone-faced, related his failure to find her, Guillaume affirmed with determination and finality, "Sarah will turn up, Everett. Magic is on our side."

Everett found he had nothing to say to that. "Monsieurs Von Gylg and Mindelsen will from time to time send silver that I've earned. I'd like you to put it aside for me and use it if there's a need."

"Gladly, but I take that to mean that you plan to leave. You're more than welcome to stay with us here, Everett."

"Thank you, but I think it's time that I moved on."

"Will you be going south to join the forces of the Grand Alliance?"

"No, the Zherians and the Alarsarians will have to sort things out without me. I'm going back to the east."

Sarah's father shook his hand. "Good luck, Everett."

The magicker cast and bounded away.

He crossed over the Grand Duchy of Filingham and the battle torn eastern provinces of Alarsaria by the end of the day but continued on into the night, stopping only when he was well into the Shadowed Hills. Along about ten o'clock the next day, he reached the Edze. On impulse, he gravitated toward the Barony of Heimgelberg and after some searching, located a steam grader working along a back road within sight of Pylton. When he landed alongside it, the operator waved; it was indeed Bob.

After much valve twisting and lever throwing, Bob brought his mechanical beast to a halt and hopped down with a grin.

"Glad to see you again!" The road worker indicated Everett's method of arrival by a quick glance at the sky. "Looks like you've gotten some new magic!"

"Yes, a bit."

The man got a gleam in his eye. "Any improvements in the wine spell?"

"Maybe. Want to give it a go?"

"Of course! Come around to the stern!"

At the barrel fastened in a frame aback of the rear platform, Bob took a mug from a hook, filled it, then held it out expectantly.

"I bid cool water become sweet wine."

After the water darkened, Bob knocked back a swig. "Mmm, not bad."

He took another much longer draught. "You know, in fact, I'd say it was half decent."

He finished the mug and placed it back on its hook.

"Would you like me to transubstantiate the whole barrel?" Everett offered.

"No, that'd just get me in trouble with the wife. She'd have thrown a wheel if I came home soused. Well, what have you been doing with yourself?"

"I met a woman, lost her, saved the world."

"Regular day's work for a magicker, eh? Shame about the woman. Every man needs one whether he wants one or not. Don't mind me being nosy, but did you just misplace her or did she take up with another fellow?"

"I just can't find her."

"Oh, if that's all then that's an easy fix. Just go looking where she aught to be and she'll turn up sooner or later."

Everett stared at Bob for a lengthy moment, dumbfounded. He suddenly knew where he would find

Sarah.

"Thanks Bob! You're exactly right! See you later!"

"Anytime!" the operator shouted as Everett bounded away. "Don't forget me and the wine if you happen to swing back through!"

Everett traveled without stopping and reached the eastern coast by evening. When he walked down the cart trail from the main road and into the shaded front court of the main house, his nieces and nephews, who had all grown a foot in the years since he had seen them last, ran screaming to hug him. This commotion drew his sister and brother-in-law from the house and Everett found himself completely enveloped in family.

Later, he wandered onto the sun-lit terrace and sat at the round, pedestal table where his father had always read on spring afternoons. Now, instead of a pile of half-finished, dog-eared books, a glass bowl filled with early green apples resided in the place of honor. He took an apple from the bowl, inhaled a savoring whiff of its fresh, sweet aroma, and took a large, very satisfied bite.

When he had transported Sarah, he had been thinking of a place of unquestioned safety, a place where neither the Esatis nor Technology could reach her, a place beyond the grasp of the slightest peril or the greatest magic. The spell had done what he wanted, instead of what he intended. It had taken her out of a time and place of danger and want and sent her to one of security and plenty.

And then Sarah appeared right before him, just as he had seen her last: dressed in the sheet, holding the lantern, hair disheveled, with smears of soot on her forehead. And thoroughly angry.

"—doing?"

She stopped, took quick stock of her surroundings, then demanded, "Where in Magic's name are we, Everett?"

He smiled. "Home."

www.ingramcontent.com/pod-product-compliance
Lightning Source LLC
Chambersburg PA
CBHW060545180626
46817CB00002B/735